# ORDER OF THE DRAGONBONDED
## BOOK OF AIR

Dragonbonded®

**THE DRAGONBONDED RETURN Series**
*Call of the Dragonbonded*
*Order of the Dragonbonded*
*Army of the Dragonbonded*
*Omen of the Dragonbonded*

**THE NEW CRONOAN CHRONICLES Series**
*Chronicles of Nartesis Shazarack: Father of
Necromancy*
*Chronicles of Alicia Farclave*
*Chronicles of Tatem Creeg*

**THE FIRST DRAGONBONDED Series**

Visit **www.thedragonbonded.com** to get the latest information on these books and other works by JD Hart, to subscribe to the author's newsletter, or to contact the author.

# ORDER OF THE DRAGONBONDED
## BOOK OF AIR

*Book 2: The Dragonbonded Return*

## JD Hart

Dragonbonded
Press

First Printing: June 2018
Fourth Printing: June 2020

9 8 7 6 5 4

ISBN: 978-1-949101-01-0

All Artwork by J.D. Hart
Cover Design by Meg Cowley

# Acknowledgments

This work, along with the entire Dragonbonded Return series, would not be possible without the support, encouragement, and suggestions of many people who have participated in making this work what it is. First, a very special appreciation goes to my amazing editor, Maya Myers.

Also, special thanks go out to the members of our small, local writers group: Matt Myers, Andrea Reimers, and Amy Kuney.

And finally, thanks to the many reviewers who provided valuable feedback on this work, including Pablo Corea, Angel Haze, Carol Klingler, Bill Loggins, Carol Raedy, Vicki Watchorn, Karyn Williamson-Corea, and Loren Zenker.

The HAR...
REAL...

ANTARIC SEA

Port Fount

Stronghold
of Aldemeer

Ashecombe
CASTLE

Emb...

D...

Moorestone
CASTLE

Darmascus

Shan' Grail
RUINS

Grim...

Mazer's Sanctuary

Manor Caltarus

Blackmarke...
CASTLE

LAKE
LOCKS

Graystone

REALM OF
GRENETIA

Cleft
CASTLE

Stonewell
CASTLE

Moonslayer
CASTLE

REALM OF
ELVENSTEIN

Char...

RMONIC
LMS

Thanatos

Xylor

Farlorde
CAMP

r's Keep

Elmsdorf

Dreadcreck
OUTPOST

Lake
Ontor

BORDERLANDS

Dragongarde
CAVERNS

Gravenrock

Coven
of Alcorn

Pennington Point

Lincolnton Point

Striker's Keep

Creeg's Point

amley's
ome

Bell's Ferry

Kallzwall
CASTLE

Loren Canyon

Labyrinth of
Armeaus

REALM OF

GRIFFINROCK

Brightmead
Estates

Harmon Keep

Warstag
CASTLE

League of
Conjurers

BORDERLANDS

Wright's Keep

iper's Glen

Stone Garden

Everbright
CASTLE

Soul's Edge
OUTPOST

Alzabar

LAKE
DONOGAL

MWELL

Chateau of
Brionne

Horken's Well

Derry's
Bridge

# Contents

Biographer's Note ...................................................................... x
Part I .......................................................................................... 1
First Flight .............................................................................. 3
A Foretelling ......................................................................... 10
Undercurrents ...................................................................... 22
Grimmley ............................................................................... 30
A Queen's Demand ............................................................... 38
Dream Vision ........................................................................ 43
The Price of a Shaman's Help ........................................... 61
Tying Off Loose Ends .......................................................... 67
A Band of Anarchists .......................................................... 69
A Dangerous Quest .............................................................. 78
A Payment Made ................................................................... 84
Part II ....................................................................................... 95
Homeward Bound ................................................................ 97
One Little Hurdle ............................................................... 103
Dreadcreek ........................................................................... 114
An Evening Affair .............................................................. 122
Sowing Seeds ....................................................................... 129
An Early Change in Seasons ........................................... 138
When a Third Time Is Not So Charming ...................... 151
An Assassin's Aid .............................................................. 157
Battle for Elmsdorf ........................................................... 162
Bloodbond ........................................................................... 181
Dragon Wind ....................................................................... 185
Part III .................................................................................... 191
A Course of Action ............................................................ 193
One Plausible Explanation .............................................. 197
Dragongarde ....................................................................... 202
Fortress Sanctuary ............................................................ 221

Old and New Wounds ...................................................................229

Unfortunate News .......................................................................235

A Dark Premonition .....................................................................242

Amid a Nest of Spies ...................................................................250

A Journey into the Dark Unknown .............................................267

Tournament of the Realm ...........................................................272

Ripples ..........................................................................................276

Grimmley's Ruse ..........................................................................283

Part IV ...............................................................................................295

Conner's Trial ...............................................................................297

Awakenings ...................................................................................305

Coronation ....................................................................................309

Clarity............................................................................................311

Imprisoned ...................................................................................316

A New Promise Made...................................................................321

An Old Promise Fulfilled..............................................................324

Two May Be Company, But Three's a Pack ................................328

Tangled Knots...............................................................................333

In the Light of a New Day ...........................................................338

Epilogue—Homecoming...............................................................345

# Biographer's Note

All historians hold to the belief that we, as a species, spend too much of our precious time looking over our shoulders and seeing what might have been instead of looking ahead and seeing what could become. Some of my friends like to jest that we settled on this common idea because we much prefer arguing why it is so. My most stalwart colleagues argue the reason is clear—we have no choice because we only learn from the past, and learning is an essential part of our survival. Yet others of my prestigious profession say we obsess over the past because it is engineered into our very makeup, like a branding imprinted upon our spirits when we are drawn at birth into this Physical plane.

I do not hold to such unfounded beliefs. If my studies into the lives of those living before the great transformation have taught me anything, it is that we all possess the capacity to create a vision from the great expanse of possibilities. I am confident that the parchments that follow will bear witness to this claim: that it is only through the fires of our struggles that we burn away the many layers of doubt and fear. Only then, when the raw beauty of our unique essence is exposed, can we discover the courage to turn away from the hypnotic falsehoods of our pasts and build our future. Maybe I am a fool, as my colleagues declare me to be, to cling to such an ideal. But as the Modeic maxim goes, "If the Cosmos had wished us to walk into our future with reluctance and dread, it would have given us eyes in the backs of our heads."

So I ask you now: when we all are called to face some formidable challenge, from what do you draw your faith if it is not the belief that someone borne from the inferno of their struggles will step forward, ready to lead those with eyes cast behind them?

- JD Hart

# Part I

*There are crossroads in a Being's life where the choices made define who they will become. Fools seek a signpost to point them down the path they were meant to take; the wise hope merely to be awake when they arrive.*

—*The Modei Book of Water (Third Book)*

# First Flight

Pennington Point◆

Conner Stonefield climbed the rough steps carved into a large boulder, then glanced timidly over the side of the gorge. Nearly three hundred paces below, a rocky river roared past. On the far side, two hundred paces away, the tattered remains of a suspension bridge dangled down the cliff, its wooden slats swinging with the gorge's gentle updrafts.

A long, scaly, black neck craned past Conner's shoulder and studied the scene below. "It seems this human structure did not fare so well with the storm," the two-legged wyvern noted with indifference. Conner neither moved nor spoke, so his bond mistook the human's silence as consent to share one of his newfound insights about the small bipedal species. "It surprises me that, for creatures incapable of flight, you humans willingly trust your lives to such precarious contraptions. In fact, I am beginning to understand this feeling you have about heights."

Conner pursed his lips, trying to shake off the growing despair that they might never reach the home of Grandmaster Shaman Grimmley Rollingsworth. For nearly two days, Conner had fought through rich vegetation growing along the westerly trail he had selected, one he expected would take them out of the Dragon's Back Mountains and on south to where—he hoped—the Shaman would break his bond with the misfit adolescent dragon. "Maybe it is time we named the feeling, Skye. It is called *fear*."

"Fear." Skye-Anyar-Bello Cloudbender recited the word as if struggling with its meaning. "Until we bonded, I never thought about fear." After a long pause in which he considered the emotions flowing from Conner, Skye wagged his head and added, "I do not like this feeling."

Conner sensed no anger or disgust through their link in the Mental plane, just distaste. They had only been bonded for four days, so neither was used to the emotional connection they shared through the link. Still, his cheeks reddened. "Few creatures are fearless like dragons, Skye. I'm sorry you have to experience my fear. Sometimes I wish I could be fearless, even for a day."

The black dragon's head swiveled about as he considered his human bond's wish. "Then we shall work on that now."

Conner stared into the beast's blazing blue eyes. "What do you mean?" he asked suspiciously.

The dragon eyed the distance across the gorge. "We are going to fly across," Skye stated with a nod.

Stunned, Conner shuffled back from the edge of the boulder, hazel eyes widening as he waved his hands before him. "Oh no! I am not going to—"

"Conner," the wyvern interrupted, turning toward his bond. His thorny head rose to twice Conner's height, as if height would give weight to what he was about to say. "I have seen this feeling of fear reflected in the eyes of creatures before I ate them. Some fought back, but none let their fear consume them. In the moments before they died, they all faced their fear. So I understand this need. It is time you faced yours."

If the dragon was attempting to boost Conner's confidence, his reference to death did not help.

Skye unfurled black leathery wings, each the length of a horse. "For once, do as I say. Wrap your rope around my chest and behind my wings, and then around my neck. Then climb on my back and loop the end around your waist. We will be on the other side in a moment."

Conner was struck with a memory of the day his best friend, Pauli, had convinced him to sneak a ride on Old Man Fairstein's plow mule while the farmer was hoeing his garden. Pauli had no more than given Conner a leg up when the mule bucked, sending Conner flying unceremoniously face-first into the mud. It was the last time Conner had tried riding anything. "Skye, there is no way I am going to let you leap from this cliff with me strapped to your back."

"Do you want to see this great Shaman or not?" the dragon puffed back. "Because getting there is going to require we cross this gorge at some point."

Conner's mind worked desperately to find another option. He knew enough about Griffinrock's territories to be certain this gorge fed the Aradorm River to the south. With the recent storm, the Aradorm would be swollen. That meant backtracking east away from the gorge, then heading south more than fifty miles to Bell's Ferry before crossing to the west. Having already been away from home for more than a fortnight, Conner was homesick and growing desperate to return to Griffinrock Realm's Eastlands, where he was to begin his studies as an apprentice in the Apothecaries Guild.

The dragon stared at him impatiently.

Finally, Conner acquiesced with a sigh, then lifted the rope from his shoulder. "I suppose a life of suffering with the Yearning would be a fair reward for getting me killed." Conner spoke flippantly, though he knew that the unstable state brought on by the death of one's bond was nothing to laugh about.

The dragon extended his neck and gave the deepening blue sky a long snort-sniff laugh.

Hemera had sunk below the tall mountains to the west before Conner sat strapped to the black creature's withers, his slender legs pressed tight against Skye's bulky neck. He could sense the dragon's heightened impatience, but that was not Conner's concern. He needed to feel confident the dragon's idea would work. This had resulted in several heated discussions, from how best to wrap the climbing rope around Skye's girth, to how tight it should be, to what kind of knot to use, to even where Conner should sit so the dragon's many sharp barbs did not jab him in any soft spots while Skye fidgeted about.

At last, Skye stepped to the edge of the cliff and opened his wings.

"Wait, wait, wait!"

Skye waited. "What now, Conner?"

Conner gripped the rope until his knuckles lost their color, unwilling to tear his eyes from the cliff descending directly beneath, his feet dangling two paces above the rocky steps. Dark, wavy hair whipped around his sixteen-year-old face from the strong updrafts. "Are you s-s-sure you can carry my weight?" he stuttered. "I mean, from up here, those wings don't look so big."

"I carried you for several miles when I saved you from the human trackers that captured you, didn't I?" the dragon asked—but he did not wait for an answer.

Conner was about to mention that the ends of the bridge's thick ropes appeared to have been hacked with an axe, not rotted or torn by the storm, when Skye leaped from the boulder. All of Conner's lucid thoughts vanished. A blast of air whipped at his long hair and tore at his clothes. The rocky river below grew alarmingly larger. He opened his mouth to scream, but his lips flapped wildly in the gale, so he clamped his jaws tight. His eyes stung, but he could not tear them from the horrific scene before him.

The high-pitched ripple of air rushing over Skye's wings changed, and Conner groaned. He fought to keep his body erect, but his head and shoulders sagged. His grip slackened on the ropes, air forced from his lungs. Sheer rocky cliffs blurred past.

Just as quickly, his body lifted off the dragon's back. He pulled hard on the ropes to keep from falling. Then everything went still.

Conner leaped from Skye's back, tumbling into the grass on hands and knees.

"Wasn't that fun?" the dragon bellowed, wings spread wide in jubilant victory.

Conner let out the scream that had been building since Skye took flight. He tried to stand but tumbled back to the ground again. "*What* were you *thinking*?"

Skye blinked, confused. "Helping you face your fears."

Conner rose on shaky legs. With jaw clenched, he stated slowly, to remedy Skye's confusion, "You didn't have to scare me to death, Skye! A gentle crossing would have worked just fine!"

Deflated, Skye's body and wings sagged. "How was I supposed to know?" he asked sullenly.

It took several minutes for Conner to regain the mental capacity to study the terrain around him. When he did, he found more bad news. The storm a few nights before had apparently caused a rockslide along the southern edge of the mountain west of the bridge. All that remained of the trail was a soup of mud and boulders.

Skye slipped next to Conner while he examined the devastation.

Conner sighed. "Every step of this journey has been fraught with delays. For once, I'd like to take three steps forward without risking my life or having to retrace two!"

"We could fly to the other side of the rockslide, then pick up the trail from there," Skye offered.

Conner placed his hands on his hips and gawked at the dragon. He must have been delirious, because his bond could not have suggested that Conner ride him again. There would be a Midsummer's Day Parade through the Borderlands before he got on that manic beast's back again! He shook his head and walked back to the gorge.

"What?" the dragon asked, shadowing his bond.

Pausing by the bridge's landing, Conner pointed to an overgrown trail running the edge of the gorge. "We'll go south from here."

Skye eyed the trail suspiciously, then grunted. "That path does not appear to have been used for a very long time."

Conner ignored the dragon. "If we don't find another route heading west soon, then this way should drop us out of the mountain range. We can hug the southern hills from there and travel at night by the light of Erebus. Besides, we'll make better time once we're out of the mountains." He glared one last time at the rockslide, his confidence returning. "That route would have probably taken us north anyway. We'll be fine."

"What if someone sees me?"

Already picking his way south over slippery rocks, Conner offered back, "Then you can give them a ride. I can think of no better way to quell a loose tongue."

South of the bridge's eastern base where Skye had leaped, Wallis Arkman sat on a large oak branch that hung precariously over the deep river gorge, his back resting comfortably against the tree's thick trunk. He gave Maestro, his gray squirrel bond, a hearty, but soft laugh, then tapped his short wooden cane against the branch with delight, nodding at the Eastlander's attempt to ride the dragon. He was quite pleased with the afternoon's turn of events, even considering his actions. He thumbed the sharp edge of the hatchet he had brought from Pennington Point, where he had given the young lad a needed nudge to save Griffinrock's young Princess Veressa from being kidnapped by Bargo and his hapless Sorcerer accomplice. The resulting ripples of chaos from his work were far from palatable. Nevertheless, they were insignificant compared to what might have happened if he had done nothing. The lad and dragon needed to test their mettle, to see what they were capable of. The planetary alignment of just four days ago was shifting farther out of his favor. Time was critical.

Arkman hated the thought of leaving so soon, but he had a long journey ahead and much to prepare in the coming months. He cleared his mind and pulled his broad-brimmed hat over his eyes, letting the echoing sounds of the raging waters below lull him into a deep, contented sleep.

# A Foretelling

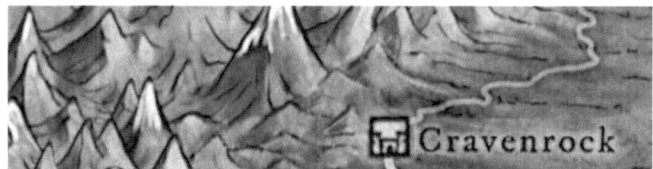

**P**rincess Veressa of Griffinrock, heir to the largest of the three Harmonic realms, paused to stretch away a weariness greater than she had ever known. With all she had endured since receiving the Calling six days before, her youthful body was nearing its physical limits. Muscle cramps and tension took hold of her legs and back more frequently, nagging at her with each stuttered step, pleading with her to stop. Yet with each step, she was getting closer to her bond; she could sense its presence nearby. So it was excitement and anticipation of what lay ahead that won the battle, commanding her legs to do what her mind could not. She shuffled forward once more.

Finding the silence unbearable, she pushed back an annoying mat of muddy blond hair that had broken free from her Ranger-apprentice braid and examined her sullen companion. "How is your head?" she asked the master Ranger with the same exhausted rigidity.

"Better." Annabelle Loris ran fingertips along the knot on her temple, a gift from a burly fighter's axe during his botched attempt to abduct the princess two nights before.

Veressa sighed, casting her blue eyes to the rocky mountain terrain ahead. "You're still angry," she stated, knowing that Annabelle regretted having caved in to Veressa's demands to go on her bonding trek without more protection … against the wishes of Veressa's mother, the queen. Both knew that it was a matter of time before the king sent a company of Defenders to escort Veressa on her trek.

Of course, Veressa's disguise as Annabelle's apprentice was actually not far from reality. After nearly a year of clandestine training in the basic combat skills of the Rangers Order, and with a surprising approval from the order's council, Annabelle had begun to secretly train the princess in the advanced arts of using Air and Earth, the elementals of the Rangers Order.

"No, Veressa, I am not angry. But you have to admit we haven't exactly had the luck of the Cosmos with us since we departed Graystone."

"Well, except for the Eastlander boy who came to our aid." Veressa's cheeks burned under her protector's sudden stare. She had not meant to ever mention the boy again, but she seemed incapable of shaking the young Conner Stonefield from her thoughts. It was more than his success at thwarting the brigands that night in Pennington Point, or at helping them flee the city under the cloak of darkness. Something had happened when Conner had sheltered her from the Sorcerer's spell of binding. She could neither explain nor rationalize the feelings away. The experience had shaken her to her roots.

Though they had lost their horses and nearly creating a royal incident of calamitous proportions in Pennington Point, Annabelle nodded her agreement. "Yes, I suppose we can thank the Cosmos for that." The Ranger took a moment to shift their few remaining supplies to her other shoulder, then scanned the Narwalen Plains to the south, where Peron, her brown falcon bond, dipped and fluttered joyfully through the high grass. "But let me be forthright on this, Veressa. When you have bonded, we are going to return immediately to Graystone Castle, where you are going to focus your energies on becoming the next queen of Griffinrock. There will be no more adventures. You are not going to put me into another tenuous predicament by going against the bidding of the queen or king. Do I make myself clear?"

Veressa hung her head at her preceptor's rebuke, then nodded her muted consent.

The next morning, Veressa and Annabelle came upon an old sorrel gelding grazing on thick summer grass near a wood-shingled farmhouse. After a brief discussion, Annabelle convinced Veressa to remain near the gate while she approached the farm in hopes of acquiring the animal. And though she paid several times what the horse was worth, she had to give a Ranger's vow to the farmer's three young daughters to take good care of their beloved Chester before they would part with him.

At first, Annabelle thought they had been fortunate to acquire the gentle creature while they continued their journey. But with the gelding's rough gait and no saddle or blanket to soften his protruding backbone, the short turns they took riding did little to ease the tension in their tired bodies. It was only Veressa's growing urgency to bond that kept the two moving at a swift pace.

Late that afternoon, Veressa came to a halt, her blue-eyed gaze turning up toward the southern face of a mammoth granite mountain she had been eyeing for several hours. Annabelle reined the gelding in and slipped lightly to the thick grass, taking a moment to study the princess while she shook blood back into her legs.

Chester twisted his neck around to consider his rider through milky eyes, then nuzzled the Ranger's empty hand with a droopy lower lip. Annabelle giggled in response as the last of the carrots the farmer had supplied for their journey appeared in her hand, then vanished into Chester's waiting mouth. She squinted up at the scenic beauty while gently rubbing the contented horse's forehead.

At first glance, the mountain appeared to be similar to others they had passed since leaving Graystone six days ago, only larger. From the mountain's base, the rocky terrain jutted formidably into the cloudless afternoon sky while strong winds blew wisps of snow from its peak. Peron circled overhead, sharp falcon eyes scanning for food.

Annabelle stepped next to the princess and sighed. "You're sure your bond is up there and not on the other side." It was more cautious statement than question. For the past day, she had dealt with Veressa's steadily growing crankiness and tension, and she did not wish to aggravate her further.

Veressa responded by giving her preceptor her first smile since Pennington Point. Her eyes sparkled with excitement.

Annabelle continued. "Great. Reminiscent of my bonding experience, only it's not a tree we have to climb."

Veressa met the Ranger's stare with determined pursed lips. "You don't have to come with me."

"Don't be foolish, Veressa. I didn't let you drag me all this distance to leave me waiting at the mountain's foot." She pointed along the desolate granite wall halfway up the side of the mountain. "Besides, you're going to need me if you have to negotiate that rock face."

"I was hoping you'd say that. So let's see what's up there before we lose the light of Hemera." Without looking to see if her protector followed, the princess attacked the mountain with her usual spirit.

Annabelle hesitated long enough to gather the climbing equipment they had remaining, suddenly wishing she'd had more foresight not to leave so many supplies back at the bank of the Aradorm. With a resolute sigh, she shouldered the bag and followed close behind.

Annabelle ran her hand over the smooth rock surface extending vertically nearly twenty paces over their heads, then slapped the rock with frustration. "I don't see a way up from here with these supplies. If I had been more thoughtful after the storm ..."

"Then we would probably not have made it this far," Veressa finished from behind. "Covering every possibility would have required keeping everything, Annabelle. So, let's not revisit that. The important question is, what do we do now?"

The Ranger regarded her apprentice with pride, taken aback by how much Veressa reminded her of the queen. "You're right, of course. But I am not sure there is anything we can do. I could use Air to levitate, but it requires elemental control you have not yet mastered. For you to attempt levitation would be pointless ... and much too dangerous." Annabelle removed several rations from her pack.

"I am not going back down, Annabelle. For me, there is only one route!" She jabbed her thumb toward the sky with determination, only to have her protector quietly stuff a ration into her hand.

"Whatever we decide to do will require energy, so you'd best eat." To make the point, Annabelle bit calmly into her ration.

The princess's defiance shifted to desperation. "Can't you levitate up and throw down the rope?"

"The rope we have is too short to reach from the top. Besides—"

"Then teach me how to levitate high enough to reach the rope," Veressa interrupted, ignoring the food offering in her hand.

"Which shows how little you understand about elemental control. Levitating five paces requires twice the control you need for two. Twenty paces would tax even my skills of twenty years." Annabelle waited to finish off another bite while she considered the options. "I think the only choice is for me to ride to Cravenrock and return with the necessary equipment."

Veressa scanned the Narwalen Plains to the south. "It would be nightfall before you returned. Then we would have to wait until morning to continue." She paced along the rock wall. "There has to be another way!"

The Ranger's eyes followed the princess while she chewed the last of her ration. Veressa's response was as expected. The princess was accustomed to being in complete control, and therefore was incapable of dealing with situations when she was not. Annabelle had learned it was best to give the girl plenty of rein until she was fully winded. "So what do you suggest?"

The princess studied a fist-sized rock at her feet, as if preparing to kick it. Instead, she picked it up, then bit her lower lip, giving Annabelle a triumphant grin.

The Ranger had seen that look before. She swallowed her last bite of ration hard. "What?" Annabelle asked with trepidation.

Tossing the unopened ration back to her preceptor, Veressa stepped away from the granite wall. Then, facing the wall, she held the rock in her outstretched palm.

The Ranger felt the gathering force, first of Air, then Earth elementals. She could sense the power building, intensifying and coalescing around the princess. The air crackled. Sand and bits of dirt shifted at Veressa's feet. Annabelle had had no clue the girl could draw so much power. She wanted to shout a warning, but was afraid distracting the princess at this point would be disastrous.

Veressa spoke the Modeic words as Annabelle had taught her: *"Outher ousia synchropetra."* There was a sound like a whip cracking, and the rock vanished from Veressa's hand. An explosion against the granite wall sprayed dust and rock debris outward. Annabelle spun away, rock bits pelting her back and arms.

"What in the ...?" Annabelle shouted. She rushed to the princess, who was bent over, coughing and gagging into her hands. Chunks of gravel filled the princess's windblown hair; tears streaked her dust-splattered cheeks. "Veressa, what did you think you were doing!?"

Veressa waved her protector away, blinking and staggering forward into a cloud of dust near the wall. Through another fit of coughs, she pointed at the rock half-buried into the granite wall. "This!"

Annabelle stepped closer. It took several moments to recover from the shock of what she saw. The rock was not so much buried into the granite as *fused* to it with a precision she had seldom seen even among Ranger warders. And the princess had not bonded yet! But as the girl's plan sank in, she glared at her delighted apprentice. "Veressa, your talents never cease to amaze me." When the princess rewarded her with a smug smile, she continued. "Nor does your penchant for harebrained ideas! And this one ranks up there with levitating to the rim!"

Veressa's smile vanished. In silent defiance, she tested her grip on the rock protruding from the granite face, then began gathering more rocks along the wall's base. "I told you: I am not going back down. Besides, you did ask for suggestions. So you can either help me finish what I started, offer a better suggestion, or stay clear of the wall. It would truly ruin my day if I accidentally hit you with one of these rocks."

Annabelle ignored the princess's threat, choosing to use the opportunity to teach her ardent student better mastery of the elementals. Veressa clearly possessed a surprising amount of raw power, but she was clumsy and impatient when it came to control. To Peron and Annabelle's relief, within an hour, Veressa had completed her rock steps to the top of the granite wall without significant injury to any of them.

The princess nodded with self-approval at her handiwork, ignoring the falcon's screeches of relief. "That required a few more rocks than expected, but it is definitely climbable." Noting the length of her shadow, she stepped to the wall and found a strong handhold to start her ascent.

"Wait, Veressa! I go first. I can drop the rope down. Then you can use it to negotiate the last few paces. Besides, we have no clue what is on the other side of that rim."

Given the means to make the climb, the princess was already a pace up the wall. "My bond is up there, Annabelle. I can feel it. Besides, I would rather have you under me than on the rim where you would be of no use." Over her shoulder, she added, "In the ever-so-slight chance I get in trouble, of course."

"Of course!" Annabelle shot back. But the princess was already out of reach.

Annabelle signaled Peron. Sensing his bond's concern, the falcon shook ruffled feathers and took flight, climbing rapidly into the late-day sky. Maybe Annabelle could not assist Veressa with any dangers, but at least Peron could forewarn her. The Ranger paced and chewed her lip as the princess ascended.

Veressa's trek was taking too long. Sensing that her bond was close, her primitive needs grew to a fevered pitch. She did not hear Annabelle's nervous voice urging her to go slowly. Nor was she aware of her legs trembling from the exertion of the climb, the rawness in her fingers, spasms of pain in her back, or the cool granite sliding across her cheek. The Calling urged her beyond caution, and she drove her body up the precarious rock face.

The next thing she knew, she was lying prone along the granite rim, looking up at the steep ascent of the snow-tipped mountain into the darkening sky. Peron floated in circles over her head, while Annabelle called up to her. She started to reply, but motion drew her attention. A bear cub with bright eyes bounded her way.

Veressa laughed and ran fingers through the cub's thick brown fur. It responded with a lick and snort in her ear. She giggled. Peron screeched overhead. *What is Peron fussing about? No. Something is not right.* She worked to understand the falcon's warnings. Annabelle was shouting something from below. The cub licked her face playfully and she pushed it away. But it leaped back, ready to continue their game.

At last, Veressa understood. She would not be bonding with a cub. A bond would be an adolescent, nearly grown. She pushed the cub away again. This time, it grunted irritably at its new playmate.

Then Hemera and the sky turned dark overhead.

Peron's persistent warning calls and Veressa's unresponsiveness from the rim were all Annabelle needed. Air and Earth elementals formed around her and she bounded lightly up the protruding rocks. She was halfway up the granite face when she heard the princess scream.

Several nobles at Graystone's court had grizzlies for bonds, so Veressa was not facing a complete unknown. But stories about their short tempers and how mother grizzlies protected their young had done little to prepare her for this beast's ferocity. The huge bear roared in irritation over her, descending to crush the life from the creature poking at her cub.

Veressa rolled just as the rock beneath her quivered from the force of the bear's massive paws. Hot breath coursed down the nape of her neck. She continued her roll, twisting out of the grizzly's reach. Huge jaws snapped, ripping part of a braid from her scalp.

A blur of white streaked across her vision, and she felt fur brush her extended arms. Her mind reeled as she lost all sense of balance. Too late, she remembered the granite face. With nothing to stop her momentum, she quietly spun out over the ledge.

Whether by chance or luck, motion over Annabelle's head caught the Ranger's attention. Veressa's body shot out from the rim, descending rapidly in a spinning flurry of waving arms and legs to the rocky base below. She wanted to grab for her, but knew the princess would be out of reach. Ignoring the pain from the half-healed wound in her palm, Annabelle tightened her grip on the rock steps. Then, closing her eyes, she drew hard on Air and Earth elementals and projected them outward with an incantation. *"Aerora energi stereoproaspi!"*

Annabelle grunted from the impact of Veressa's body against her barrier. She struggled to maintain control of her hold on both the rock and elemental forces, sensing Veressa's body slowing. But her grip weakened, and she lost her tenuous footing. With feet dangling, Annabelle clawed wildly to regain a foothold. She drew even deeper on the elementals to counter Veressa's weight. Her head throbbed in response.

Peron screeched and fluttered past in a helpless attempt to protect his bond from some unseen threat.

At last, Annabelle's link with the elemental snapped and she gasped at the force of the recoil, driving her body hard into the wall. Just then, she heard the muffled sound of Veressa's body striking the hard base below. "No!" she shouted.

Sobbing and shaking, Annabelle descended to the base, calling out again and again to the motionless form below. Stumbling over rocks, she ran to Veressa, then clutched the lifeless form to her bosom. Ignoring her bloody hands and Peron's screeches above, she wept uncontrollably. "Oh, Cosmos, what have I done!?"

A swirling blast of sand whipped across Veressa's face, stinging her flushed cheeks, forcing her to close her eyes. Grit filled her nostrils and mouth, and she coughed and sneezed reflexively. She raised her arm, but the sand flowed like silk around her naked body. There was a sound like granite boulders grinding, yet somehow, in the crunching sound, she heard her name. The cold stone under her bare feet vibrated with the deep groan of the voice. She spun around, trying to locate the sound emanating from everywhere, but swirling sand filled the void.

Memories flowed across her mind, of the grizzly mother and cub, of slipping over the rim of the granite face, of falling to the base below. She touched her temple where she remembered striking a rock, but felt neither pain nor knot. "Am I dead?" she asked in fear.

"Listen carefully, cousin of the Air, if you are to remember," the granite voice ground out. "The time of the Cosmic juncture has passed. You have only begun to play your part in what must unfold. There is much that you must accomplish."

*Cousin of the Air? Cosmic juncture? My part?* None of what the voice said made sense. She masked her mouth with her hand. "Who are you?"

"I am Ourea, vessel and spirit bearer of Earth elemental," rumbled the voice. "I am to send you my young brother Antilles so that he may bring you strength and aid you along your path."

"My bond," Veressa stated at the memory of white fur flashing past, though she was bewildered by everything else. "I have a bond. Antilles," she said, a warm joy flooding through her. "Path?"

"Everything you hold dear is but desert sand, Veressa. Soon you must choose among many difficult paths. Some would bring you joy, but only at great sorrow to your world. Others you would take alone, bringing great sacrifice and suffering to those you hold dear, but the choice would heal your world from seeds of travesty yet to be sown. You must prepare for the journey ahead."

Veressa felt the tugging at her mind, her feet sinking into the stone. "No! Wait! What path? What journey? I don't understand!" She screamed at the churning grit, but the stone became quicksand.

"In time, all will be clear," the granite groaned.

Veressa feared leaving without knowing the full meaning of this foretelling. She was not ready to face whatever future the voice prophesied, so she labored on, fighting against the stone as it sucked her into the blankness beneath. Demands to the moving sand became requests, first desperate, then pleading, until the very moment she vanished. And silence once more filled the swirling void.

Annabelle hugged the princess's body to her, rocking gently. A battle raged within her, between her inability to let go and the need to accept Veressa's death. Tears of self-torment mingled with blood from scratches across her face, etching long red lines of incrimination down her neck and chest. Peron perched in a dead tree nearby, relentlessly scanning for the enemy causing his bond such grief.

Hemera had not moved in that eternity between when Annabelle first held Veressa's form and when she heard the princess's soft groan. The Ranger gasped, gingerly relaxing her grip to examine the body she held. A bright red streak matted the tightly woven Ranger-apprentice braid along Veressa's temple. The princess's eyelids were closed but fluttered; her cheeks flushed. Annabelle exhaled hard, trembling in wild exultation at the sight.

A quick search of the area yielded a handful of ripe burrberries, which she crushed and lightly pressed against the head wound, then wrapped Veressa's forehead tightly in cloth. By the time the wrap was secure, the princess's cheeks were cool, her breathing normal.

Urgency drove Annabelle now. She lifted the unconscious Veressa into her arms and started down the mountain pass toward Chester wading contently through a thick meadow.

Peron squawked and winged swiftly south to guide his bond.

The Ranger was so intent on Veressa's welfare that neither she nor Peron noticed the sleek white form trailing stealthily behind.

# Undercurrents

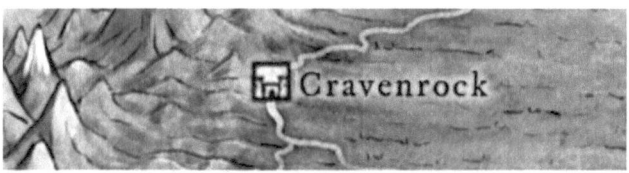

Marcantos Evinfaire slid his bare legs quietly from under the light bedsheets, then ran stiff fingers through his long, ruffled hair. The warm predawn air in Cravenrock Keep was as stale and dismal as his life had become the past fortnight, occupied completely by a daily ritual of intense workouts and training, first as student, then as instructor to the Warriors assigned to Cravenrock. Yet, in spite of the exhaustion that nagged his body, his mind refused to settle. Sleep came in stuttered fits. He studied the half-healed cuts along his muscular forearms. His speed and agility were clearly improving under the guidance of his preceptor Blake Friarwood, as was his skill at manipulating Water and Air, the elemental forces of the Warriors Order. But Marcantos had never felt so impaired. And though his preceptor dismissed his budding anxiety as a natural side effect of the Narwalen summer heat and his mentor's strenuous regime, he could not help but worry about his recent mental and emotional restlessness.

Foxy's body moved next to him, and she moaned softly in her sleep. He studied the curves of the bedsheets outlining her sleek Warrior form, then smiled—a rarity for him of late. At least one distraction offered solace in this Cosmos-forsaken place. He took a deep breath, pushing away his doubts. Foxy—no, he shook his head, reminding himself to use her real name now that he knew it—Trista, one of the four master Warrior instructors assigned to Cravenrock Keep, did not seem to be concerned about his shifting temperament. Maybe she was right; maybe he was overreacting.

Marcantos rubbed his feet over the motionless mass of thick fur beside his bed. Copious, his brown bear bond, grumbled and twitched in sleepy response. In the growing predawn light, Marcantos stretched his lithe body before he dressed and headed for Cravenrock Keep's ward. With Hemera breaking the eastern plains, he found Friarwood waiting along the northern parapet. His pace slowed as he neared.

Friarwood studied his grandmaster Warrior student with folded arms, cool eyes, and a calculating stare. His preceptor wore his usual loose-cut black robes. A massive bow hung from his right shoulder. "How good that you decided to join me this morning," Friarwood said with a smile contradicting his impatient stance. "Perhaps your evening diversions have taken priority over your morning training?"

"Of course not," Marcantos retorted irritably. He nodded toward the fiery orange ball in the east. "I am only a moment late from—"

"A moment can be all that separates the living from the dead, Marcantos!" Friarwood snarled, then visibly relaxed with a sigh, raising his palms disapprovingly before his student. "Never mind. We have much to do before your *voyeurs*"—he nearly spat the word—"arrive for their daily show. First, I want to see if you have progressed with the forms we started yesterday." He waved brusquely for his student to begin.

Marcantos did not hesitate for even a heartbeat. Without thinking, he crouched. His fingers flicked, and a sharp, short dagger appeared in each palm. One blade pointed forward toward his preceptor, the other back, protecting his wrist and forearm.

Friarwood studied him closely, then nodded.

His student responded, drawing deep on Air and Water elementals. *"Ponther ousia odigosepithesi."* His body blurred, moving through the Dance of the Tiger forms, shifting between the churning torrents of energy around him. The blades swirled rhythmically in Marcantos's hands, first up, then to the right, each stroke in perfect counterbalance. Without warning, he struck out fiercely. The student spun and jabbed, and the preceptor danced back. Each killing stroke of the blades slipped just beyond the reach of the preceptor's shifting body.

"Good, Marcantos. You are fluidity in motion, molten lead cutting through a soft breeze, piercing your enemy's defenses." Across the parapet the two danced, whirling blurs of the student's attack in rhythm with the mentor's retreat, until Friarwood's heel struck the parapet's back wall. With his Sight, Marcantos sensed a change in the swirling eddies chewing at the patterned Harmonic fabric of the Mental plane and reacted to the shifting currents. Consumed by the bloodlust of the fight, he drove both daggers forward toward his preceptor's chest.

Friarwood pressed the sole of his left boot against the parapet's sidewall and pushed out, driving his body sideways and out of reach of Marcantos's blades as his student leaped past. Friarwood grinned at the expected advantage. He shrugged, and his heavy Grenetian longbow slipped into his waiting palm. But his advantage was lost with this action. The student spun, reversing his momentum with a kick against the back wall. Friarwood used his bow like a quarterstaff, and each fierce stroke of the bow was met with precise defensive taps from the younger grandmaster's blades.

The preceptor laughed with intense pleasure and jumped out of reach of Marcantos's spinning daggers. "Now, be mist from the elementals you draw upon." A steel-tipped arrow appeared in Friarwood's hand, the black shaft spinning between the preceptor's dexterous fingers. He continued, the heavy bow leveled at his student's chest. "Your foe strikes, but you are a phantom. Your enemy swings, but his blade meets only air where you were an instant before." Without warning, Friarwood's hand flowed from bowstring to quiver and back again, firing a dozen arrows in rapid succession.

Marcantos responded to the changing Mental flux, and he spoke a spell: *"Aetos ousia odigosproaspi."* His blades flashed. Working through a complex defensive weave, the blades precisely deflected each deadly arrow. But Friarwood's aggressive attack inflamed him. His eyes blazed with fury. Crouching once more, Marcantos prepared to leap back into the battle.

"Enough!" Friarwood commanded, his hand raised as if staying a maddened dog.

Moments passed while Marcantos fought to regain control. Illusory spots swirled in his tunnel vision. His chest heaved erratically, thighs trembling with unspent energy. Finally, the student rose as if waking from a dream, tranquility returning. With a calm smile, he removed one of the dozen black arrows protruding from the parapet's walls and walkway, then ran his thumb over the sharp tip. "Did you forget to bring practice arrows, Blake?"

The other man smirked in a way that inevitably disarmed and infuriated its recipient. "It is time we put such childish toys away, Marcantos. You cannot find your true mettle without a little risk."

The side of Marcantos's mouth twitched at his preceptor's response. *Is he questioning the strength of my character?* He tossed the arrow to Friarwood. "Dead men have no mettle."

Before Marcantos could say more, the sound of soft-soled boots in the ward below drew their attention. A moment later, Trista appeared at the stairs along the far end of the parapet. She wore a dark, sleeveless jerkin tight at the waist and loose at the chest, leaving plenty to the imagination for what lay beneath. Marcantos locked eyes with her and was rewarded with a warm smile as she lingered in the morning light. Time stopped. He wondered whether her glow was from Hemera's orange color or the feelings he hoped she shared with him. Maybe he would never know. Undaunted by his stare, she moved like a cat toward the two men, in control of every aspect of her body, with a touch of seduction added for good measure. In his mind he still called her Foxy for many reasons; how unfortunate that she had nearly weaned him of using that nickname aloud.

"Why are you not dressed for our morning exercise?" Marcantos inquired.

"A rather winded manor guardsman came to your bedchamber moments ago carrying this." Trista extended a rolled parchment bearing a flowery script—*Grandmaster Warrior Evinfaire*—and sealed with Countess Garlander's ring.

"Manor guard? I am of no import to the countess." Taking the message, he broke the seal and scanned the finely scripted lettering. "I have been summoned to court by Contessa Garlander. I am to go immediately."

Friarwood held a restraining hand to Marcantos, then turned to Trista. "Did the guardsman say anything when he gave you the message?"

"No, Grandmaster," she murmured, her eyes never leaving Marcantos. "Only that the message was important."

"A moment of your time, Marcantos." Friarwood drew his pupil to the side and whispered an incantation: *"Aetha energi kalyptholos."* The air shimmered about them, creating a dome of silence. "Before you go, I must tell you of some news I received in the middle of the night that is likely related to the countess's summons."

Marcantos did not know how his preceptor acquired the information he always had at his disposal, nor did he care to know. Friarwood seemed to have eyes and ears everywhere about him. Marcantos suspected this was partially the reason his preceptor had advanced so quickly through the Warriors Order. He nodded, then waited.

"A man ... let's say, in my service ... came to my chambers in the middle of the night while I worked, to recount to me a very peculiar tale he had personally witnessed. It seems late last evening a master Ranger rode through the Cravenrock gate clutching an unconscious female Ranger apprentice in front of her. My man says he would not have thought twice about it, being that this is Cravenrock, if not for a few oddities. First, he noted that the two were riding a rather bedraggled old nag, clearly not requisitioned by their order. But what really drew his attention was regarding some trouble between the gate guardsmen and the unconscious Ranger's bond. Of this, he said no more. But it was enough to elect him to follow the pair from the shadows of Cravenrock's buildings. It is here the story grows more intriguing.

"The master Ranger rode immediately to the countess's manor, where she briefly exchanged words with the manor guardsmen stationed outside. The shadows from which my man had chosen to observe these events prevented him from hearing what was said, but it clearly sent the guardsmen into a tizzy. Within moments, the manor was alight with guardsmen running hither and yon with the countess's conciliator directing the mayhem. Immediately after the unconscious Ranger was gingerly carried inside, a runner was dispatched to retrieve the countess's personal Physician, Onorus Dankmar, who returned and stayed through the remainder of the night."

"All of this is fascinating, Blake, but what does this have to do with me?"

"I was getting to that, Marcantos. I then inquired with my man for a few details about the Ranger who brought this evidently important Ranger apprentice to the manor. Tall for a woman, she had shoulder-length black hair, smooth dark complexion, and piercing green eyes. But maybe most telling was the master Ranger's bond." He paused for dramatic effect.

Marcantos grew impatient. "Yes?"

Friarwood's eyebrows lifted. "A male brown falcon."

Marcantos's mind reeled, refusing to take the implications further. "There must be more than one female master Ranger fitting such a description."

The preceptor grunted his annoyance at Marcantos's refusal to accept the obvious conclusion. "Maybe. But who else would be riding with a young woman who could command such response from the countess and her retainers? The implications are quite clear, Marcantos. Whatever the countess wants with you, it most certainly has to do with an injured Princess Veressa ... and her personal protector and guardian, Master Ranger Annabelle Loris."

It had been years since he had heard that name. It was another life, a younger, wilder day at Striker's Keep, when Marcantos and Annabelle had been together. The light grip of Friarwood's hand on Marcantos's shoulder pulled him from the memories.

"I should not have to remind you to be mindful of what you commit yourself to this time. The countess is not the keep's commander." The comment was to remind Marcantos of the day he'd made a promise to train young Warrior recruits after he had injured their four preceptors in a mock fight. Friarwood released his grip along with his hold on Air elemental. The shield of silence fell away.

Marcantos smiled faintly at Trista, then walked toward the keep.

Copious met Marcantos with a morning yawn while crossing the ward, then lumbered after him into the keep's cooler hall.

Friarwood's eyes shifted from his departing pupil to examine the exquisite lines of Trista's body before him. A person in his position could not afford to let his mind wander to such physical pleasures; still, the thoughts were tempting.

"I doubt Marcantos would appreciate you looking at me that way." Trista did not take her eyes from Marcantos's back. After Marcantos disappeared into the ward's hall, she turned to study the grandmaster.

Friarwood grunted. "Do you think I am concerned about what Marcantos likes or doesn't like?"

Trista's eyes glistened. "Maybe that is exactly what should be foremost on your mind. I would think what he likes *should* be your concern."

Friarwood stepped closer, menacingly. Trista cowed in response. "Do not attempt to dictate to *me* what I should be concerned with. I was told in good faith by Barbarian Barcleave that you were the right choice for this assignment. We spent years getting you into this position of responsibility. But it seems your Barbarian skills are not up for the task." He measured her stoic reaction, then redirected his attack. "Or are your feelings for this man getting in the way?"

The woman shook her head solemnly, cheeks flushed.

"I ask because I need to know where your true allegiance lies, Trista. It concerns me that Marcantos is having difficulties adapting to my unique style of training. It is your responsibility to ensure his transition to the Anarchic ways is a smooth one. You are running out of time to assist him in this adjustment." He turned his gaze to the portal Marcantos had disappeared through. "A change is coming. I can feel it."

"He will be ready for you."

This time, Friarwood let her watch his eyes scan down her body. "Good, because if you cannot assist me in his transition, I will be forced to find another assignment for you to make up for my displeasure. Do I make myself clear?"

Blood ran from Trista's cheeks. She understood what was necessary for those of Friarwood's true order to experience pleasure. She nodded her acceptance, then took her leave.

# Grimmley

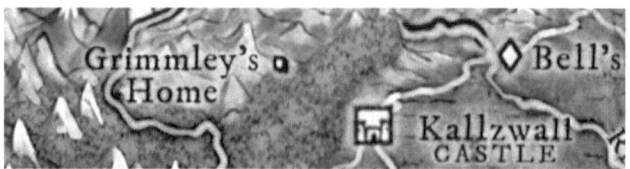

Early on the morning following their crossing of the Aradorm gorge, Conner and his scaly, black bond stopped on top of a hill and gazed down into a shallow valley to the south. The scene was as Jess Tandoor had described. The valley was situated in the middle of several hills, forming a natural bowl that spanned more than a thousand paces in diameter. Along the inner regions of the hills, several dozen groves containing every type of tree in the known world encircled the grassy valley like a summer wreath. The trees had been meticulously planted in rows and sectioned by type. To Conner's left was a grove of large-leaf maple trees, and beyond that, a grove of dark oaks. To his right were groves of hickory and walnut. Beyond those on either side, he could discern pine, spruce, noble fir, alpine ash, and cherry gum.

At the heart of the valley was a white stone cottage about the size of Conner's home, with a clay-shingled roof. From what appeared to be the back door of the cottage, a stone walkway meandered through a large, well-tended garden, ending at the bank of a clear, blue lake. A wooden walkway extended out over the lake, connecting the path to a white gazebo built precisely over the middle of the water. The only visible signs of life were a few birds and small mammals foraging through the groves and a horse grazing contently in the valley.

Conner led the way, keeping the dragon hemmed in the shadow of the maple trees. Approaching the cottage, he caught movement of someone through the open windows. He faced his large shadow. "Skye, I need you to stay out of sight until I have talked to the old Shaman. The last thing we need is for him to take a hard look at you and keel over in shock. So let me prepare him for what he's about to see. Then I'll bring him out to have a good look at you."

Skye tried to blend into the trees, nearly uprooting a thin maple. The feeling of slightly restrained excitement through his connection with Skye fed Conner's anxiety. "But Conner, few of my family have ever seen a great Shaman. It is sung that they are spiritual beings like us. I have always wondered if they see the Cosmos as we do."

Conner ignored the creature's refusal to accept the fact that Shamans were of the same race as other humans. He was beginning to think it impossible to deflate the intrepid creature's enthusiasm, so he decided it was no longer worth the time or trouble to try. "I am sure the two of you will have wonderful chats about the mysteries of the Cosmos, but you need him alive and lucid to have those discussions. So please, for once, do as I ask. And don't destroy anything or burn down one of his groves. Okay?" He waited to see if anything was seeping into the wyvern's thick, horned skull.

Skye's eyes darted between Conner and the cottage while debating whether to heed Conner's request. Rolling his head to the side, the dragon squinted. "Okay, Conner."

Conner was not sure what the head turning meant, but he sensed the beast's reluctant acquiescence. He nodded with satisfaction. "Okay, I will try to be quick." Not wanting to give the dragon an opportunity to reconsider his promise, he hiked hastily down the hill toward the cottage.

Passing the garden that took up most of the yard between the cottage and lake, Conner recognized nearly every type of plant he knew to be for medicinal and herbal use. And he named them as he walked— tanglewood bush for muscle soreness, dreamweaver to induce sleep, balsemium for toothaches, haggleweed for exhaustion, even the very rare sternwall vines used to ease the ails of whooping cough. The exotic plants grew seemingly at random about the garden, a stark contrast to the precise rows of trees surrounding the cottage.

At closer examination, the cottage was smaller than he had first thought. The outer walls were constructed of white boulders roughly honed into large blocks. But what Conner found most fascinating was that every boulder had been cut into a unique size and pattern. Each one interlocked precisely with the next, creating a perfect seal with no need for mortar. Several large, wood-frame windows with finely polished glass were opened wide along each side of the cottage, giving the home a sense of both the simple and the elegant.

Around the front of the cottage, the clay-shingled roof covered a slate-floor porch extending several paces in front of a large wooden door and another window. Conner stepped to the entrance. This close to the famous Shaman, his sense of urgency waned as his doubts took root. He stared at the polished brass ball knocker hinged to the door.

Before he could grab the knocker, the door swung wide. In the doorway stood a thin, elderly man wearing bright green flowing robes adorned with images of tiger swallowtail butterflies that seemed to flutter as the robes swayed in the gentle breeze. His round face, which contradicted his narrow frame, was set amid long, curly white hair and a bushy white beard that covered most of his chest. Wire-rimmed glasses were set between prominent eyebrows and a button nose. And between his teeth, he held a long-stemmed pipe, which he puffed vigorously while examining his uninvited guest—reminiscent of Apothecary Guildmaster Cleaverbrook examining the physical condition of his plants.

Conner cleared away the knot in his throat that had developed under the man's intense scrutiny. He began, "Excuse me, sir, for the bother, but would you be Grandmaster Shaman Grimmley Rollingsworth?"

The aged man ran his fingers through his beard as if pondering a perplexing problem. Conner waited, the delightful aroma of pipe smoke soothing his nerves and removing the edge from his exhaustion.

"I am not sure if I am defined by a name, but Grimmley Rollingsworth is the name my parents gave me. The rest is really rather trivial."

Uncertain how to interpret the Shaman's odd reply, Conner continued. "I seem to have acquired a problem that I hope you can help me with, sir. I was told by Student Jess Tandoor from the Apothecary in Pennington Point where I could find you."

The Shaman's bushy eyebrows rose in recognition of the name. "Hmm. I see. Yes, I know Student Tandoor. A fine young lad. But boy, who are *you*?"

"Oh! I am so sorry, sir! Yes, my apologies. My name is Conner Stonefield. My problem—"

"Stonefield?" the Shaman interrupted, his gaze floating to the porch awning as he tapped his pipe bowl. "Conner, you say? Why, I have heard that name somewhere before. But I am not young anymore, so memories come and go as they will." He waved Conner to follow him into his home. "I am sure someone as young as you knows nothing of such things, so you'll have to be patient with me for a minute while I ..."

Conner hesitated before stepping through the doorway, glancing in the direction of where he'd left Skye. But he found no trace of the black beast. He glanced across the yard and then up the long rows of trees to the north and west, to no avail. *How does something so big disappear so quickly?*

He was so engrossed in looking for the infuriating creature that he failed to notice that the Shaman had stopped talking and was staring at him from the middle of the cottage. "Did you lose something, boy?"

Conner jumped. "I'm sorry, sir. Yes, it seems I have, but I am sure I will find it again soon." He actually was a bit relieved that he did not have to worry about Skye scaring the old Shaman to death before he had a chance to prepare him. He stepped through the wide portal.

The entire cottage was one large room, or more precisely, a number of sectioned areas with no walls. To Conner's right, under one of the cottage windows, was a large, finely carved wooden desk covered with scrolls and parchments, all neatly stacked. A soft fire burned in a granite fireplace that filled much of the remaining wall. Farther on, a hearth of the same stone extended nearly to the middle of the cottage, where a short, square table containing a three-tiered board of the game Crowns separated two well-worn padded brown chairs. Behind the Shaman was the back door, a small breakfast table under another open window, and an iron stove and cabinets. To Conner's left, a steep, narrow staircase led to a small wooden platform extending above several more large windows. Here, the cottage walls were lined with stuffed bookshelves, a busy workbench, and a large wooden rack holding hundreds of labeled vials and glass containers. A number of potted flowering plants and knickknacks hung from the upper floor's bracings and columns. The scent of burning hickory, mixed with a number of fragrances Conner did not recognize, filled the cottage. The overall gestalt was that of a well-organized and immaculate mess.

"Hoot! Hoot!" A large barred owl studied Conner from a worn perch near the fireplace.

The Shaman stared contemptuously at the bird. "Don't mind Barthox. She doesn't mean most of what she says, and says even less of what she means, especially before she's eaten." The owl stared back.

Ignoring the owl, the Shaman settled in one of the well-worn chairs in the middle of the room. "Well, while I try to place where I have heard that name, why don't you tell me about this problem of yours." He pointed to the chair across from him with his pipe's mouthpiece, apparently unconcerned about Conner's scruffy appearance.

"Thank you, sir, but if it's all right, I will stand."

"As you wish," Grimmley shrugged as he relit his pipe with a spell: *"Hem pheto anaptofotia."* He exhaled smoke through his nostrils, still studying Conner. "Your problem?"

"Oh, yes, sir. My problem ..." Conner started nervously. "Well, sir, I was on my trek from my home in Creeg's Point when I—"

"Creeg's Point! That's it!" The Shaman interrupted Conner triumphantly. "Now I know where I've heard that name before. Why, you are the new apprentice to Guildmaster Cleaverbrook, aren't you?"

"Yes, sir, I am. But how did you know?"

The Shaman's scrutiny intensified. "My boy, it is my responsibility to know everything going on within the Apothecaries Guild." He waved away the smoke impeding his clear view of the boy. "But I don't get mixed up with any internal guild affairs. If you have an issue with your assignment or studies, you will have to take that up with the guildmasters."

It took a moment for Conner to understand what the Shaman meant. "Oh, no, sir! I am quite happy with my assignment. In fact, I am excited about being selected for the guild. I want nothing more than to be an Apothecary guildsman."

"That's good, boy. Then I am sure you will do well. So I fail to understand what could possibly be the problem."

Conner breathed deep to calm his nerves. "Let me start again. You see, my trek led me deep into the Dragon's Back Mountains, where I was pursued by a group of trackers. There, I found the remnants of what I think was an abandoned mine."

"Pursued? Why were you being pursued, boy?" the Shaman asked, his interest suddenly piqued.

"Well, sir. That is a long story for another time." Conner very much wanted to keep the discussion away from what had happened during his time in Cravenrock, which could do nothing to gain him favor with the Shaman.

"It has been my experience youths on their bonding treks are not chased without fair reason. Maybe you should take the time to fill in some details so I can better understand how I might assist."

Conner wanted to kick himself for having a tired, flapping tongue. He sighed. "I was falsely accused of a crime and arrested while I was traveling through Cravenrock."

The Shaman's forehead wrinkled, his bushy eyebrows floating above his spectacles. "Arrested?" He puffed vigorously on his pipe. "I see. But that doesn't explain why you were being chased if you committed no real crime."

Conner decided it best not to lie to the orderman, but did not want to mention anything about falling in with the Thieves Guild to collect enough coins to continue his trek. "I escaped," Conner stated simply. He winced, not sure how the Shaman would react.

"And this has nothing to do with the problem you want help with?" He leaned forward, eyeing Conner with sudden fascination. "Maybe it is best to leave that tale for later. I can hardly wait to hear what kind of trouble surpasses being a fugitive."

"Well, as I was saying, I was chased into an abandoned mine. There, in the large main cavern, I found this ..."

Grimmley patiently studied the boy.

"... this, well, this ..."

Grimmley let out a long puff of smoke, then rose slowly. "Dragon."

"Yes! Well, no! Not exactly. Well, to be honest, maybe? You see, *he* thinks he is a dragon. Well, no. He calls himself a wyvern, and he does kind of *look* like a dragon ..." Conner's words fell off as he realized the Shaman had named it. "Wait—how did you know?"

Grimmley removed his pipe and pointed over Conner's shoulder, repeating the word, "Dragon."

Conner turned. Half of a horned, black head containing a bright blue eye peered through the open window.

"Skye! I told you to stay hidden in the trees until it was clear for you—"

"But Conner, I could feel you were ... what was that word? Anxious? I was worried something was wrong."

Conner became aware of the Shaman standing next to him, staring at the head that filled the window. The Shaman eyed Conner with still greater interest, his bushy eyebrows ever higher. "Yes, boy, I see what you mean. It seems you do have a problem."

Conner furrowed his eyebrows at the beast with fists on hips. "Oh, you don't know the half of it!"

# A Queen's Demand

King Jonath stepped from the Royal Scrying Chamber he used to communicate with others who had access to similar rooms around the three realms. Taking a moment for his consciousness to settle, Jonath cast an intricate Fire and Air spell of warding to seal the chamber doors: *"Heter ousia kleidofylaxi."* He sighed deeply, then started down the long hall with hands clasped at the small of his back. He hardly noticed the finely etched gold in the gray marble floor, the ornate paintings lining the walls, or the brightly colored ceiling sparkling in the ambient morning light. He would have gladly traded them all for a single fortnight's reprieve from the string of troubling reports he had received concerning his daughter, Veressa.

Beggar, the king's white spotted owl bond, fluttered behind, her perpetual worried frown worsened by Jonath's heavy heart and unsettled mind.

It was bad enough that he had held back telling his beloved wife and queen about his visit with his lifelong friend Dane Norterry at the Mystic Chamber of the Oracles, and about the discovery of the Cosmic alignment on Midsummer's Day. All attempts to uncover any details about the Cosmic event foretold by the Mystic oracles had produced nothing useful. But having the queen uncover that bit of news paled to what would happen if she discovered that he had been withholding important information about their daughter. Jonath had gone out of his way to convince Izadora not to send a legion of Queen's Defenders after Veressa when the princess snuck away on her bonding trek with only the Ranger Annabelle Loris to protect her. He had held to the faith that the Ranger, Veressa's assigned protector since the princess was five, could control the girl. Jonath had been terribly wrong.

It was possible that he had successfully kept news of the princess's mishap at the Aradorm contained, along with the unexpected return of Veressa's gelding back to Graystone without his rider. It was conceivable that Queen Izadora would not link word of a botched assault on a Ranger apprentice in Pennington Point to their daughter. But nothing would prevent this most recent calamity from reaching the queen's ear in quick order. Well, it might as well be his report she received. He picked up his pace, proceeding to the queen's reception hall, where his wife would be preparing for the first High Law grievance of the day. It was best to get this over with before she was distracted by her regular duties. They tended to make her irritable.

He stepped past the two royal guardsmen, their mongoose and raccoon bonds frolicking in the corner. Before either guard could react, the king drew upon Air elemental, and the heavy mahogany doors to the reception hall groaned and swung open in response.

Inside, two more guardsmen stood near the door. Izadora stood before a mirror, making final adjustments to hair and crown while Tyresus, her noble goshawk bond and self-appointed guardian, perched next to her throne.

The queen offered her husband a radiant, regal smile. For the first time since leaving the Scrying Chamber, the rhythmic beat of the king's boots faltered. After all their years together, she never ceased to have that effect on him.

"What a pleasant surprise, my king. Have you come to observe your queen in royal action?" Izadora's melodic, commanding voice possessed the hint of tease Jonath found alluring, heightened by a piercing gaze and long, flowing dark hair. But when Beggar, Jonath's bond and harbinger of feelings, floated through the portal and took her usual perch near the door, the queen sighed. With a signal to the guards, she waited until she was alone with the king before speaking further. "I should have known you came with business in mind, and bearing bad news at that." She nodded at the bristled owl and exhaled slowly to brace herself. "You know I do not like to keep my people waiting, so out with whatever you have to tell me."

"I have been withholding information from you, Iza."

"Do you mean your outing with Dane Norterry to the Mystics' temple several days ago?"

Jonath tensed. "So you know about that?" he noted with surprise.

"Of course," she responded, as if thinking otherwise was absurd. "What I don't know is what was so vitally important that it could pull you away just hours before the Midsummer's Night Festival. You know how important the festival is to me, so don't try to dismiss this as trivial."

Jonath hated the rapid shift in winds, but the queen would not change course until she was satisfied she had all the details. With a deep breath, he started in about his meeting with the Mystics Order's College of Doyen and the Mystic oracles. He made only a passing note of the celestial device in the oracles' chambers, but went into great detail about their description of the Cosmic alignment and the oracles' interpretation of its meaning, ending with the location of the event inside Griffinrock's realm. Jonath recalled Oracle Gildamare's description of their system's planetary bodies struck in such perfect balance that the effects of the Cosmic laws no longer apply. A *singularity*, she had called it. He shook off the feeling this event was an ill omen. "Given that my order's oracles consider this one of the greatest events of our time, I have since approached all six order councils with requests for information. After nearly a week, I have still to receive any news. I fear it may be too late to know what the Cosmic event was." He sighed.

The queen listened intently without speaking, fingers moving lightly through his shoulder-length black hair. When he had finished, she said, "And you withheld telling me about the most significant event in a millennium occurring in our realm because ...?" Certain that her husband was properly baited, she wagged a finger his way. "Be careful how you finish that sentence, Jonath."

"Because, at the time, I thought it best," he responded confidently. "And I still do. There was enough happening at the time that you did not need to worry about this as well."

"So, you're telling me you didn't think I could handle the news."

"Of course not!" He realized the trap he was about to step into and redirected his response. "It is my way of helping you, Iza, by shouldering some of your responsibilities. Sometimes, I feel like a third eye."

The queen smiled back, releasing her tension and anger. "Jonath, I know your motives were honorable and in my best interest. But give me credit to handle more than one problem at a time. You are not my protector; you are my husband and Champion. I will keep telling you this until you truly believe it. We are monarchs together. That is how I want it, to share everything in life. And that is how it will be. As your queen, I demand it!" Though she spoke roughly, she never lost her smile.

The king studied his hands. No matter his motive, he had been wrong to hold back the news. For the first time ever, he wondered if he had been right telling her he could successfully be both her lifelong Champion and her husband. Maybe maintaining this balance was not possible. "Yes, of course, Iza. It seems my love for you has failed you in my duties."

"That is nonsense, Jonath! From the day you became my Champion, you have been more than I ever thought possible." Pressing closer, she touched the slight graying at his temples he referred to as Veressa's Mark, gazed into his steel-gray eyes, and added soothingly, "In every way."

It was her way of telling him, once again, that she forgave his imperfections. It was never easy loving someone incapable of error. He sighed. "Maybe you should hold judgment until you hear everything."

Her cheeks flushed and she slapped his chest in frustration. "Why is life with you like being constantly tossed in the air? Every time I find solid ground, you throw me up again. What else have you to tell me?"

How he loved his queen. "I just left the Scrying Chamber, where I talked with Master Ranger Loris. Veressa is bonded."

"That is wonderful news, Jonath!" Relieved, she continued. "Finally, our daughter can return home ... and be done with all those crazy thoughts of becoming a Ranger. Maybe now she will settle down and take her responsibilities seriously." She caught his pursed lips and froze. "What is it?"

Jonath cleared his throat. "While bonding, Veressa fell and struck her head." He raised his arms to stem the alarm swelling in her. "Veressa is fine, Iza; don't get upset! She is in Cravenrock Manor, under the supervision of Countess Garlander's personal Physician. She expects her to be fully recovered within a day."

The queen bit her tongue. Jonath knew she wanted to say *I told you so!* Instead, she asked, "And what do you plan to do about this?"

Jonath considered how best to summarize the actions he had taken to remedy the situation—ones that would minimize the political fallout that would certainly come. "Everything has already been taken care of."

# Dream Vision

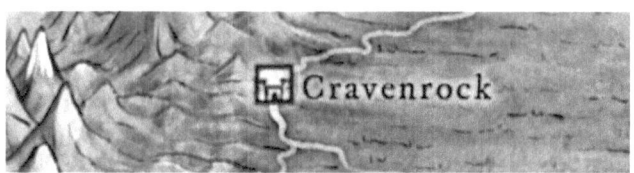

The gentle whisk of a warm breeze across Veressa's cheek brought her from a fitful sleep. She opened her eyes, letting them adjust to the room's sparse lighting. The ceiling was painted with a mural of Kallzwall Castle atop its lone mountain, protectively overlooking the western Narwalen Plains. The castle's signature traits—its massive oak doors, four corner towers capped with cone-shaped copper roofs, and a central square keep and tower extending fifty paces above the castle grounds—were meticulously portrayed. Yellow and white spring daffodils dotted the bright green Narwalen carpet while snow blanketed the rough mountain terrain about the castle walls. Those in the region often used this image to signify the return of life after a rough Narwalen winter.

The room's walls, decorated with elegant patterned paper, gradually shifted into focus. Several large, scenic paintings were hung about the room. Thick drapes to her left shunted most of the bright light streaming through an open window. The dark mahogany door beyond, with its flowery carvings and polished bronze knob, was closed. A crystal pitcher, a matching goblet, and an unlit gold-and-copper lantern sat atop a marble inlaid table between her bed and the window beyond. Peron sat nervously on a perch near the door while Annabelle's head, with its tightly woven master Ranger braids of black hair, rested on the bed. Her bandaged hands lightly held Veressa's forearm.

Veressa tried to sit up, but dizziness and a throbbing in her right temple forced her back down. Fingertips ran delicately along the gauze wrapped tight about her forehead as she struggled to sort through the memories of the last few days.

Annabelle raised her head. Red, swollen eyes were filled with a mix of exhaustion, worry, and something else. There was sadness in the Ranger's eyes that contradicted her thin smile.

*What could she be sad about?* With a start, Veressa struggled to sit up once more. "Where is Antilles?"

"Who?" It required little force for the Ranger to hold the princess to the bed.

"My bond! Where is he? Is he hurt?"

Annabelle gestured to a large, sleek form lying stretched out comfortably along the opposite side of the bed. "*Antilles* is doing quite well at the moment, though he did not particularly want to follow us into Cravenrock last night, nor did he appreciate the manor guardsmen getting too close to you. It will take a while for him to adjust to being around humans."

*Cravenrock?* So she was in Countess Garlander's manor. She cautiously rotated her head. Two small, trim ears set high on her bond's rounded head perked forward, while emerald eyes set wide on a large tan face stared serenely back at her. A crown of black spots extended back, expanding into small round rosettes that cloaked its thick tan-and-white fur. Stocky legs ending in large paws seemed discordant with its trim yet powerful body. It was the largest cat she had ever seen.

Reading the princess's thoughts, Annabelle continued. "Conciliator Barlock believes it to be a snow leopard, though it appears no one in the manor has ever seen one. Whatever it is, it is a rare creature indeed." She eyed the princess skeptically. "So you've been awake a few moments and already have a name for your bond?"

The mix of emotions flowing from her bond—concern, apprehension, contentment—confused Veressa, yet she also felt calm and settled for the first time since receiving the Calling a week before. But her dream eroded the edges of her peace, fraying away corners of her serenity. She needed to understand her dream's meaning. "What can you tell me of Illric's theory of bonds?"

Annabelle was surprised by the seemingly random question, but leaned back in her chair to study the ceiling mural while she called forth old apprentice studies. "Illric, a cleric before the time of orders, was the first to put forth the notion that two elementals could be combined to create more powerful spells. Her pioneering studies and experiments in using Fire and Earth together formed the foundation for today's Shamans Order. This idea became the impetus for the Progressive Period, and ultimately the creation of today's six advanced fighting styles."

The Ranger noted the princess's eagerness to hear more, so she continued with a shrug. "In her later years, Illric shifted into more fringe notions, even by today's standards. It was during this time she proposed that, while humans possess the ability to use all four elementals, we are each born with a predisposition toward one over the others. She further believed it is the connection we share with our bonds that gives us the ability to combine two elementals. To help give credence to this theory, she developed a classification to attempt linking each animal to an elemental. Our selection for bonding is based on an inner need to fulfill some destiny we each possess. That is, she believed that the powers we use today would not be possible if we had no bonds. She also suggested that this theory explained the Yearning a person feels if the bond dies, caused by the lost connection with an elemental force rather than simply the loss of an animal bond."

"What do you think of the theory?"

Annabelle shrugged, then waved a bandaged hand. "I'm no scholar, Veressa. I don't have much need for theories. I prefer dealing with things I can see, hear, touch, and feel. Theories won't change how the

Cosmos works, so I leave such thinking to the intellectuals who have the luxury of time to consider such notions.

"Still," Annabelle continued, "Illric's thinking did form the foundation for the Orderman's Code we use today. Her theory of bonds has dropped out of favor among most scholars. Yet it is the reason why apprentices are not accepted into an order or guild until they have bonded—except, of course, for a few special occasions."

"Why did the theory fall out of favor?" the princess persisted.

"Mostly because everyone who ever attempted to map species to elementals failed. For example, according to Illric, not all birds are creatures of Air elemental. Now, why are you asking me about this?"

Veressa fidgeted. "I had ... a dream, where a voice ... spoke to me."

Annabelle grunted skeptically. "A dream? Veressa, you hit your head pretty hard. I wouldn't let some dream disturb you."

The princess shook her head. "No, Annabelle. It was in this dream I was told my bond's name. The voice also called me 'cousin of the Air' and told me that my bond was an Earth elemental gift from the Cosmos."

The Ranger leaned forward to study Veressa with pursed lips. "Did this voice have a name?"

"It called itself Ourea."

Annabelle inhaled sharply and leaned back. "Ourea, the Mountain? Ourea, the Djinn? Ourea, the keeper of Earth elemental?" When she spoke again, it was with a wispy voice. "Princess Veressa of Griffinrock had a dream vision."

"A dream vision? I have never heard of such a thing."

"Maybe not, but you have heard of Antorio Bestigee, Tatum Creeg, Krygus Armamore, and Maria Woodbriar."

"Of course. With Marci Illric, they are the five paragons: the only ordermen ever raised to the rank of supreme grandmaster within their orders in posthumous recognition for acts deemed transformational in the world."

"Yes. They are also called Harbingers of the Eras, and were some of only a few in recorded history known to have been visited by one of the four elemental Djinn at the time of their bonding, though none ever spoke of what these spirits said." Annabelle leaned close to study Veressa's face, then nodded with satisfaction, if not awe. "Exceptional abilities to use elemental forces, a rare bond, *and* a dream vision! Veressa, it seems you have been chosen to play a vital role in the future of the realms. And to say we are in a transformational moment would be an understatement." She poured water from the crystal pitcher into the goblet. "But you can't be a paragon if you don't get well. Thank the Cosmos the Physician's herbs and spells were adequate. She will return shortly. Once she is certain your head wound is healing properly, food will be brought."

The princess attempted to sit up again, this time with more success. "I am feeling better," she said, more wishfully than factually. Eyeing the exquisite creature stretching the length of her bed, she took the offered glass with shaky hands, then emptied its contents. She felt very hungry. "I am glad I have you with me as my guide and teacher, Annabelle. There is no one in the world I trust more."

Annabelle did not reply, so Veressa studied her protector. Though she looked less worried, something still tugged at the edges of the Ranger's mouth. "What is it? What's wrong, Annabelle?"

Annabelle opened and closed her mouth several times, considering how best to tell the princess something grave. At last, she found the words. "I brought you to Cravenrock under the cloak of darkness last night, Veressa. Once you were seen by the Physician, I used the countess's Scrying Chamber to speak to your father."

"You did what?" Veressa nearly screamed, then grunted at the throb of pain.

"The pretense of our secrecy is no longer critical to maintain, Veressa. It has served its purpose. You have your bond. The king had a right to know of the situation. And I ..." She glanced away. "I had an obligation to inform him."

A feeling of foreboding flooded over Veressa. "What did he say?"

Annabelle's expression chilled. "I have been relieved of my duties as your protector. I will be leaving this morning to Dreadcreek for a new assignment."

Veressa went cold. Numbness obliterated the dull pain in her head. Dreadcreek. The perfect name for the most dismal place in Griffinrock, it was the Rangers' northern outpost near the eastern edge of the Dragon's Back Mountains. Close to the Borderlands, it was the spearhead of many skirmishes with Anarchist forces refusing to acknowledge the neutral lands farther north and east of the hold. "I can't let this happen, Annabelle. I will contact Father. Once I have explained what happened and about my dream vision, he will have to reinstate you as my protector. My studies *must* continue."

"You will do no such thing," the master Ranger commanded.

"I can and I will! If anyone is to blame for what happened yesterday, it is me. You saved my life! I will not allow you to take unjustified blame for my actions."

The Ranger gripped the princess's hand in hers. "Veressa, you must listen to me. For once, do as I request. Whatever Ourea spoke of is very important. Of that, I have no doubt. But you must not tell *anyone* about your dream, not even your father. If the Anarchists acquired this knowledge, your very life would be in danger."

Veressa sat shaking her head while Annabelle spoke, considering the political consequences of her father's actions. "Once news of your dismissal gets out, it will damage the status of the Rangers Order with my mother. And it will certainly end your hopes of ever becoming grandmaster. I cannot let that happen."

"It is too late for that." Annabelle stated calmly. "Others have been told. Once released, there is no sending the nymph back to its plane."

"Others? What do you mean, *others*? Who else needed to be told of this?"

Annabelle glared at the princess over folded arms. "Do you think you could take one single breath without having a protector assigned to you? To release me from the responsibility means another must assume it. I would think you understood that."

"Another protector? I don't want another protector, Annabelle! You have been with me from the time I started walking." Veressa's eyes filled with tears as sadness and anger fought for control. "How will I be apprenticed as a Ranger?"

"Enough, Veressa! It is time you stopped acting like a spoiled, hurt princess," Annabelle exclaimed to stem the princess's emotional tide. With a glance, the Ranger gestured to the large cat taking a sudden interest in its bond's flood of new emotions. "You are bonded, so start acting accordingly. I understand it will take time to adjust to this new stage, so I will forgive you this time for your outburst. But I will have no more immature talk about what you will do."

Veressa sniffed and rubbed angrily at the tears streaming down her face. Her cheeks stung as if they'd been slapped, though Annabelle's words had hurt more. "This is not fair," she mumbled.

"Yes, well, welcome to being an adult. You must let go of the notion that life is fair. Such a belief only leads to pain and sorrow. It is time you realized that as queen, you will be forced to make decisions that affect the lives of those around you, some of whom you care for deeply. Sometimes those decisions will bring harm, so learn to choose wisely. That is an essential part of being a great queen."

Annabelle's words were strikingly close to those Ourea had spoken. If this was the difficult path the Djinn had foretold Veressa must take, she did not want anything to do with it. How would she know which path would bring great sacrifice to the world and which great suffering to those she loved? Which was better? How was Antilles to aid her on this journey she must take? And how did the Cosmic juncture signify a new era in which she would play an important role? She was just a princess. What could she possibly do to bring about a new era? The force of the questions she couldn't even begin to answer made her lightheaded. She ran trembling fingers along her bandaged temples. The tight Ranger-apprentice braids were gone. Her stomach knotted in response. "What will you do? What is your assignment?" she asked softly.

"I have no details yet. Besides, it is an assignment from the Rangers Order and likely does not involve matters of the realm. I cannot share what I do not know, Highness."

Annabelle's unexpected formality dug deep into Veressa's soul. Her fingers combed gently at the residual kinks from her braids. "At least tell me who has been assigned as my new protector."

"That I do not know either. Your new protector will visit you shortly," she continued. "You must surely understand, Highness, that I can no longer be your preceptor." The Ranger rose and pulled her dark-green hood forward to hide her facial features. "I will inform the countess you are awake." Stealthily, Annabelle moved to the door, but stopped, her palm resting on the handle. "I have always been proud of you, Highness. It has been an honor to serve as your protector ... and as your preceptor."

Antilles rested his chin on the side of the bed, looking at his new bond with a thoughtful expression. Veressa ran fingers down the long lines of black spots dotting his cheek. He began to purr, and her heavy heart lightened, troubled thoughts fleeing. When her eyes were dry enough to look up, Annabelle and Peron were gone.

Annabelle pressed her back against the outside of Veressa's bedchamber door to steady her raw nerves. She had not been certain she could steel her emotions against the princess. Knowing that this was in the princess's best interest did nothing to ease her sorrow. Veressa could be frustrating, but Annabelle loved the girl with all her heart.

She paused to smooth Peron's ruffled feathers with a shaky hand, then started down the long hall of bureaus leading to the countess's reception chamber. In a way, she was glad Veressa had told her about the dream vision. Annabelle had failed the monarchy four times as

Veressa's guardian since leaving Graystone, the last time nearly costing the princess her life. She could imagine no greater travesty to bear than to have caused the death of a future paragon—by fault or intention, it did not matter. She could only hope her new assignment would offer an opportunity to atone and restore some measure of balance to the Rangers Order.

At the end of the hall, Annabelle turned left and ran headlong into a tall, well-built man coming the other way. Having been self-absorbed in remorse and foreboding, she rocked back on her heels in astonishment. She looked up, straight into the hazel eyes of ... "Marcantos," she whispered before she could stop the name from escaping her lips. Immediately, her defenses went up. She bowed slightly with a jerk, hoping her smile did not look like the grimace it was. "Grandmaster Warrior Evinfaire, deepest apologies for not being more attentive."

The man gifted her with the same smile that had both infuriated and melted her heart all those years ago. "Master Ranger Loris," he responded with intense formality and a supple bow. "How good it is to see you again. Of course, apologies are never required from you."

Annabelle fumbled, choosing to ignore his last statement. "I had no idea you were in Cravenrock."

"I told you a long time ago, our paths are inexorably bound to cross many times."

"Yes, it does seem to be my fate." She left her meaning ambiguous, and much to her satisfaction, she noticed him stiffen. "What is it that has forced us to cross paths this time?"

"Why it is you, Annabelle," he answered with a precise counterstroke.

*So, after all this time, you want to play parlor mind games, Marcantos? Very well.* Her mind worked quickly. Judging from his reaction to their encounter, the man was not surprised to see her. Since she had arrived only hours before and had not reported to the keep's commander, she surmised the countess had seen fit to inform him of

Annabelle's arrival at the manor. But the countess had no motive or interest to do so. That meant instead he had been informed of the princess's presence. Of course, he knew Annabelle had been assigned as the girl's protector and would make the connection. Only one plausible reason explained why he would be told of the princess's arrival. "So *you* are Veressa's new protector."

For just a moment, there was a look of surprise on Marcantos's smug face before he masked it with his confident smile.

"Yes. It seems my destiny is to come to the rescue of ladies in distress."

His words bit hard at her, and she fought back a scowl. Peron squawked irritably at the man. Old memories of their days together at Striker's Keep flooded back, ones Annabelle would rather have forgotten. It was her first assignment, soon after being raised to the Ranger rank of watcher, brash and fearless, ready to defend the Harmonic Realms. During her four long years at Striker's Keep, many good friends and comrades died in skirmishes with Anarchic forces—so many that she soon stopped counting. Like Annabelle, those who survived the day, by luck or talent, learned to live the night like it would be their last. For some, it was.

It was into this live-by-the-moment existence that a rash young Warrior named Marcantos Evinfaire appeared. His early mastery of weapons and commanding presence on the field were becoming legend among his order, and his noble ways were seductive to Annabelle's yeoman upbringing. She had been unseasoned and impressionable, flattered by the nobleman's attention. And he took full advantage of the situation. For the first time, she'd thought she was in love.

One spring morning of her fourth year, the keep's commander received word that a band of Anarchists had ransacked a village to the south. A battalion of Defenders was dispatched under Marcantos's command, while Annabelle was assigned to lead an attached company of inexperienced Archer guildsmen. They rode hard that day. Before dusk, the battalion came upon the lead party. Marcantos ordered

Annabelle's company to swing around in front and engage the party while he swept his battalion in from behind, boxing in the trailing party of raiders.

That evening and on into darkness, her small company of Archers fought off wave after wave of Anarchist assaults attempting to break through their line and return to their Anarchic lands. Warned only by the dying embers of the fires before them, they fought valiantly, calling for their comrades' help. In a final act of desperation, the raiders mounted an all-out attack and overran the Archers' hastily constructed fortifications. Combat shifted to melee; the Archers' missile weapon advantage had been lost. Her company fought heroically for life and realm, swinging throwing knives and unstrung bows to fend off Anarchist longswords. So focused was Annabelle on the raiders that she did not hear the screams and wails of those dying about her, though the sounds would haunt her in dreams for months to come.

Annabelle could not recall when Marcantos's battalion had appeared to scatter what remained of the two raiding parties to the winds. One moment she was striking a raider with her bloody bow; the next, she was surrounded by Defenders. Only then did she collapse from her wounds. She awoke days later in the Striker's Keep dispensary to discover she had been the only one in her company of Archers to survive.

When Marcantos visited, she inquired, then demanded, to know what had taken him so long to come to her company's aid. His refusal to answer enraged her, so he never came to visit again during her long recovery. After that, they hardly spoke. It was after her reassignment to Dreadcreek later that summer that she heard Marcantos had received a decoration of honor for heroism in coming to the aid of fallen comrades that gruesome night. It was a harsh way for an idealistic girl to learn the true ways of the realms.

"I always knew you to be a fool for thinking yourself some chivalric orderman," Annabelle replied. "But you have truly outdone yourself if you think, even for a moment, that Princess Veressa needs rescuing."

Marcantos stiffened. "That is how we differ, Annabelle. It is just such a perspective that nearly got the princess killed. Threats come from *many* sources. Surely you can see she needed to be rescued from one of them."

Annabelle inhaled hard. Yes, the Warrior had always been self-centered and conceited, but she had never known him to be cruel. The years had sharpened his tongue into a knife. Very well. She would let the abominable man discover for himself whom he'd been assigned to protect. Maybe there was balance in the Cosmos after all.

Copious, bored by the repartee, rolled on his back and yawned noisily, looking at Annabelle upside down. She pitied the animal for having to suffer a life with such a repulsive human. Like many times in years past, she squatted and scratched the big bear briskly under the chin, and was rewarded with a familiar grunt and twitching hind leg. "Take care of your bond, Copious, my old friend. It seems he will need it one day."

With nothing more to say, Annabelle stepped past the bear, who called for her to come back for another scratch. She did not look back, her eyes locked on the reception chamber doors on the other side of the foyer.

To think she had once loved this man. But that foolish, innocent child was no more.

Marcantos brooded while the green-cloaked Ranger walked briskly away, Peron winging stealthily behind. She had been so full of life and adventure in their youth. *I can't let feelings of the past distract me from the task at hand. Annabelle is gone; what is done is done*, he noted sadly.

With a deep sigh, he took the long hall of bureaus to his right. The echoing tap of his polished steel-heeled boots brought relief from the strangely quiet corridor accommodating an endless supply of doors. In the hall's adjacent offices, many well-dressed administrators and clerks worked diligently through stacks of parchments, handling state affairs for the eastern region of the Narwales fiefdom. To fight off his darkening mood, Marcantos read the signs as he walked: *Sheriff of Cravenrock, Office of Order Affairs, Captain of the City Guard, Office of the Regional Guard, Office of Taxation, Office of Accounts, Office of Chancery, Office of Civil Justice, Office of the Treasury*. On and on the doors went until he reached the far end of the hall, where he came to a lone female manor guardsman at attention.

He went left into the chamber hall reserved for those of nobility and lurched to an awkward halt. Someone ahead was gathering a considerable amount of Air elemental. But the princess was supposed to be alone! "The princess is in danger! With me!" Marcantos yelled over his shoulder and dashed ahead. He jabbed his left arm forward, fingers spread wide as he drew upon Water elemental. Five steps from the princess's bedchamber, Water flowed around the doorknob's metallic lock. *"Pon ousia xekleidothyra!"* Three steps away, he shifted the elemental flow, and the lock's gears clicked mechanically. At two steps, his right hand came up. He pulled Air to him and his sword leaped into his ready palm. *Aetos ousia llisixifos!"* One step away, he drove a wall of Air into the thick mahogany door. The heavy door responded with a groan and burst wide. He dove through the portal, hoping the surprise would give him an advantage over the princess's assailant.

Since Annabelle's departure, Veressa had contemplated Ourea's words from her dream vision, considering them from every possible angle. Nothing made sense. Her head was beginning to throb again, and she grew tired of thinking about it. Elemental practice seemed the perfect distraction.

Clutching her empty goblet in both hands, she drew upon Earth elemental and focused on the crystal pitcher. *"Ora ousia anakametallo."* She sensed the elemental's attraction to the material.

The lead within the glass sparked as Earth coalesced around the vessel. Veressa closed her eyes, focusing on the sensations of the pitcher—its size, bulbous shape, and smooth handle. Somehow she knew its weight, its temperature; she could even sense the base pressing on the marble table. Intrigued by the sensation, she drew on Air and wove the two elementals into a dense mesh, completely encasing the crystalline object with the energy. In her mind, she sensed that she could have drawn much more Air and Earth, felt the incredible wellspring surging from within and through her new link with Antilles. *"Outher ousia anapsokrystallo,"* she said, and guided the elemental force upward to make the pitcher levitate from the table. She directed it gracefully toward her. With but a thought, the mouth tipped forward, and her goblet filled with water.

The delightful moment ended abruptly when the hinges on the door behind her groaned under the stress of a great force and the door burst wide. She turned just as a well-built man leaped through the entrance and went into a tight body roll. Veressa's Ranger training seized control. With detached interest, she tracked the flowing motion of the man's perfect rotation. As the man completed his maneuver, rising up in the middle of her bedchamber with sword raised high, she recited a spell— *"Outher ousia kinokrystallo"*—and sent the crystal pitcher hurling at his chest.

The intruder reacted with stunning agility. Leaning back slightly, he spun on his heel. The pitcher whirled past, striking the back of the open door. Shards of crystal and water sprayed everywhere, creating the moment of chaos the princess needed. She was already gathering Earth and Air about the only loose object remaining nearby—the metal lamp.

"Highness!" The man raised his left arm toward the princess, though his eyes were glued on the heavy lamp floating above the table. "It is I, Grandmaster Marcantos Evinfaire of the Warriors Order! My sincere apologies for disturbing you in this manner, but I thought you were in danger. When I felt the elemental powers in the room, I expected someone else to be here." The man scanned the room.

Satisfied no one else was present, he signaled the winded manor guard outside, who relaxed but kept a diligent eye along the hall. Marcantos bowed, his intense gaze shifting from the floating lamp. "I did not expect you to be so skilled in elemental power and control. It really is quite impressive for someone just bonded."

If the intruder thought a few words of adulation would be enough to appease the princess for his rude entrance, he was sadly mistaken. Besides, Veressa was used to such talk from noblemen. Unaffected by his praise, she struggled to understand the significance of the man's most unwelcome appearance. She offered Marcantos a faint smile of recognition. "Yes. Grandmaster Evinfaire. It has been a few years."

Marcantos rose from his crouch, a warm smile parting his lips. "Your Highness was but a young girl half your size when last we met. I am flattered you remember me."

The princess tensed and sensed Antilles crouch at her side, ready to attack with a mere emotional cue. Everyone in Griffinrock had heard of Grandmaster Warrior Marcantos Evinfaire, the man most likely to be Veressa's Champion of the Realm. *Does the man think me to be such an imbecile? Or could he be the only male nobleman left in the entire realm with even a single grain of humility?* Veressa found the thought entertaining as she studied the man. He was indeed a fine specimen, truly gentle to the eyes. Any woman would find him more than attractive. She gently rubbed Antilles's ears, and the cat relaxed. But she was not any woman. "What makes you think I need the attention of such an esteemed orderman to provide protection in this manor? Is there cause I should not be safe in my bedchamber?"

The Warrior cleared his throat. "It is in the king's duty that I am here, Highness. King Jonath requested that I personally see you safely back to Graystone."

Veressa's cheeks flushed. "I see. So *you* are my new protector." She stiffened with embarrassment, fighting back the anger flowing through her. Not only was this new protector male, he was from an order whose current standing with the monarchy was something less than pitiful! If her father wanted to punish her for her actions—as if Annabelle's dismissal were not enough—he could not have selected a more appropriate means!

"I have received approval from my order's council, so yes, I have assumed responsibility as your personal guardian and protector." Marcantos eyed the floating lamp as it rattled in response. "You must understand I am simply carrying out the king's orders, Highness."

"So then, it seems I have a trained monkey for a protector." She would most definitely have a few harsh words with her father when she returned home. Of course, there would be no recourse if she was unsuccessful in swaying his decision, for her mother would offer no support in this matter. Livid, she continued. "But, then again, I suppose my father was short on choices this far from the central realm."

Marcantos hid a snarl with a rigid bow before he continued. "It seems the knock on Your Highness's head has not affected her lucidity … or her tongue. This is clearly good news. I see no reason we cannot begin our journey back to Graystone with morrow's first rays."

The princess had no intention of letting the infernal man take control either the discussion or her actions. She was a bonded woman of royalty. "Unless you have also appointed yourself as my personal Physician, Grandmaster Evinfaire, I believe the decision as to when I can leave for Graystone belongs to Grandmaster Guildsman Onorus Dankmar. I will ready myself when *she* says I am well enough to do so."

"Why, of course, Highness. I merely suggest that if your spirit is any indication of health, I should go prepare my bags this very hour. I will see to it personally Physician Dankmar comes immediately to ensure Your Highness is fit for travel." Marcantos marched through the open door, then turned. "You may not enjoy the fact that I have been tasked as your protector, but I have never failed an assignment. And I will not fail this one. You are under my protection now, Highness, by decree of the sovereign king of Griffinrock. I truly hope you come to appreciate our relationship and can learn to be amiable to the situation."

Veressa called forth Earth. With one quick spell—"*Ora ousia kinothyra*"—she slammed the door in Marcantos's face before he could say anything else or even bow in parting respect. How dare the insufferable man turn his back on the future queen of Griffinrock! And how disappointing that he was no different from all the other men she had known.

Caught up in her misery, she was unaware that her eyes scanned to the west. The Eastlander, Conner Stonefield, once more invaded her thoughts and her heart skipped a beat. *No,* she corrected herself. *One was different.*

Marcantos pursed his lips, watching water droplets trace long lines down the princess's bedchamber door. Crystal shards protruded from the finely carved griffin relief. How impressive! Princess Veressa's use of elementals would become as legendary as her temper. He had no doubt both would long be thorns in his side. No matter. She would come around once she appreciated his worth. And when that happened, he would be there, a ready receptor of her gratitude.

The sound of Copious's yawn and the awkward fidgeting of the female guardsman waiting patiently at his back brought him from his thoughts. Maybe Physician Dankmar did not fully appreciate her role in this matter, a problem he was about to rectify. He had stayed way too long in this miserable city. A caravan was leaving in the morning for Pennington Point, so the Queen's Defenders would bolster his protection for the princess. They *would* be on the road for Graystone with the morrow's first light.

"See to it that Princess Veressa's bedchamber is cleaned up before I return." He did not wait for the guardsman's nod before he disappeared back up the hall. The perfect rhythm of his steel-heeled shoes on the hall's marble floor soothed his growing impatience.

Veressa flung open the thick drapes to let the afternoon heat dry away tears that refused to stop. Ourea's words echoed in her mind: *You must prepare for the journey ahead.* "So this is my path." She sighed.

Motion drew her from the painful thoughts. A green-cloaked figure crossed the courtyard below, where two more Rangers waited on horseback.

The hooded figure mounted a third horse. Glancing her way, the figure gestured in the secret Rangers' hand language Annabelle had taught Veressa. *My heart goes with you, always.*

With the Ranger's falcon bond taking his normal scouting position overhead, the three hooded riders moved slowly past the guardsmen at the manor entrance, then turned south toward Cravenrock's city gates. Beyond those gates, the trio would ride northeast. Soon, they would be beyond the borders of Veressa's knowledge. She wondered what wild adventures awaited the Ranger in Dreadcreek. Veressa felt a sudden thrill and wished she could travel with Annabelle once more out on the open plains, even if the Ranger was heading to that dreadful and dangerous place. She shook away the unusual sensation flooding through her. "My heart goes with you as well, Annabelle," she whispered.

The riders were long since lost among the busy streets and tall buildings before the princess answered the gentle tap at her bedchamber door.

# The Price of a Shaman's Help

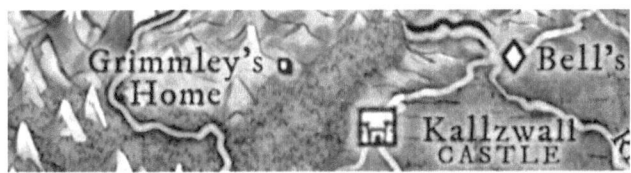

**G**rimmley spent the rest of the morning after meeting Conner and his dragon asking the boy pointed questions about the events of the last fortnight. And though the young man provided amazing details, a large gap of unaccounted time in Cravenrock still existed. But he saw no reason to turn the discussion into an inquisition. The last thing he needed was to alienate the boy by forcing him to talk about something he was dodging, which was in all likelihood irrelevant to the situation at hand.

*A young lad and his adolescent dragon bond here at my home!* It was too much for Grimmley to get his mind around. Until he did that, he doubted he could formulate a viable plan for what to do next. And that was his first problem. Worse, he knew absolutely nothing about human-dragon bonds, other than that very little was known. But he was not ready to let the boy in on that secret. So while he pondered the situation, Grimmley carefully watched the boy and dragon's interactions. By late afternoon, he had made only a few useful observations.

First, the two spoke to each other in a language with which Grimmley was unfamiliar, yet they conversed as if they had spoken it their entire lives. Second, it had been a complete surprise to the boy that Grimmley could not understand a tad of what the dragon was saying. Further at this point, the dragon had seemed extremely disappointed. And third, even though he did not understand what was being said, there was no question that the two carried on like headstrong siblings, each wanting to have their way.

It was, in fact, in the middle of one of these heated discussions that Grimmley remembered why he preferred a life of solitude. Growing weary from their racket, he went inside to start preparing a dinner that would soothe his unsettled, aged spirit. By dusk, the noise had died away. Through the open window, he caught sight of the dragon flying north. Within a few moments, the creature had disappeared over the hill.

When Conner's lanky figure appeared in the doorway, Grimmley said, "I fixed a soufflé. I hope you like fish."

The silhouette did not move. "Yes, sir. But I am not very hungry."

"You make a terrible door, boy. Besides, I have one. So come inside and sit. And stop calling me 'sir.' You're starting to make me feel old," Grimmley grumbled. The feeling was more due to what the Cosmos had dropped into his lap, but he did not want to think about that right then. "If I am going to help you, you might start calling me Grimmley. After all, that is my name."

Conner ambled across the cottage floor to stare solemnly out the window in the direction the dragon had disappeared.

Once two plates were set on the small table, Grimmley broke the silence. "I assume he went off to find something to eat."

The boy nodded absently.

The Shaman grunted in response, holding the hot soufflé in his hands. "Well, I appreciate that he chose not to partake of any of the local delicacies."

Barthox hooted her agreement from her fireplace perch.

"Grimmley," the boy stared at him with intensity. "I want you to break our bond."

After the boy's request made its way into the Shaman's conscious mind, the Shaman set the baking dish down before he dropped it. "You want to me to do *what*?"

"I want you to remove the bond between Skye and me."

Having Conner repeat his petition did not help. "Boy, I don't think you understand what you are asking."

"I am willing to try anything you think might work."

For the first time Grimmley could recall, he was without words.

"I can't go back home with"—the boy gestured out the window—"*that*! How do I become an Apothecary and raise a family when I have to look after a dragon?"

"Ah." Grimmley nodded his head. He ignored Barthox's long hoot of *I told you so*. "Well, it is true you can't go home with the creature. Perhaps you should—"

"I knew you would see it my way. I should be bonded with a squirrel ... or a raccoon like my dad. That is the kind of bond an Apothecary should have."

It was time to correct Conner's childish notion that certain people were *meant* to have a certain type of bond. "Wait, boy, let me finish. I—"

"Tell me what we need to do. I will try anything!" Conner's voice had an edge of desperation.

"It's not a matter of—"

"Grimmley, if anyone can remove this bond, you can. I know that. I can feel it."

"Well, if anyone *could* remove a bond, I would be the one, but—"

"So wave your hands, cast a spell, or give me a potion to drink. I don't know what you will charge, but I will pay what I can. You have my word, as an Eastlander and future member of the Apothecaries Guild."

Conner's constant interruptions were starting to grate on Grimmley, which was not easy to do. "Shaman spells are never about waving hands, my boy! And, as far as payment, there is nothing I need that you could provide ..." He hesitated midsentence and reconsidered what he was about to say.

Conner picked up on the Shaman's hesitation. "What? What is it?"

Grimmley waved his hands in front of him as if erasing his last thought. "Oh, never mind you that. I will help you the best I can. There is no need for compensation."

"No, Grimmley. I cannot accept your help without some kind of payment. It is a principle my father taught me and the way among freemen of the Eastlands. Besides, it is the least I can do. So what is it?"

The boy seemed quite emphatic on this point, so Grimmley considered the idea again at the boy's persistence, then jiggled his head in an attempt to shake the crazy notion away. "No, Conner. It is much too dangerous to ask you this favor."

"By the seven planes, it is a fact that in the last fortnight I have had a lifetime supply of danger." Conner's eyes went northward. His voice softened. "But Skye keeps telling me that I should face my fears. Perhaps he's right. At least tell me what you need."

Maybe it was not Grimmley's place to make decisions for the boy. After all, the lad was bonded and therefore an adult. "All right," he started. "There is a valuable box that might contain something even more valuable. But it was lost a long time ago. And I am not even sure precisely where it is."

"Wait. Are you saying this box you want would be useful in helping Skye and me?"

After some consideration, Grimmley decided it would not hurt to take the boy literally. "Well, yes, Conner, retrieving the box would be helpful. But I cannot emphasize enough the danger the two of you could face."

"We'll do it."

The Shaman raised his palms to the boy. "Not so fast. Maybe you should talk this over with your dragon before you commit to something this drastic."

Conner hesitated, then bobbed his head. "I think ... no, I *know* Skye will want this too."

That evening, Skye winged back from the north, dipping silently above the tree line, and settled near the bank of the lake. The dragon could sense Conner's mind was still restless from their last argument, so he waited patiently for Conner to begin with whatever was in his thoughts. His belly was full, so he was feeling less cross. If another fight broke out, it would not be his doing.

Finally, his human bond spoke. "The great Shaman says he can help us break our bond, but we must retrieve an important artifact first."

Skye twitched with a spasm of irritation, unable to stop the grumble escaping his full stomach. "You are still set on going through with this?"

The question earned him another of Conner's incredulous stares. "I thought that was all settled. Are you having second thoughts *again*?" After further consideration, the human elaborated. "I thought you wanted to remove these shackles as much as I do."

True, like Conner, Skye was feeling homesick. Images of returning home sometime soon frequented his thoughts. But to refer to their bonding as "shackles" seemed a bit harsh. "The meaning in what the Cosmos offers depends on our attitude when we receive the gift."

The human shook at the dragon's response, on the fringes of erupting once more. Skye's bond might not like being reminded their bond was a gift, but that was not his problem. Besides, after five days of being bonded, Skye still did not understand the constant urgency his bond had for rushing into action without adequate analysis. At least dragons understood that some things needed thorough deliberation.

The dragon continued with hardly a pause. "Since it seems you have not figured this out on your own, I feel obliged to tell you that I am my own being. Bonding does not mean you can drag me along into whatever adventure you concoct just because it suits your fancy."

"Oh, you've made that lavishly clear on more than one occasion," huffed the irascible human. "But there is no way I'm ever going to return home like this." He waved his arms between them.

"And you are convinced this is going to work?" Skye was certain that whatever the Great Shaman said was irrefutable. He sensed vast power in the Shaman, which bolstered his confidence that the early dragonsongs of the Shaman Shazarack creating the race of dragons told the truth. But he wondered if Conner's frantic desires to break their bond made him susceptible to misinterpreting what the Shaman had said. He had never heard of a device that could break bonds, or any other method for that matter, but then again, he was new in dealing with this strange bipedal species.

"Grimmley is, and that is good enough for me. But if you're going to drag your feet with every step of this journey, I'll be an old man before I get back home. Now, are you with me on this or not?"

Skye considered telling Conner to go off on his own so he could nap amid the oaks, but given what he had learned about his impetuous bond, Conner would likely need Skye along to drag him out of whatever trouble he fell into. Besides, the success of collecting this all-important device should not be left to a human alone. With a slight nod and tilt of his head, the wyvern succumbed to Conner's unrelenting demands once more. "Okay. I will go along with you on this. What do we do now?"

# Tying Off Loose Ends

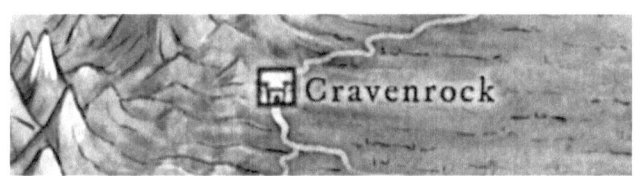

$\mathbf{B}$lake Friarwood stared out onto the Narwalen Plains from his Cravenrock tower bedchamber. His thoughts floated through the various tasks he had yet to complete before the royal entourage left for Graystone at morrow's first light. But he was in no hurry. He had packed his belongings days ago, expecting an assignment like the one his young pupil, Marcantos, had been given that morning.

Once again, the Anarchic oracles had been right. But all Sarmenion, brother of the Kindred, had said was that Friarwood should travel to Cravenrock with Marcantos, then await for something momentous. Gratified, he gently rubbed the onyx ring on his left forefinger. The balance of force was indeed shifting in the Kindred's favor.

Carnia's loud squawk broke his concentration.

Living in the Harmonic lands was like dealing with a rash that would not go away. So the thrill of being on the road again stirred his feet to action. Just a few loose ends to tidy up, and he would leave this wretched city behind. Maybe getting away from this place would help Marcantos adapt to Anarchic ways. Friarwood moved swiftly down the stairs of the keep, on past the large main hall, and down another set of stairs into the tower's basement, his falcon bond grudgingly in tow. Toward the back wall, he pressed his palms simultaneously on two bricks. He spoke an ancient incantation, *"Outher ousia xekleidothyra,"* and was rewarded with a muffled click. A portion of the wall swung his way. Looking over his shoulder one last time, he slipped into a small antechamber, then waited until Carnia flew through and took the perch he had added when he constructed this secret room long ago.

*"Outher ousia kleidothyra,"* he incanted to relock the hidden door, followed by *"Outher ousia thetopagida"* to set a series of traps. The cramped room flared to life. He slipped into a black robe that he removed from a wood cabinet. Attired once more in his true form as the Assassin Lacerus, he took a cleansing breath to calm his nerves.

There had been no word in the four days since Morgas and his Alpsland trackers had been sent to apprehend and return the young thief Vault after the young lad absconded from the city. That meant either Vault had single-handedly taken care of Morgas and his trackers or Morgas had elected to desert his assignment. Lacerus would discover which scenario held the truth once the two companies of Anarchic soldiers dispatched to Morgas's village home of Elmsdorf returned with news. If Morgas had deserted, the Anarchic force would eliminate the problem.

Lacerus hesitated at the spiral iron stairwell that would lead him deep into the Cravenrock undercity. No matter how hard he squeezed, no one could even provide the Eastlander boy's true name. And there was still the mystery of the dragonfire imbued in the stone Morgas had brought him during his hunt for Vault. But he was simply out of time. He would leave the investigation of that enigma in Brother Groegan's capable hands. Without more information on the Eastlander, Lacerus's priority was to pick a reasonable replacement for Pirate, the current Thieves Guildmaster. He pulled the black hood forward to hide his malicious smile, his black onyx ring faintly aglow. The pleasant thought of ridding himself of Pirate was all Lacerus needed to take the stairwell with zeal and complete the work at hand.

# A Band of Anarchists

"Cha Kohm! Cha Kohm! Cha Kohm!" The wild exaltation rose hot from the throats of the throng encircling the two combatants. Cha Kohm—*Free Honor*—was the traditional manner through which Anarchic Barbarians established rank among their order.

Groegan Briarmede licked a thin red line along his muscled forearm, a twin to the wound he had, moments before, received on his other arm. That made two cuts, and he had yet to touch his opponent. One more and Groegan's challenge would be concluded. He pushed back long, wavy hair clinging to sweaty temples and cheeks. Groegan snarled and rounded on his adversary once more, this time drawing Air and Water elementals to him. *"Ponther energi tachyprosopo,"* he incanted. His draw upon elemental forces surprised the throng of Barbarians about him, choking off their exuberant chant.

Barcleave Tallenia, commander of the Farlorde forces, also felt Groegan's unexpected elemental call and lost his sporting smile. He crouched at the ready, his stance wide, mass low. The commander's imposing voice filled the hushed silence. "You might rethink whether you are ready to take this to the next level, Groegan."

Groegan had to be cautious. Much was riding on what happened next. Still, he was growing tired of these incessant games, the parade of endless frays in a never-ending cycle to claim what should have always been the Kindred's. His black onyx amulet felt cool against his sternum; the thick leather grip of his sword was hot in his palm. "There is nothing to rethink," he said through his gritty smile.

Barcleave bared his teeth, then licked a streak of Groegan's blood from his blade, bloodlust and elemental force filling him. *"Aetos stoicheiodis fainaspida,"* he said, forming an elemental weave of Water and Air. "Then show me what you have, young one."

The black mass surged once more about them, raising their chant of approval into a frenzy and feeding the contestants' rush.

Groegan responded to chant and commander's wish.

He came at Barcleave with sword held wide. The commander's elemental weave shunted his attack. But Groegan's deception had done its work. Shifting Air beneath him, the young Barbarian cartwheeled over the commander. His blade flashed downward to trace a line along Barcleave's neck. Groegan kicked out to slow his spin and found solid ground a heartbeat later. He had made his first mark.

The commander spun, noting a severed lock of hair drifting from his shoulder. He measured his young opponent, reassessing his opinion of the man. They circled. Barcleave did not have to wait long for the opening he hoped would put a decisive end to the contest.

Barcleave lunged and incanted *"Ponther ousia odigoxifos"* to guide his blade. Barbarian steel blurred in Hemera's midday light, forcing Groegan to keep his blade close, his feet dancing as he deflected each of the commander's whirling strokes in a rising tempo. Modeic symbols along the blades burned bright blue, then white, then blue again as Water and Air flowed around the combatants. Shouts from the throng reached a fevered pitch, drowning out even the blades' rapid reports.

Barcleave felt the other man's stutter-step, sensed Groegan's defenses buckle. With bloodlust pumping hot through his veins, the commander seized the advantage. Forming another elemental shield before him, he came in high. With weight and elemental force, the larger man ground the young upstart to his knees. Victorious, he sneered down into the quiet eyes of Groegan ... and knew instantly he had been deceived yet again.

With elemental forces in reserve, Air flowed from Groegan. *"Aetos ousia anypsopetra,"* he said, weaving a web beneath a thumb-sized rock at his feet. The stone shuddered, then shot upward, slipping behind Barcleave's shield and striking the commander hard on the temple.

Barcleave staggered back, blood trickling from a growing welt. His head throbbed, but he held tenaciously to his elemental shield in preparation for an onslaught that did not come.

In combat, as was the standard with all Anarchic orders, Groegan had been trained to be in the moment, to let Anarchic bloodlust guide his actions, to exploit every weakness without hesitation. But something about the commander's elemental shield gave him pause. A heartbeat later, he understood.

Leveling his blade before him, palm against the pommel, Groegan spoke the Modeic spell, *"Aetos stoicheiodis odigoxifos."* The symbols along his sword ignited. The point of his sword shifted as it probed for the slight flaw he had felt in the commander's shield, and Groegan slid his sword tip through Barcleave's imperfect weave.

The commander's eyes widened, first with surprise, then wider with distress, as the point of Groegan's blade probed deeper through Barcleave's elemental shield. He fought to tighten his weave, but his efforts were useless. Just as the point pressed against his sternum, Groegan's blade stopped. Barcleave gave a swift twist of his shield to the right, torquing the young Barbarian's sword from his viselike grip. Groegan's blade tumbled to the dirt. Spinning on his heels to the left,

Barcleave stepped up beside Groegan, pressing the edge of his dagger against the side of the younger man's neck.

Groegan raised his arms, palms out, signaling that he yielded his challenge.

The surrounding Barbarians pushed and shouted at one another, some yelling that the commander should leave Groegan a scar as reminder of his brashness, though a few shouted the cut should go much deeper.

Moments passed, challenger's and commander's eyes locked. Around them, several arguments churned into fistfights. At length, Barcleave stepped back and sheathed his dagger and sword, then walked from the field, leaving the band of Barbarians to sort out the details.

The night was deep when one of Barcleave's lieutenants, a barrel-chested man named Engert, slipped into the commander's tent and stood stiffly before the large desk. After being recognized, the stocky and seemingly unsettled master Barbarian announced, "A grandmaster Necromancer from Thanatos and a master enchantress have just arrived. The Necromancer says she must speak with you regarding an urgent matter."

Barcleave understood the man's tension. Citadel Farlorde was a defensive fort near the Borderlands north the Dragon's Back Mountains. It seldom drew high-ranking orderman visitors. He leaned back and gestured his invitation. "Show our guest in, then."

Before Engert turned fully, a woman pushed through the tent flaps. In her mid-thirties, with dark complexion, she was dressed in a traveling version of the usual long, flowing, black Necromancer robes. Coal-black hair was pinned back at the scruff of her neck. She would have been soft to the eyes if not for the impatient and weary expression she wore ... and the two undead standing protectively at her heels— personal guardians common among Necromancers while they journeyed. "I am Grandmaster Necromancer Meera Asheborne from

Thanatos, second to Breanen Sagamore, counselor and wife to the Sovereign Prince of the Necromancers."

Barcleave stood and bowed. "It is an honor, Grandmaster Asheborne. I am Master Barbarian Barcleave Tallenia, Commander of Citadel Farlorde."

Asheborne was not impressed. "My time at Farlorde is measured in but hours. I am tired from my long ride, commander, so let us dispense with formalities. I want to rest before I leave early on the morrow." She shoved a rolled parchment at the commander.

Barcleave took the scroll and stared at the three wax seals securing its edge. They had been pressed with rings from members of the Conjurors', Necromancers', and Barbarians' order councils, signifying that all three councils concurred with whatever instructions were scribed within. The commander had never seen such a sealing. For even two councils to agree on an action was rare. The scroll was clearly of vital importance to the Anarchic Lands.

Satisfied with the commander's reaction, the Necromancer proceeded. "Now that I have your full attention, commander, let me describe what is written on that parchment. We would not want any misunderstandings as to what the three councils have agreed upon."

"No, of course not." Barcleave broke the seals and scanned the lettering as the Necromancer continued.

"You are to supply troops for two critical missions across the Borderlands. I will lead one mission, a small band of eight seasoned Barbarians dressed in mountain attire who know their way about the central region of the Dragon's Back Mountains. The other mission is to be led by Master Conjuror Deatrice and her apprentice." Asheborne nodded toward a tall woman in robes and a young man waiting outside near one of the fires. "The Conjuror will require two full companies of Barbarian trained soldiers to deal with an insurrection near the Borderlands."

The commander stiffened. "Two companies? But that would deplete my forces by nearly a third."

"Thus you begin to see the magnitude and import of our missions," the Necromancer proclaimed, sounding both irritated and tired. "Or maybe you would prefer to take this matter up with your order's council?"

The edge of Barcleave's mouth twitched. "That will not be necessary. The instructions are quite clear. I will have my lieutenants prepare you tents for tonight's rest."

"That is not required, though I will require Alpslander clothing. Have the men and supplies ready with Hemera's first rays," the Necromancer demanded before stepping through the tent's portal. Her undead escorts lurched stiffly behind her.

Engert reappeared with a questioning look, drawing the commander from brooding thoughts. Still, his eyes remained glued on the backs of the Necromancer and enchantress weaving their way back through the maze of tents and fires.

Barcleave rubbed his fingers along the Modeic etchings on his sword as he considered how best to handle this new matter. "The young one I fought this morning. Bring him to me."

Groegan was sitting by the fires near his tent, bantering with new friends, when Engert appeared with his perpetual disapproving stare. "The commander *requests* your presence."

Of course, the statement was anything but an invitation. The commander had elected not to kill him on the field, but he could have changed his mind. Refusing the commander's request would ensure that a line of Barbarians would await him by morning, ready to make bloodlust with him in defense of Barcleave's honor. Groegan rose. Expressions of respect on the Barbarians around him bolstered his resolve. It was time to see if the suggestion Brother Sarmenion of the Conjurors oracles had made to challenge the commander had paid off. He nodded to the group in recognition, then trailed Master Engert.

The two Barbarians wove through the concentric rings of tents toward its epicenter. As was common across the Anarchic Lands, the position of each Barbarian's tent signified their status in the order's hierarchy. Those allowed to lay stakes nearest to the commander's tent were those Barcleave held in highest esteem.

Groegan did not wait outside Barcleave's tent, but slipped confidently between the flaps.

Barcleave sat sharpening his blade. "I would have thought, for such a young Barbarian, you were not ready to make your move. It seems I was mistaken."

"I hope I did not surprise you too much."

Barcleave chuckled heartily. "You may no longer lay stakes near my tent, Groegan. Find an open field if you choose, or I will see that you are reassigned to another station."

Groegan's challenge had established him as a contender for future commander of the Farlorde forces. As was custom, he could no longer declare direct fealty to Barcleave. Bowing low before the commander, he said, "I have been honored to serve under your command, Master Tallenia." Also as tradition dictated, he could no longer recognize Barcleave as commander. It was time to see if other Barbarians would lay stakes near his.

"Only time will determine whether your move was brash or brave, Groegan. In either case, you showed exceptional talent on the field. It is possible I might yet take you as a student," Barcleave said, nodding approvingly. It was the Barbarian way of saying why he had let Groegan live. There was no honor ending the life of a young challenger with innate talents; nor was there any in training a young Barbarian who had none. In time, Barcleave would know where Groegan's future lay.

Groegan bowed again with respect.

"For now," Barcleave continued, "I have an assignment that might help your cause." The commander measured the young Barbarian's reception of the news before continuing, disappointed the young man showed no surprise at the offer. "A Necromancer is on a mission through the Borderlands to track an animal of some sort. I have need of someone I can trust to command the Barbarians I am to send with her."

Groegan took his time replying. "I would take oath for you if ..." He was taking a gamble, bartering with the commander's freely offered gift.

Barcleave's eyes widened in unmasked surprise. "Yes?"

"... if you take me as your student when I return."

Outside, several lieutenants took note of the rare mirth emanating from their commander's tent.

Meera Asheborne stepped from her tent, letting the cool morning air dissolve her tension. Hemera's rays were just lighting the citadel walls on the green hill to the north. She had heard that mountain people had customs as strange as their dress. And given how she had struggled to don the Alpslander clothing, that was not a good sign. She was a Necromancer, not a Barbarian. She would have to adapt quickly or risk putting her mission in peril.

Two companies of black armored Anarchic soldiers stood in tight formation before her, obscuring the sea of tents and morning fires blanketing the open field beyond. The master Conjuror and her young apprentice were weaving through the tight lines, inspecting those who would accompany them.

Meera looked to where three women and five men lingered, each attired similar to her.

"Grandmaster Asheborne of the Necromancers Order?" asked one of the men, tall and well-built, with flowing blond hair. The man moved like a tiger toward her, then bowed low. "I am Barbarian Groegan Briarmede. Master Barbarian Tallenia requested that I be your second on this mission. I have considerable knowledge of the mountain regions and of those inhabiting them. I have personally chosen the Barbarians you requested for their skills in scouting, espionage, and interrogation. They await your directions."

Meera nodded at his efficiency. "We are to travel southwest from here. Our assignment is of the utmost importance and secrecy, so I cannot offer further details until we reach the Borderlands. For now, know this. No one can discover our presence. We are to eliminate anyone we meet whom you cannot personally vouch for."

Groegan's sea-green eyes surveyed the Necromancer's guise. "You did well with the attire. However ..." Stepping closer, he pointed at the shoulder strap for her longsword's scabbard. "May I?"

Suspiciously, Meera nodded, then watched as the Barbarian adjusted her belts and straps. She had not let a man touch her so in many years. Most male ordermen were repulsed by her occupation, and male Necromancers were ... well, lifeless. Yet, this Barbarian did not seem bothered either by her proximity or by the two undead protectors lurking at her back. He bent to tighten the calf buckles around her fur leggings, and she caught a faint blue flash from a gold amulet stuffed between his chest plate and furs. She had seen only one such amulet before—one worn by her liege, Breanen Sagamore, who had once told her of its rarity. Who was this man with just such a rare stone, assigned to a distant outpost, and so stalwart near a Necromancer and her personal guards? And what was his connection to Breanen? She shuddered at the stone's possible significance.

Once the small troop had moved several miles south of the citadel, Meera sent her undead guardians' spirits back to their plane. Free of the undead, the Barbarians' mood lifted, and they picked up speed along the trail leading south to the Borderlands and the mountain range beyond.

# A Dangerous Quest

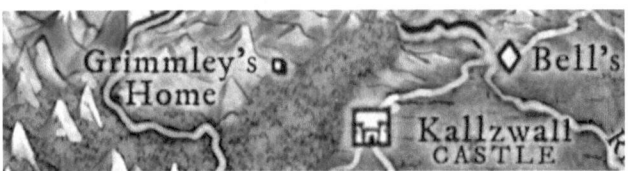

Conner awoke to the smell of frying eggs in butter and onions, and the soft sound of Grimmley humming a lively but unfamiliar tune. Occasionally, Barthox hooted her approval of Grimmley's work while the Shaman rummaged about the kitchen, making no attempt to be quiet. Before getting up, Conner instinctively searched his mind and felt Skye's presence not far from the Shaman's cottage.

"For a farmer, you do sleep late. No wonder you're thin as a sapling, boy! You'd let all your crops turn to seed before you got them to harvest," Grimmley grumbled without looking up from his cooking. Barthox hooted her agreement. "I was starting to think I'd have to pry you from those covers."

Conner's stomach grumbled its irritation at having refused Grimmley's soufflé the night before. He rose and stretched, content to note no aches or stiffness in his body. He ran fingers through his messy hair, then stumbled across the floor, sidestepping the small desk's mound of parchments near the cot he had taken for the night. "My apologies, sir. It has been a long time since I slept in anything resembling a bed." With more than a fortnight of sleeping on the hard ground, cavern floors, rooftops, trees, even a smelly stockade cell, he had forgotten how a good night's sleep affected his mood. He was no longer sure he could sleep on anything but a bed again.

With a cooking pan in one hand and spatula in the other, Grimmley examined his guest with a disapproving frown and crumpled white eyebrows. A white apron covered the front of his bright Shaman robes. Finely stitched across the apron in colorful thread were a chef's hat and the words *You can fool me once, but I am still the Shaman.*

Conner was pondering its meaning when the orderman responded. "Don't blame the guest bed for your laziness, boy!" Gesturing gruffly to a chair at the small, cluttered breakfast table by a window, Grimmley continued. "So sit before everything gets cold and I have to feed it all to Stomper." At the sound of his name, a raccoon appeared in the windowsill by the table, chattering at the appetizing spread of toasted bread, marmalade, and hot tea. "Besides, you're going to need the energy for what you have ahead of you," Grimmley warned.

Conner did as he was instructed.

Grimmley unceremoniously dumped a mix of eggs, potatoes, and goat cheese onto the plate before the boy. Noticing Conner's eyes as large as tea saucers, he grunted. "I suppose it has been a long time since you've had a real meal too," he stated factually. "Well, don't wait for me to say go, boy. Dig in."

Silently, Conner obeyed. With the first bite of eggs, Conner's mouth exploded with a tingling sensation that made his jaws ache and his eyes water. Stars danced across his vision, and he nearly dropped his spoon.

The Shaman beamed at the boy's reaction. "You like it?"—though it wasn't so much a question.

Conner coughed slightly before attempting to respond. "This is amazing, Grimmley. I've never tasted anything like it," he affirmed.

"I spent years perfecting the fourteen herbs and spices needed to bring out the true flavor of an egg," Grimmley said proudly. He settled into the chair across from Conner and watched his guest while he ate sparingly at his own small portion. Conner had cleaned his plate of eggs, along with the saucer of toast, the container of marmalade, and the pot of tea before Grimmley spoke, for once with an edge of seriousness. "How is your dragon, boy?"

Conner stopped mid-chew, then swallowed hard. He stared out the open window before speaking with a distant voice. "He spent most of the night to the north with some agitation, but returned before dawn quite pleased. I can assume he found another late-night meal."

The Shaman examined the bowl of the dark pipe he had removed from his pocket. "I wasn't asking for a weather report." He lit the tobac with a flint, drew hard on the long stem, and exhaled slowly. The smoke drifted lazily out the window. "Did you talk to him about the plan for today?"

"We discussed it again last night. As I mentioned yesterday, sir, he is willing to do this."

Grimmley continued to examine the boy as he puffed on his pipe, then nodded. "Okay, then. Let's get down to business for what you have ahead of you."

It was several hours before Conner stood in front of the cottage holding the reins of Grimmley's sorrel mare. The Shaman checked the saddle cinch and straps holding the pack behind the seat. "You would recognize the box if you saw it?" the Shaman asked for the umpteenth time.

"Yes, sir. It is a silver box the length of my forearm, about one hand thick and tall. It has rounded edges and sides, and is likely sealed with a silver lock that has no keyhole. And there are Modeic symbols etched across the top," Conner repeated for the umpteenth time. "I am not to attempt to open it, or to damage it if at all possible."

Grimmley examined the boy, grunting his approval. An emphatic hoot came from the cottage. "Very well, then. Travel due west to the Falmere River. Turn north into the mountains. East of the river, you will find a narrow trail winding along the river gorge. The crescent moon–shaped cavern you are seeking should be in a mountain near the gorge about thirty miles north. At least, that is where it allegedly resides." He patted the mare's rump lovingly.

The horse bobbed her head several times and nickered softly.

"Sara here knows the trails well, so give her plenty of rein. She'll do fine." Grimmley leaned close and whispered even though the dragon could not understand him. "Don't take your eyes off the horse whilst the dragon is about. You don't know what kind of eating habits the creature has."

Conner scrutinized Skye over Grimmley's shoulder.

Lolling back on his haunches, the dragon blinked innocently at the two humans.

Conner glared at the black creature disapprovingly. "He'd better not try to eat my ride." Noting this did nothing to boost Grimmley's confidence, he tried again. "Don't worry, sir. I will bring Sara safely back with the metal box."

Grimmley waved his arms at Conner as if shooing chickens from a seeded garden. "Yes, well, all that depends on you actually leaving, doesn't it? Just mind what I said and keep your wits about you. You both should do fine."

Conner climbed into the saddle and, with the late morning glow of Hemera at his back, urged Sara at a trot uphill between the thick, well-tended groves of spruces and pines. Now that Conner was finally on the move, Skye eagerly leaped into the cloudless sky, and with a few powerful beats of his leathery wings, drifted above the tree line to the west.

With hand tucked under his arm, Grimmley tapped his pipe stem against pursed lips as the two disappeared over the hill. He had hardly slept, spending much of the night debating the logic of sending them on such a dangerous quest. But sometimes, tests were needed to discover the true stature of an adolescent human, and in this case, an adolescent dragon. He could sense an abundance of raw power yet to be awakened in the boy. But that was just the first problem.

There had been no known human-dragon bonds in over five hundred years. It was bad enough that the Dragonbonded had been such a secretive order. Whatever knowledge they had acquired about bonding with dragons, or more precisely, their powers through those bonds, had died tragically with the last of their kind. But working through that problem was insignificant if neither human nor dragon wanted to keep their link.

Grimmley bit the pipe stem and puffed vigorously. Of course, there was no way to break a bond, a fact the duo were clearly not prepared to accept. Working through this situation would require boundless persistence and infinite patience. No wonder the Cosmos had dropped Conner and the dragon into his lap. He grunted at the empty western sky and ignored the pointed hoot from within the cottage. On the far side of ninety years, Grimmley had long since retired from assuming such responsibility, quite happy to let spry youngsters take the demanding reins. But he could not turn these two away. And he certainly would not pass this on to someone who would stir it into a bigger mess.

What Grimmley needed was a brilliant scheme, carried out with secrecy, exceptional wisdom, deception, and finesse. To execute such a scheme, he would need not only a willing accomplice, but a great scholar, preferably one who knew more about the subject of dragons than anyone else alive.

Of course, at some point, he would need to consider yet another salient point. Shortly after the Dragonbonded had died, bringing about the end to the Anarchic War, a Mystic oracle had predicted their return. Most considered her mad, for her cryptic poetic quatrains, now known as the Omen of the Dragonbonded, spoke of how the Dragonbonded would one day return and herald a new beginning borne from the fires of a power that would destroy everything. Many had futilely attempted to decipher the verses' meaning. After five hundred years, few still believed in the Omen of the Dragonbonded. Did he count himself among them? Grimmley wondered. No. That was best left for when he and his cohort could ponder the Omen in light of this recent revelation.

An admonishing, "Hoot! Hoot! Hoot!" from the cottage broke him from his thoughts.

"Yes, Barthox. I will rest up before I use the Transit Stone. Don't get your beak all in a kink." He ambled back into the cool cottage and closed the door.

# A Payment Made

For the fourth time that morning, Conner reined Sara to a stop on the narrow trail winding along the eastern edge of the river gorge. He crawled gingerly from the mare's back and pulled at pants crimped in his crotch. He had ridden most of the previous day and all that morning. Now, his stiff legs and back were hampering their progress. The dragon's growing frustration made Conner wish he had hiked instead of ridden.

Skye eyed the sorrel mare. "Why don't you let me eat the horse? Then you can walk from here. I am sure we would get there faster, and I won't be hungry anymore."

Conner bent backward, driving his knuckles into the small of his back. "I have told you a dozen times why you can't eat Sara, so stop asking. Besides, you can't find the mountain with the crescent-shaped cavern if you're busy eyeing the horse's haunches." He shook stiffness from his legs. "We have to be getting near," he added longingly. With a grimace, he climbed back into the saddle. "From the way Grimmley was talking, the cavern we're looking for is big. It should be easy to use your mountain breathing technique to find it."

Skye snorted and started forward again, his wings slightly spread to maintain his balance along the uneven trail. "Mountains have many hollow areas. There is a big difference between finding *a* cavern and finding a *specific* cavern."

"Well, your constant gawking is spooking the horse and making me irritable. Fly on ahead and take another look so my back can take a rest from the mare's skittishness." To Conner's surprise, rather than giving his usual retort, Skye leaped from the side of the gorge. The dragon dropped like a rock toward the ravine. At the last moment, his wings unfurled. His long tail skimmed the fast-flowing river below, picking up speed as he scanned the mountain cliffs.

But the solitude was short-lived. Within a few minutes, Sara jumped at the approaching black creature, sending another spasm of pain up Conner's back. The dragon fluttered to a stop on the trail ahead.

"I believe I found the mountain we are looking for. There is a large crescent-shaped crevice carved through the middle of a mountain to the east. Unfortunately, I see no trail for your pack animal to take. Conner, climb on my back so we can get to this place and find the Shaman's box," he pleaded.

Grateful for the excuse to walk, Conner dismounted and moved stiffly toward the dragon. "You want me to trade one pain in the back for another? No thanks, Skye. I have a better idea. Spot a route for me to the cavern entrance. I'll leg it from here." He led Sara off the trail, tied her reins to a small tree, and removed the saddle. Donning the equipment Grimmley had packed, he regarded the scaly black mass before him.

Skye's stare was a piercing blue blaze. "Your stubbornness makes no sense. If we do not reach the cavern before nightfall, we will be forced to wait out the night before we can retrieve this item, thus delaying our return."

Conner thought what the dragon did not say: *To break our bond.* "Then you should find me the quickest route to the mountain, don't you think?" Conner knew his bond's irritation was feeding his own. When the dragon did not respond, he gazed up at Hemera, measuring its progress across the sky.

Skye responded sparingly. "I will dip low to signal the direction you should take." With a few quick beats of his wings, the black shadow was gone.

It was late afternoon before Conner clambered onto a large rock halfway up the southern face of a mountain. There, he found his bond waiting. Above, a desolate scene of rock and dirt continued nearly vertically to a sharp summit against a cloudless sky. Below, to the south and on west to the Falmere River gorge ran the rugged, treeless gulch he had traversed to the mountain's base. The sight reminded him how much he hated heights, wiping clean any curiosity he might have had looking for the route he'd taken in his arduous ascent. He did not venture near the rock's edge.

Instead, Conner worked to remove his gear. "How do we get into the cavern?"

Skye lifted his head lazily as if suddenly realizing he was not alone, then delayed his reply with a lethargic yawn. "The only entrance large enough for us is a short distance along that rocky depression to the left. At the rate you are moving, it will take another of your hours." The dragon examined him with what Conner could feel to be disdain. "Of course, we could reach it quicker if we flew."

Conner ignored the last comment, choosing to pursue an earlier statement. "You said 'large enough for us.' There is another way into the cavern, then?"

"There is a gap leading into the cavern behind that large boulder." He pointed with his thorny nose at a tall rock pitching to the side. "But it is too narrow for my frame. We will need—"

Conner did not wait for Skye to finish. Moving around the boulder, he found a dark, shoulder-width fissure in the rock face. He returned and removed a torch and flint from his pack.

"Why are you wasting time exploring that route? It is too narrow for me to negotiate and we do not have time for me to widen it. Our only way into the cavern is along that trail."

Conner pointed at the listing boulder. "I believe this route is big enough for me to take. If so, we can save an hour by going different ways. I'll meet you on the inside."

The dragon summoned the energy he needed to pull himself from the rock. He moved with amazing agility to block his bond's return to the boulder. "Conner, we do not know what is inside that cavern. Splitting up is the worst possible maneuver. Some caverns this high in a mountain are labyrinths of traps and winding paths. You could get lost. Besides, we will not know which path to take to meet up, even if there is one connecting the openings."

"If the two entrances don't meet up inside, then we may need to search both sides of the cavern, right? So stop being my keeper. I only want to take a quick look. If it helps, I promise not to go far. So please move aside." Conner slipped around the reluctant barrier. He held the torch before him, gave the dragon a reassuring wink, and disappeared into the fissure.

At first, the crevice was large enough for Conner to walk upright, but the split in the rock narrowed. After ten paces, he was forced to lean forward. After twenty, he had to twist his shoulders and crouch. After thirty, he was crawling on his stomach, pushing the torch in front of him. A light draft from within blew torch fumes into his face. He coughed and sneezed. His eyes and nostrils burned. Forty paces into the fissure, Conner came to the end and triumphantly crawled out onto a rocky surface. He wiped tears from his eyes, then held the torch in front of him. But the cavern absorbed the feeble light. His irritation grew as he squinted into the darkness.

Fear of stepping on or into something pulled at his mind, so he leaned the torch against the cavern wall next to the fissure and incanted the Night Vision spell: *"Ora energi anakafanos."* The cavern sprang to life. Conner stood in awe of the cavern's sheer size.

He was standing on a small, rocky platform extending outward and to his right several paces. At the other edge was a narrow, manmade bridge constructed of large rocks and gray mortar. Roughly hewn stone blocks rested on unevenly chiseled spindles to form a rail of hip height along either side. At the base of the rails, two boulders were crudely carved into snarling, winged gargoyles. The bridge spanned a dark chasm, connecting the platform he was on with a flat, rocky floor twenty paces away. Along the cavern floor, a wide alley extended directly from the bridge and ran between a number of old buildings; the effect was that of a street in a small town. He was certain he had found the crescent-shaped cavern.

Conner's gaze followed the jagged edge of the cavern floor into the abyss below, but even with his unnatural vision, he could not measure its depth. He pressed his spine hard against the wall and diverted his eyes upward to help steady himself. Long, pointed cones hung like bony fingers from the rough, uneven ceiling more than a hundred paces above.

"Conner, are you all right?" Skye's concerned voice reverberated through the crack behind him.

He hesitated, thinking through how to proceed before he responded. If the silver box they sought was in one of yon buildings, Conner could be in and out of the cavern in a few minutes. That meant they could be heading back to Grimmley before dark. Conner bent down to keep from raising his voice. "I'm fine, Skye. I need a few more minutes before I come out."

Fighting back his fear of the black chasm below and ignoring the warning stares of the gargoyle statues, Conner placed a foot on the bridge's landing, testing the walkway with more weight. Its solidity bolstered his confidence, so he stepped onto the bridge, cautiously sidestepping any stones that appeared too loose even for his light frame.

Conner was more than halfway across when the first stone cracked and fell from the middle of the bridge. He watched in terror over his shoulder as more stones broke free of their mortared bonds and vanished into the darkness below. The bridge quivered under him and he ran. Sounds of grinding and snapping destruction reverberated off the cavern ceiling and walls as the abyss chewed away ever larger chunks of the bridge. Two paces from the far landing, the last of the bridge disappeared from under him. Conner leaped, hooking his arm around a stone gargoyle, which held the weight of his body dangling over the edge.

Moments passed while Conner struggled in the darkness to hoist himself up, until he lay on the bridge landing trembling with exhaustion and fear. He heard the distant echo of Skye's concerned voice: "Conner, I am coming around to find you." In the silence of the cavern, Conner clung to that reassurance.

At last, he sat up to find that the landings and four angry gargoyles were all that remained of the bridge. He was trapped on the cavern floor. With only one route remaining, he rose with a sigh and faced the structures ahead.

Unsure how long Skye would need to make his way into the cavern, Conner decided not to wait to begin his search, hoping he would find their treasure by the time his bond arrived. Three small buildings on either side of the wide alley had been constructed of a mix of tightly packed clay and stone bricks, long since crumbled with age. The petrified remains of wooden doors littered each entryway, and remnants of gray cloth hung sadly from the sparse windows.

The air reminded him of Cravenrock's undercity, only worse—stale and thick with the smell of mold, dirt, and death. He tried to shake the feeling he was being watched. Stumbling upon the gruesome remains of a human corpse sharpened the strange sensations. It sat slumped against one of the buildings, legs splayed wide with a metal helm drooping forward, as if it had died in its sleep. Ancient chain mail sagged loosely from what remained of its torso. An intricately carved broadsword leaned against the brick wall just within arm's reach.

Conner's fascination with the grotesque figure overpowered his revulsion, so he crouched to take a closer look. What he beheld made him gag. The body was only partially decomposed. Pasty gray skin glistened across half the face. A glassy, opaque eyeball dangled from one hollow socket while the other held the shriveled remnants of an eye frozen in an eternal stare. Cartilage and ossified muscle along the left side of the face were all that kept its jaw from falling away. Conner's stomach tightened and he pulled back, then stumbled forward into the first building.

He rummaged through it, and several more buildings, but all he found were more corpses, each wearing various types of armor or clothing deteriorated beyond recognition. Like the first, none were completely decomposed. One corpse lay sprawled on its back in a grotesque pose, gripping a rusted longsword with sinewy hands, its dark skin stretched tight over the bones. With lips eaten away by worms, the corpse bore blackened teeth in a horrific grimace. Another, in rusted chain shirt, stood at rigid attention, a helm tilted awkwardly over a face with pockmarked skin and a thick brown beard, but with empty eye sockets and a nose long without flesh or cartilage. Its leathery lips were drawn up tight and pursed as if it had passed deep in thought.

Conner wanted nothing more than to be away from this dismal place, so he shook off the shudder at each of the bodies and moved on in search of the box. Still, he was meticulous in ransacking each building. He called Skye's name repeatedly, but the cavern was as quiet as a crypt.

After completing a search of the buildings, he proceeded farther up the wide alley, where he passed two more cadavers—one splayed across the floor, the other sitting in a decomposed chair nearby. These were different. Nothing but bones and decayed cloth remained of the first. A woman, possibly, given the strands of hair about the skull. From the other, thin, wispy white hair flowed from under a gray hood, while the tattered vestiges of flowing, gray robes hung from its inert body. Sagging, ashy skin covered a face that still held clumps of a beard nearly to its emaciated waist. Part of its nose was gone, and two lidless eyes seemed to stare back at him. The hilt of a gilded dagger protruding from its withered chest drew Conner's attention, and he reached out to touch it. A bright white spark arced from the red-gemmed pommel and he pulled away, shaking numbness from his hand.

Bewildered, he left the corpses and continued down the alley until he came to two massive cages on each side of the alley. Each had been constructed entirely of dark metal bars thicker than Conner's arm, reinforced with several horizontal beams of the same metal. Huge cage doors hung open. Conner searched through the first cage, finding nothing except several thick chains of the same dark metal attached to shackles larger than plow harnesses. He was pondering what morbid use such shackles had served in this place when a muffled noise from the alley drew his attention. He whispered for Skye again, but again was rewarded with silence. *What is keeping that dragon?*

At the end of the alley, Conner came to a large building. A rusted, metal door hung at an angle from its hinges. He pulled on the handle and the door fell away with a metallic snap and resounding crash. Conner peered through the rising cloud of dust and decay, then cautiously stepped through. Rotted wooden tables and benches littered with metal tools and leather straps filled a large room. He did not want to imagine what most of the tools had been used for, but he did recognize a rack of sharp knives and spools of decayed thread near one bench. A dozen snake hides and skeletons hung on the wall nearby.

Toward the back of the room, Conner came upon a tall metal cabinet. The door on the front was slightly ajar. His heart leaped into his throat. Several Cravenrock thieves had once described such cabinets, used for holding valuables. Taking a deep breath, he pulled hard on the gold handle. The door groaned as it opened. Inside, he discovered a number of books. But when he tried to remove them, they dissolved into clouds of thick dust. After the paper grit settled, his Night Vision caught the muted gleam of dull metal in the back of the middle shelf. Reaching in, he gingerly removed a metal box matching the size and shape Grimmley had described. He ran his fingertips over the finely etched Modeic symbols barely visible through the tarnish. He smiled victoriously.

Another muffled sound near the door drew his attention, but again, nothing was there. Still, a morbid chill ran through him. This time, he was certain he had not imagined it. With prize in hand, it was time to go. He left the building and hiked with a sudden urgency back up the alley, repeatedly calling and scanning the cavern above for his tardy bond. Conner returned to the large cages and bolted to a stop. The blood in his veins turned to ice. The chair that had held the gray-robed corpse was empty!

There were more muffled sounds at his back. Conner turned, and he was filled with a terror greater even than that he'd felt in the presence of the Assassin in Cravenrock's undercity. Ten paces away, half a dozen corpses stood staring blankly at him, and before them, the stiff, gray-robed figure. Conner began to quake violently. From the creature's emaciated chest came a rustling rasp as it exclaimed, "How wonderful it is to be awake again!"

Conner scanned the cavern in hopes of seeing a dark-winged savior descending to his rescue, as it had the night after they had bonded, when Skye had descended to steal him away from his captors. Instead, he spied more undead creatures crawling from the buildings about him. The sounds of a hollow laugh filled the cavern chamber.

Something brushed against his side and he spun. Three more half-decomposed bodies gripped and scratched listlessly at his arms. His mouth opened, but he could not find the air to make a sound. He shook free of their clinging grasps and staggered back, clenching the box tight to his chest.

To his right, he caught the fluid motion of a large, black form flying toward the robed corpse. "Skye! Over here!" he shrieked. Again, he shrugged free from bony hands tugging at his clothing and clawing at his arms. He shuffled back another step. When he thought his nightmare could get no worse, he watched in shock and horror as Skye fluttered to a stop near the gray-robed corpse and, unfurling his wings, bowed to the creature!

Stunned, Conner stepped back again, but his heel slipped from the edge of the abyss. So caught up with the nightmare before him, he had forgotten about the chasm behind. Gangly hands pulled tenaciously at him. He tried to get a solid foundation to fight back, but his foot slipped again. "Skye! Help me!" Conner screamed in growing desperation. But the dragon was unresponsive to his pleas, his head bowed submissively before the corpse while it croaked its laugh even louder.

Twisting, he swung the box at a corpse. The undead's head lolled back from the sickening crunch, its one eye staring dully at the ceiling as it continued blindly gripping at Conner's shirt. Conner swung again, but his other heel slipped from the edge. With the last of his energy, he screamed, "Skye, please! I need your help!"

Conner's feet slipped from the edge and he went down hard on his chest and knees, the box he refused to relinquish taking his air. His ribs ached, but he fought to regain ground. He thought of his parents in front of their house that bright morning he left. That day seemed so long ago. He pined to be there with them now. He let out a sob as he slipped farther over the edge, his legs flailing wildly while claws dug into his back. He thought of Pattria as she had been that night in the Palaver Room, leaning against him, her comforting smile reassuring him nothing in the world could ever change. How foolish he had been to believe that he was the master of his own destiny!

With his one free hand, he clawed at the cavern floor. Panic became hysteria. And there was Pauli, his eyes ablaze with an eagerness to find some new mischief. Who would drag his best friend from trouble now? Conner let out a sharp laugh at the macabre humor.

Silently, he lost his grip on the rocky crevice and disappeared into the darkness below, clutching the silver box to his chest with nothing but the robed corpse's laughter to mark his passing.

# Part II

*Great wisdom is born not from the desire to always be right, but from overcoming the fear of being wrong.*

*—The Modei Book of Fire (First Book)*

# Homeward Bound

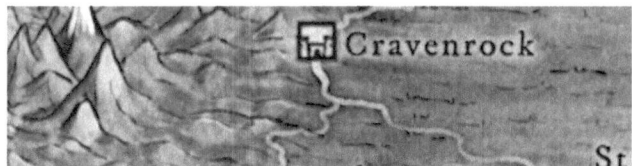

Two hours from breaking camp, and already Hemera was heating the back of Marcantos's dark leather jerkin. Dust borne by the company of mounted Defenders ahead hung lifeless in the warm air. The grandmaster Warrior twisted in his saddle, then squinted in dismay at the scene behind. It would be another in an endless stream of oppressive and cloudless Narwalen days. He counted the long train of thirty laden wagons rumbling at a snail's pace along the road—the first leg of their journey to Graystone.

His gaze fell upon the lead wagon. He met Martyn Cornwell's intense scowl with a measured glare, heightening Marcantos's irritability. The pathetic high merchant had been brooding since the previous morning, when he had been told that the princess and her royal entourage would be accompanying his Merchants Guild caravan to Pennington Point. Cornwell had been livid to the point of absurdity, ranting for more than an hour about how the princess's presence would only invite trouble for his troupe. Once Marcantos explained that he would also be using the caravan's company of Queen's Defenders to bolster the princess's personal protection, color drained from the merchant's face. And when the Warrior suggested Cornwell could proceed without his usual safeguards, the ungrateful man could not find words to slip between his flapping lips.

The loud crack of leather reins in Cornwell's fists over the rumps of four draft horses made it clear who the lash was really meant for. Marcantos smirked at the impotent threat. Copious growled as he waddled beside his bond's warhorse.

"You really should learn patience, Marcantos," teased the black figure next to him.

Marcantos wiped beads of sweat and dirt from his brow with a kerchief, then examined the narrow waist of the woman riding at the head of the Defenders. "Patience has its place. Too much can be as deadly as too little. You taught me that, Blake." He attacked each word with an annoyed vengeance.

Friarwood smiled, eyes habitually scanning the open terrain ahead. Marcantos's preceptor never tired of knowing he had been heard.

"Maybe it is time to put an end to at least one person's sulky mood," Marcantos grumbled to himself. He spat grit from his mouth. *And get some relief from this accursed dust.* Marcantos spurred his black steed out of its slumbered step. He did not rein him back until he was next to the princess.

"I hope Your Highness slept well last night," Marcantos commented facetiously with a slight bow. After camping next to the road, he was sure Veressa would be wishing she had not been so quick to refuse a royal carriage for traveling and sleeping comforts.

Instead, she scowled, easily eclipsing Cornwell's distaste. "Does my protector think me incapable of sleeping between anything but a plush mattress and quilted blanket?" She gestured up the empty road ahead. "Maybe my guardian should ride on ahead to ready my sleeping space with soft, cool leaves and dried grass before my arrival."

Marcantos sighed. Pennrock Road had never appeared to be so long or bleak. "I know we did not begin this ... arrangement ... on solid footing, Highness. But I do hope you will not judge me solely on my actions at the manor. At least give me a chance to gain your trust before you pass sentence on me."

Veressa fought back an impulsive response. It was the first sign of progress since leaving Cravenrock the previous morning. What he said next would likely determine their relationship in the days to come. Unfortunately, he was not well versed in waving a flag of truce. "I can only imagine how hard it must be to accept your father's decision. I know how close you were to Master Loris." He hesitated, chiding himself for using past tense. "But this will be a very long and taxing journey if we continue this way. Please understand I am as bound to carrying out King Jonath's orders as you are bound in returning home. Your security and well-being are my only concern until you are safely within Graystone's walls."

The princess exhaled forcefully, but rode on in silence.

His eyes followed the large white cat stealthily shadowing Veressa thirty paces north of the road, ears back, a vigilant eye on Marcantos's unexpected appearance near the princess. Marcantos tried again. "I see your bond is getting accustomed to humans. Yesterday, I hardly saw him."

The princess flashed a warm smile at her bond. "Maybe his aloofness is for the best. I think even my mother's fearless Defenders are frightened by him."

Marcantos nodded. "A creature like that is to be respected. I heard once the Modei worshipped the leopard for its fierceness and fury."

The princess gazed at her new protector as if seeing him for the first time. "Yes, Grandmaster Evinfaire, the early Bremenn scholars thought thus. But later scholars discovered that the leopard really signified the Modei's reverence for nature's guiltless and impetuous way of life." She studied his surprise-filled eyes. "I suppose from our understanding of the world, we are incapable of distinguishing spontaneity from ferocity. However, the Modei knew the leopard did not kill out of anger or fury, but purely for necessity. The Modei believed people could learn a great deal from nature. That is why the symbol of the leopard was so prevalent in their writings. No one understood the Cosmos as did the Modei."

Marcantos met her gaze with a smile. He was genuinely impressed. "I did not know Your Highness was a scholar in the teachings of the Modei."

Veressa let out a singsong giggle, reminding him of her days of youth. "Every Griffinrock matriarch since the Armistice of the Orders has been schooled by Paladinian nuns."

The Warrior glanced away to hide his revolt at the mention of the clergy guildsmen. The friars and nuns of the guilds were self-proclaimed experts in the Modeic writings. As curiously enigmatic and idealistic as their parental Paladins Order, they preached absolute peace and equality to all who would listen, be they queen or serf. At least Paladins had no problem smiting with their sword hand while they prayed for the vanquished spirits with their other. "How unfortunate that the Modei's understanding of the Cosmos could not prevent their destruction. What we could have learned from them if given a chance."

The princess bristled. "You can execute a man, you can eradicate an entire race, but no sword or arrow ever killed an idea once seeded. We have had many chances to learn, but instead, we further the injustice of our deeds by heedlessly ignoring the Modeic words of warning left at Shan-Grail. How many of our follies could have been prevented if we had listened to the ghosts of our past? No, Grandmaster Evinfaire, ignorance kills ideas. And whether for man, race, or idea, we Cronoans have been excellent killers."

Marcantos knew Veressa neither lectured nor admonished him. She spoke with the force of an inward conviction that reminded him of his own just-bonded youth. Where was that boy now? "Of course, Your Highness is right," he said, this time with heartfelt emotion. With the moment lost, he was content to ride in silence. For once, the princess did not seem to mind him near.

Marcantos's actions more than his words left Veressa deep in thought. She had heard the troubling stories about the man who many believed would be her Champion someday. Most of what she had heard she did not like. He was impulsive and quick to anger, traits not valued among the Harmonics. But those qualities did not seem so bad. The man's abrasive blend of superiority and rudeness far exceeded the mind-numbing dullness of noblemen whose actions and words she could predict ... or who wilted under the heat of her determination. For the first time she was intrigued by what she sensed in this grandmaster Warrior. He showed genuine emotions.

She glanced his way, pretending to check on her bond, and caught his piercing gaze. Her cheeks burned. She felt his intense scrutiny. What were all those faults she had been told about him? Oddly, nothing came to her except that he was the youngest grandmaster Warrior in centuries, and a decorated, valiant soldier.

The thoughts were a welcome distraction from other troubles that had gnawed at her through the early morning hours. Marcantos had been right in one regard. She had hardly slept, but not for the reasons he surmised. Through most of the night, her mind had been consumed by sensations and desires she did not understand, leaving her exhausted and raw. She had always enjoyed being away from Graystone and the pressures that weighed on a future queen. But this was different—new, and far more profound.

She was reminded of when she had watched Annabelle depart for Dreadcreek and the strange exhilaration she had felt at the thought of running off with the Ranger. She was suddenly aware of all of her physical senses—the creak of her saddle, the feel of leather reins in her damp palms, the smell of horses, the wind blowing through the thick grass alongside the road, the taste of grit in her mouth. There was a certain clarity of being there, in that moment. She had an exhilarating vision of leaping from her horse and sprinting away across the plains, her leopard bond leading the way. She wanted to laugh at the idea, but there was nothing comical about feeling her heart start to race.

Seeking solace from the energy beckoning to her spirit, Veressa broke the silence with the Warrior. By late afternoon, she was surprised to discover how swiftly the day slipped by.

Forgotten behind the company of Defenders, the Anarchic spy Lacerus observed everything. For the first time since departing Cravenrock, the princess had begun to relax, even occasionally to laugh. And Veressa's ease had a calming effect on Marcantos, which would make the young man all the more receptive to the Assassin's special training. Lacerus was overcome with pleasure. If his continued efforts kept Marcantos on his current path, everything would fall in place perfectly.

## One Little Hurdle

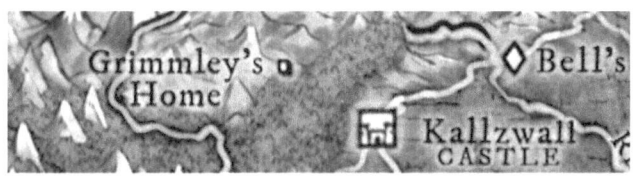

**"Y**ou nearly let me die back there!" Conner forced the words through clenched teeth to keep them from clattering in his skull. Neither the thick sleeping blanket nor the evening fire helped ward off the cold horror gnawing at his bones.

After a long pause, Skye replied, "I would not have let anything happen to you, Conner."

"How am I supposed to believe you?" he asked with a molten glare at the radiant blue orbs over the dancing flames.

Dragon eyes stared back in unblinking silence.

"At least explain what happened, because I really think I deserve to know. I could understand that the sight of "—Conner shook visibly again, forcing down his rising fear—"*undead* coming to life might be bewildering. By the light of Erebus, it was for me!" *First, an Anarchist Assassin, and then the walking dead! The world is mad!* Conner pulled the blanket tighter around his shoulders. "And for the first time ever, I sensed confusion in you. But there was more, Skye. I felt your"—he shivered at the memory of the emotions that had flowed through their bond while the black dragon bowed before the undead—"*reverence* for that creature!" A laugh near hysteria escaped his lips.

The glowing blue eyes glanced away.

*Say something, beast!* he wanted to scream. Even now, ripples of turmoil flowed from the wyvern—uncertainty, doubt, confusion, even a hint of embarrassment. Of course, not fear—never fear! But Skye's persistent silence did nothing to alleviate Conner's accusations. His growing distrust in his bond began to overshadow even the terror of what he had experienced earlier that day. Conner cradled the silver box as if it possessed his very redemption. He ran trembling fingers over the cryptic symbols visible in the flickering firelight. "I only hope this box was worth the trouble," he mumbled to the dark.

The sounds of night filled the void between the two oppressed spirits. Sleep did not come to Conner until the waning crescent of Erebus rose into the starlit sky.

Late the next afternoon, Sara crested a rolling hill and stopped, ears perked forward. Conner rose stiffly in the stirrups, craning his neck to have a better look at the sight consuming the horse's attention. Over the tops of the perfect rows of spruces, gray smoke curled from a cottage chimney. The smell of hickory and spices attacked his nostrils. Grimmley was cooking some wondrous delicacy for dinner. He swallowed hard to quell an empty stomach. He could only hope the Shaman was making enough for four, because he could surely eat enough for three! Ignoring the yawn coming from the black creature behind, he urged Sara forward. The last four hundred paces of his quest were likely to be the hardest.

Before he reached the clearing at the edge of the spruces and pines, a loud hoot from the cottage brought a haggard but relieved Grimmley to the door.

The Shaman caught that the boy had noticed his worried expression and waved his arm. "I was concerned you wouldn't make it back with my horse, boy. It would be hard replacing such a fine animal." Stepping stiffly from the porch, he gently rubbed the mare's muzzle. The Shaman stood silently sizing up Conner and Skye's condition.

Conner dismounted with the stiffness of three days' riding. "I'd think you'd be more relieved to know that I was not merely successful at keeping Skye's talons out of Sara's haunches, Grimmley," he stated smugly, ignoring the dragon's snort. Smiling, he removed the silver box from the saddlebag and handed it ceremoniously to the Shaman.

Grimmley gasped, eyes wide. "You found it," he whispered, cradling the box. He ran calloused, shaky fingers over the symbols. "Conner, you do not know what this discovery means."

Conner shrugged. "Sure I do, Grimmley. It means Skye and I can go our separate ways."

Again, the dragon snorted, this time with emphatic agreement.

The Shaman glanced up, then blinked. "Ah, yes, breaking the bond. About that, Conner," he coughed. "So, you two are still set upon severing your ties?"

"That is why we retrieved the box, Grimmley."

The old man grunted. His face was masked with a peculiar expression, so Conner added for clarification, "We wouldn't have risked our lives or journeyed so far."

"I see. Well, I was hoping this quest would have convinced you otherwise."

"Why would you hope that?" Conner asked, growing suspicious of Grimmley's odd behavior.

"Well, my boy, there is something you need to know." It took several moments for the Shaman to find words—disconcerting, since in the short time Conner had known the Shaman, finding something to say had never been a problem. "You see, boy, there is no way to break a bond."

Conner stiffened. "Wait. What? No! You said this box would help us break the bond."

The dragon sensed Conner's shift in mood. "Conner? What is the Shaman saying?"

Grimmley eyed the dragon with uncertainty. "No, my boy, I said the box would be helpful for you two. What I meant—"

"You tricked us!" Conner screamed.

"Conner?" Skye shifted anxiously. "What is it?"

Grimmley found what moments before he had lacked—the ability to speak. "I had to go along with the pretense, Conner, because you were not listening to reason. In fact, you weren't listening at all, always interrupting, going on about how you deserve a certain kind of bond. If you had listened, I would have told you: there isn't a way to break a bond. Period. No one in recorded history has *ever* broken their bond."

Conner shook his head. "No! This isn't right! I nearly died getting that box. Now you stand here telling me it won't sever our bond?" Images filled his mind of half-decomposed undead gripping at his clothes, the stench of death about him, and his descent into the abyss. "I did all that for nothing?"

Conner's shift in emotions was all Skye needed to fill in the blanks. Unfurling his black wings, the dragon erupted. Fire spouted from his gaping mouth. His head and neck whipped about, scorching dirt and grass. The beast danced uncontrollably in swirling spirals, flames shooting in every direction.

Sara bolted at the wyvern's explosion and disappeared around the far side of the cottage, her eyes white and nostrils flared.

Through all of this, with mouth agape and fists of rage, Conner ignored both maddened beast and frightened horse.

Grimmley raised his hands in an attempt to calm the bonded pair. "Not for nothing, boy! You have done the Harmonic Realms a great service by retrieving this box, one greater than you could possibly imagine! For that, I am truly indebted to you."

But Conner was no longer listening to the Shaman. His thoughts were all about what he had endured since leaving his home over a fortnight ago. He had placed his trust in Skye and Grimmley, and both had revealed their true character. A grandmaster of the order governing the guild he was to be a member of should be greater. But the old orderman would do and say anything for personal gain. Conner had been naïve, gullible. Disgust and rage boiled through him and through his link with Skye. *Why me?* he wanted to scream. He stared up at the darkening sky, tears of anger welling up.

"Conner, I will do everything in my power to help you—" Grimmley was saying.

Conner shook in rage at the old man. "I don't want anything from you! I trusted you, and you betrayed me! You are no Shaman!"

Grimmley tried to break through the boy's anger. "—everything in my power to help you understand how to use this gift the Cosmos has seen fit to give you."

"I don't want this gift!"

"Conner, control your temper! Your dragon is feeding on your anger. It is going to destroy my forests!"

"Good!" Conner's eyes were aflame. "I hope Skye scorches every last tree for what you did to us!"

Grimmley stepped forward threateningly, his haggard appearance gone. "Don't test my patience, boy." A worried hoot came from the cottage, quite similar in tone to an *uh-oh.* "Even with your dragon, you are not ready to take on *this* Shaman. So take control before I do! And you had better learn how to curb your temper before you get into a situation you cannot bluff or strong-arm your way out of!"

Conner blinked and stepped back. "Fine." He called Skye away from several smoldering walnut trees. Finally, he asked, "If a bond can't be broken, then just tell me how did you expect this box to help us? How?"

The Shaman held his right palm up and mumbled an incantation: *"Ora energi pnigofotia."* The patches of fire among his trees and grass snuffed out. "By getting you to work together on a common goal, boy!" he huffed emphatically. "From the moment you two arrived, you have done nothing but nip at each other's heels, bickering, arguing, and complaining like two spoiled children who aren't getting their way! Well, it is time you both realize that life doesn't always work the way you want. So grow up!" He poked a finger at the black beast still dancing about irritably. "Accept that you are bonded with a dragon, and get on with your life!"

After a long silence, Conner mumbled, "There must be someone out there who can help us." His watery eyes searched the wooded horizon.

"There is no one, my boy," Grimmley said with absolute confidence. He gripped the boy by the shoulders, holding Conner's gaze. "I am truly sorry. *No one.*"

Conner shook free of Grimmley's grip. "I need time to think."

"I understand." Grimmley nodded solemnly.

Conner shuffled past the dragon and the columns of smoke rising from the patches of scorched grass and trees, then around to the Shaman's garden in the back.

Grimmley grunted in frustration. After Conner and his dragon had disappeared around the cottage, the Shaman removed his pipe from his pocket and lit it with an incantation. His ruse to get the two to see the Cosmos's gift for what it was had ended in dismal failure. *Energy is wasted on the blindness of youth*, his preceptor had liked to say.

After a few hard draws on the pipe, he declared through the open door, "Well, Barthox! That did not go so well." The barred owl hooted her concurrence. All Grimmley could do now was hope he had not made things worse. Regardless, the pair had to move past the barrier they were beating their heads against. Too much needed to get done, and Grimmley had no idea how much time he had to work with.

*Give the boy some space*, he chided himself. To fight a brewing anxiety, Grimmley went inside and set the silver box on his desk, then went back out to find Sara. After unsaddling and feeding the mare, he returned to his desk and thoroughly examined the box. Drawing upon Fire and Earth elementals, the Shaman cast several powerful spells of detection, which revealed no traps. The lock could have been set with traps of Water or Air, but if his theories were correct, that was not possible. With a deep breath to steady his nerves, he incanted a command spell. The latch clicked in response. He gently slid the top back with trembling fingers. Nothing happened, so he peered cautiously inside.

The Shaman relaxed back in his chair with a sigh, scowling at the box as if the metal device had bitten him. He puffed on the pipe until smoke hung about his face. "Well! That is not what I expected!"

"Hoot-hoot," came the solemn reply.

Near dusk, Skye found his bond sulking near the lake's edge. The dragon lumbered closer, then settled near the foot of the walkway. For a while, the two sat in silence, the tip of Skye's tail thumping out the minutes as they passed. Finally, he swiveled his head to take in the motionless lad with shoulders slumped forward. "I do not understand why this great Shaman sent us off on a quest without divulging everything he knew about what we were seeking ... or that it would not be useful in breaking this bond." Skye's leg twitched uncontrollably. When his bond offered no argumentative response, the wyvern concluded, "Dragons would never consider holding back important information."

Conner huffed without taking his eyes from the sparkling water at his feet. "Then it seems, Skye, that you have learned another wonderful human behavior. It's called *deception*."

Skye grunted with an effective twitch of his tail at the word. "Deception makes no sense. We are not responsible for how another responds to a situation. Honesty is essential for others to learn how to survive in an impartial, dangerous world. Deception only takes away that opportunity for growth." The longer Skye thought about it, the more cross he became. And Skye realized Conner had been right all along. Shamans were just humans. He averted his eyes from Conner, blazing even brighter under the heat of his rage. "Conner, let us go back into the mountains and work out what to do without the help of any Shamans or other humans. I miss the breath of the mountains to awaken me in the mornings."

The long silence permitted Skye to remain attentive to the ebb and flow of emotions coming through his link with Conner. He knew Conner wanted to return to his home, wanted to find a way to live out a normal human existence, but could not envision how to get there attached to a dragon. Skye recalled the first time that, as an amphithere, he had snuck past the Keepers standing watch over the den, climbing on rising columns of air through a shaft that vented out the top of his island home. It had been his first sight of Hemera, a large golden orb rising over a dark blue ocean. He could just make out the massive lands to the south. He had heard the dragonsongs and knew great adventures awaited him there. But his wings were wet and weak. He had lain stretched across the rocks through that morning, imagining the day he would reach those far-off shores. Conner's feelings seemed to match those he had that day.

Conner broke the long stillness. "I'll think about it," he mumbled.

Skye rose and stretched, noting Hemera dipping low among the trees to the west. "Okay. Just do not take too long." With that, he leaped into the deepening blue sky and flew away.

Conner sat on the side of the lake's wooden walkway, feet splashing in the cool water. Around him, the sounds of a summer evening were coming to life. Hemera had disappeared beyond the hills to the west. Golden rays streamed through gaps in the slow-moving clouds painted a wondrous blend of deepening reds and purples. If it had been any other evening, he would have found the experience a Cosmic inspiration of joy. But Conner was on an inward journey, a journey that sapped him of all will and hope, in a darkened and bleak mindscape holding no chance of Hemera's rise.

Conner jumped with a start at a gentle hand on his shoulder. Deep in thought, he had missed the Shaman's approach. Kind eyes and a warm smile met his hopeless glance.

"I think it is time you and I had a serious talk, boy," Grimmley said softly. When Conner said nothing, Grimmley sat next to him, removed his silk slippers, and dipped his toes into the water. For a few minutes, only the sounds of crickets and splashing feet filled the void. At last, he broke the long silence. "I am an old man, Conner. Many years ago, I gave up trying to influence the ways of the world. This place was to be my personal sanctuary, a peaceful spot where I could live out my remaining years in relative solitude, helping those in need the best I can … with the skills I remember how to perform, of course," he chuckled, giving the boy a wink. "But it seems the Cosmos has a different plan for me as well."

Conner's face flushed. He had never considered the onus of responsibility he was placing on the old Shaman's shoulders.

"My preceptor once told me, 'The Cosmos was kind enough to give us wit to help us deal with dreams that will never see the light.' You know by now that becoming an Apothecary is not on this life's journey for you." Grimmley relit his pipe—*"Hem pheto anaptofotia"*—then waited.

The Shaman's observation wormed its way into Conner's soul. Conner nodded, feeling the heat from the raging fires burning the bridges of his once-future life.

Grimmley spoke again. "What I know about human-dragon bonds can be scribbled on a potion label, and I suspect most of it is wrong. But it does not take Shaman foresight to know"—he held Conner's gaze with a look of foreboding—"that you cannot contain this secret of yours for long. Soon, someone will discover the first human-dragon bond in five hundred and fifty years has occurred. And when that secret gets out, you had better be prepared to deal with the consequences that will most assuredly come your way."

"You're right, of course, Grimmley. My apologies for getting you involved. This is not your problem. I should not have saddled you with such a burden. Skye and I will leave with first light." Conner started to stand, but Grimmley's hand held him firmly in place.

"Don't be so quick, boy. I'm not done, so settle." The Shaman waited. "That's better. What I am getting to is this: I am going to be your preceptor." Grimmley worked at getting the tobac fully lit again, giving time for Conner's mouth to close. "Of course, it has been thirty-some years since I had an apprentice, so I forget all the details about how this is done. Besides, it won't be official, since the Shaman Dons would never approve of it, even if I *were* to tell them I was guiding you." He leaned closer and winked, oddly reminiscent of Pauli. "So it seems we both have secrets to share."

"Grimmley, that is incredibly nice of you, but I can't accept your offer. I would be devastated if the Dons discovered you were secretly-"

"You think I'm too old to handle those crotchety old men and women? By Ourea's elemental, I taught most of them everything they know about being grumpy!" The Shaman's hearty laugh made his entire narrow frame bounce, though Conner failed to see the humor. "Besides, who else do you know who is willing to risk teaching you how to control elementals? Or cast incantations? Hmm? Because I can tell, boy, you have potential like black clouds hold rain!"

"I do?" Conner was surprised. "Wait! No! What am I thinking? I am not an orderman! I am a freeman, an Eastland farmer. That is all I have ever been." Fear began to bubble up through the remnants of the nightmare he had the evening before meeting Grimmley. The dream had begun with him being one of the legendary Dragonbonded, standing tall on a castle wall with the Ranger apprentice he had assisted in Pennington Point by his side. But the Assassin he had met in Cravenrock appeared on the horizon, coming for him on a great warhorse. He tried to run in fear, to climb on Skye's back, only to be pummeled with accusations and jeers from those around him. Luckily, Grimmley pulled him from the disturbing memory.

"Oh, you are right. It is all you have ever *been*, boy. That ended the day you touched that dragon. It would serve you well to get over that little hurdle."

*"Little?"* Conner shook his head tenaciously. "No, it would be best if I go find a secluded place in the mountains somewhere until I can figure out what to do. Skye is happy there."

Grimmley's eyebrows furrowed over wired glasses. "You *are* truly as stubborn as I have heard Eastlanders to be! Very well! I wasn't going to do this, but you leave me no other option!"

"What are you talking about?"

"Do you remember what you said when you asked for help in breaking your bond? You said you would not accept my help without some kind of payment—'a principle among freemen of the Eastlands' I think were your words, or thereabouts. Well, if I'm not mistaken, the opposite is also true among your people. To refuse an offered payment for a deed completed dishonors the giver, yes? So I offer payment for recovering the silver box." He leaned back, nodding triumphantly.

"That's ... that's not fair."

"Harmonics is not about fairness, boy. It's about balance." He offered Conner's shoulder a few hearty pats, then rose, taking a moment to admire the starry sky. "After you talk to your dragon, I suggest you come inside and have some dinner. You're going to need a good meal and a long night's rest if we're going to start your training in the morning."

With a lively tune to help carry his step, the Shaman disappeared through the back door. Soon, the sounds of banging pots, verses from songs Conner had never heard, and emphatic hoots from Grimmley's personal choir filled the cool night air.

The scaly black beast had long since vanished on silent wings north toward the mountains in search of a meal. Still, a cascade of emotions flooded through their link. The dragon was angry. Conner would need to spend time with the dragon in the morning to begin mending their relationship. It seemed they would have to deal with each other for a very long time to come.

He had no idea how long he stared into the dark northern sky, but it was hunger more than anything that drew him back into the cottage.

# Dreadcreek

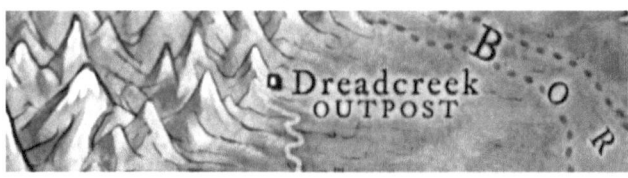

Lanchus Lendfeather sparked flint into the copper burners, then sat impatiently watching the orange-and-red flames lick at the oil-soaked wood chips. Slowly, Dreadcreek's command terrace came to life, the dancing fires casting eerie shadows into the cool night air. Beyond the thick granite terrace pillars, ice-capped mountains were silhouetted against a panoramic night sky.

Though the Ranger's thick green cloak easily concealed his wiry frame, the hood did little to hide his aged features. Long gray hair braided in grandmaster rank hung about his narrow face, recessed eyes, and bony cheeks. The figure leaned comfortably against a bristlecone pine, its thick, twisted trunk and rambling gnarled roots creating a throne-like chair. The terrace's marble floor and the roof ten paces overhead had been constructed around the ancient tree, believed to have been old even when the Seven Realms had formed over a millennium ago. Ranger and tree were suitably matched.

At last, he broke the wax seal on the rolled parchment he'd been handed and leaned forward to let the burners' glow illuminate the finely scripted lettering.

*To Grandmaster Lanchus Lendfeather of the Rangers Order, Commander of Dreadcreek Forces, from King Jonath of Griffinrock.*

*With this dispatch, I deliver into your capable hands your order's loyal agent, Master Ranger Annabelle Loris, who henceforth is released from her services these past eleven years as protector to our daughter, heir of the Griffinrock throne. Master Loris has served the crown with honor.*

*I also beseech unto you a solemn and urgent request as the faithful right hand to the Queen of Griffinrock and servant of the three Harmonic Realms. Our realms are in need of information regarding an unknown but momentous event that occurred seven days ago at a location approximately forty miles to the west of Dreadcreek. The Griffinrock realm would be in your debt if you retrieved any facts through which we could gain an understanding of this event. I trust you will keep this petition for your personal eyes only.*

*Scribed, signed, and sealed as the humble servant of Griffinrock,*

*- Countess Garlander of Cravenrock*

Lanchus read the parchment a second time, dissecting each sentence to be sure he understood the intricacies of the letter's meaning. First, Sovereign Lady Kyles, head of the Rangers Council, had already informed him of Master Loris's dismissal by the Griffinrock crown and of her reassignment to Dreadcreek. With the way the appointment had been handled, it was clear even to a simpleton that Loris's eleven years of Griffinrock service had ended poorly. The king's flowery praise for the Ranger could not cover that stench. But the circumstances surrounding the situation were neither his concern nor interest. The question was purely one of deciding how best to use an orderman tainted by a royal scandal. He had learned early in his career to avoid such fellows like the plague. No hurry. He was sure something appropriate for a branded Ranger would come to him.

What was most unexpected in the letter was the king's request for his help in a matter of state, which made the request both intriguing and troubling from several angles. First, appeals for assistance were handled through official channels. As mandated in the Armistice of the Orders, each order's council approved all petitions from the realms and made decisions about how to deal with them. Extensive analysis, examination of secondary, even tertiary effects of each option, and measurement of gains and losses were needed before a council made a decision.

But King Jonath was petitioning him directly. Of course the king knew any actions Lanchus took without approval of his order's council would be prohibited under the Orderman's Code, and would thus be of paramount risk to Lanchus's career, if not his life. For this reason, Jonath was offering a debt of payment for taking such personal risk. With the increased number of skirmishes to the north of late, nothing would suit Lanchus better than to be free from the miserable assignment he had held for more than a decade. Performing the king's request could mean a position in Griffinrock's royal court, or possibly even as a landed knight. Freeland regions in southern and eastern Griffinrock needed the experienced hand of a strong lord baron. This brought a smile to his otherwise tired, wrinkled face.

And second, whatever this unknown event, coinciding with Midsummer's Day, the king clearly believed it vital to the Harmonic Realms. Yes, Jonath would grasp at any clues thrown him, anything out of the ordinary, but what ...?

Lanchus tapped a bony forefinger over pursed, dry lips. It was shortly after Midsummer's Day that he'd begun receiving reports of a winged monster spotted by transients west of Dreadcreek. Of course, he had done nothing. He did not have the manpower to chase every apparition and fantasy manifested by the fools in the region. The reports were merely mad rants of mountain people too long in the wilderness and hallucinations of skittish travelers frightened near the Borderlands. Still, these reports offered the perfect guise for the plan taking shape, one that would ensure Jonath's indebtedness, and with minimal risk to Lanchus's personal safety.

He studied the long columns of black braids on the female Ranger bowed before him, marking her master rank. She had not moved nor spoken since her arrival, her right hand and knee pressed to the marble floor in humble servitude. Further, he foresaw how his plan would take care of the blight with which he had been assigned. He held the scroll casually before him. "Are you aware of what this letter contains, Master Loris?"

The middle-aged Ranger with dark skin and solemn green eyes glanced up from the floor. Even though she was weary from the long ride from Cravenrock, he thought her a lovely woman.

"No, commander. I was told only to deliver it personally into your hands, then await your instructions."

*Good.* The grandmaster dropped the parchment into one of the burners, then grunted in satisfaction. Any evidence of the motivation behind his plan disappeared into green flames and ash. "Henceforth, you are assigned as the Ranger consul to the scouting patrol under the command of Guildmaster Scouter Gertrum Smelterman. With morning's light, you will travel west with his patrol to investigate reports I have been receiving of late concerning a large winged creature. It is likely the only things flying are people's fancies, but I want to be sure these reports are not about a vanguard force of Anarchists attempting to mask their movements within the region." Lanchus pressed a small gold ring firmly into Annabelle's palm. He waited until she had thoroughly examined the ring's enchanted green-emerald inset. "You are to report—immediately, and *in secret*—anything you discover. Are my orders understood, Master Loris?" he whispered.

"Yes, commander." She bowed her head.

"Very well. I suggest you get plenty of rest this night. You will most certainly need it."

Lanchus sat back and waited until the cloaked Ranger vanished down the terrace steps to the hold's camp far below. He would need to report something to his council. He carefully examined his plan from every perspective, looking for holes, probing for flaws. Once he was confident the plan was solid, he pressed his left heel against a metal bar under the pine chair. *"Outher ousia afairopagida."* The Rangers Order emblem embossed in the marble floor slid away to reveal stairs made from the roots of his bristlecone tree. A smile parted his thin lips. *Lord Lanchus Lendfeather has an exceptional ring to it*, he thought pleasantly, then disappeared into the Scrying Chamber below.

Annabelle had slept little since Veressa's accident three days before. Yet despair more than the hard ride from Cravenrock sapped energy from her body. She ran through the litany of nightmarish features of her new position—a Ranger consul assigned to a scouting patrol under an Alpslander guildmaster investigating sightings of a large winged creature. By the sons of Chaos, she could not imagine a worse assignment! Grandmaster Lendfeather, or possibly the Sovereign Lady Kyles, was certainly creative. And "a vanguard force of Anarchists"? Surely Lendfeather knew she could see through the pitiful attempt to sugarcoat this task. One thing made no sense: Why waste an entire patrol of men to get her out of the way? Whatever this excursion was truly about, chasing phantoms through the mountains was not going to restore the Ranger's status with Griffinrock.

Thinking it through while she rubbed down and fed her gray gelding produced no new revelations. Far beyond numbed exhaustion, she procured a vacant tent, ate, and retired for the night. But sleep did not come to her restless mind. She never liked change, but going from the princess's protector to consul for a guildsman?

*No*, Annabelle corrected herself with a wag of her head. *I am looking at this new position wrong.* This was meant to be her yoke of shame, punishment for her failures. She checked on Peron, who had taken a perch near the tent flaps, before pulling her blanket high over her shoulders to stave off the cool mountain air. No more complaining. As willingly as a serf accepted bondage to a landed lord, she would wear this burden of guilt.

Shortly after first light, a low voice woke Annabelle from a deep sleep that had been fleeting.

"Master Loris, are you awake?" After a brief hesitation, the voice continued. "I am sorry to disturb your slumber, but daybreak has passed. My patrol grows impatient to be on the trail. We have far to travel in the coming days."

She rolled stiffly from the hard cot and stepped from the tent into the cool, bright morning air, her sleeping blanket hanging loose about her shoulders. She was met by a stocky middle-aged man dressed in mountain fashion of summer pelts and deerskin boots. The hilt of a two-handed sword common among Alpslanders extended from behind his right shoulder. His bare arms were thick and muscular, sporting a number of scars. Four gold bars sown into dark leather wrist bands marked him as a guildmaster in the Scouters guild. Long, wavy, salt-and-pepper hair and a bristled short beard hung about a round face set off by a flat, small nose and deep blue eyes.

The Alpslander raised his palm toward her, then, pressing his forearm across his chest, tilted his chin down in a sign of respect. "Welcome, Master Ranger Loris. Honor be to your home," he said, offering the customary greeting of the Narwalen people. "I am Scouter Foreman Gertrum Smelterman of the Gilstadt region." He gestured toward the large brown grizzly at his side. "Targon is my bond."

"Well met, Alpslander. May the mountains always be the bedrock of your strength," Annabelle responded with equal formality and a friendly smile.

Gertrum seemed genuinely surprised by her greeting. "You know the customs of my people?" He shadowed the Ranger to a large iron kettle hung over the smoky remains of a morning fire.

Annabelle ladled the cooling stew of local roots and spices into a wooden bowl she found hanging on a metal rack nearby. "I spent two years at Dreadcreek as a warder." Inhaling the aromas steaming from the bowl, she took a stump with a slight groan, then smiled up at the Scouter. "Of course, that was more than a few winters ago."

The Alpslander's calm blue eyes measured her condition while she ravenously emptied the bowl and refilled it. "Master Ranger Loris, we will need to move fast if we are to discover the true nature of these reports. Our tracks may take us down hazardous paths not journeyed in several winters, making it hard for a horse to traverse."

It had taken a year at Dreadcreek for Annabelle to understand the ways of Alpslander talk. It would have been improper for the guildmaster to state openly that he thought her incapable of keeping up on foot. She had seen knife fights break out over less. So words were spoken for the receiver to properly interpret their meaning, and to respond appropriately. "Guildmaster Smelterman, I trust you will not underestimate the strength of my legs or my resolve. We share a common mission, and therefore a common path. My feet tread but a step behind where yours lead."

For the first time, a friendly smile broke across the guildmaster's broad face. He bowed with respect. "Then you must call me by my given name."

Alpslanders were slow to trust flatlanders, and rightfully so with their strange flatland customs. She suspected Gertrum had many concerns for why a master Ranger had been assigned as consul to his scouting patrol. But he had made the first of many steps they would need if they were to develop a healthy relationship. It was early progress, truly a welcome sign. "As you must also, Gertrum of the Gilstadt region," she replied.

"So you say, Annabelle of the flatlands. When you have finished, I will introduce you to my guild patrol. They may not look like much, but they have ended more Anarchic savagery than any orderman in

Dreadcreek." It was another good sign. Mountain people never boasted in formal company. "Then we take the Shadowside trail."

With formalities dispensed, Annabelle washed and placed the bowl back on the rack, but paused before heading to the tent to gather her supplies. "Why do we head north along the Shadowside trail? I understood the sightings to be west."

"Most of our time of late, we have been scouting along the eastern Borderlands for your Griffinrock forces. We must go first to a village near the northern Borderlands to acquire the services of someone who has more knowledge of the region to the west. Sometimes the fastest way is not by the shortest route."

When Annabelle returned with Peron, she asked him skeptically, "So you believe there is something behind these reports?"

Gertrum's eyes went skyward to the command terrace. "Your Grandmaster Ranger Lendfeather does not leave his terrace anymore, so we interpret these stories differently. I have seen too many strange things in my life to discount these tales as pure hallucinations. Besides, even if they are, we can always hope the trail leads us into a battle with Anarchists somewhere." Eyes glistening with excitement, he started toward the hold's northern gates.

With Annabelle and Peron in tow, Gertrum and Targon soon reached the Shadowside trailhead, where a dozen Alpslanders milled about waiting impatiently for their foreman's arrival.

## An Evening Affair

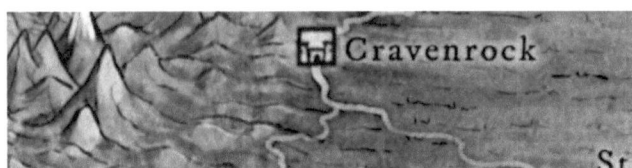

The embers of the campfires along the side of Pennrock Road cast a deep reddish glow about the long line of heavy wagons and sparse trees. As with the previous two uneventful nights, Lacerus unfurled his bedroll at the edge of camp near the road, though he suspected tonight would be different. He settled in, his eyes on the slender blanketed form near the middle of the camp, then waited.

Lacerus knew patience, and not just as one of the Kindred. Patience was an Assassin's greatest weapon, instilled from the first day of training. He recalled the night he'd completed his apprenticeship—a day that had begun with a hard boot to his bruised ribs. He had quickly wiped sleep from his swollen eyes and squinted up at his black-cloaked preceptor in the late afternoon light.

Dark, brooding eyes hidden somewhere beneath his master's black hood measured his worth. "It is time, Lacerus," was all the master Assassin had said before walking away.

Lacerus had understood. With many different faces using many different names, he had completed this test before. Feigning bewilderment, he worked stiffness from his body and stumbled after his preceptor, who stood by a rusted metal door. There, they waited in silence while eleven other Assassin apprentices with their bonds and preceptors gathered. There was a loud metallic click. Lacerus ignored the door's irritable groan as he tested the balance of the small blade offered by his preceptor. The door swung open. Signaling his new Peregrine falcon bond to remain, he slipped stealthily into the Assassin's labyrinth. Through that evening and on through the night, the newly bonded youth ran, climbed, and crawled his way through the labyrinth, killing savage beasts, avoiding undead creatures, and disarming lethal traps.

At dawn, the four remaining apprentices staggered back through the door, exhausted and hungry, where they were given chairs for rest. For hours they waited, fighting off sleep, until their preceptors appeared, black hooded and silent before them, each sporting a powerful Assassin's bow. In unison, the Assassins nocked black arrows and drew hard on their bows, tips pointed at their apprentices' chests. Time ground by, the apprentices waited for the subtle signs their preceptors would release their arrows. Catching an arrow aimed at one's heart required instincts sharpened only by patience.

By afternoon, one full day from when their test had begun, two of the twelve apprentices still drew breath and were added to the Assassins ranks as slayers. Lacerus kept the arrow he had caught; his preceptor had only nodded his silent approval. Two survivors. It had been a good day for the order.

The bay of a dozen wolves far to the north floated on the late night breeze. Veressa shuddered in her blanket, but not from the chill in the air. The pack had found their prey's scent; the chase had begun. Excitement welled up in her. Every muscle in her body tensed, fighting the primitive urges stirring her heart to race once more. She recalled the nearly forgotten dream she'd had a week before, the night of the storm by the shore of the River Aradorm. In the dream, she had hunted a great stag. Now, the memory of that dream beckoned to her, urging her to join in the hunt. She hungered to revel in every detail of that night's apparition, from the moment she took up the chase to the feeling of bringing down the stag.

She fought against these urges by concentrating on the senses of the night—sounds of crickets and the light wind in the trees, the smell of burning wood from the campfires, the sight of a million stars in the moonless sky. But these only heightened her awareness, cutting away at the thin veil of her humanity and leaving her as naked as she had been in her dream vision.

Nearby, several sentries chatted in complete disregard to the alluring sounds and smells filling the night. *How could they not be moved by the beauty of such sounds? How can they not want to be part of that hunt?*

She worked to quiet her mind as Annabelle had taught her. She had been successful the previous night when the impulses had visited her. *Annabelle, why are you not here? I need you to help me understand what is happening.* She was not afraid, just confused, alone, bewildered by the addictive energies igniting her senses. Some part of Veressa could feel her resistance to these urges weakening, buckling to the primeval passion that beckoned her to escape into the wilderness. To become one with it. Just beyond the fires' lights, Antilles's high-pitched bark called to her.

A faint twitch from the bedroll by the fire drew Lacerus's attention. He counted the heartbeats, waiting for an alarm by one of the thirty sentries on duty. But one never came. His eyes shifted north across the road, measuring the seconds. It was not long before a slim figure outlined in starlight crouched in the tall summer grass next to the large white cat that had lingered there since evening. Veressa had escaped the camp without notice, surrounded by an entire company of highly trained Defenders.

*Very impressive! She indeed has Ranger skills of evasion!* Excitement coursed through Lacerus. After the figures had disappeared to the north, he slipped from his bedroll. The man known by those in camp as Grandmaster Friarwood vanished into the dead of night to shadow the bonded pair.

Veressa ran with an unbridled swiftness she did not know she possessed. *Where am I going?* she wondered, but in truth, she did not care. Earth and Air elementals coursed freely through her. Through their link, Antilles was feeding the thrill of the night adventure, and with her bond as her guide, she felt at home. A barred owl on silent wings snatched a rodent scurrying across the lush summer woodland floor; a raccoon chattered as she ran past, annoyed at the disturbance while dipping a half-eaten frog into a fresh stream; a mother opossum with her six babies peered down from a branch above. The forest had never felt so alive. Veressa drew from her bond's link, feeding the thirst. And the two ran on through the night.

She had no idea how much time had passed. But all too soon she stood north of the road again. The smell of the sentries and fires to the south assailed her nostrils. She gave Antilles a loving pat, for he understood she had to return before her absence was discovered. Marcantos would have no such mischief under his tight watch.

Veressa moved with the stealth of her leopard bond across the road, slipping easily between the Defenders standing watch. Several paces from her blanket, she grew overconfident and reckless. A dead twig snapped under her step, and she cringed in anticipation for the sentries to shout an alarm. But no sound broke the silence of the night. A moment later, she was back in her bedroll. And for the first time since leaving Cravenrock, she slept.

Lacerus waited, hidden behind an oak at the edge of the camp's clearing, until Veressa was safely back in her bedroll, considering all he had observed. Maybe the Kindred had set their sights too low. Why had

Brother Sarmenion not foreseen this? What if Marcantos was only a stepping stone to a worthier prize? If Lacerus could turn Veressa as he had his current pupil ... Excitement at the thought boiled in him, and he considered how their plan could be revised. The loss of Annabelle as her preceptor had clearly left the young girl wanting, even hungry for more. That made her susceptible. And she held such potential! He would work out the details before he proposed anything to his Brothers. For now, he had work to complete before dawn. Messy details to clean up.

Lacerus stared down into the dead eyes of the sentry he cradled. The man had seen Veressa return and had nearly sounded an alarm. It was risky, but Lacerus had been forced to act swiftly. After all, he could not let Marcantos find out about the princess's evening outing. His student's mental instability was making him rash. The young Warrior would have prevented her from relishing any further evening affairs. No, Lacerus needed Veressa to continue her nightly jaunts into the wilderness, at least until he knew how best to turn this to his advantage. He retrieved the sharp blade from between the Defender's ribs, then wiped it clean on the man's cloak. Hefting the dead weight over his shoulder, Lacerus slipped quietly back into the night.

"Yes? What is it sergeant?" Marcantos blinked up at the muscular young Defender standing over him, nervously wringing his hands in the morning light. Clearly it was bad news.

"I'm dreadfully sorry to bother you, Grandmaster Evinfaire, but I thought you should know one of my men has gone missing this morning. No one noticed until a half hour ago, so the exact time he vanished is unknown."

"Princess Veressa!" Marcantos jerked his head toward the middle of the camp.

"Rest assured, sir, the princess is asleep and unharmed," the sergeant interjected. "I had the morning sentries check the camp the moment I received the report. Everyone else, including horses and supplies, is accounted for. Further, we found no signs of a struggle."

Friarwood appeared next to Marcantos, having taken an interest in the camp's sudden flurry of activities. The preceptor appeared exhausted in the dim dawn light.

"Everything untouched," Marcantos rubbed at his face. "That makes no sense."

"Well ... actually, sir, it does," the sergeant stammered, unsure how to proceed. "Occasionally, we get a bad egg in the Cravenrock company. It's not common, but Defenders have been known to run off when they've had enough of the queen's service."

"Had enough?" Marcantos snarled. "Your men's responsibility is to protect the princess. Any soldier in dereliction of this duty will be severely and immediately punished. Is my position clearly understood, Sergeant?"

Friarwood cleared his throat before the young Defender could reply. "If our truant friend has wandered off somewhere, Marcantos, there will be signs of his departure. No offense, sergeant, but more trained eyes might prove useful."

"No offense taken, Grandmaster Friarwood." The soldier bowed humbly.

Marcantos turned to his preceptor. "Yes, Blake, you are right. Would you mind having a look around while I check on the princess?" Taking in the scene, he sighed. "Since it seems most are rousted, we might as well break camp. We can make Pennington Point well before dark."

"I found a single set of tracks leading back east off the road," Friarwood lied. "It seems the soldier had a change of heart about his service to the queen after all."

Marcantos did not respond, his eyes flicking about, never settling, as if he was unsure how to deal with the situation.

Friarwood grew concerned as Marcantos became more pensive by the moment. "If you want, I can bring him back. Maybe you need to make an example of the man in front of the others," he suggested.

"No, Blake. I see no need to alarm the princess. Such matters are best handled discreetly without royal influence. When we arrive at Pennington Point, I will dispatch a message from the station. He will be dealt with in due time."

"Of course." Friarwood smiled.

## Sowing Seeds

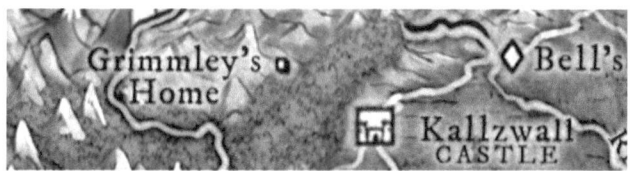

Grimmley's new apprentice stared out the back window with a brooding, forlorn expression. The boy's lack of progress during their first training session was clearly eating at him. The Shaman had hoped the tantalizing smells of the breakfast feast being set on the small table would pull him from his depression spiral. But the haggard lad did not even seem to notice.

Stomper was not so predisposed. The raccoon appeared in the windowsill, chattering and staring longingly at what the boy failed to notice.

Conner absently rubbed the raccoon's ears. "I'm sorry, Grimmley," he said, breaking the silence.

The Shaman dumped whipped, spiced eggs from a hot iron skillet onto two waiting plates. He had concerns about Conner's missteps earlier that morning, even finding the session bewildering. But he would not let on about that yet. Maybe talking would shake the boy from his sour mood; food was clearly having no effect. "For what?" he asked nonchalantly.

"It seems I fail at everything," came the boy's mumbled reply.

Grimmley poked a long wooden spoon under the boy's nose. "It's much too early in the season to judge your progress by the harvest you reap, boy. You'd be in a better mind if you judged it by the number of seeds we plant!"

"Seeds we plant?" Conner laughed and held his arms wide to give the Shaman a good look at his disheveled appearance. "It seems this soil is barren, Grimmley! You're wasting your time with me."

Grimmley grunted. "Why don't you let me be the judge of when I'm wasting time. And I'll have no more negative talk in my house, boy! Besides"—he scanned the cottage for something to bolster his argument—"you're offending Barthox's ears!"

"Hoot?" The owl stared at him wide-eyed.

"Ah!" Grimmley dropped the skillet on the stove and fanned a dish towel in frustration at his bond. Count on her to miss an important cue. Whoever started the myth owls were wise had obviously never attempted to converse with one.

Grimmley needed to get Conner's mind off the morning's failures before he sank beyond his reach. The Shaman took the seat near the stove, then waved at the chair across from him. "Why don't you sit, Conner? While we're eating, you can tell me how you retrieved the silver box. I think we're both in need of a good story."

Conner's emotions were dry leaves in a winter storm, spinning and churning him into cold, dark despair, consuming mental energy he needed to spend understanding what had gone wrong with his training. Last night, he had been lost, with no trace of a future. That was, until Grimmley had offered—no, demanded to take him as his apprentice. Just a month ago Conner had been excited about becoming a guildsman. What had made him think he could succeed as an orderman? He should have known better. Now all he wanted was to go home, and to take on the simple life of a freeman farmer working the soil like his father. His family, Pattria, and Pauli filled his thoughts. Would he ever see them again?

He had found Grimmley at dawn sitting quietly in his gazebo over the lake. The training had started well enough. The Shaman had been first surprised, then troubled to discover Conner already knew several spells, describing how Night Vision and Cloak were basic clerical spells of the Earth elemental. But they were supposed to be known only by certain ordermen and guildsmen. Grimmley wanted to ask where he had learned those spells. But much to Conner's relief, the Shaman pressed on, teaching him several more basic spells, ones his new preceptor referred to in a grumbling voice as "more useful to a Shaman."

He was quick to learn the Earth elemental spell Detect Plant, then the Fire spell Detect Heat, successfully casting both on his first try. Grimmley was elated, even to the point he could not sit still. So the Shaman hopped about energetically, going on about how he had never known an apprentice to successfully cast these spells even in the first dozen attempts. He then proceeded to describe how Earth and Fire were the elemental forces through which a Shaman drew his powers. Through all of this, Grimmley kept slapping Conner proudly on the back, calling him truly the most promising apprentice he had ever known.

But the training turned sour when Grimmley described to Conner how he could draw upon both Fire and Earth elementals simultaneously to cast more complex Shaman spells. Detect Life Force, the simplest of advanced spells taught to Shamans of seer rank, was used to reveal any living creatures within the vicinity. The preceptor was undaunted when Conner's first dozen attempts ended in dismal failure. But after another hour, Grimmley was running out of ideas why Conner could not even get an elemental spark casting the spell. Though the Shaman attempted to hide his reaction, constantly encouraging him to continue trying, Conner could hear the growing frustration and concern in Grimmley's voice. By the time Hemera was halfway to its zenith, Conner was too hungry and exhausted to try anymore.

"What?" Conner asked when he realized he had not been listening to Grimmley. He blinked, staring at the steaming breakfast that had magically appeared on the table before him. "Oh, the quest. Yes, of course." He took the chair. After twitching from a sharp stab of hunger pains, he dug in.

Reticently, he began to recite the events about his trip to the cavern, using the time he chewed his food to select which parts of the tale to leave out. He described how Skye had led him to the mountain and how he'd come to the crescent-shaped cavern and a bridge spanning a deep chasm. To Conner's frustration, Grimmley appeared more interested in hearing details about the ancient buildings he had searched than about how he'd nearly died crossing the collapsing bridge. Grimmley interrupted his tale with several pointed questions, only grunting at Conner's responses with his pipe stem clenched between his teeth. He finished by describing briefly how he had found the box in a cabinet at the far end of the makeshift street and how he had relied on Skye to fly him back out. Fearing he would be forced to try to defend Skye's unjustifiable actions in the cavern, he excluded any references to the undead and his drop into the chasm.

After the tale was done, preceptor and apprentice finished their breakfast in silence, enjoying what serenity remained of the cool and quiet morning. Sara pranced and bucked among the dark oaks, scattering a small herd of white-tailed deer farther up the hill. "Skye is returning," Conner warned. The dragon had been gone since his angry departure the previous evening.

"Yes, well, I suppose you two have lots to discuss. I'd say helping him through his anger is more important than continuing our lessons at this point. I don't have time to play fireguard over my trees for the next fortnight, you know."

Conner nodded resolutely. "Grimmley, I do appreciate all you are doing for me." He gestured toward the black shadow that appeared over the northern hill, winging toward the cottage. Sara bolted out of the oaks, preceding the dragon at a full run, her tail high in the air, snorting her warnings of the beast's arrival. Skye dipped lower. Tilting his wings back, he hovered teasingly over the frightened horse's haunches. "For us," Conner corrected with a smile.

"Conner, do not let this morning's training drag on you. No matter what you may think, you did well. Real wisdom comes from understanding the full extent of our limitations."

Conner's smile split his face. "If that was true, I'd be a genius!" The Shaman apprentice vanished through the back door to meet the dragon. Somehow, he would have to fit in a good scolding for scaring Grimmley's mare yet again.

Late that afternoon, Barthox swooped through the front window to her perch near the fireplace. With a "Hoo-hoot ta-HOOT!" she announced the arrival of a new guest.

Grimmley peered out the back window to the north. He had a good idea who the visitor might be, but it was best to be prudent when it came to having his company spotted. Conner was in the lake gazebo, where he had been since lunch, endeavoring to cast the Detect Life Force spell still eluding his mental grasp. Farther on, the boy's bond was attempting to hide in the late afternoon shadows between the large-leaf maples and hickories. Crouched with wings folded tight against his body, the dragon wiggled on two powerful legs. His tail snaked to adjust his balance. Blue eyes blazed at Sara grazing on thick green grass nearby, completely unaware of the creature's presence. Grimmley scowled. Tranquility was nothing more than a fleeting memory in his once blissful utopia. With a sigh of resignation, the Shaman crossed the cottage and opened the front door.

On his lawn, a tall figure gripped a twisted wooden staff next to a lanky and winded dapple-gray stallion. A dark blue robe, tied with a gold sash and embroidered in golden Modeic symbols that sparkled in Hemera's light, hung loose about a thin frame. A deep hood hid the visitor's face.

The figure bowed wearily. "Well met, Grandmaster Rollingsworth. It has been too long since last I gazed upon that old Shaman face of yours."

"Well met, Grandmaster Newstone. No longer than the last time you amazed me with your powers of Sorcerer perception." Grimmley stepped aside, waving a path through the doorway.

The robed form stiffly crossed the porch and stepped through the door, stopping in front of the three-tiered board of Crowns in the middle of the cottage. "I see the board is as we left it. How long have we been playing this game? Six years?"

"Seven," grunted Grimmley.

A hearty laugh came from under the hood. "Yet you cling to the false hope that Shamans can develop a sense of strategy." The figure bent to examine the wooden pieces closer.

Grimmley removed his pipe from his robe pocket and lit the tobac. "Not at all! Shamans have little use for hope. We rely instead on the enduring truth that the spirit's will to overcome adversity can withstand the cold logic of Sorcerer thought." The Shaman grinned ominously at the cloaked figure. "A demonstration I am prepared to continue tonight." Then the Shaman's smile faded as the gravity of the moment settled between them. "But, alas, there are matters more urgent we must attend to first."

The robed figure nodded. "My dear Grimmley, it may be a while before my bond forgives me, for I urged him at full speed nearly nonstop for three days. Horasius has never sensed such a state of excitement as I have been in since you told me of the good news."

Wild snorts and pounding hooves drew their attention to the back window. A moment later, Sara galloped wild-eyed past the lake, her tail a flag in the wind. "Well, *good* is not the word I would use, but I leave you to draw your own conclusions." His spirited mood extinguished, Grimmley preceded his guest out the back and along the garden path leading them to the lake gazebo.

"Boy!"

Conner jumped. Deep in concentration, he had missed the Shaman's three previous attempts to get his attention. "I'm sorry, Grimmley. Something occurred to me about this spell. I thought I might ..." He noticed they were not alone.

"Never mind that." Grimmley waved at the new guest. "Conner Stonefield of the Eastlands, this is Grandmaster Newstone of the Sorcerers Order."

"Well met, sir." Conner started to bow, but faltered when the robed figure pushed the hood back, revealing a slender feminine face with dark olive complexion. The Sorceress's straight, shoulder-length hair, coal black to Grimmley's white, was hooked behind her ears and hung forward, accenting a sharp jaw line and chin. Her hair was pulled back along her temples, the hint of gray heightening the illusion that she wore a silver tiara. A fine gold chain threaded through five gold rings spaced evenly down her left ear marked her rank in the order. Her hazel eyes seemed to sparkle with an inner wisdom beyond her years.

The Sorceress chortled. "It is nice to meet you, Conner Stonefield of the Eastlands. Why Grimmley, you failed to mention how polite a lad he is!" The wink she gave his preceptor made Conner's cheeks burn.

Grimmley cleared his throat, scrutinizing his apprentice as if struggling to decide whether he was worth the cost. "Considering the boy's progress the past day, his Eastlander upbringing may be his only endearing quality." Having decided further teasing might send the boy into another tailspin, he continued with the introductions. "Conner, Grandmaster Newstone is the foremost authority on dragons."

"Yes, Conner Stonefield, I am quite excited about meeting this bond of yours," the Sorceress added.

"Oh, good!" Conner exclaimed. "Maybe you can show me how to teach the beast some manners. I haven't had a lick of success so far."

"By the way, where is the annoying black beast?" Grimmley was at least relieved to find Sara once more grazing near his grove of sweet chestnuts.

"Skye? He is right over—" Conner pointed toward the large leaf maples across the lake, suddenly void of animal life and dragon.

A gurgling sound near the gazebo drew their attention. A scaly black head broke the smooth surface of the lake, the rainbow tailfin of a fish longer than Conner's forearm dangling from the side of his mouth. The dragon flipped the fish into the air and swallowed it whole. "Yes, Conner?"

"Oh no, not my lake bass!" Grimmley cried out.

"Hoot!" Barthox added from the branch of a small maple tree in the garden.

Conner sighed. "I thought you said you didn't like water! And what have I told you about eating animals in the Shaman's valley? Now come out. There's someone here who wants to meet you, but for the life of me, I don't know why she'd bother."

"I do not mind water. It is rain that I don't like." Skye's head vanished once more, leaving only ripples to mark his passing.

Conner led the two ordermen back to the end of the walkway, arriving as the dragon stepped to the lake's edge. Water streamed from the black leathery wings unfurled before them, his horned ebony head lowered. "I am Skye-Anyar-Bello of the family Cloudbender."

The visitor spoke in a stuttered melodic voice. "I am Layna Mariya of the family Newstone. May your days and deeds add honorable verses to your family's dragonsong, Skye-Anyar-Bello of the family Cloudbender, as your father did before you."

Eyes blazed between double lids. "You know of my father?"

The Sorceress bowed with respect. "The name of Anyar-Bello Cloudbender fills many verses of our humansong. You are truly a fine wyvern, Skye-Anyar-Bello, with exceptional teeth, sharp talons, and powerful wings. Your name shall someday do the same."

Skye puffed out his chest at the Sorceress's string of compliments.

Conner thought the display childish, but he could sense the Sorceress had truly delighted his bond. Conner started to mention he had heard of no songs of Anyar-Bello Cloudbender, but decided silence was the better option. The Sorceress was clearly going out of her way to stroke the dragon's ego. Then Conner's jaw sagged, large eyes studying the orderman. "You can speak to dragons?"

The Sorceress beamed. "I once came across a book in Darmascus written during the Anarchic War. It had been used to teach Elvenstein's royal family basic dragon speech." She sized up the wyvern before her. "But to be candid, I was not sure I could speak it, since I have never spoken to a dragon before."

Of all the feelings flooding through Conner at that moment, relief was foremost. At last, he would not be the only person who could translate his bond's incessant and intrusive questions!

## An Early Change in Seasons

"**W**ell?" Grimmley asked the Sorceress after recounting a thorough tale of everything he knew about Conner's adventures leading to his arrival at the cottage. He had followed up with a detailed account of how the boy showed a natural genius in manipulating Earth and Fire elementals, but failed miserably at casting even the simplest advanced spells. He stared at her from under furrowed eyebrows. The flickering firelight from the hearth at Layna's back accentuated the Shaman's ragged lines of exhaustion. She could not remember him looking so old. "What do you think?" He prodded Layna when she offered no immediate response.

Evening air cooled by the lake floated through the open window, giving Layna a slight chill. She leaned forward, moving one of her knights toward the center of the board of Crowns. Thick tobac smoke floated across the board like fog on a morning battlefield. "I think you're in trouble."

"I wasn't talking about the game," Grimmley complained, but could not resist frowning at the new location of the Sorceress's wooden knight.

Layna sat back and studied the Shaman while she lit her pipe. *So much for injecting a little levity into the discussion.* "And I wasn't talking about *this* game." She drew on the pipe stem before continuing. "The Shaman Dons will be angry when they discover you have been keeping a secret from them—especially one, I might add, this significant." None of what she had to say would be a surprise to the old orderman, but it was always best to study the board before considering the next move.

"No, I suppose not," the Shaman grumbled, intense eyes on the board. "But given what I must do, by the time they learn of the boy, that point will be the least of my concerns."

"No. You can't contain this secret for long. I would bet my battlestaff that dragon sightings have been reported to at least one person who has a keen interest in this matter. For all you know, the creature is already being hunted. And those from Cravenrock may still be on the hunt for Conner."

"That is why I must act hastily—something I am not familiar with." Grimmley gestured toward the gangly form at the far end of the room. Conner had not flinched since collapsing across his cot shortly past supper. "The boy is but a lamb among packs of hungry wolves. He must be ready to stand on his own if he is to have any chance against those who would use him in their games of power. I don't have time or energy to remove every obstruction presenting itself."

"You need my help, Grimmley," the Sorceress stated with a nod. "You can't do this by yourself."

"Layna, I cannot deny I could use your historical understanding of dragons and the Dragonbonded. Those who know anything on the subject could be counted on a single hand, and you are the only scholar among them." The Shaman shook his head resolutely. "But what I do is risky at best, and more likely dangerous. I cannot ask for your help."

"Ha! Me? The scholar? That statement alone should give you an indication how dire this whole situation is! But I don't see that I have a choice in this matter."

"There are always choices."

"'Choices are myths borne by the foolish and simpleminded. A disciplined wise man discerns the path meant to be taken from all others, then continues without hesitation,'" Layna retorted in a deep, grumpy voice. She leaned over the board, smiling. "A very wise old Shaman taught me that. Think of it, Grimmley!" whispering excitedly. "The first human-dragon bond in over five hundred years dropped out of the skies, here, in your hidden garden oasis! That is the fortunes of fate, my dear old friend."

"Or misfortunes." Grimmley waved irritably at the smoke. He countered his opponent's move decisively by shifting his crown prince in a feint to the left. "How secret is this place if that boy could find it so easily?"

"You don't think it a tad peculiar? He possessed everything he needed to locate the only person in the Harmonic Realms powerful enough to help, yet not motivated by self-interests." Grimmley did not answer, so she continued with an edge of enthusiasm. "Yet here we sit"—she gestured grandly—"the self-ordained preceptor and the only living scholar on Dragonbonded. You offer a bowl of rice to a starving traveler, then act surprised that the traveler takes it? How could I possibly refuse such an opportunity?"

Grimmley's unease hung in the air like his thick smoke.

"How many times have you come to my aid, Grimmley?" she persisted. The two had first met when Layna was fifteen, by which time her parents could no longer control the spirited and tumultuous girl. Grimmley, traveling through the southern outlander region on a quest for a rare herb root, had understood that the girl's disruptive behaviors were driven by an early awakening of her powers to use elementals. He volunteered to take her away, saving her from a certain stoning by the villagers. For nearly a year, he trained her on how to focus her abilities, until she bonded with her horse Horasius and was accepted into the Sorcerers Order. "Your words swayed Grandmaster Rossengale to accept me as his apprentice."

The Shaman flushed at her gratitude. "Your order would have been left wanting without you, girl! Rossengale saw that. Your supercilious old Sorcerer preceptor needed someone to force him to see what was already there. You did the rest."

Layna laughed. "You are as cantankerous as you are old! Even after I completed my apprenticeship, you were always there for me. No, Grimmley. Either way, it is time we find balance in our relationship. It is the Harmonic way." Everything settled in her mind, she nodded with satisfaction. "Bound by the Orderman's Code, I freely offer you my assistance, Grandmaster Rollingsworth." It was the pledge from the Code of the Orders. "Now you're just going to have to accept it!"

Grimmley exhaled a ring of smoke with a sigh. Standing, he drew his gaunt form up and bowed. "Then by the Code, Grandmaster Newstone, I accept your offer." He shuffled to his desk, then returned to stand before Layna holding a metal box. Though she could sense the box was not heavy, Grimmley held it like it possessed the weight of the world.

The warm glow from the fireplace brightened and flickered as flames danced wildly. Dry hickory logs popped and hissed. Layna waited until Grimmley spoke the Fire and Earth spell that sealed the cottage from any unwanted ears and eyes: *"Hemea ousia fragidomatio."* The old orderman knew how to hold her interest!

"Now that we both are bound as brother and sister by the Code, I can trust into your hands a most intriguing tale, one I believe may prove critical to our unraveling a riddle lurking in the shadows before us." He held the box out for Layna to take. "A most mysterious account that forces me to do something I could never have dreamed." With brows raised and a distant gaze, he said as if with his last breath, "To break the Code's most sacred of laws."

The first law of the Orderman's Code, to never reveal a secret to one of another order, was punishable by the most horrific death the order could devise, and Layna did not doubt the Shaman Dons' creativity in the matter. She took the box carefully and examined it. Leaning forward, firelight illuminated the finely etched Modeic symbols across its top. She read aloud, "'Fettering Stones'? I'm sorry, Grimmley. That only makes sense to a Shaman. It is surely not a secret I care to know, nor one that appears relevant to our situation."

"Yes. I suppose the relevance is not so clear." Grimmley spoke as if a great journey loomed into the night. "A context would be helpful, though the meaning of the symbols also eludes me." The Shaman sat and checked his pipe before beginning his story.

"The evening our two interlopers arrived, I spent some time talking to the dragon with the boy providing translation. It seems the creature was quite impressed to be in the presence of what he called a 'great Shaman.' The beast was filled with questions about the Cosmos for which he believed only my 'kind' possessed answers. While I clearly had no problem with a dragon calling me *great*, I found his manners rather intriguing. So I endeavored to understand the reason for his reverence, prodding the beast for information amid the endless stream of questions he was capable of producing. After several hours, I pieced together an understanding of his peculiar behavior." Grimmley puffed on his pipe. "You see, Layna, according to his family's dragonsongs, the first dragons, what he called the Ancients, were created out of nothingness by a great Shaman god named Shazarack."

"Shazarack," Layna repeated. It was a name she recalled from her studies of early New Cronoan history. But little about the necromancer's life must have escaped the confines of the Shamans Order. Since the man had lived nearly a millennium ago, most of the information that remained about him had been lost or misinterpreted. Even so, she was quite sure of one thing. "His name never appeared in relation to any known writings about dragons."

The Shaman nodded. "Yes, well that was to be my first question."

"Your second?"

"Is it possible that the dragon's assertion could be true?"

Layna shrugged. "Nothing I know contradicts that thesis, Grimmley. Dragons weren't known to exist until the first human-dragon bondings, which came two hundred years after this Shazarack lived. However, that is insufficient proof. No one thought dragons had survived these past five hundred years. Yet, here one is! For all we know, they could have predated humans.

"But there is a ring of truth to the dragon's beliefs," she pressed on. "Several volumes I have read contain brief passages about dragons called the Ancients. And there is the question of how dragons came to know the name Shazarack.... So, are you telling me this Shazarack may have possessed the ability to create dragons? If so, then he truly was a god."

"No. Not without some kind of help. This is where the box enters our story. But first, I must tell you a bit about Nartesis Shazarack, so you can better appreciate what this early Necromancer was capable of. Harmonic Shamans do not speak of these things because of the Code's first law, Layna. His story is a dark one, embodying what we Shamans consider to be the very essence of the shadow side."

Layna's thoughts strayed to the unspeakable horrors perpetrated by Warlocks of her own order before and during the Anarchic War. She reached across the board and soothed Grimmley with a light pat on his arm. "Every order has its dark side, my dear friend," she noted sadly.

The Shaman thinned his lips, then began. "The early Shamans, even before the time of Shazarack, had the power to summon spirits, life forces from another plane, into the Physical using command spells of calling. Once called, the summoned spirit was required to do the bidding of the shaman. But these biddings had limitations. The spirit was without physical form, so the shamans possessed very little power to persuade or threaten their enemies. Besides, the spells did not last, so the spirits soon returned to their planes of existence.

"Shazarack was not satisfied with this. Through many years of painstaking study, spawning unimaginable horrors and grotesque atrocities, he learned how to cast command spells binding a spirit to a human cadaver. These spells of resurrection solved the first of the two problems in callings. But he did not end his research there, striving to discover new, more insidious ways to extend the time these spirits were trapped in their human cadavers.

"Soon, he resolved to train other Shaman Necromancers in the nuances of his discovery. Thus, the Academy of Thanatos was born. Many Shamans studied under Shazarack. Over time, his so-called academy forged a necro-army of undead, nightmarish abominations that formed the basis for many of today's tales and myths. Oh, in those days, he was a god to his students all right, drunk with power. And their necro-army grew until it was formidable even to the entire forces wielded by the seven monarchies.

"The seven monarchs sent emissaries to Thanatos, along with other Shamans, in hopes that they could address their growing anxieties for what was being created. But Shazarack's intentions were made evident when the emissaries returned home … as undead. To avert an all-out war, all the other orders were forced to side with the monarchies. It was a move even the great Shazarack had not predicted. A great army, the Army of the Seven Realms, was forged with pacts between monarchs and the fledgling orders. They laid siege to Thanatos, scorching the lands, destroying the city, and turning the academy to ashes, along with all its books and parchments. Since then, my order has maintained that Shazarack died at the Battle of Thanatos."

"But you believe differently."

"Yes. I formulated a different theory based on ten years of detailed research, one the all-wise Dons have continued to deny as plausible." The Shaman puffed irritably on his pipe.

Layna nodded. "That is why you refused a position on the board."

"Hmm?" Her statement had disrupted Grimmley's thoughts. "Well, I certainly couldn't imagine spending the rest of my days with a group of closed-minded authorities suffering from false beliefs!" He waved at the cloud of smoke around his face. "Now, where was I? Ah, yes, Shazarack's death." He pointed at the silver box resting in Layna's lap. "Open it," he commanded.

Layna fumbled with the latch until she heard a metallic click. She lifted the lid and peered inside. "It's empty."

"Yes." Grimmley drew the word out ominously.

Layna drummed her fingernails on the side of the box, then bit her lip. "Okay. Tell me there's more, Grimmley."

"Of course there's more! Have you ever heard of Cleric Stones?"

"No. Should I have?"

"They're the rarest of gems in the known world. Let me tell you about what I discovered in my research many years ago." He repacked his pipe and settled back.

"The Modei's great city of Shan-Grail was discovered deep in the Dragon's Back Mountains one hundred years after the last of the Modei perished. It was only then, to our misfortune, that our ancestors understood the full extent of the Modei's knowledge of the Cosmos. For two years, various guilds of the time fought for the rights to ransack the city, their spoils hastily loaded and carted away across the rugged terrain—items of untold value swallowed up or dispersed among the guilds' highest-ranking members. The guilds were in such a hurry to grab what they could that little was documented."

Grimmley breathed deep. "But what you may not be aware of is that the guilds that acquired these relics were those later consolidated into and under the Paladins Order with the Armistice of the Orders. And while you can fault the Paladins for many failings, organization and bookkeeping are not among them!

"My part in this story began when I was a young man, having advanced to the adept rank of seer under the tutelage of a very fine master Shaman. My first assignment was to travel into western Elvenstein to assist the Paladinian Clerics of Moonslayer in reclaiming what they could from a most dreadful fire that had consumed a third of their monastery's library. It was while I was in this service to repay a debt held by my preceptor that I came upon a bundle of parchments tied and pressed between two unmarked marble plates that had protected the documents from being consumed by the fire's hunger.

Little did I know at the time, nor did the clerics of the monastery, but this bundle possessed nearly all the known records regarding the Cleric Stones.

"It was the first parchment that drew my attention. Recorded even before the Seven Realms were established, it told of a black onyx stone possessing the power to extend life—stones forged in the very heart of the greatest mountains and imbued with concentrated levels of Earth elemental. These stones were so rare that only the high priests of Shan-Grail were allowed to possess them."

"So the legends of Modei's high priests living three hundred years or more were not imaginative stories created by proselytized Cronoans?" Layna interjected.

"No. So you can imagine an impressionable Shaman seer's excitement in discovering such a treasure! Of course I could not tell the Clerics of Moonslayer of my find, for they would surely have taken it from me. So in the fortnights following, by day I worked diligently to assist the clerics as best I could in their work. By night, I studied the documents between those marble plates, committing to memory all I could in the time given, for the parchments soon hooked me into their strange and mysterious path. Contained between those plates were the names of the greatest of Bremenn masters who had acquired the forty-four stones known to exist, followed by a series of other names: their most promising students, who, over nearly one and a half centuries, had been the heirs to the stones and the knowledge about them."

"How does all this relate to our dear old Necromancer, Shazarack?" Layna asked.

Grimmley poked an index finger into the air. "In the timing, my dear Layna. You see, since the heirs of the stones were those who retained the greatest knowledge of the Modei, their names were meticulously documented. The Bremenn Cardinals wanted some way to track down each and every stone. Some years later, the Cardinals discovered that the lineage of fifteen of the stones had come to an abrupt end, without even a trace as to where they had gone.

"In the rising chaos and uncertainty of the War of the Orders, the Cardinals recalled the remaining twenty-nine stones, which were locked away in the cellars of the Stronghold of Aldemeer. How could they have known the war would last nearly twenty years? Thirty-seven years after the structuring of the new orders, the new Paladins Order conducted a full inventory of the cellars at Aldemeer. To their dismay, they found only eleven of the twenty-nine stones remained; that is, eighteen more gems had disappeared, along with a silver box the Modei priests had used to hold them. Any trails that would have served in determining what happened to the stones had long since gone stone cold. Figuratively speaking." Grimmley winked.

"I have since held to the belief that Shazarack survived the siege on Thanatos, and that he was the one responsible for the disappearance of the stones. Through later research and some reasoning, I converged on the region where Shazarack's lair should have been. The dragon's account, which we should assume is accurate until we have proof otherwise, fills in a missing piece to the story. It gives some credence to why the Necromancer needed the stones."

Layna opened the box again. She had not noticed the nine thumbnail-sized indentations along the base. "How did you come by this box?"

Grimmley nodded toward the cot.

Layna was stunned. "*That* was the quest you sent Conner on? To retrieve the stones?"

Grimmley raised his hands in his defense. "It was a calculated risk, I know. But a quest the pair proved worthy of, don't you think? The fact they found the cavern where I predicted it was and successfully retrieved the box proves Shazarack survived the Battle of Thanatos and that it was in the Necromancer's possession at some time. Besides, we needed to know what these two are capable of, Layna. In two days, they did what I failed to accomplish these last twenty years. It seems the Cosmos has something very important in store for them."

Layna didn't want to let Grimmley's enthusiasm distract her from filling in a few gaps. "What of the eleven stones remaining in the possession of the Paladins?"

Grimmley shook his head sadly. "Yes, well, the last parchment in the bundle described how those mysteriously vanished later, about fifty years before the Anarchic War. From what I know, no other Cleric Stones have ever been found. It seems I will never have a chance to study their extraordinary powers."

"You just don't want to pass up the opportunity to be a thorn in the side of another generation of Dons," Layna quipped. She would never doubt the old Shaman's ability to be thorough in matters of importance, but it was too wild a leap for Layna to go from accepting that Shazarack had taken the Cleric Stones to believing that he had created the race of dragons. True, Layna was not a Shaman and likely did not appreciate what was required or possible in performing such acts of necromancy. But she was not yet convinced of the stones' importance. They were discussing how to survive the winter when they needed to put game on the table tonight.

Layna emptied ash from her pipe bowl. "What do you suggest we do?"

Grimmley rested his head back and closed gaunt eyes. "Considering the ease with which the boy learned basic spells of Earth and Fire, it is clear he has exceptional raw talent. But he is totally inept at combining elementals. I have spent most of the last two days trying to understand what is blocking him. It's as if the boy has no talent at all—which is obviously untrue. I know I am rushing his training, but time is not on our side."

The Sorceress could see that it was time she started pulling her share of the load. "Perhaps you are wrong about his ability to use Earth elemental, Grimmley. I say this because I sense a strong aptitude in him to also control Water elemental. And it is simply not possible to have the natural ability to control *three* elementals. Let me try training him tomorrow to see how he responds to advanced spells of my order." She waited.

Grimmley bobbed his head.

"But I won't coddle the boy, Grimmley. He needs to see the urgency of the times. By morrow's eve, he'll think tilling his father's fields would make a nice furlough from my training. I will break through this barrier, or he will regret that I didn't."

Grimmley nodded again, weakly. "It has been a long time since I've been part of an adventure. I'd forgotten how exhausting they can be. Maybe a good night's sleep will shed new light on the situation." Their game of Crowns forgotten, he rose and ambled to the narrow stairs leading to the balcony above and his bed. "Till morning then, Layna. Sleep well." And he climbed the steps and was quickly in bed.

The Sorceress went outside and found Horasius near Sara's pen, comforting the mare whose nerves were worn raw from the dragon's presence in her valley home. For the first time since the bonds' arrival, Skye had not flown north into the mountains. The mare could sense the dragon watching her, hidden somewhere among the many groves of trees.

Layna sniffed the light breeze; the night's cool air carried the promise of rain by dawn. Dragons did not like rain. Nearby trees shuddered from a gust and she glanced to the west. The air was thick and humid.

Horasius bobbed his head anxiously and nickered, his ears back.

"No, Horasius, this storm does not bring normal summer rain. I sense this one, like the dragon, is a forerunner for an early change in seasons." The trees would soon mark the transformation, like the Omen of the Dragonbonded would mark the end of an age. She pulled her hood forward at an unexpected chill. She could only hope they would be ready.

Grabbing up her supplies, she returned to the cottage. Barthox, the Shaman's personal sentinel, glared down from her post along the railing near Grimmley's bed. Layna untied her bedroll, spreading it out in front of the fireplace. Letting her restless thoughts skim across all she had learned that day, she settled in with the fire at her back. The sounds and smells of night through the open windows and Grimmley's soft snores overhead carried her into a welcome sleep.

# When a Third Time Is Not So Charming

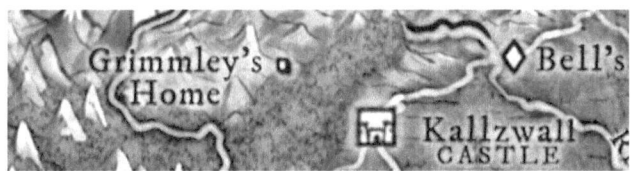

**G**rimmley stared out the back window, scratching at a nonexistent itch on his bearded cheek. The three plates of dinner he had prepared lay cold and forgotten. A distant flicker of lightning illuminated the outline of the lad sitting where Grimmley had left him hours before, slumped forward along the side of the gazebo walkway, leggings rolled up and feet dangling in the water. Dark gray clouds and a gentle rain that had persisted since dawn deepened Grimmley's sullen mood. Thunder rolled through the valley.

The Shaman sighed. He tried to ignore the pacing behind him, but in truth, he would have joined the Sorceress if he'd had any energy left in him. He understood completely her sense of helplessness. "Well, all things considered, that went well."

"How can you even think that? It was a complete disaster!" came the mournful response at his back.

"No one died," Grimmley shrugged.

Count on the Shaman to find bars of gold in a bucket of sand. "What happened today is unimaginable. Or should I say, what didn't happen."

"Now you see my quandary."

"Hoot!" Barthox concurred.

"No, this is worse, Grimmley! Yesterday, it wasn't even imaginable a person could control more than two elementals. Even the cleric Illric didn't consider it possible. And if it wasn't enough to have a human-dragon bond materialize at your door, we find ourselves facing a mystery as baffling and enigmatic as the Modeic hieroglyphs."

"Yes, well, telling the boy he is the first person ever known to control three elementals didn't improve his mood, did it? After your attempts today, I think we can agree. Working with two or three elementals doesn't matter; the boy doesn't have a glint of ability in combining them. I sense his will slipping further from our reach, Layna."

"I am not one to give up easily on a plan of action, but it doesn't take an oracle to see that this approach is not working."

Grimmley nodded absently. "Given the recent turn of events, I doubt a lifetime would be adequate for this plan. I can't even begin to consider how to use the knowledge we gained today. One thing is for sure. Whatever solution we happen to stumble upon, it certainly won't be one about fine-tuning what we are doing. I fear we are fish attempting to walk. Our method of teaching is designed to fit a world where an apprentice can manipulate only two elementals. Antorio Bestigee had to completely rethink how to manipulate elementals when he discovered the means to prove Illric's theory. What if the same is necessary to manipulate three?"

"Then we need an unorthodox approach," Layna submitted.

More than her Sorceress powers and the knowledge she possessed about the Dragonbonded, Grimmley appreciated Layna's tenacious spirit and creative mind. He was ready to grasp at anything she threw his way. "Go on," he nudged.

"Getting a clear picture of what the Dragonbonded were like six hundred years ago is like looking at a stained-glass window with most of the pieces missing. You can see practically any image you want with what remains. One of those many missing pieces relates to how the Dragonbonded learned to use their extraordinary powers. I never found anything written about Dragonbonded preceptors, not even a ranking like those used by the other orders. I assumed it was because the Dragonbonded were secretive, and that knowledge was either lost or never shared. A third possibility had never crossed my mind."

"Which is what?"

"That the Dragonbonded had no preceptors, at least not in the sense our orders function. What if the Dragonbonded were on their own to discover how to use their powers? It would explain how the first Dragonbonded developed their powers without any guidance, which has baffled me from the beginning. We can be certain they were not trained by other ordermen."

"No," Grimmley agreed. "No orderman of the time would have helped the people they most feared." He sensed more was behind Layna's words. "What is it?"

"What if Conner is not the first with the ability to manipulate three elementals? What if it is something all those who bonded with dragons shared?"

For a moment, Grimmley was stunned by the idea. "That would explain a great deal—why they were feared so by the other orders, and why they were considered harbingers of the Anarchic War. Given the turmoil within the orders at the time, what orderman wouldn't find it disconcerting to know someone else could create more powerful spells than those used by the orders?"

Layna nodded. "We could be trying to force this boy down a path he is clearly not intended to take, Grimmley. Maybe it is time we give him some room to work this out on his own."

Grimmley did not adore the idea. He had faith that the lad possessed the inner strength to find his own path. But did he have the courage and will to walk it? They were pinning their hopes on a phantom's tail.

Barthox ruffled her feathers and shook, then offered her bond an encouraging wink.

Grimmley, with no other ideas to offer, grunted acquiescence.

Layna pursed her lips. "We should get Conner in and make him eat. He'll need his strength. When these rains let up in a few hours, I will take the boy and his bond to Dragongarde."

As if to critique their decision, thunder groaned deep across the valley. The cottage windows trembled on their hinges.

"You're sure of this?" Conner asked for the fifth time. The two ordermen seemed less confident of this training method than they had been of the previous two. "How will I know if this is the right thing to do?"

Grimmley checked the girth on Sara's saddle. Satisfied, he patted Conner's shoulder gently while inspecting the boy over the rim of his glasses. "It's one of the Cosmos's greatest gifts, my boy, not knowing the future. Otherwise, the future might be too intolerable to consider. Think of this as another exciting adventure, and you will do fine."

"I've had enough adventures, thank you." Conner did not know how far they would travel, but judging by the food they'd packed, it would be no jaunt. He climbed into the saddle, adjusted the reins, and felt his heart start to race. His Sorceress preceptor was taking him to Dragongarde, the famed, ancient fortress of the once Dragonbonded. It was hard not to contain his excitement as childhood stories of that majestic place came to him. But there was something more, just below the surface of his excitement. Unlike his failed attempts to cast spells under Grimmley's and Layna's tutelage, this felt right. For once, he did not mind the thought of a long ride.

After a final good-bye, the Sorceress and her stallion bond led the way north at a gentle canter between the maples and dark oaks, with Sara a few strides behind. Conner sensed his bond near and met indigo eyes as the winged specter glided silently overhead, outlining the black velvet sky of diamonds beyond.

Sara snorted and bucked to the side.

The eastern sky would lighten soon. It would be a hard ride after all. He heeled Sara faster to keep pace with Horasius's rhythmic hoofs. The Sorceress's robes fluttered in the wind, braided symbols of gold catching the silver light of Erebus's thin splinter hanging like a beacon in the east. The damp wind was cool on his face. Yes, it would be a hard ride through what remained of the night, but for the first time in days, he did not mind not knowing what lay ahead.

Leaning against the back door, Grimmley relit his pipe as he watched the night take riders and dragon. The task ahead overwhelmed him, but it was the urgency of the moment that drove him. He retrieved the silver box, then removed his staff from the corner of the room. "Take care not to leave any pellets on the floor, Barthox."

"Hoot!" the owl exclaimed, indignant.

Grimmley took the path to the circular granite table at the center of his lake gazebo. He worked swiftly, lighting a green candle on a large Cosmic Star etched deep into the tabletop. He removed four colored incense sticks from a box nearby, ignited the ends, and placed them on the four stands at the tips of the star's points. With a stave in one hand and the box in the other, he stepped carefully over the star and began to chant. The candle's green flame popped and ate hungrily at the herbal wick and beeswax. Smoke from the incense swirled and clung to his robes, skin, and stave, the pungent odors deepening the Shaman's trance.

Grimmley's incantation grew louder. He raised his glowing stave over his head, shaking it with each tonal inflection of the spell that drew Earth to him. Each tree in his thick, lush wreath of groves, painstakingly cultivated and attuned to his spirit, began to resonate as minute amounts of Earth were drawn from each leaf. The inner band of trees began to shimmer. The next band followed, then the next, continuing outward in an accelerating procession of bands until the entire ring of trees glowed. Earth elemental flooded into the roots and surged beneath the lake like a raging river over a broken dam.

Grimmley's voice grew to a fevered crescendo. Finally, he jabbed his arm toward the night sky, using the lake to magnify and focus the Earth energy toward the Cosmic Star at his feet. The granite table trembled. The outline of the star turned molten; the incense sticks sizzled in their stands. Smoke thickened about the table, burning brighter and brighter, until the gazebo columns and the trees beyond cast deep shadows outward across the entire valley and up the hills. *"Ourera eftos taxipyli!"*

Grimmley vanished in a bright flash. There was a sucking pop as air rushed to fill the void. A sudden gust extinguished the candle flame, leaving only the residual glow of the Cosmic Star to mark the smoke rising in gentle curls from the glowing wicks. Then, even that faded into darkness.

The valley calm once more, a disparaging hoot came through the cottage window beyond the walkway and garden.

# An Assassin's Aid

**V**eressa stood alone on the eastern shore of Bell's Ferry landing. Across the Aradorm River, lights from the small town of Clovendale sparkled off the crystal waters, adding to the evening's serenity. The night air was cool, a relief from the long days of riding, but not from the urges that grew stronger with each nightfall. Twice so far on the journey home she had slipped away into the night to run free with Antilles. But these escapades offered only temporary comfort, for the next evening, the strange desire to be one with the wilderness would return. *What is happening to me? Am I losing my grip on sanity?*

"Truly a tranquil scene," came a deep voice at Veressa's back.

Veressa jumped and spun to find Grandmaster Friarwood staring at her with his usual unreadable expression, hands clasped behind his back. "It seems Narwales has many such scenes," she said.

Friarwood bent at the waist slightly, wearing a smile that did not seem genuine. "But none to rival those of Graystone, I would say, Highness."

"No. I suppose not." Veressa forced herself to relax. There was something she found ... *off* about the orderman, so she had made it a point to keep her distance—not always an easy task; after all, he was her protector's preceptor.

Antilles sensed Veressa's wariness of the Warrior and crouched.

Friarwood caught the leopard's motion, and his counterfeit smile faded. "I have not had an opportunity, Highness, to congratulate you on your bonding. It seems the Cosmos has seen fit to offer you a most magnificent—and powerful—creature." When the princess offered no response, he proceeded. "Such a bonding is a very rare gift."

Still, Veressa did not reply.

"I hope this does not seem too forward, Highness, and I mean no disrespect, but I must confide that I am most sincerely concerned for your safety."

"Safety? From whom?"

"Not so much a *whom* as a *what*, Highness. You see, I cannot help but notice a change in you since we departed Cravenrock three days back."

Veressa's eyes narrowed at the man. Already, the Warrior had broken several rules of orderman protocol, and he was quickly edging toward insolence. "I am not sure I know to what you are referring, Grandmaster."

Friarwood cleared his throat. "Desires, Highness. Strong impulses to do what most would not consider ... *normal*."

Veressa's body tensed. Her heart thundered in her ears.

Friarwood nodded at her reaction. "I must say that the signs were most subtle. If we had not been traveling together, I might have missed the cues. I can sense these ... desires ... are causing great distress within you."

*I have been discovered!* Veressa thought. Her eyes darted over Friarwood's shoulders to the camp of Defenders nearby. Marcantos was near one of the fires, giving orders to several of the guards, oblivious to his charge and his preceptor out on the dark landing.

"Do not worry, Highness. Marcantos is blind to such things. When he becomes singularly focused, as he is now, all else recedes from his vision. I do not fault him, of course. Such extreme drive has served the

Harmonic Realms well, and will no doubt continue to do so ... and serve Griffinrock, too, if that is to be his destiny."

Veressa certainly needed no reminders that most in Griffinrock expected Marcantos would one day become her Champion.

"It is for this reason that the man is incapable of protecting you from what you may be experiencing. His involvement in this matter would only prove meddlesome."

Veressa considered walking away. But Friarwood held the advantage. If she were to slight him, he might be vindictive enough to report what he knew to Marcantos after all, feigning concern for her best interest. That would end her sneaking away from the camp unhindered for the remainder of their journey. That Friarwood had approached her with such confidence meant he held no doubts. Denying the truth would have been useless. She tilted her head upward. "But *you* can help?"

Friarwood gazed at the white leopard at Veressa's side. "I have seen such behaviors before, Highness. What you are experiencing is quite rare, though it is not unique. And left to your own devices, there is some chance you will find yourself in danger. A different kind of danger, Highness, than that you might encounter on your ... adventures—as you have the last two nights."

*So he knows of that as well!* Any words she spoke against his claim would only make her seem weak. So she waited for him to expose his intentions. Blackmail?

"I understand your hesitation, Highness. I can sense that you do not trust me; you do not know me well enough yet. Please understand that I would not offer my assistance in such an intimate matter if there were someone else—a preceptor, perhaps?—nearby that you could turn to."

Veressa's cheeks crimsoned. Yes, her growing urges were a matter most intimate, especially for a future queen.

"I imagine these compulsions can be quite alarming. Not understanding where they come from might even make one question their own sanity. Perhaps I can offer some advice, Highness. I can sense that elemental forces have already awakened within you—strong forces at that. It is your mindfulness of the Mental planes ... and of Harmonic Sight ... along with your extraordinarily powerful bond that are the source of any impulses you may be feeling. Of course, there are ways to deal with them. And it would please me greatly, Highness, if you were to allow me to humbly offer just a few suggestions that have helped some I have known in such a state of stress? You may do with them as you wish, and I will say nothing more about this matter"—Friarwood's eyes flickered toward the camp—"to *anyone*. But if you find my suggestions helpful, then I would be at your disposal to offer further assistance."

"And what would you suggest?" Veressa asked hesitantly.

Friarwood cleared his throat. "For one, Highness, I would suggest that you do not fight what you are feeling, but instead flow with it. As much as you want to turn away, that is fear speaking to you. You should expand your uncomfortable feelings, embrace them. Let them direct you. There is nothing to fear, Highness. It is simply an inner part of who you are calling to you. Learn how to use it to your advantage."

There was a seed of truth in Friarwood's words. Her intuition *had* been to turn away, to run from these feelings, to fight them with all of her will. But that was not working; in fact, trying to deny them had seemed to make the urges stronger. What could be the harm in letting go? She found great exhilaration in that question, and with it, a feeling of breaking free from a losing struggle. She nodded slowly. "Anything else?"

As the two stood on Bell's Ferry landing, Veressa listened intently, nodding as Friarwood offered several other suggestions. When he was done, he took his leave and slipped away as he had arrived. She combed her fingers through Antilles's thick fur. She could sense no ill will or harmful effects in what the grandmaster suggested. Maybe she was overreacting; maybe he did have her best interest in mind. Veressa's thoughts went to Annabelle. She could have used the Ranger's reassuring words right then.

Alone once more, Veressa turned her gaze toward the Aradorm and the lights of Clovendale, considering the road ahead. At first light, her entourage would cross the river and, if all went as planned, in two days arrive at Kallzwall Castle, home of her aunt, the Duchess Mariette. As she returned to the camp, she found herself eager for the moment she could slip away into the night to test out Friarwood's advice.

# Battle for Elmsdorf

**O**n the morning of the third day out of Dreadcreek, Gertrum Smelterman signaled to hold up, then turned toward Annabelle. "We near the village of Elmsdorf. From here, be mindful not to take any actions that could be considered unfriendly." Gertrum gestured to his patrol spread out down the steep trail behind and waited for each to nod their understanding.

"That confirms what I have been sensing for the past hour." Annabelle glanced around. "These people don't fight for the Harmonics? Do they not know they live within the realms?"

"They consider themselves freemen. You cannot draw lines between Harmonic and Anarchic Lands in mountain granite. The Alpslanders of this region do not recognize any rule or authority other than that of family and bloodbond."

"That sounds strangely Anarchic," Annabelle noted.

Gertrum flashed an angry look her way, but it vanished so swiftly Annabelle thought it could have been a trick of the morning light. "Trust that these people hold no warmth for the Anarchists. But you should understand, they are as apathetic of the Harmonics."

"What have we ever done to them?"

The guildmaster reflected on the Ranger's question while rubbing his grizzly bond's ear. "The true convictions of a people are sometimes measured more by what they don't do."

Gertrum and Targon crested a knoll, then waited for Annabelle to catch up. He gestured before him with a thick, scarred arm. "Elmsdorf."

The scene was not what Annabelle had expected. The narrow trail they had taken out of Dreadcreek snaked down a steep hillside, ending at a long stone bridge that spanned a ravine shrouded in thick summer vegetation and morning mist. The other end of the bridge opened onto a wide, oval ledge extending across the entire southern section of the mountain.

Farther on, the smooth face of the mountain extended upward a hundred paces, pocked with cavern entrances and interlaced with a maze of stairs and terraces carved from the mountain rock. Vines and plants with colorful fruits and vegetables fingered outward from the central base, where water flowed freely. In the center of the ledge, a monolithic stone totem rose a dozen paces. Chiseled, painted faces with grimacing expressions ran the length of the totem.

Gertrum studied Annabelle's reaction. "The people who live here did not build this place, Annabelle, though they do maintain it. No, all this was built probably two millennia ago. It marks some of the vast treasures left behind with the passing of the Modei."

Annabelle pointed at the long structure spanning the gap. "But that bridge defies everything known about bridge building. My father was a Mason Guildmaster's assistant, so I know that a stone arch cannot support such a span. There are neither columns nor trusses beneath, nor beams nor cantilevers above to offer the necessary support. By all that is rational, that structure should collapse under its weight."

"Well, then, it seems someone's thinking is not rational." Gertrum laughed. "I know nothing of what you say, though I believe your knowledge is as you think it to be. But the difference between what we believe and what is real is often wider than this chasm. The dead do not willingly give up their secrets; it seems the Modei are especially stubborn in that matter. It does seem to destroy most theories I've heard about the ancient nomads being heathens. I suppose it will remain a mystery for some time to come." Gertrum started down the slope toward the bridge. "Now we see if our path to this place was worth our time."

A small group of Alpslanders met Gertrum's patrol at the bridge. All wore summer clothing and longswords like those of the patrol. At the front stood a tall, muscular man with a distinguished nose and brown hair hanging free over his shoulders.

"I am Morgas Terranus, tomal of Elmsdorf." The large man waved at the white wolf at his side. "This is Valmer."

Gertrum placed his forearm across his chest and bowed. "Honor be to your home, Tomal Terranus. I am Gertrum Smelterman of the Gilstadt region, Harmonic guildmaster scouter, and leader of this patrol. This is Targon." He gestured toward the grizzly nearly half the width of the bridge. "Terranus ... I visited this village once years ago. Perom Terranus was tomal then. He was your father?" he asked. "You would have been a young lad then, but I do not remember you."

Morgas stiffened. "I was ... away."

Gertrum nodded as if the tomal need say no more. He opened his arm toward Annabelle. "This is Master Ranger Loris, consul to our patrol."

Removing her hood, Annabelle saluted. "May the mountains always be the bedrock of your strength."

Morgas nodded, then turned to Gertrum. "You are a long way from the Gilstadt region, Guildmaster Smelterman."

"We have come from Dreadcreek in hopes of acquiring the assistance of Elmsdorf in an important matter of the Harmonic Realms, Tomal Terranus."

"Then we shall retire to my home, where food and drink can be properly offered. We can discuss this matter in privacy and comfort."

Annabelle leaned close to Jerad, the young, wide-eyed guild apprentice next to her. The youngest in the patrol, the lad was exceptionally gifted at scouting. "Tomal is not a title I am familiar with," she whispered.

Jerad smiled at the Ranger. The Scouters apprentice had taken a liking to Annabelle shortly after departing Dreadcreek and was always underfoot. "It means 'pathfinder.' It is similar to your titles of chief or leader, but more subtle. The tomal is the guide for a village's path through life. But even that description does not give it justice." He shrugged, absently petting his gray mountain squirrel bond.

Annabelle patted his arm while studying the broad-shouldered Alpslander leading the way into the village. "That helps, Jerad. Thank you." The tomal did not seem enthralled with any Harmonic matters, urgent or otherwise. She followed the greeting party into the village.

"I would ask what you have to offer in exchange for our help," Morgas said to Gertrum and Annabelle as they sat in front of bowls of fruit and water, customary midday food for Alpslanders. The three were alone to discuss a possible arrangement.

Gertrum bit into a fist-sized apricot. "We do not have anything of Alpslander value to offer, but—" Gertrum slurped and was cut short.

"You come to our village, sit at my table where I offer you fruits, and ask for our assistance, but you bring nothing to bargain? You are no different from those north of the Borderlands who visit our village."

"Of course there is a difference, Tomal." Gertrum's voice bit with a flash of anger. He wiped juice from his stubble. "Anarchists don't ask."

Morgas leaned forward, his fists pressed to the table. "You speak as though that counts for something. Harmonic demands are bitterleaf chilled in honeysuckle wine; it is sweet to the tongue at first, but hard to swallow once the savor wears off. Every man, woman, and child has a purpose in our village. To remove even one would cause undue hardship on those remaining. All we ask for is ... compensation ... for our help."

Before Gertrum could reply, the deerskin hanging at the cavern doorway fluttered. A tall woman with thick-braided golden hair entered.

"This is Pallia, my wife, and her wolf bond, Galven."

Pallia studied the faces of the newcomers at the table, then nodded. "Husband, I will speak with you. Outside."

"Make yourselves comfortable. I will return momentarily," Morgas said.

After the tomal left, Annabelle sighed. "Well, that didn't go so well."

"Sure it did!" Gertrum rebutted, then scratched his glistening chin. "We're still guests of the village, aren't we?"

"That could change at any moment. If he refuses, we will be without a guide."

"Then we must make sure he does not refuse. Besides, the negotiations have just begun."

Jerad appeared at the entry and gestured to Gertrum with his hands, then vanished again.

Gertrum grinned at Annabelle. "It seems we may have something of value for the tomal after all." Then he, too, stepped through the entrance, with Annabelle quickly on his heels.

Jerad urged them to follow him up a steep, winding staircase that led over a small waterfall. Nearing the upper end, he slowed and extended his arm back and down, then crouched behind a natural wall of rock and vegetation. Guildmaster and Ranger joined him, peering over the rim of the wall to the eastern side of the mountain.

There, Morgas and five villagers took a long, stone bridge spanning a deep ravine farther to the northeast, a twin to the bridge they had crossed to the south. Amassed near the far end of the bridge, a large number of well-armed soldiers stood in perfect columns along a grassy ridge. Light glistened off their studded armor and black shields bearing the emblem of a steel-gray cross overlaid on a blood-red ring.

"Anarchists," Annabelle ground her teeth. Her hand went instinctively to her staff.

"I would estimate one hundred fifty—two full companies." Gertrum beamed his jubilance at the chance to fight Anarchists. "It seems the carrion will feast well this day."

The three watched as Morgas's small band approached a gray-cloaked figure at the front of the Anarchists. After a few moments, the cloaked figure started making threatening gestures at the tomal. Morgas remained at ease, feet spread wide and arms folded while the figure continued its animated monologue.

Morgas shook his head defiantly.

Tensing, the figure removed its cloak to reveal a slender, dark-haired woman in flowing pitch-black robes. A handsome young man stepped to her side and handed her a staff as Morgas and his band started back across the bridge.

Annabelle sighed and sank down onto the stone step the two Scouters occupied. "A dark Mystic. Looks like the serenity of the morning is going to be fleeting."

Jerad stared back. "A what?"

"A Conjuror, or more precisely, an enchantress. And a master by the looks of those robes. That makes the young man next to her her apprentice."

"A dark orderman." Gertrum hammered the wall with his fist. "It's been a long time since I faced off against one of them."

The Ranger grunted at the audacious statement. "I'm surprised you're still around to talk about it."

Gertrum backed from the wall and studied Annabelle, then rubbed his chin with thick fingers. "Well, I wasn't alone. I suppose the grandmaster Mystic with us had something to do with the creature's demise. It is a tale worth telling over an evening fire and spit. For now, let's go find a way to send these atrocities to their reclamation." He bounded down the stairs with an energy belying his size and their long journey from Dreadcreek.

Annabelle glared at the guildmaster's back. "Is there anything that dampens that man's spirit?"

"Only going too long without quenching his sword's thirst for Anarchist blood," Jerad said with a chuckle. He retreated from the wall, tailing his guildmaster down the stairs.

"No, no, no!" Gertrum practically stomped his foot in protest. "We can take them, I say. The Ranger can handle the enchantress, and our fighters will dump the trash she dragged along into the ravine."

Morgas frowned at the simplicity of the scouter's strategy, glancing at those gathered in counsel near the stone totem. "There are not enough fighters in our village to ensure such a victory, and even that would come at a heavy cost. I appreciate your eagerness to assist, but it won't be enough. There is another way, but it will require more subtlety."

"What are her demands?" Annabelle interjected before Gertrum could argue with the tomal.

Morgas hesitated before answering. "It is tradition that the Anarchists send forces to villages along the Borderlands. She has come to take three of our youth to be trained in the Anarchic ways—twenty years of servitude. She has granted me one hour to realize the foolishness of resisting." His frown became a snarl mimicked by his wolf bond.

Pallia touched his shoulder and he relaxed.

"She could wait a month. It changes nothing," Morgas growled. "Since returning to my village, I have sworn my life against the ways of their orders. They shall have no more of our generations. The cycle ends here, and it ends this day!"

"What, then, is your strategy, Tomal?" Annabelle asked.

Morgas described how he planned to deal with the force outnumbering his village fighters four to one. Then he detailed how the enchantress would deal with the situation once she learned of the tomal's decision; he clearly had extensive knowledge of Anarchic tactics.

Annabelle interrupted. "We will need to modify your plan slightly if it is going to work, Tomal. There is some information you lack that is critical to our success. The Conjuror, her pup, and I share an elemental force." Noting their bewildered faces, she elaborated. "All ordermen possess the ability to manipulate two of the four elementals, so we all share some basic powers. The enchantress and I both manipulate Air. Once I cast a spell, she will know of my presence. Then you will have lost the element of surprise."

Morgas nodded. "Once the enchantress discovers a Harmonic orderman is among us, she will order a full-scale assault. She will show no mercy and offer no quarter to any left standing. I cannot allow you to engage in the battle until it is clear we have the advantage."

"Therein lies the problem," Annabelle said. "How can you achieve an advantage without my help against such a force led by a master Conjuror?"

Gertrum broke the long silence that followed. "Anarchist soldiers are skilled fighters. I will grant them that. But they have one flaw we might work to our advantage. In prolonged battle, they can be overcome with bloodlust. Once that happens, the enchantress will have little hope of controlling them."

"Yes," Morgas said, catching Gertrum's direction. "I looked into the eyes of those in their ranks. They have traveled a great distance and hunger for battle. If we can hold them long enough to work them into such a frenzy ..."

This was what the council needed to complete their plan. Morgas used the time the enchantress had afforded rehashing details until everyone understood their part. When the hour was up, he raised his hand. "There is one thing more. The enemy must be defeated without mercy. We cannot take prisoners or show mercy. If but one reports back, they will return with a greater force to make an example of us to all who would dare defy their authority. May the mountain give us strength."

"May the snow be our blood," the Alpslanders responded, then dispersed.

Annabelle noted Jerad standing to the side wringing his hands. "Are you all right?"

"I've spent most of my time scouting the Gilstadt region. I've never seen so many Anarchists at one time before."

The Ranger nodded. "When the time comes, you'll know what to do. If you want, stay close to me until we engage in the fight."

"I'd like that," he smiled. Even his squirrel bond relaxed.

The two walked toward their waiting spot, a boulder north of the totem.

"You have to admire the tomal's mettle," Jerad said, shaking his head.

"Conviction for a way of life is easily confused with courage," Annabelle replied. She bit her lip as Morgas walked toward the north bridge, passing more than thirty village fighters hidden behind other boulders. Pallia was among them, her face filled with concern for her husband. Annabelle, too, loathed the thought of the tomal facing two companies of Anarchists alone, but it was the only way.

Morgas waited at the foot of the north bridge, Valmer bristling at his side. His blue eyes narrowed at the blackness before him. He'd known this day would arrive ever since he and Pallia returned home a fortnight ago. The enchantress's demands were but a pretense. The real message was from his former liege, Lacerus, the Assassin who had sent him to track down and return the young thief named Vault. When Morgas had decided to return to his home instead, he had done so with the full understanding that his disloyalty would not go unnoticed. This Anarchic force was a statement: *Disobedience will not be tolerated.* It was time to see if the village's preparation had been sufficient.

Reaching over his shoulder, the tomal unsheathed his longsword. He knew he taunted the enchantress, but his mind walked elsewhere.

Lifting the blade to the light, he studied the many small notches along its edges, the pitted groove, and the wide point that refused to remain sharp. Big hands tightened on the thick leather grip. He tested its balance, making smooth arcing circles.

The sword was not a finely forged weapon. It was heavy and off balance. But it was one Morgas could trust with his life. He read the words etched by his father's hand before the old tomal quenched the blade in the winter snows: *Mountains will crumble before a father's love passes.*

He did not wait long for the Conjuror's reply.

The enchantress jerked her hand forward and down. As one, the company to her right dropped their shields, drew their blades, and marched forward, their bonds remaining behind. The rhythmic pounding of polished swords on studded body armor made the sound of whips cracking. Abruptly, they halted. They leaned forward, hard leather armor creaking in strained anticipation.

With a nod from the enchantress, a short, bulky woman with feral hair raised muscled arms. Tilting her head to the midday sky, she screamed an Anarchic war cry. It was an eerie warble, a blend of angry howl and mournful wail. The tomal had heard that baleful sound many times. He did not flinch. The ordered columns cascaded into a churning mass of black chaos, spilling out onto the bridge in raw fury. He raised his lone sword to the ready and licked his lips in anticipation.

The battle for Elmsdorf had begun.

Before the front line of Anarchic fighters broke across the center of the bridge, a salvo of arrows and rocks rained down from the mountain's eastern rise with devastating effect. Those who faltered were quickly trampled or swept over the side of the bridge by the agitated tide of darkness rushing from behind. A second and third volley descended into the chaos. With the flight of the fourth, the village fighters sprang from their hiding places. With Morgas leading, they took to the bridge and met those who had weathered the aerial barrage.

Morgas's fighters buckled under the impact of the Anarchic force, but the enemy's advantage was short-lived. The narrow bridge did not allow many Anarchists into the fray. Those in the front soon discovered the difficulty in getting a killing stroke while their comrades clambered from behind for their chance to draw blood.

"Keep the line tight!" Morgas cried out to the Alpsland fighters about him as they stabbed and stepped in rhythmic precision, using their longer swords to deadly advantage in the close quarters. The exhausted and wounded retreated from the line while fresh fighters stepped in to continue their assault. Unprepared for this unusual defense and able to return few lethal blows, row after row of Anarchists fell at the villagers' feet.

Thick blood pooled around the Anarchist bodies littering the bridge, and Morgas struggled to keep solid footing on the stones. His back and legs cramped; his sword was lead. But each wound he delivered was payment for the many scars he bore—acts the Anarchist orders had perpetrated on him during those years of servitude. A tall soldier with wide, hazel eyes reminded him of his first of many brutal instructors. He found an opening and stabbed upward into the man's throat while Valmer bit into the man's boot, pulling him off balance. Morgas was rewarded with a shower of warm blood across his face and chest. The soldier tumbled backward into the seething ebony mob, clutching at the gaping wound. Morgas stepped forward, eagerly greeting the next in line.

From behind her boulder, Annabelle watched the wounded retreat from the mayhem on the bridge. Village elders rushed to assist those unable to walk to the makeshift clinic at the base of the village caves while fighters sporting bandages returned to the bridge to bolster their dwindling defense. Those suffering light wounds were attended first, forcing those with more serious injuries to wait. One Alpsland woman with a chest wound cried out, then slumped forward.

The sound of a ram's horn drew Annabelle's attention back to the north. There, Morgas's fighters had driven the line of Anarchists back to the center of the bridge. In unison, the first company of Anarchists withdrew and reformed their ranks, leaving behind a third of their force dead or dying. The enchantress had been probing for any weakness in the villagers' will to fight. But there had been none.

In response, a cheer rang out among the Elmsdorf fighters on the bridge.

Unmoved by the loss of soldiers, the enchantress raised her staff and jerked it forward. The second company of Anarchists advanced onto the bridge in tight formation. According to Morgas, the second round would test the villagers' might.

The rhythmic pounding of swords on polished armor quelled the proud Alpslanders.

As before, a volley of arrows and stones rained down from the mountain. But the second company had been observing the villagers' tactics. The feral-haired woman cried a warning and the soldiers lifted their shields over their heads. Arrows and rocks glanced away harmlessly with the clamor of clicks and thuds. Undaunted by the barrage, the company marched toward the center of the bridge, where the Alpslanders waited.

Annabelle understood the danger. The archers needed to thin the attacking force, and quickly, before they entered into melee. Making her way to the eastern ridge, she gestured to the archers above. A dozen boys and girls descended and rallied around the Ranger while the younger ones remained, seeking cracks between the square shields.

Under the cover of boulders, she guided them closer to the bridge. "See if you can take out the leading row of soldiers," she said, pointing at the exposed thighs and calves beneath the wall of shields.

The oldest archer, no more than fourteen, signaled, and the others fanned out to begin the gruesome task. Several soldiers went down with well-scored hits; a few tumbled over the edge of the bridge to disappear into the gray mist below. Those behind the front line lowered their black shields and pushed forward to fill the gap, stepping over their fallen comrades.

A young fighter named Trayos pushed forward to stand next to Morgas and wiped blood from a cut at the base of his neck. Hefting the large, bloodied sword the boy's father had handed him, he winked up at the tomal with a glint in his eyes.

Morgas nodded back with Alpslander pride.

A moment later, the Anarchists reached the center of the bridge and met the awaiting village fighters.

The Alpsland fighters forced the horde of black to remain shoulder to shoulder. Swords and shields ineffective, the close-quarter melee ground to a stalemate.

"Tomal!" Trayos shouted, then pointed to the north. "The Conjuror is casting a spell."

The Enchantress was losing control of her troops and had decided to end the conflict decisively. To the astonishment of the fighters about him, Morgas yelled, "Retreat!"

Annabelle sensed the strong pull of Air. White clouds turned dark overhead as they frothed in wild, chaotic motion.

Morgas and his fighters were making a fast withdrawal with the second company of Anarchic soldiers close behind, their bloodthirsty faces contorted in exaltation. Farther on, what remained of the first company had perceived a coming victory. And fearing being left out of spilling more blood, they rushed the bridge once more. None seemed concerned for the rain of arrows and rocks continuing unabated from above. The Anarchic ranks thinned further.

At the base of the bridge, just as Hemera vanished behind a dark haze boiling overhead, Morgas and his Alpsland fighters turned and met the soldiers once more.

And the world spun into bedlam.

Several boulders hiding young Alpslander archers exploded in a blinding flicker and thunderclap. Gravel rained down on Annabelle and those around her. To her left, all that remained was a cloud of thick dust. Before she could shout a warning, another flash streaked down the side of the mountain, bringing more rocks on the heads of those waiting eagerly for a signal to join in the battle. The high-pitched wails above echoed across the steep incline.

*The children,* Annabelle thought in horror. *The enchantress is targeting the children!*

The bridge was the only access to the village. As long as the Alpsland fighters controlled the bridge, they controlled the battle. So Morgas's tactical retreat had succeeded in giving the archers an opportunity to thin the second wave's ranks. But it had also left his fighters in a strategically poor position. It had been a desperate move.

A flash of lightning drew Morgas's gaze, where he witnessed the devastation along the base of the ledge. Out of time, the tomal raised his left arm high, then, clenching his fist, pulled down hard.

The remaining fighters, led by Pallia, rushed in to bolster the exhausted ranks. When the reinforcements reached the base of the bridge, the Alpslanders formed a spearhead with Morgas at its point. Together, the band surged forward, driving a wedge into the middle of the Anarchists. It seemed nothing could slow the tomal's blade; more Anarchists went down and the wedge widened.

But the resulting gap had given the second Anarchic wave an opportunity, and they seized it. A number of black-armored soldiers rushed forward to fill the vacuum left behind Morgas's spearhead, and they formed a portal at the base of the bridge. Before the Alpslanders could stem the flow, several dozen Anarchists broke through and ran toward the unprotected clinic of wounded and elderly.

Morgas's spearhead continued forward, breaking through the back of the second wave. Unimpeded, Morgas's fighters swiftly traversed the bridge littered with bodies, some writhing from wounds. With a deafening roar, they met what remained of the first wave returning to get in on the fight.

Thunder from another series of lightning bolts drowned out Annabelle's warning to the Scouters. She turned to gaze at the motionless body at her feet, a thin trail of smoke flowing from a large hole in the middle of Jerad's back. His squirrel bond lay dead at his side.

"This fight will be over before we get started! We can't wait any longer," Gertrum shouted.

"Then enough of this," Annabelle responded, and stepped back to the stone totem at the center of the village ledge where she could see the battle playing out before them. More importantly, she would soon be the enchantress's target. There was no need to risk further collateral damage.

Gertrum offered her an encouraging nod and led his Scouters out to join in the fight.

Taking a deep breath, she plunged her staff into the dirt. *"Outher pheto afyravdos."* Symbols along the base of her staff flared. Air and Earth coursed up the wooden shaft. And it sprang to life, warping and bending from the torque of Air tugging at its ends, forming into her elemental bow.

The enchantress's eyes went wide, first with surprise, then with fury. For a moment, the two ordermen appraised each other across the wide divide. Then, turning, the dark Mystic spoke to her apprentice.

The young man bounded away, disappearing over a ridge to the north.

Before Annabelle could murmur the spell intended to slow the Anarchists sprinting toward the clinic, a great wellspring of Earth swirled beneath her. She hesitated. Instead of drawing Earth to her, she fought to control the elemental force gushing up through her like a geyser. Earth surged up her bow, searing her palm. The marrow in her bones burned hot and she cried out in agony. She had never held so much Earth, had not known such energy could be tapped. Forced to use it quickly, she incanted the only spell that came to her. *"Outher ousia plattopetra!"*

Morgas did not slow when his band met the returning company of Anarchists. His sword arced first in a long upward stroke to his left, followed by a downward stroke to his right. One Anarchist fell away with a severed arm; another staggered back, attempting to keep his entrails from spilling out across the bridge. The tomal fought with singular purpose, hacking at any who dared stand before him, heedless of the steel flashing about him. He heard Trayos shouting, "Tomal! Tomal, wait!" But words and the clash of metal behind lived only at the fringes of his mind. He sensed Valmer at his thigh, snarling and biting. He found solace there, measuring each moment with step and stroke.

When Morgas broke through the back of the first wave's line, his dreamscape evaporated. He was standing on the northern foot of the bridge. Fifty paces away, under a large oak tree, stood the enchantress, alone.

He was set to give the last signal, but from the enchantress's gaze, he knew that the Ranger had already joined the fight. Their element of surprise was no longer his. He had simply taken too long to get there.

Morgas twisted the blood-drenched hilt in his palm. The enchantress had not noticed him yet. He could hear the wolf's pant, feel the rush of his bond's excitement, sense the tension in Valmer's legs. Morgas crouched. Man and wolf attacked.

Annabelle held her Stone Wall spell as she watched Morgas's futile attempt to slay the enchantress. *The man is mad!* she thought. Then she understood. Morgas was sacrificing himself to give the village a chance. Ten paces away, the enchantress flung her arm forward. Tomal and bond froze midstride, trapped in a bubble of Air. At least Morgas had succeeded in disrupting the enchantress's spell. Not wanting to witness his gruesome end, Annabelle turned her attention to the Anarchists who had broken past the bridge. The thick wall of rock she had summoned had stymied their vicious assault, but it would not hold them for long. She needed to thin their ranks to ensure the village was safe.

Annabelle's arm blurred and a half dozen Anarchists fell before a gleeful Gertrum and his Scouters could reach them. With the Harmonic patrol in the fray, Annabelle continued to fire shafts into the skirmish with deadly precision whenever a target presented itself.

Just as a victory cry rang out among Gertrum's patrol, thunder rumbled, and the Ranger dove to the side. A nearby boulder exploded into dust and grit. Annabelle rose amid the dust and uttered another spell: *"Outher ousia odigovelos."* Five arrows in quick succession arced across the chasm to the north.

Morgas struggled against the vise crushing life from him. His ears popped; his eyes bulged and bled; his ribs buckled under intense pressure. He could no longer draw breath. His vision was failing. Through his link, he could sense Valmer also dying. Then as quickly as the force had taken him, it was gone.

Morgas staggered forward and inhaled deeply. His opportunity would be fleeting. Stepping and spinning to his left, he whipped his sword around. In one last gasp of desperation, his sword slipped from his sticky grip and careened toward the enchantress.

Distracted by the Ranger's arrows, the enchantress had failed to anticipate Morgas's maneuver. The dull sword tip pierced her chest, puncturing heart and lungs and severing her spinal cord. The impact of the massive weapon lifted her off the ground, impaling her to the oak tree behind. A moment later, she expired.

With the enchantress dead, Annabelle cast another Stone Wall spell at the northern foot of the bridge. The Anarchists were trapped, and the Alpsland fighters routed the remaining soldiers back to the middle of the bridge where, with the aid of the young archers above, they finished the grisly task of dispatching the last of them.

When everything fell silent, Pallia exhaled. "It is done," she said, nodding to the Ranger. "Thanks to you and to Gertrum's guildsmen, we remain free another day."

"No," the Ranger shook her head. "Not done yet." She moved in front of the stone totem once more, drawing on Earth and Air.

The power from the totem was frighteningly intense. Again, Earth flowed unabated from the obelisk. Annabelle was but a moth fluttering dangerously near a raging flame. She forced her eyes closed to sustain the concentration she would need if her spell was to work, a spell that should have been far beyond her elemental abilities. The right amount of Air had to be mixed with Earth. She called upon Air. Bits of dust swirled around her legs, popping and sparkling like diamonds. The Modeic symbols etched the length of her bow flared to life.

Peron's circling motion in the sky guided her.

In one fluid motion, the Ranger notched an arrow, raised her bow, and pulled the magical string taut. *"Aerora ousia odigovelos!"* she exclaimed, releasing the elemental cord. The projectile arced into the bright sky, though the Ranger never saw it. The intense release of elemental force slammed her back into the obelisk, her shoulders sliding down the stone structure.

Pallia helped her stand on wobbly legs.

Annabelle nodded solemnly. "Now it is done."

The enchantress's apprentice, Yergen Kelmer, held his Air and Fire illusion spell as his deerskin shoes danced lightly over mountain terrain. It was a complex spell, the first he had learned since starting his apprenticeship in the Conjurors Order a fortnight ago. But it would be enough to keep the Alpslander dogs off his heels.

He had considered returning to his preceptor when the thunderclouds dissipated, the battle surely won. But the enchantress's command had been specific: He was to return to Citadel Farlorde and report what he'd seen to Master Barbarian Barcleave Tallenia. On he ran.

The young apprentice bounded a wide, flat boulder like a deer. He smiled. It was hard to contain such youthful pride, though none within his order appreciated physical strength. Conjurors relied on the prowess of missile combat, not the strength and endurance Warlocks used. He doubted any in his order could outpace him. So the sudden impact of a sharp force between his shoulder blades astonished him. He fought to maintain his footing on the rough terrain. Stopping, he glanced down.

Trembling fingers slid along the smooth arrow shaft protruding from his sternum. He marveled at the bloody metal tip made by a guildmaster smithy. There was no pain, only a soft rattle in his chest while he labored for breath. He felt tired, and his legs buckled under the weight of his light body. Knees struck the rocky terrain. He sat back on numbing legs.

Yergen's gaze turned skyward. And as for the very first time in a long while, he noted soft, white clouds floating gently on a canvas of bright blue. *So incredibly peaceful*, he thought. Then the bright sea of blue and white dissolved into dull grays as Yergen tilted forward.

# Bloodbond

It was nearing dusk when Morgas appeared in the entryway of his home, staring down into the village circle where a funeral pyre was being prepared. Soon he would speak final rites for those villagers whose spirits had been reclaimed that day. He had lost several good friends and a few young fighters, among them Trayos, the youth who had stood with him on the bridge and eagerly met Anarchist savagery with his father's steel. Many others had been wounded. Yet, with all the sadness, this was not what weighed heaviest on his mind.

Through the late afternoon, he had returned to negotiations with Scouter Smelterman and Ranger Loris. They had explained that they were on an expedition to discover the source of alleged dragon sightings southwest of Elmsdorf and needed an expert to guide them through that region.

When the Ranger had first mentioned dragon sightings, Morgas recalled the events of a fortnight ago. He, Pallia, and the Narkain brothers had chased a boy named Vault north out of Cravenrock only to lose him in a cave. Suddenly, everything fell into place—the sounds and sights of the cave's destruction, the odd pulsating rock he'd retrieved from the cave, Lacerus's reaction when he'd handed the rock to him, the blinding flash from the Assassin's ebony ring, even Carlon's injuries and the boy's ability to vanish without a trace or track. Memories of stories he had heard as a boy flooded back—ancestral stories of dragonfire, rock temporarily imbued with the essence of a dragon, seen throbbing a cobalt blue from caves near his village home.

It all pointed to only one plausible explanation. The timing of the sightings Ranger Loris mentioned was no coincidence. Vault—the boy Pallia had later discovered to be named Conner Stonefield—had stumbled into a cave with a dragon. Morgas was certain this Conner Stonefield was connected to this beast. And this led him to a more chilling thought.

Morgas had seen the look in the Assassin Lacerus's eyes when he handed him the rock. Lacerus had known the rock was imbued with dragonfire. That was why he was so eager to get the boy back, alive ... and at any price. It also meant Lacerus had a fortnight head start tracking this creature down. If the Anarchists got their hands on a dragon ...

Pallia stepped up close behind him. "So, my husband, what have you decided?"

He pushed the unsettling thoughts away and gazed into her eyes. "There is nothing to decide. This patrol of Harmonics came to our aid today and surely made the difference in the battle. I am bound by the bloodbond to repay."

"What if you had no bloodbond, Morgas? What would you do then?" Pallia asked harshly.

Morgas was shocked at Pallia's flash of anger. "I have been away from our home too long, and today we lost family and comrades. I belong here, as tomal, with my people. What would you suggest I do?"

"I do not ask you to not consider your bloodbond to these people," Pallia replied, waving her arm at the room where the Scouter and Ranger awaited Morgas's decision. "Only that you think of this as an opportunity."

Morgas could not hide his confusion.

Pallia sighed. "Yes, some very dear friends were lost today, the price for taking our first step to a new freedom. But that freedom also comes with a responsibility to choose our path wisely. Elmsdorf needs a strong tomal who has a vision to make the right choices. They will look to your wisdom."

She swallowed hard. "There is a change coming to these mountains, my husband. I hear it in the songs of life around us, see it in how the wind moves through the trees, smell it in the smoke of our evening fires. Everyone will be swept into this change. We cannot hide or run from it. I know you sense it too, though you do not speak of it. When this change comes, you must be prepared to choose a side. *This* is why you must go, not for some bloodbond. Walk with them, work with them, with open eyes and ears. Once you have listened to their hearts, then, my husband, you will understand what is in yours. Then you will be ready when this change comes."

Relaxing at last, Morgas smiled. "It seems I already am a very wise man."

"You praise yourself too much, husband," Pallia scolded, but had to bite back a smile of her own.

Morgas nodded. "I praise you, wife, for truly I was wise to have married you. Bloodbond will make for a good pretense. I will walk with these people. I will listen to their words and watch their deeds. Then I will return home to you and my people, and we will make ready for winter's change." But he would not yet speak of what he speculated about either dragon or Eastlander. Not until he was more certain, and his heart guided him to do so. It seemed this Conner Stonefield was not yet finished forming ripples in his life.

"By the Cosmos's will, how fortuitous that enchantress and her pups appeared when they did!" Gertrum slapped his hand on the table. "And I don't mean purely for the joy of spilling some Anarchic blood. Morgas will have no choice but to assist—not to offer a few young scouts, mind you. No, *he* will come with us." Annabelle did not respond, so he went on. "Did you see the way that man fought? He will be a great tomal someday. I frankly can't think of anyone I'd rather have in our service."

Annabelle could no longer sit listening. "I did not participate in that battle for the glory of killing *or* to create a bloodbond pact with the tomal, Gertrum. My motives were simple. I fight for the Harmonic Realms. And do not forget Jerad, or the good Alpslanders who died today with motives just as simple—in defense of their home. At least give Morgas the honor of your silence while his village grieves."

The guildmaster clamped his mouth shut. After a moment, he murmured, "But of course you are right, Annabelle. I meant no disrespect. And I have not forgotten Jerad. He was a good lad, and I will miss him dearly. I suffer from my own lust for blood. You honor me with your honesty and sincerity. You truly are a good advisor."

Annabelle let her thoughts flow while the two waited in anticipation of Morgas's decision. The events of the day were indeed fortuitous, but for a different reason—one eluding her mental understanding. There had been a force behind the events that guided her to this place, as though she was being directed here.

For the first time since being assigned to the scouting patrol, Annabelle understood that she was right where she was needed. There was purpose to their work. From the seed of that purpose sprang the hope she would one day reclaim the Rangers' honor lost through her misdeeds as Veressa's protector.

# Dragon Wind

Layna studied Conner's sullen expression in the flickering glow of the campfire. In the two days and nights since they'd left Grimmley's home, the Sorceress had learned how to read the boy like a scroll. "What's on your mind, Conner?"

The Eastlander jumped. "What do you mean?"

"I know that look. Something weighs heavy on your thoughts." She rose, stretching away stiffness from the day's long ride. "Sometimes it helps to talk about it," she prodded.

Conner scrutinized the snoring black mass at the edge of the firelight. At length, he asked, "Is there any truth to the Omen of the Dragonbonded?"

Layna leaned against a rock and sighed. "So that is what troubles you. Yes, I can see how the foretelling of the Dragonbonded returning might make you restless." She studied the star-filled sky overhead. "Have you ever heard of the Oracles of the Mystics Order?"

"Of course. Who hasn't?" Then Conner's cheeks flushed hot from his tactless response. "I'm sorry, my lady. I didn't mean anything—"

Layna's hearty laugh cut him short. "No offense taken, Conner." She drew deep on the stem of her pipe, the light evening breeze whisking smoke into the darkness beyond. "Did you know not all of their prophecies come true?"

Conner was shocked. "No."

"Of course not. You don't hear of those stories, do you? And why is that?" The Sorceress waited while her new apprentice chewed on the question. "Because people have come to accept the oracles as infallible. Yet there are imperfections in their arts. To give them credit, they are correct quite often. But their divinations are not based on certainty, Conner. They are based on known laws of the Cosmos, laws that can be misread or, more precisely, interpreted without full knowledge of everything affecting the future."

Layna tapped ash from her pipe's bowl. "Funny things, prophecies. It is not so much about whether a prophecy is a foretelling of what will come, but rather about those who believe in a prophecy so strongly that they bring about its certainty. No, Conner, prophecies only point the way to what *may* be, not what *will* be. But people can be so single-minded they accept a prediction offered by the mighty Oracles as the only possible truth. And they will do nearly anything to ensure its outcome, no matter the consequence, all so they can hold to the comfort of their belief in the all-powerful Oracles. It is a sad reality, Conner, but people like being wrong less than they like being unhappy." Layna thumbed more tobac into her pipe and relit it with a stick from the fire. "Of course, you didn't hear that from me." She winked at her young apprentice.

Conner eyed his mentor skeptically. He did not have to believe in Assassins and undead for them to be real. "I never believed in the Dragonbonded, but now I know they were real. It seems they will be again."

"Conner, each of us chooses how we contribute to the circumstances through which the future takes shape. No omen can dictate that. When you make your choices based more on what you believe is right than what you fear is wrong, or on what someone else tells you, then you will be on the path to freedom."

A long silence followed. Layna thought Conner did not want to continue the talk, so she retrieved her lute and began to strum the strings absently.

Finally, the boy responded with gentle conviction. "I believe in a simple and fair world, Layna. I believe people are good and caring. I believe we possess the potential to settle our differences with compassion for everyone involved, no matter how bad things become. I believe that conflict only brings about pain and suffering. And I believe suffering never mends a tattered fence or a broken heart."

Layna nodded with satisfaction. "Those are all noble beliefs, Conner. Truly, they are. But what do you do when those beliefs conflict with your very survival? Sometimes, one must set aside such lofty ideals to do what is necessary so they will flourish again another day. What good is a wonderful dream if it is swept away before its time of fruition?"

"So you believe the omen is true. You're saying there is a chance that the Dragonbonded"—Conner struggled to finish the sentence—"*will* be the bringers of war?" He broke the stick he had been poking at the fire and threw the pieces on the blaze, watching flames lick hungrily at the dry bark. "I don't want to be the one who drives the world into a war that destroys everything I know and love. I, for one, am not willing to pay any price for such a foretelling of the future."

Layna sighed. "It is not up to you to determine such a fate, Conner, so do not carry the weight of the realms' future on your shoulders. It is possible the world will need you to survive a calamity brought on by another source." The Sorceress eyed the wyvern twitching in his sleep. Her words were doing little to soothe the boy's doubts.

"Have you ever heard of dragon wind?" she asked, picking at a solemn tune on the lute.

Conner shook his head.

"During the time of the early Dragonbonded, it was commonly thought that the wind from a dragon's wings was what brought change to the world, thus the term 'dragon wind.' I have often wondered if the roots of the Dragonbonded's omen sprang from that belief."

After a long silence, she began to sing.

*In the glade by the brook, where a humble cabin stands,*
*A mother's eyes are lost to empty skies.*
*She pines for the son she lost to distant lands,*
*So to the southern wind she cries.*

*"Oh, dragon wind, where'd you blow?*
*You carried away my son. And I don't know where he sails.*
*With outstretched arms, he rode on great black scales.*
*Oh, dragon wind, where'd you blow?"*

*On the hill to the east waits a pretty young lass,*
*Her arms stretched up to empty skies.*
*She yearns for her love, while lovely days do pass,*
*And to the western wind she cries.*

*"Oh, dragon wings, please blow your wind my way.*
*I don't know where you took my love, for he did not want to stay.*
*Can't you see that I'm lost, so to the Cosmos pray,*
*That you will bring him back to me someday."*

*Outside a timeworn cottage, the winter wind moans,*
*While inside a roaring fire licks the skies.*
*But the warmth cannot reach the chill in his old bones,*
*So to the icy north wind he cries.*

*"Oh, dragon wind, where'd you blow?*
*You carried away my love. And I don't know where she sails.*
*With outstretched arms, she rode your great black scales.*
*Oh, dragon wind, where'd you blow?"*

*On the edge of a cliff, near a small cave I stand,*
*Where the snowcapped mountains greet the sky.*
*Humbled by the beast, I reach out with trembling hand,*
*And while stroking her black scales, I cry.*
*"Oh, dragon wings, please blow your wind my way.*
*I don't know where we will go, but please carry me away.*
*Just spread your wings, and to the Cosmos I'll pray,*
*That I will become Dragonbonded someday."*

Conner did not speak again, so Layna checked on her bond once more, then prepared their camp for the night. It would be another hard ride on the morrow, but they would reach their destination the day after. She could only hope the boy would be ready. By the time she returned, Conner was asleep.

Not far from the fire, half dreaming, Skye lay listening to the Sorceress's voice. He had picked up enough human speech to catch the essence of her humansong. But more than the words, it was the feelings coursing through his bond's link that drew him into the strange ballad. He felt an emotion stirring there, something new. He could not name it, but understood its effect—reverence and respect. And for the first time since the day he'd bonded with Conner, he slept deeply.

# Part III

*Life's meaning can be found in the relationships one develops. Bonds are but one way to guide a being toward a deeper understanding and expression of self. Family, friends, even strangers—each relationship is like a mirror into the being's soul. If one wants to truly see their essence, they merely need to examine the relationships they cultivate.*

*—The Modei Book of Air (Second Book)*

# A Course of Action

The grandmaster Necromancer Meera Asheborne surveyed the devastation about her and sighed. What remained of the rover camp was a disheveled mess of collapsed tents and supplies littering the site in random fashion.

"Which one?" came Groegan's deep, Barbarian voice at her side.

Meera flicked a burning log back onto the smoldering fire with her boot. "That is a challenging question. Your band of Barbarians was a little overzealous."

"You did say our mission is to remain a secret and to eliminate anyone we meet."

Meera stepped over the mangled remains of a young woman—well, she thought it was a woman. "Yes, but I would have thought it obvious we needed one of them alive to gather any useful information they might have had." She ignored Groegan's dismissive shrug, flittering about the carnage until she came upon the cadaver of a middle-aged man. Chunks of lung, stomach, and intestine dangled from exposed ribs splayed wide from the blast of a Barbarian's spell. Still, everything from the shoulders up looked to be intact. "This one will have to do."

As Groegan dragged the body to the edge of the campsite, and away from the other Barbarians, Meera considered how best to proceed.

Spirits called from another plane were compelled to carry out the orders of the Necromancer who summoned them into a physical vessel. But most were devious beings, relishing any opportunity to exploit ambiguities in the summoner's commands. Meera would be exhausted from her summoning spells, and from the past week of hard travel. She did not want to risk failing to uncover information vital to their mission. No. The Necromancer needed the assistance of a special spirit, one she had come to trust in such times of dire need.

The many summoning spells she would need to cast were complicated and required her undivided attention. While the Barbarian band worked to clean away evidence of their bloody deed, Meera went to work on the cadaver. After nearly an hour of incantation, she bent over the mangled body. "Spirit," she called.

The dead man's eyes opened and turned slowly toward the Necromancer. "Asheborne," he slurred, then smiled, though it looked more like a cringe.

"I need your assistance, dear friend, to know something about the one who owned this body."

The man's eyes looked down at the gaping hole in his chest. Fingers picked at the bloodstained entrails while it worked to call forth the dead man's memories. After several moments, he spoke. "He and his itinerant friends came here from the Narwales region of Griffinrock in search of gold."

"Good. I need to know if this man knew anything about any strange sightings, any reports he might have heard about a great flying creature. Perhaps he saw such a beast?"

The man's expression shifted, like dark clouds obscuring a clear sky. Finally, he rasped, "He saw no such creature. But there were rumors ... gossip from those he passed along the way ... sightings of black flying monsters."

"Where? Where were these sightings?" Meera urged the man, leaning closer, eager, not wanting to miss anything.

"Along the southern central region west of here. This man did not hold much faith in these strangers' lore, so he did not inquire further."

Meera nodded appreciatively. Placing her palm to the cadaver's forehead, she spoke softly to release the spirit back to its plane of existence. *"Ourera psychi apostelpsychi."*

Groegan, having heard the exchange, grunted at her back. "I do not understand this desire to put oneself at risk so recklessly over shiny metals. As my preceptor was fond to say, 'Strange are the ways of the Harmonics.'" He looked hard at Meera, then asked, "You trust this spirit's words?"

"I do." Meera stood and faced the Barbarian.

"So you would suggest we alter our course of action? You believe our path lies farther to the south?"

Meera hesitated, considering the spirit's words, then nodding. When Groegan did not respond, she decided to share a secret she had surmised about him. She knew she was taking a risk. But she had become close to him with her feelings the past week, a rare sensation for her, and she fancied he held a similar attraction. "Groegan, I know you are a soothsayer."

Groegan tensed as if she had called him an oathbreaker. "What do you mean?"

"I have watched how you interact with the other Barbarians," she said. "You are not like any Barbarian I have known—more aware of what is about you, more attuned to what lies beyond your senses, more ... grounded. A skilled Necromancer picks up on such things. I have known only one other as you—my Lady Breanen Sagamore, to whom I am devoted completely, counselor and wife to the Sovereign Prince of the Necromancers. She is renowned among my order as a clairvoyant of sorts, one who has access to knowledge others are not privy to. Before sending me on this mission, my lady told me that I might meet a man like her—someone in whom I should trust." Meera pointed to his chest. "And I know you wear a rare black gem attached to an amulet beneath your armor—one exactly like the stone my lady wears. I sense its power.

I mention this only because we should hold no illusions between us. I know now she spoke of you. So I ask you here, what path would you suggest we take?"

Groegan moved closer, his eyes hard on hers. "I say we continue as planned. I say Dragongarde is where we will find what we are after."

Meera ran her palm down his Alpslander overcoat and smiled. "Then that is what we shall do."

## One Plausible Explanation

"Just like the last two." Frustrated, Gertrum kicked at the elk carcass.

Morgas gazed at the vultures circling overhead. "We were fortunate this time to find it before any scavengers arrived. This one was killed late last night."

The guildmaster waved at the bloody mess. "Muscle and fat picked clean from the bones, with hide and entrails left untouched. We can be certain our carnivorous friend is picky about what parts he eats and what he leaves for others to sort through."

Annabelle scanned back up the narrow canyon, where the rest of their patrol waited. "None of this makes sense. There is only one set of tracks. A female elk would never willingly enter a blind pass alone."

Gertrum followed her thinking. "Given the length of her stride, she was chased or herded. Yet, there are no other tracks." Bending, he poked his thick thumb through a hole in the hide dangling from the hipbone. "These puncture wounds are from a creature with large talons. Our quarry is a huge bird of some kind. At least that matches the reports of a winged black monster."

"There is one flaw in your theory." Morgas squatted, then gestured for the other two to inspect the carcass closer. "These deep gashes along the bones are marks left by large teeth from ripping chunks of flesh away, not by a bird's beak. These marks, like the ones on the other carcasses, were made by our beast, and not by a scavenger after the kill."

"Well, I am sure there is a perfectly natural explanation for this." Gertrum waved at the confusing evidence. "There is yet a possibility two different kinds of creatures were involved in these kills."

Morgas laughed at the Scouter's suggestion. "What? A large cat riding on an eagle's back?"

Gertrum snorted, then scratched uneasily at his bearded chin while he struggled to find a better explanation.

Annabelle turned the discussion in a new direction with a question. "Gertrum, do you recall what you said to me when we first arrived at Elmsdorf? 'The difference between what we believe and what is real is often wider than this chasm.'"

"Yes, I recall. But we weren't talking about winged monsters then."

"No. We were talking about something just as implausible. My father was fond of saying, 'Certainty in one's beliefs is the enemy of truth.'"

"You aren't seriously suggesting ..." Gertrum started.

"I'm suggesting there is something significant going on here. And I'm suggesting we need to change our strategy if we want to discover what this creature is."

"Go on," Morgas nudged before Gertrum could debate her.

"Our goal is to determine if these dragon sightings are real, but our premise has been that there are no dragons. For the past five days, we have been chasing phantoms, reacting to each new report, splitting up our patrol to cover more ground. This is taking too much time, and unless we gain the luck of the Cosmos, that is unlikely to change." Annabelle pulled out the map they had made to track the sightings. "But what if we assume dragons *do* exist? We could draw new conclusions from what we know."

Morgas's tracking skills kicked in. "Which raises a whole new set of questions that could lead us down a different path."

Gertrum licked his lips. "Okay, I'll play along with your hypothesis for a minute. How do we fit the knowledge we have into such a theory?"

Annabelle ran her finger along the ink marks representing the known sightings. "First, we can assume we are dealing with one dragon. If there were more, we would have had more sightings, or at least different sightings occurring about the same time."

"Okay, agreed. So why would a dragon show up here? And why now?"

Annabelle raised her palm. "Let me continue. Second, there is a pattern to the sightings and animal killings. They started moving southwest along the southern edge of the mountains. Then they clustered for a week here. And now they are on the move again, this time northward. There is a clear pattern here, one I think we can predict. But it isn't so much the pattern that is interesting as it is the speed."

Gertrum scrunched up his face. "I don't follow."

"It is said that dragons were known to fly many miles in a single hour. Mountains would offer little if any impediment. Yet the general pace of our friend is that of a human."

"Wait," Gertrum urged. "Are you suggesting this dragon is traveling with someone?"

"I am merely offering a viable explanation for what we know. But this leads us to yet another conclusion." Annabelle chewed on her lip while considering what she was about to say. "There is only one rational explanation for why a dragon would be traveling with a human."

After a moment, Gertrum waved his arms as if warding off a vexatious spirit. "That's insane!"

"Is it? Really? Well, there is one more piece of information you must consider before you commit me to an asylum." Annabelle pointed at the map. "We are here; this is the current direction of the latest sightings …" She traced her finger northward. Tapping a point near the top of the mountain range, she studied the faces of the two men. "And this is Dragongarde, home of the once-great Dragonbonded."

Neither man could find the words to utter his disbelief.

Alone, Morgas gazed out at Hemera tilting toward the ragged snowcapped skyline to the west. Fog was settling in the valley below. Though a few scattered thoughts floated through his mind, he was as certain as the granite beneath his feet of a few things.

First, any doubts he had as to what they tracked were gone. Morgas was certain that the dragon they were tracking was what had been inside the cavern the day he'd nearly captured Vault, what had aided Vault in his escape later that night, what had injured Carlon Narkain, and what had been and still was in the company of the boy, Conner Stonefield.

That meant Vault, this Conner Stonefield, was one of the long-forgotten Dragonbonded. Morgas could not explain why, but he needed to find this boy, if for nothing more than to warn him of Lacerus. Something about the secretive grandmaster Assassin concerned him— concern not only for Vault's safety, but for the safety of everyone Morgas cared about. And therein lay his struggle. He had spent many years in the Anarchic Lands and had a great sense of connection to their natural way of life. Yet in the days since joining Gertrum's band, he had walked the trails with Ranger Loris, had seen the goodness in her heart, and through her words, was learning that the Harmonic ways also had merit. Morgas was running short on time; he would have to decide soon what to do with this knowledge. But for now, he would continue to hold his tongue.

The miniature projection of Ranger Loris holding the enchanted emerald ring wavered before Grandmaster Lanchus Lendfeather while he reflected on her report. "You are sure of this, Master Loris? I do not want to be embarrassed before Lady Kyles and the council over half-baked notions, yet I cannot sit on this news if it holds an element of truth."

"All the evidence points to only one plausible explanation, Commander," came the faint reply. "The sightings are almost certainly a dragon and its bonded human."

"Very well. You were correct to report this to me. Continue as you proposed."

"We should reach Dragongarde in less than a week. I will report again on what we discover." The Ranger's image bowed, then dissolved.

The grandmaster pressed his bony frame into the massive tree chair and drummed his fingers. He had considered recalling Ranger Loris and that gullible Scouter Smelterman, but after further deliberation, he'd concluded it best to give the two even more slack. How better to quench King Jonath's thirst for meaning about "an unknown but momentous event" than with a fantasy about a Dragonbonded? And when the Ranger's story did not pan out? How could he be held responsible for the imaginative psychosis of a tainted orderman?

Lanchus stepped spryly into the Scrying Chamber. He would contact the king of Griffinrock immediately with the news. Maybe his sights for becoming the next Griffinrock baron had been too low. With a little time to work out the details of his story, he would report to the Rangers Council as well. He could only imagine the pandemonium this tale would cause across the realms.

# Dragongarde

Conner had been absorbed with gloomy thoughts of dark ordermen for several hours when Layna's bond, Horasius, came to a sudden halt on a large, grassy bluff.

"We have arrived," Layna declared without fanfare, then dismounted.

"We have?" Conner blinked. He glanced around in confusion, as if waking from a long sleep. Fifty paces farther to the north, the bluff came to an abrupt end. In Hemera's late afternoon light, he could make out a large river basin beyond and far below. And farther was a vast expanse of thick, green forest. They had reached the high northern edge of the Dragon's Back Mountains, and the Borderlands. A steep rocky incline jutted sharply up to the east while another sloped gently down and away to the west. "This is it? I was expecting a city or a castle, or at least the remains of an ancient village."

"I'm sorry to disappoint you, Conner." Layna gave him an understanding smile. "We'll set up camp here and enter Dragongarde in the morning."

His mentor was being purposely cryptic again, and that annoyed him. Maybe she hoped the continuing mystery would keep him from dying of sheer boredom. Knowing that further questions would yield nothing productive, Conner slipped from Sara's back and helped prepare the camp for the night.

Later that evening, Conner returned to the fire. "I don't get it. What's up with Skye?" He waved his arm in the direction of the rocky ascent to the east. "He refuses to come over here. You'd think he was afraid of this place, but that's not possible."

Layna asked, "What are you sensing?"

Conner turned his thoughts inward. "He feels honor, or more precisely, homage toward this place."

"Yes. I had not thought of that, but it's understandable."

Conner shrugged his bewilderment.

"Dragons have a heightened sense of respect for all beings, things, and places historic. And have no doubt that this hallowed ground fills more than several dragonsong verses."

Conner studied the large bluff with what remained of Hemera's light. "It's only slightly more than a grassy knoll. What's so special about that?"

"For one, it is where Skye's father died."

Conner could not find the words to reply, so he squatted next to the fire. He wished he had been more attentive about Cronoan history, but he'd only studied it as a farmer's son, and freeman farming was far removed from realm concerns. Certain Layna was as tired of his questions as he wearied of Skye's, he chose to use his tongue for something more immediately gratifying—eating. He ladled hot stew made from roots and rations into his wooden bowl and filled his mouth.

Layna stepped around the fire and sat next to Conner. Ladling out a bowl for herself, she spoke. "Life was much different six hundred years ago. Yes, the Armistice of the Orders had solidified the six orders that survive to this day, but the Third Age following was a turbulent period. The War of the Orders in the Second Age had left the realms in disarray. And while the period of expansionism and the rebirth of the guilds in the sixth century helped, there was growing unrest, not between the orders as before, but within them. Soon, the monarchs discovered the order councils, mandated by the crowns under the armistice, had done little to stabilize their orders. Maintaining agreements with the six order councils was becoming increasingly difficult. This was the state of affairs when the first humans bonded with dragons.

"To be sure, those original Dragonbonded were a very powerful gaggle of youths. A collage of all the social classes, they were enigmatic and secretive. After bonding, most simply vanished from their homelands, never to be seen or heard from again. Of course all this heightens the mystery around them, the kind that imaginative souls use to fuel folklore and ballads. But except for the occasional story of another human-dragon bonding, life in the Seven Realms went on. That is, until fights broke out within the orders and rifts began to form.

"After the seven monarchs discovered Dragongarde here on this mountain, they sent emissaries to garner Dragonbonded support. The crowns hoped that respect for the elemental powers of the dragon-bonded humans would help hold the orders together. But hope eroded as negotiations stretched on for years. Nothing exists today to explain why it took so long, but in the end, an agreement was finally struck, including monarchic recognition of a seventh order, the legendary Order of the Dragonbonded.

"When the Anarchic War began, the Seven Realms were pulled into the conflict, and the monarchs were forced to choose sides. Griffinrock, Grenetia, and Elvenstein sided with the Harmonic faction, and the Harmonic Realms were born. The smaller realms of Gorgonia, Dristonia, Tanzanar, and Andorea to the east sided with the Anarchic faction to form the Assembly of Anarchists. With lines drawn, the Anarchists within the six orders declared secession and formed six new orders, the ones we now call the shadow orders.

"Those within the Order of the Dragonbonded attempted to resolve the growing unrest and keep a semblance of peace among the realms, but the damage had been done. An army of Anarchists marched on the royal castle of Grenetia, burning Darmascus to the ground and murdering the patriarch and most of his family, tipping the scales. So the Dragonbonded chose to side with the Harmonic Realms. Bands of Dragonbonded were dispatched to help defend the castles across Griffinrock, Grenetia, and Elvenstein. Castle dungeons were reworked and expanded to become living quarters for the dragons and their human bonds.

"The hundred years of war nearly annihilated what remained of our once-great Cronoan civilization. In the end, the Assembly of Anarchists amassed a vast army in the forests north of here in preparation for an all-out assault on Grenetia to the west. Only one obstacle remained in their path." Layna jabbed her spoon to the east. "Dragongarde. The home of the Dragonbonded had to be destroyed if the army was to ensure their supply lines to the east would not be severed. So the Anarchic army marched out across the vale below, now called the Valley of Souls, and laid siege on Dragongarde. And though the Dragonbonded were vastly outnumbered, they flew out and met them.

"The shadow orders in those days were very powerful in the use of elemental forces. Eventually, what remained of the Dragonbonded were driven back to this grassy knoll, as you called it. This is the place of the final battle, where the last of the human-dragon bonds died."

Layna pondered on Conner's long face and placed her hand lightly on his shoulder. "But their sacrifice was not in vain. The Anarchists had won the battle, but with severe losses. The Dragonbonded had destroyed the Anarchists' will to continue their campaign. Here, on this very spot, five hundred and fifty years ago, the Treaty of Alignment was signed by the seven monarchs, the heads of the six Harmonic order councils, and the six Anarchic order councils, formally recognizing the two factions, establishing the Borderlands as a neutral zone, and ending the Anarchic War.

"No one, not even those who despised and feared the Dragonbonded, could dispute the fact that the Order of the Dragonbonded, with their unwavering vow to defend the Harmonic

Realms, had brought about the end to the Anarchic War. That was the true legacy of the Dragonbonded. That is, until you showed up at Grimmley's door." Layna smiled with a mouth full of stew, then offered Conner a reassuring wink.

Conner stared into the flickering flames for a long time, mulling over Layna's history lesson until he could no longer keep his eyelids up. He thanked his preceptor, bade her good night, and tromped off to find a grassy spot to throw his pad. Lying under the brilliant night sky, he listened to Skye's guttural rhythmic dragonsong echoing down the incline from the east and wondered why humans did not bless their ancient fallen with similar regard.

The next morning, Conner woke to find the Sorceress standing over him wearing a peculiar expression. He bolted from his blankets, knees wobbling while he tried to clear sleep from his mind. "Many apologies, my lady. I have overslept." Exhaustion and lack of sleep was no excuse. "Grimmley has warned me many times that an orderman's day begins early," he admonished himself before his mentor obliged him with her own rebuke.

The Sorceress placed a firm hand on his arm to steady him. "Slow, Conner. You did not oversleep."

This gave him time to study the lines on her face. Her perpetually upturned lips had been replaced with an expression of ... concern. In an instant, Conner was fully awake. "What is it, then?"

Layna cleared her throat. "Early this morning, I received a message from my order's council. I am to return to Brightmead Estate at once to address them. I am sorry, but I must depart immediately."

Conner blinked, stunned. Behind Layna, Horasius was saddled and packed. A rope extended from the saddle, tied to a halter on Sara's head. "But Dragongarde—"

"Is in safe hands. This is your journey. I have complete confidence you will find your way."

"But …" Conner needed time to focus. He shook his head hard. So many questions clamored to be the first off his tongue, all afraid they might never get answered.

"Please understand. I would not leave you thus if I had a choice." She waited until she had his full attention. "There is something you need to know. It seems the Rangers Council has discovered your existence, or at least that of a human-dragon bond. No Orderman's Code could ever hope to contain such news. Word has spread like a brushfire throughout the six orders. I am my order's only scholar on Dragonbonded, so the council has turned to me to offer guidance while they consider the meaning of this untimely information. The sooner I arrive in Brightmead, the greater the chance I can contain the damage. But it is many days' ride from here."

Layna swung into her saddle, the urgency palpable. "I truly am sorry to leave you with this burden, Conner, but your days are limited before everyone across the realms knows of our secret. It is possible I can redirect the news, or impede its progress if you are endangered. Be comforted to know that I will do everything conceivable within the Code's boundaries to give you time. You are a brilliant lad. It is time to put that mind to good use."

"And Sara?" Conner felt the weight of a great trap closing around him. How was he to make it out of the mountains again? Or did she expect him to stay hidden here?

His mentor's incredulous stare and glance to the rocky cliff where a large black form warmed his body in the morning rays told him what she expected. "Do not concern yourself with Sara. My path will take me near Grimmley's home. She will be safely in her valley soon enough and in good health. Oh, and I almost forgot. One more thing." The Sorceress tossed Conner a thumb-sized rock hastily tied and hung from a thin strip of leather.

He dangled the rock in the morning light, noting small flecks of sparkling greenish mineral. "Oh, look! You made me a going-away present!" he retorted, and stared up at the hooded woman. He caught her slightly upturned lips. "What is this for?"

"Hopefully, nothing," came the expected cryptic response. "But keep it with you for a while." She adjusted her weight to ease her bond's trek down the long, winding slope. "Sometimes the best preparation for the path ahead is to just take it." And with grim determination and a nod farewell, she rode south.

Within moments, Conner was alone, staring at the winding path that had taken his preceptor. "Great! Just great! The first human to have mentors from *two* orders, and I get dumped by both of them!"

Conner waited until he was sure Layna was not going to reappear, laughing and telling him it was all a big joke. Then, with a sigh, he slipped the makeshift necklace around his neck, collected his few belongings, and hiked east to the rocky incline. "It seems we're on our own."

Skye added, "Again."

"Yes, well, do you suppose you could—"

"Find where the caverns are? Already done. There are a number of entrances along the vertical northern face of this mountain to our east. Inside, I detect a labyrinth of rooms and tunnels, but there is one large cavern not far below the mountain's crown. It is certainly the central quarters of this fortress."

"Then can you—"

"Find a way for you to get into the central room? I scouted ahead and found what appears to be the humans' entrance to Dragongarde. It is at the same elevation as the main hall."

"That's great, Skye." Conner was pleased with the dragon's initiative. "So then, will—"

"Will I direct you there? I can if you don't argue about where I guide you."

Conner decided it best not to start a quarrel so early in the day. It was clear the dragon's ego still smarted from their quest for Grimmley's silver box. He felt bad for his behavior that day, so he responded with a humble bow. "Then I leave the path of our expedition in your capable hands … er, claws."

Skye opened and closed his jaw several times as if considering whether Conner mocked him. Conner knew the wyvern was waiting for him to suggest they fly rather than take the precarious trail on foot, but such a request would not be forthcoming. Finally, with an emphatic "Humph!" Skye led Conner up the steep incline and through a maze of boulders and brush. The climb was slow at first, but soon the duo came upon a series of several hundred broad rocky steps ascending farther upslope. At the upper end, much to Conner's relief, the trail leveled out. Surveying the long staircase from the higher altitude, Conner noted a rockslide had destroyed the lower portion that had once extended to the grassy knoll below. Left to his own devices, it would have likely taken him days to find this path. Conner would have been grateful for his bond's talents if not for the fact that he would not even be in this situation if he had bonded with another creature. With no worthy excuse to dally, he followed Skye in silence.

Nearing a half hour of hiking, Conner's patience waned. Layna's warning ate at him, and he was eager to get started—with whatever lay ahead. But the wide trail snaked between massive boulders, trees, and shrubs, thwarting his attempts to predict how much farther they had to go. He was thankful when they rounded a boulder to find the trail's abrupt end under a large half-circular hole in the mountainside.

Without hesitation, they eagerly stepped through the portal. Inside, Conner waited to let his eyes adjust to the darkness. But the seconds were like hours, so he invoked Night Vision.

Conner blew air through pursed lips as he surveyed the room. If he had been expecting a grand ballroom or spacious auditorium, he would have been sorely disappointed, but as he'd had no expectations, he was only terribly discouraged by what he beheld. The circular room was large enough to hold at most fifty people, and then only if they did not mind getting very friendly. Several simple paintings and unrecognizable symbols adorned the roughly hewn walls. Remnants of what appeared to be wood chairs and tables littered the rock floor. Worn by over five hundred years of weather, they crumbled at his touch. Conner fought back a growing fear that the trip had been in vain. What was he supposed to do with this? How was this to help him?

Skye's deep voice echoed from the other side of the room. "Conner, maybe we should find the main hall. This antechamber is not worth our time."

"Antechamber," Conner spoke the word like he was trying on new shoes. "Of course." He shook his head, then barked a short laugh.

From the far end of the antechamber, the two proceeded down a long hall wide enough for Conner to walk next to his bond without worry of getting trampled. After fifty paces, the other end of the hall came into view. Fueled by anxiety, concern, and excitement, Conner's heart began to race. He picked up his pace, dwarfing Skye's sluggish step.

"Conner, wait. I think you—"

Conner sensed Skye's wariness. "We don't have time to worry about what kinds of animals live here, Skye. Besides, if we encounter anything deadly, I'm sure you can scare it away"—he flashed his black bond a mischievous smile—"or eat it."

"But Conner, you should—"

Skye never had a chance to finish the warning. A blinding flash exploded in front of Conner, followed by a loud pop that lifted Conner off the ground and snapped him back into Skye's chest with a thud. Moments passed before Conner could focus and hold more than a fleeting thought. "Maybe I should have taken it slower." Conner shook off lightheadedness, blinking up at the glowing blue eyes over him. "What was that?"

"It seems your predecessors decided an elemental shield was needed to protect the fortress from unwanted guests."

"I think it's still working." Conner sat up with a groan.

Skye snort-sniffed. "Yes. I can see the shield. I thought you could as well."

Conner squinted at the spot where he had been struck. "Nope. Maybe my Night Vision is blocking my sight. Can you do something about it?" Conner asked hopefully.

The dragon stepped forward, and after several minutes, gazed back at Conner. "Whoever erected this shield knew what they were doing. It appears to be designed to stop only humans." To prove his point, Skye stepped past the invisible shield, then turned to his bond. "Since it does not affect me, there is nothing I can do against it. It seems you will have to work through this on your own." He thought for a moment. "Though I can offer to guide you."

With a reluctant sigh, Conner crept closer. Recalling Grimmley's lessons, he let his consciousness slip from his physical senses and sensed the dancing patterns in front of him. "I see it!" He inched closer. He had expected the shield to be like a hard surface, impervious like a metal plate or stone wall, but the shield was soft, like a permeable cloth waving gently in an ethereal breeze. The iridescent surface shimmered though there was no light in the hall to reflect. "This is stunning, Skye. It's like it's alive."

"In a manner of speaking, Conner, it is. Elemental shields work much like sound and light. They can be created to have a natural modulation using a unique combination of elementals and tension in the weave. Dragons, humans—everything exists on a unique frequency. When something with the same frequency encounters the shield, it creates a resonance that feeds back on the shield. This shield is set to modulate at the frequency of humans. So when you interacted with it ..."

Skye noted Conner's gaping mouth and sensed his bond's confusion. "Let's see if we can get you through."

"Yes, thank you," Conner said with a grateful exhalation.

"First, you will need to find each of the shield's four elemental threads. Start by picking one of the threads, and take hold of it with your thoughts."

Conner wondered how a wyvern could know of such things. Adjusting his stance to fight back the doubt building in him, he followed his bond's bidding. Soon he could discern the threads weaving the elemental fabric. "Okay. I have one."

"Good," Skye nodded. "Which elemental?"

"Earth."

"Now you must grip another one, without releasing the one you have."

After a few moments, Conner flashed a triumphant grin. "I have Water." Anticipating Skye's next instruction, Conner was working to grip the next thread. But each time he got mentally close, his concentration on the other two waned, and his hold loosened. Skye waited until Conner continued with a strained crack in his voice. "I have Fire."

Skye extended his head and closed his eyes, clearing his mind of emotions that could prove distracting to his bond. "You are nearly there."

As Conner worked, he discovered holding four elementals simultaneously was like trying to drink from a goblet while wrestling Pauli, a sure way to get soaked *and* battered. Worse, Conner knew the three elementals he held from his studies under Grimmley and Layna. But he had never worked with Air, and it was proving to be quite elusive. He could sense the thread's presence, but he might as well have been trying to grasp fog. Conner was growing tired, his head throbbing. But he ignored the pain, recreating that same mental focus and intensity he'd had the day he'd scaled Cravenrock's wall. He studied the final thread—and a revelation came to him.

Each elemental exuded a unique sensation, like different foods having distinct flavors to the palate. In Fire was the sense of energy, a vision of constantly flickering light. He had come to know Water by its mutability, like something morphing to fit the shape of everything it touched. And Earth gave him a taste of stability, of permanence. Air activated a different quality, one of sound, light and spacious. Sight, touch, taste, and sound. The elementals worked off different senses. Conner knew what to do.

A moment later, triumphant if haggard, he declared, "I have all four!"

"Now push the threads together. You must force them to overlap."

Conner's inclination was to pull the threads apart, but so far Skye's directions had been sound, so he ignored the impulse. He closed the gap between the threads. They resisted his efforts. Ignoring the growing vibrations assaulting him, he willed them together. Abruptly the threads dissolved, and the elemental shield crumbled away. With a hint of surprise, he said, "I think I destroyed the shield."

Skye snort-sniffed at his naïve bond. "No, Conner. It is still there. But you no longer are affected by it. We now can explore the main hall." The dragon squinted down at Conner with excitement. "You did quite well."

Conner tried to recall a time in his brief time with Skye when the wyvern had actually given him a compliment, but nothing came to mind. With a satisfied smile, he stepped lively after the dragon and crossed the portal into the hall.

A moment later, Conner stood in awe. The main hall was as large, elaborately decorated, and stunning as the antechamber they had first entered had been small, sparse, and drab. The circular room measured well over a hundred paces in diameter. Around the wall were a number of other entrances of varying size, including a large entrance on the far end that offered more than adequate ambient lighting for the hall. Numerous tapestries, flags, and murals depicted the castles, people, and bonds of New Cronoan life six hundred years ago. Except for the many images of humans and their dragon bonds, the scenes looked entirely familiar. Above the wall, an immense domed roof with intricately painted false vaults and reliefs extended up to the ceiling's apex sixty paces overhead. It was clear the inhabitants of this ancient fortress cared more for their aesthetic senses than those of any stately guests they might have entertained outside. But that was not surprising given what he had heard of the reclusiveness of the Dragonbonded.

What was surprising was the condition of the tapestries and flags in this hall: they could have been made a year ago. The fortress's protective shield must have been preserving its contents.

The other surprise was the sheer spaciousness of the hall. There were no columns or other buttresses obstructing the enormous open room. Dragonbonded could have flown in and out of the cavern without fear of decapitation. For a moment, Conner stood lost in visions of young men and women on the backs of dragons swirling above in gleeful tourneys of tag like those depicted on the tapestries. Then he shook himself free of such childish fantasies. It was time to explore what lay beyond the other entrances.

In the midday hours that followed, Conner and Skye were able to visit only a fraction of the incredible web of rooms and corridors spiraling out and down from the main hall. Conner had always been keen at memorizing details, but he would have easily gotten lost in the maze if not for Skye's sharper sense of direction and location.

"I could swear we've been in this room a dozen times." Conner prodded a bed of thick straw with his boot as if he hoped it would fly out the gaping hole that lit the sleeping chamber.

Once more failing to catch Conner's flippant meaning, Skye responded. "We have only searched the lower, western section of the caverns. And this chamber is slightly smaller than the previous four." The wyvern eyed the human pacing about and added, "I don't see how we can explore this fortress any faster."

But it was more than impatience chewing knots in Conner's stomach. In Conner's mind, Dragonbonded had been living legends, heroes and defenders of Harmonic life, respected by monarchs, revered by the masses, and dreaded by the most powerful ordermen of the time. Yet they had lived like reclusive beggars in caves deep in the mountains. He could not fathom why they had chosen to live this way, and that made him irritable. More to the truth, he wondered if bonding with dragons had somehow driven them mad. Would he be so inclined one day, content living out his years in such conditions? He kicked the straw bedding again and walked on through the next entrance.

Shortly, they entered a long hallway that was, according to Skye, near and at the same elevation as the main chamber. Wooden racks constructed from oak logs ran down both sides of the room. To their right, large black leather saddles hung in meticulous formation with odd symbols above each one. To the left ran an uninterrupted line of black full-body suits. Conner pointed to the right. "I think those would fit you better than me. Just don't get yourself in a ruffle thinking you're going to get me to sit in one of them."

Skye snort-sniffed while eyeing the saddles. "And do not fool yourself thinking I am going to stop trying."

Conner wagged his head despondently. The emotional link he shared with Skye offered meager help in getting through to the beast. He strolled past most of the uniforms before his curiosity became unbearable. He lifted a suit from the rack. Finely tailored for a man his size, the uniform was made of highly polished leather, layered and thick though amazingly light. Shards of dragon scale were tightly stitched into the shoulders and lower neck, forearms, hips, knees, and shins. The buttocks and inner thighs were padded with coarse hide. A bright crimson dragon was sewn over the heart.

In the silent moments that followed, Conner understood the significance of what he held. The suit had belonged to, and been worn by, one of the legendary Dragonbonded. Everything—the fortress, the elemental shield, the chambers—could have been elaborate fabrications, like stage props in a historical play. But to Conner, the suit he held was proof—the Dragonbonded were more than folklore. He reverently returned the uniform to its rack and moved on in search of something more useful.

Conner could not discern whether the device they discovered in the adjacent chamber was useful, but it was most certainly bizarre and mysterious. The cylindrical apparatus sat on a short table in the center of a small, circular room, sandwiched between two ornately carved mahogany chairs. A number of unrecognizable markings, similar to all those adorning nearly every wall and mural of the fortress, were embossed across the wood base. He slipped into one of the chairs to marvel at the device's workmanship.

Upon the base rested a precisely balanced golden wheel with a diameter the length of Conner's forearm, formed into the design of the Cosmic Star. Intricate swirling patterns had been meticulously carved or sheared into each point of the star. And embedded near the tip of each point was a thumbnail-sized gem. Ruby, diamond, sapphire, and emerald—each flawlessly cut and polished, sparkling even in the meager light offered by the small hole at Conner's side.

Skye thrust his way in, though the room was clearly not intended to hold a dragon. After examining the contraption and the tapestries on the walls depicting people studying the device, he offered another tidbit of dragon insight. "Humans truly are peculiar creatures. Maybe that is why they create such wondrous things. What is this object for?"

Conner shrugged and gestured at the walls. "The best I can tell, it is some kind of game Dragonbonded played. But I cannot discern the goal or how it was played."

Skye twitched with disappointment, already wiggling about to escape the cramped space. "Such diversions and toys are for guivre. Real games are played outside, climbing along cliffs and dancing in the clouds."

"Each of us has a different idea of entertainment, Skye," Conner called out before his bond could vanish back up the long hall. Left alone, he pondered the meaning of the Dragonbonded peculiarities. They were cave-dwelling hermits living in unpleasant conditions far from any social life. They'd left behind no books, parchments, scrolls, or writings beyond the indecipherable symbols, tapestries, and murals ornamenting every room. And the only valuable item he discovered seemed to have been used for amusement.

Just past dusk, Conner found Skye at the northern entrance of the central hall, looking out on the Valley of Souls. He sat down on the ledge not an arm's length from the dragon, letting his feet dangle over the edge. The scenic night view, the lake reflecting the bright stars above, was beyond any vision of beauty he could have imagined possible. Conner was not sure why, but Karlana Landcraft's voice came to him, and he recalled something she had said the day he attended her lesson on bonding. *Yes, Conner, you especially will do well with your bond. The important thing to remember is that there are no exceptions to the Cosmic Laws. Do not fight your connection.* Softly, he asked, "Skye?"

"Yes, Conner?"

"The dragonsong you sang last night, the one honoring the dragons who died here, can you teach me to sing it?" In the silence, Conner could feel the force of emotions flowing from his bond, weaving a mental tapestry. Dragons possessed an incredible range of feelings.

Skye's head swiveled in Conner's direction, and with double slits forming over his glowing orbs, dipped slightly. "I would be honored."

That night, the two sat on the ledge overlooking the Valley of Souls, not as bonds, but as tutor and student. Conner knew dragons learned by mimicking their elders, so he had to convince Skye he needed instructions. Skye labored to teach Conner the numerous nuances of the dragonsong, delightedly snort-sniffing at each of his human bond's mistakes and patiently offering both encouragement and correction.

Conner quickly discovered the challenges he faced. Dragonsongs were different from human songs in two ways. Once he could recite the dragon words and understood their meaning, Conner discovered the first difference—with a few minor adjustments, he could sing of honor and praise also to the Dragonbonded who had fallen on the plains below. This led him to suggest that they alter the dragonsong slightly to include the humans. But his proposal was met with the fierce obstinacy that only a dragon could muster. Skye would not even entertain the thought of changing a single word, and he was resolute on the matter. Conner refused to let any of this deter him. After a heated exchange and some colorful name-calling, Skye elected to ignore his student and instead enlighten him on the second peculiarity of dragonsongs.

Dragonsongs had no melodies. Tonal inflection, the only semblance of a dragonsong melody, came from the feelings of the singer. The same dragonsong sung angrily or sadly had different tonal qualities, and thus completely different meanings. This meant that, with the variety of emotions dragons possessed, the same song could convey an infinite variety of meanings.

Stuck on wanting to include the Dragonbonded, another round of arguments ensued. In the end, the two struck a compromise. They would leave the words intact, but instead alter the tones to convey honor for the dragons and their human bonds. Exhausted and nearly hoarse from shouting, and with the sky lightening in the east, Conner stood next to Skye, and together they sang. Conner let his link with the dragon guide his inflections, the human's throaty sounds weaving and resonating harmonic overtones on the dragon's deeper voice. The hall became their instrument, and soon, their song echoed down the immense vale below.

After the dragonsong was complete, Skye simply nodded.

Conner could not recall a time the dragon had not possessed the ability to express whatever thought or feeling was on his mind. But after a few awkward moments, Conner nodded to Skye, patted his scaly shoulder, and walked back into the hall to find some rest.

Sleep did not stay with Conner for long. By noon, he was up. He devoured a ration in silence while Skye twitched and snorted in some dreamscape. His mind was awash with the haunting images of Dragonbonded on the murals, tapestries, and paintings calling to him. He retraced his path back to the room with the device.

Later that day, Skye woke himself with an audible snort and stifled a leisurely yawn. He smacked his lips to ward off an angry, empty stomach, though his efforts were in vain. Hemera was drifting into the western sky. Conner was at the main hall's entrance, staring in deep contemplation at the vale below. The dragon sensed the fluxes in his bond's emotions. "Conner?"

Conner faced him. He was wearing one of the Dragonbonded suits and a broad smile. "Thank you, Skye."

"Hmm?" The dragon blinked. Was he still asleep? Had he finally found that altered state of blissful consciousness he had been seeking back in the cave when he met Conner? Or had the very creature that had shaken him from those elusive dreams now delivered what he had stolen by waking him so abruptly? Maybe there was truth in the dragonsong of the Dragonbonded!

Conner continued on the tail of Skye's thought. "Since the night after our bonding, you have shown nothing but patience and understanding. All this time, I have been caught up in my own problems, fighting my own demons, and failed to appreciate how you have always been there. I could not have asked for a better friend nor been blessed with a better bond. I am proud to be bonded with such a mighty creature. The Cloudbenders are truly a great race."

Skye visibly relaxed. "I have been waiting a long time to hear you say that." But he understood Conner was not done, so he waited.

"I've been looking at this all wrong."

"At what, Conner?"

"This." Conner's gesture encompassed the entire fortress. "I have always dreamed of a time when there would be no more wars, no more bloodshed, no sadness and pain, no more destruction. But in those childhood visions, I was a simple Eastland farmer. I lived on the fringes of that dream, a victim of some Cosmic story playing out, an anonymous byline or footnote in its passing. I was an observer too weak to influence the world around me. I believed if I lived a good life, and focused on helping those in my community when they were in need or sick, then the world would get along fine."

Skye shifted his position uneasily. "And now?"

"Grimmley and Layna believe I possess the power to be something more. They keep telling me if I learn to harness the abilities of the Dragonbonded, then I can direct and shape the future of the realms. Layna believes I can choose what is to come, write my own story. And if that is true"—Conner thinned his lips—"then it is time I tossed away the notion I have to become what they want me to be. It is time I embrace the unknown, and possibly the unknowable. We may never discover what these people, and their dragon bonds, were about. And for the first time, I don't really care. I cannot be one of the ancient Dragonbonded. And I don't have to try. There will be many who will see me as they imagine the Dragonbonded to have been, expecting me to be something I'm not, if only because you and I are bonded. I can't help that. I can only be true to myself."

Skye exhaled and nodded. "What do you suggest we do?"

Conner felt filled with the dragon's sudden pride. "I think it's time we find you a saddle so I can learn how to dance in the clouds. Once Erebus rises, we fly back to Grimmley's for a long-overdue chat."

# Fortress Sanctuary

**"W**ill you *please* take it slow this time?" Conner gripped two leather rings woven into the front of the saddle he straddled, the one now cinched tight around Skye's girth. His head whipped side to side as his bond waddled towards the main Dragongarde entrance.

"I cannot help it, Conner. I am excited," Skye boomed back.

"*That* I can sense." Memories of them flying across the Aradorm gorge came rushing at him—literally. "I just don't get it," he went on, in hope that talking might distract him from his growing angst. "What could possibly be so exciting about having me sitting in a saddle strapped to your back? Personally, I find it a touch peculiar that such a proud creature as you would want anyone or anything riding you like this."

Skye hesitated, teetering on the edge of the entrance as he considered Conner's question. "I do not know. I cannot explain it. It is as if I was meant to have someone on my back. It just *feels* right."

"Well, I am certain I wouldn't want someone dangling off my shoulders."

Skye craned his neck about to study Conner. "Maybe I like it because it is the only way I can be in control."

Through their link, Conner sensed the dragon's emotional shift, one he now knew to be quirky dragon humor. "Thinking of myself as a hostage to your whims doesn't exactly instill confidence in what we are about to do, you know."

Skye snort-sniffed his pleasure. "Then why did you change your mind? Until a few hours ago, you were certain you would never climb on my back again."

Conner gazed down, measuring the distance to the valley far below—half a mile at least, thrice the height at the gorge. He chewed on his lower lip. "Because I can't let doubts rule my life forever. Moving forward is going to require that I take risks I'm not accustomed to. I'm hoping this will help me better understand those who came before. Critiquing their eccentric lifestyle certainly hasn't helped. Besides"—Conner stared back into Skye's sea-blue eyes—"at least this time I have a saddle to hold me in place."

Skye took the awkward silence that followed as his cue. The dragon unfurled his wings and gently pushed away from the ledge.

Conner clamped his eyes shut. There was a sudden dip and his stomach lurched into his throat. But just as quickly, the feeling vanished. He recalled how he had tapped into his connection with Skye the evening he had assisted the two Rangers at Pennington Point. In his mind, he found that emotional conduit, a shearing ray of light. It called to him, and he stepped into it. Just as that night, his fears abated.

Skye zigzagged lazily over the valley north of Dragongarde. With each successive pass, the dragon's maneuvers became more dramatic. He would tilt his wings back, and the two rose higher over the green expanse of grass and sparse trees, until Conner was certain he could touch the clouds overhead. Then the dragon's wings would tilt forward, and they would descend gently back.

As they flew, Conner began working out hand and leg signals with Skye so that he did not have to yell over the roaring wind. This was not to say the two did not have their disagreements over who should be in control of their direction, speed, and height. Sometimes Skye would become filled with dragon rapture and forget Conner was even back there. But in time, Conner discovered that when he listened to his bond, they actually were of like minds. With considerable patience and some give-and-take, even dealing with dragon stubbornness, they were able to work through their differences. Conner was reminded why Grimmley had sent them on the quest to find the silver box and realized the old Shaman had been right all along. The two just needed to find a way to work together. Conner took mental note to be sure to thank Grimmley when he had the chance.

Conner was so focused on flying that he was surprised when Hemera dipped below the western mountains and the valley below turned dark. He had completely lost track of time. Conner tilted forward and tapped Skye's shoulder with his left toe.

His bond tilted right and the two began the long journey south to Grimmley's cottage.

Along the way, Conner watched the sky turn dark. And soon, more stars sprinkled the clear, ink sky than Conner had ever seen. Erebus, its half-face sliding slowly into the west, bathed the snowcapped mountains with a soft, muted glow.

Like a flicker of distant lightning, Conner's mind was filled with a vision of Caralynn, the young Ranger apprentice he had met in Pennington Point. He thought it odd that her image would invade his thoughts at this particular moment, yet there was something about the apparition that gave him pause.

Skye sensed Conner's abrupt feelings of concern. "What is it, Conner?"

"Caralynn. She is hurt ... or in distress. I don't know how, but I feel her anguish. And she is not far away." Instinctively, he found himself urging Skye with heel and toe. Conner sensed Skye's reservations, knew the dragon balked at the madness of his words. Still, the dragon said nothing. "Please, Skye," Conner nudged him again.

Silently, his bond turned east.

A few minutes later, the horizon ahead was awash with the faint radiance of castle lights. "There," Conner shouted, and tapped Skye's scaly neck to pick up speed.

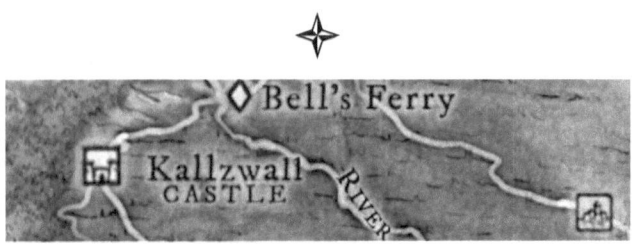

Veressa was in torment. During summer visits to Kallzwall as a child, she had grown to cherish the scenic view from the upper levels of the castle's noble towers. But now, the scene, with a waxing Erebus burning low in the clear night sky, did little to quell her anguish. More than a week since leaving Cravenrock, nearing three since departing Graystone on her bonding quest, and still she resisted returning home. In the morning, she would beg Marcantos for yet another day of rest before starting the final leg of their journey, but she knew what his answer would be. With only half their travels complete, her new protector was tired of her frail excuse of injury. Veressa was learning how soft Annabelle had been in dealing with her demanding ways.

The thought of Annabelle brought another throb to her temple, and she rubbed at the wound she'd received while bonding, one that seemed it might never completely heal. She needed her dearest Ranger friend and preceptor more than ever before. Undeniable changes were stirring in her. How could she face her mother and father before she made sense of what was happening? They could see through her like no one else could, and would question her until she broke. Only she had no answers. And if they drew from her what little she knew, would they question her sanity?

But more than being accused of madness, Veressa could not face her mother knowing she had failed to live up to the queen's standard of perfection. How could she ever fulfill her responsibilities to her people if she was busy fulfilling her own selfish desires? Her mother would have been strong enough to fight off such desires, and would surely see Veressa's behavior as dereliction of duty. Tears of shame flowed while the questions continued unabated. Was she ready to accept what awaited her back in Graystone, knowing her parents would never allow her to continue her nighttime escapades? What would happen to her cut off completely from those adventures? If she was not already insane, surely that would drive her there.

In the silent void, the night sounds from the countryside below called to her again, a craving tugging at her spirit. She shivered and pulled her robe tight, though the air was warm and dry. Only here, high in this fortress sanctuary, had she been able to find refuge from her desires.

At least one person had offered her hope. She did not know how Friarwood had sensed the restlessness stirring in her or her ability to control Earth and Air elementals—something only a Ranger should have detected. She had brushed aside her distrust for the man, and when several of his suggestions had proven useful, she had reached out for further guidance, more out of desperation than want.

Suddenly, a new thought stole her attention, one that shook away her worries. No, not a thought, and not a memory, but a presence—the presence of the young Eastlander she had met in Pennington Point. What was his name? Conner Stonefield. That night was like a dream she had had long ago. Thoughts of him often filled the corners of her mind since the night he'd helped her and Annabelle escape the town. She turned toward her bedchamber door, half expecting the young man to simply walk through. She shook her head and laughed at the foolish notion.

Instinctively, Veressa spun again, this time scanning the horizon to the west. There, she caught movement, a glittering mist of cobalt blue, sparkling like tiny sapphires floating in the sky, beating, growing ever larger. Suddenly, the stars flickered out of existence and she staggered back. She felt Antilles's soft fur against her thigh, soothing her from crying out before the great beast that had descended upon her balcony. Large unfurled wings steadied two massive clawed feet perched precariously on her banister. She heard the hard rush of air, felt the hot blasts of steam across her face, smelled the intense odor of sulfur. The sides of the creature's barrel chest heaved from the exertion of flight. Piercing intelligent eyes seemed to hold her gaze as she marveled at the magnificence of the creature's wondrous size.

Astride the beast sat a tall, thin man dressed in black, rocking rhythmically with each hard blast of the beast's breath. He gripped no reins nor other means of steering the savage aerial steed. She could sense the man's eyes boring into her, as if peering into her mind.

"Caralynn?" A familiar voice echoed across her balcony.

*Conner? Riding a dragon?* Veressa squinted up at the human apparition hidden among the shadows of her bedchamber lights. She shook her head, palm pressed to the knot behind her temple. She felt lightheaded and disoriented. The floor spun beneath her. She was indeed going mad! The world churned into empty grays, and she slumped to the cool marble at her feet.

"Caralynn!" Conner jumped from the saddle and ran to where she lay.

"You know this female?" Skye asked, his sides heaving from the extended flight.

"Yes." Hovering over her, Conner noted her night clothing, far more exquisite than any he would expect a Ranger apprentice to be wearing. Her hair was no longer braided as a Ranger. Conner looked around them. They were near the top level of one of Kallzwall Castle's towers; that much was certain. And given their location ...

"Well, Skye ... maybe I don't know her after all."

"What does that mean?"

"It means that everything I observe about her now contradicts what she—and her Master Ranger preceptor—told me she is."

Skye snorted his disdain. "More deceptions. It seems your kind is afflicted with the disease."

Conner knew Skye referred to Grimmley withholding information before sending them on their quest. "It seems so." Conner bent down and pulled Caralynn's unconscious body toward him. He gently checked her head and shoulders for injuries. He found a slight bump near her temple, from a recent wound. He could sense it was causing her pain, though again, he could not discern how he knew. In one of Grimmley's lessons, the Shaman had tried to teach Conner an advanced spell using Earth and Fire to heal such a wound. As usual, Conner had failed miserably at casting the incantation. But then, Conner had an inspiration. Recalling how the protective shield around Dragongarde was a weave of elementals, he began forming an Earth and Fire weave near Caralynn's wound, following the general idea of how Grimmley's spell was supposed to work yet without trying to force the energies to combine. He did not hold much hope that his therapy would have any effect, and there was a chance someone nearby might detect his use of elementals. But Caralynn's safety took precedence.

The Ranger visibly relaxed in his arms, color returning to her cheeks, but she did not awaken.

Conner suddenly became aware of how warm and soft Caralynn felt in his arms. He recalled the exhilaration he had felt that night in Pennington Point when he had wrapped his arms around her, protecting her from the Sorcerer's binding spell. Conner smiled at the memory.

"What is this feeling I am sensing in you, Conner?" Skye cranked his head forward and looked at his bond sidelong.

A flash of embarrassment flooded over Conner. "I don't know what you mean," he answered, unable to find a more fitting defense for the attraction he was feeling for the Ranger apprentice.

Skye snorted. "Deception, it seems, is contagious."

"Don't be absurd. I'm just worried for her safety." Skye was quickly becoming adept at seeing through Conner's thin skin of rational thinking, and that was very worrisome. One's emotions should be private. He certainly did not like being bonded to a creature who could critique not only his actions, but his every feeling as well, especially when he was at a loss to explain them. "I can't just leave her here on the cold balcony floor. But then, if she is as important as I suspect, it would be unseemly for me to be carrying her inside her bedchamber as well."

Skye snorted. "You think too much, Conner. If the right thing to do is to take her inside, then take her inside. And then we can be on our way. I am weary and grow hungry."

"And we both know how you get when that belly of yours has been empty for too long." When Conner scooped Caralynn up into his arms, the Ranger apprentice flung her arm over his shoulder and nestled into his embrace, though her eyes never opened. Conner's face flushed. With the sounds of Skye snort-sniffing at his back, he carried Caralynn inside and placed her in her bed, pulling the silk sheets over her.

*One thing is sure*, he thought as he stepped back out on the balcony, the night air cooling his burning cheeks, *I will never speak of this to anyone. Ever.*

# Old and New Wounds

"**V**eressa and her entourage reached Kallzwall Castle yesterday morning," Jonath announced with a touch of relief.

"They're making better progress than expected." Izadora entwined her arm in his and nodded. Their bonds had taken their customary perches outside the bedchamber, heralding the royal couple's approach up the long hall. "I guess her new protector is working out after all."

"I wouldn't know." Jonath waited for the queen's full attention, then continued. "Our daughter is not talking to anyone, least of all to her new protector."

The queen's step faltered, so he pressed on. "Oh, things started out all right between them, but with each passing day, Veressa becomes more reclusive, spending more time only with her bond. She hardly speaks to anyone."

Izadora flashed him her worried-mother look.

"What did you expect?" he asked the queen.

"Veressa has been gone a while," the queen answered softly, to hide her growing stress.

Nearly two fortnights—Jonath could not recall a time their daughter had been away so long. Izadora also missed the princess. But even more, the queen was starved for understanding. "Tomorrow, you can use the Scrying Chamber to interrogate her personally."

"Interrogate? You think that is what I want?"

"I think you want answers. But if you're expecting them to come easily from our daughter, you should set that notion aside. She is angry I dismissed Annabelle. Our daughter blames herself for this misfortune and me for the consequences. Maybe you should consider it a blessing she is not here exacting her wrath on any who visit her with a greeting."

Izadora grunted, but did not argue the point. "At least she is healthy, bonded, and returning home."

The king wondered whether he had chosen Veressa's new protector wisely. But he would address that concern with the queen on a different occasion. Instead, he chose another stream of thought. "Have you considered my petition to go lightly on changing the Rangers Order status within the realm? The Rangers Council did well in selecting Annabelle as the girl's protector. It would be unjust to censure the entire order for Cosmic events and our own child's foolishness."

"I should not have to remind you that taking no action against the Rangers Order could be perceived as favoritism and would surely offend the councils of the other five orders. The realm has many pacts with them, Jonath. Would you have me jeopardize those stable relations because of one person? Besides, the Rangers Council understood the risks when they agreed to offer a protector, though it is beyond me why you refused to consider a different order. They have received many years of benefit from that pact."

Jonath reached out and, placing his palm on Izadora's shoulder, shoved her roughly behind him.

"What ...?"

The king gestured up the empty hall. "The guards—" Jonath looked for them, but saw only motion from a narrow side hall. *"Aethra energi plattosfaira,"* he whispered, and an elemental sphere of Air and Fire flared to life around the couple.

The blackness separated from the flickering shadows of the side hall, knowing the king would not miss the movement. He sensed the force of Air as Jonath raised an elemental sphere of protection, effectively severing the intruder from the royal couple ... and sealing them in the middle of the hall.

The form moved forward, his lethal trap already sprung.

Jonath heard the faint metallic click over his left shoulder and knew he'd reacted too late. He spun, saw the flash of a thin needle from the mechanical device attached to the wall, and felt the bee sting. Poison coursed swiftly through his body. He wanted to pluck the steel spine from his neck, but his arms would not respond, nor would words of alarm take form. His legs went numb, and the king crumpled to the stone floor.

A different spell would have given his beloved a chance to retreat back up the hallway. But his mind worked sluggishly, and a better spell would not come without an incantation on his swollen tongue. Hopelessly committed, all he could do was hold the elemental forces he had summoned and wait for help to arrive. He fought to remain lucid, but his grip on consciousness was already weakening.

The black-cloaked figure floated into the dim light of the hall and pushed back its hood. Jonath beheld the face that had haunted his thoughts through many years.

Izadora watched Jonath tense and spin, saw his knees give way to gravity. She clutched her king to her bosom in horror, refusing even to let go when his weight pulled her to the cold floor with him. Struggling to comprehend what had happened, lost in his distant gaze, she did not see the shadow move stealthily into the light. But she did not fail to notice the recognition in her husband's gray eyes.

Hector Dellrose reveled in his triumphant return to Griffinrock. He had fought the Mystic Jonath before, and had spent the many years since studying the king. He understood how the man thought, knew his every weakness. He had picked this very spot knowing Jonath would make the fatal error of casting a spell that would prevent the queen's escape. The Champion's elemental sphere had become their tomb. Hector stepped into the light and looked into Jonath's eyes, his exalted laughter echoing down the empty hall.

Izadora glanced up. Though Jonath's spell distorted the air around them, she could not mistake the face of the man towering near. "You!"

"I told you we would meet again, Majesty. And here we are—the queen, her Champion, and his avenger."

Izadora took in the black cloak, the long bands of vertical braids that had once run horizontal. "How could you? You swore an oath to protect me. You were a decorated Defender of the Realm, a grandmaster Ranger. Now ..." She could go no further.

"Yes, Majesty, now I am a *dark* Ranger, an Assassin. Everything changed when you let this man deceive you."

Hector's words called up old, forgotten wounds, ones that had nearly put the Rangers and Mystics at war, yet Izadora would ever defend her Champion's honor. "Jonath fought within the rules of the tourney. All the orders, including yours, agreed!"

"The Tourney Council would have done anything to avert a war between the two orders. I should have been your Champion! But you let your love for this fool blind you, and you fell for his deceit. And me?" The Assassin held his arms out wide and looked to the ceiling. When he spoke again, his voice was softer, almost sad. "I was shamed by my order for having lost what should have been mine. But that was many years ago, Majesty. People change ... and mistakes change people." The old Ranger saying had never sounded so sinister.

Hector tapped on the sphere of Air and Fire and was rewarded with a weak spark. Jonath's shield was dissolving. It would not hold much longer.

Izadora rose on trembling legs, struggling to think. She was not trained in fighting tactics. Still, a desperate plan formed.

She looked up at Tyresus on his perch, knowing he could sense her growing stress. If the timing was right, maybe she had a chance. If her bond could distract the Assassin ... The goshawk took wing, moving swiftly up the hall. She stepped closer to hold the dark orderman's gaze, tensing, ready to run. "Yes, Hector, people change. And as you have shown, some for the worse."

Tyresus's wings opened, his body tilting back. Sharp talons shot forward.

At the last moment, the Assassin spun. His blade flashed in the dim light.

Izadora cried out and staggered, clutching the side of her head. Her knees went weak and she fell next to her husband again. Her eyes went to Tyresus, the goshawk's severed head and wing next to its twitching, bloodied body. And she sobbed.

"Did your husband ever tell you why he pushed you to approve a Ranger as your daughter's protector, regardless of the fact that there were more capable ordermen in the other orders?"

The queen shook her head to clear away the dizziness. The Yearning already gripped her, clouding her thoughts, confusing her. Tears pooled on her chin and dripped softly on her husband's chest.

Hector interpreted her reaction as an answer. "Of course not. And you were too infatuated with this serf to ever ask." He tested the elemental sphere again, impatience growing, his taste for blood palpable. "Remorse is a powerful emotion to those who break with their principles, don't you think, Majesty? Your husband knew how the

Rangers Council abused me in the days after the tourney. He chose a Ranger to cleanse his sin." The black cloak shook. "I suppose it was his way of finding balance for his guilt. Isn't that the Harmonic way?" The Assassin spat the question.

Izadora heard Jonath's labored, painful breaths, each giving her one more precious moment to draw hers. Even with death's call, her Champion fought for her. She peered deep into his gray eyes, and like she had so many times before, she found strength. Izadora pulled the ruby-studded dagger from the sheath at Jonath's side, and the queen of Griffinrock rose defiantly before the Assassin, teeth clenched and bared. At least she would be with her husband soon.

Hector was forced to admire the queen's tenacity. But he had never considered her capable of such anger. The snarling, tear-streaked face of the woman in Harmonic monarch's clothing left him with a rancid taste in his mouth. He sneered back. The king's spell would surely have alarmed someone. All he wanted was to be done with this assignment.

The Assassin called upon Air and Earth. *"Aerora stoicheiodis plattodory,"* he said softly, then sliced through what remained of Jonath's spell. The elemental dome crumbled into wispy gold flakes. Stepping over the forgotten form of the former serf, Hector raised the short silver blade still dripping with goshawk blood. A bitter revenge was better than none at all.

# Unfortunate News

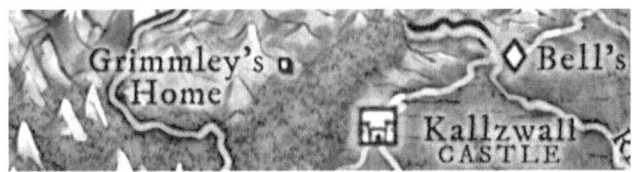

Grimmley woke to the delightful smell of eggs frying in butter and the soothing hum of an enthusiastic chef. He slipped his wire glasses over his nose and glared at his guardian bond for her dereliction in duties.

"I instructed Barthox to let you sleep," a voice called from the kitchen below.

Vindicated, the owl glared smugly at the Shaman and winked before making a speedy exit through the kitchen window.

The Shaman shuffled from his bed and clambered down the stairs grumbling about conspiracies in his own home, but settled at the table to watch his young apprentice put the final touches on the morning banquet. "You've been watching me cook."

"Told you." Conner grinned. "I'm a quick study."

"Apparently so. Didn't I just get rid of you?" Grimmley sighed. "And I was just starting to get used to the quiet again. What happened? And where is Layna?"

Conner hesitated with a spoonful of tea dangling over a steaming teapot. "We arrived at Dragongarde two nights ago, but yesterday morning, the Sorcerers Order called Layna back. She took Sara and rode south, leaving me to deal with the dragon alone."

"Called her back? She would not have left you unless it was absolutely imperative."

Conner's lips thinned. "She said the orders know that we ... well, that a human-dragon bond exists. It seems our secret is out."

The Shaman gave the young man in the skintight black suit a quick appraisal while the boy emptied hot eggs onto waiting plates, then leaned back. "Then it is good you found the back of your dragon," Grimmley stated with a good bit of satisfaction. He was eager for more news, but inquisitions did not settle well with the lad, so he filled his mouth and let his questions wait their turn.

The food vanished from the table while Conner described the previous day's events. He began with how they had found the entrance to Dragongarde and discovered a powerful shield of energy around the fortress that left its contents untouched by time. He then proceeded into describing their exploration of the massive labyrinth of halls and rooms. Grimmley was sure Conner was leaving details out, but determined it best to let the boy lead. At last, Conner pulled a tube from a leather satchel and unrolled a number of parchments covered with charcoal sketches.

Grimmley confirmed Conner's suspicions. "Modeic symbols."

"Yes, but what do they mean?"

Grimmley tapped a forefinger to pursed lips. "Deciphering Modeic writings is not about translating symbols. This glyph"—the Shaman pointed at an abstract drawing of a tree—"could have different meanings depending on the glyphs around it. And similar-looking glyphs can have quite different meanings. That is why it was a century before the early cleric scholars broke the Modeic code." The Shaman watched the boy's face grow long, so he added, "I can teach you, as all ordermen are taught. A smart whip like you could be reading Modeic glyphs in a year."

"A year," the lad acknowledged, but he made it sound more like a lifetime. And given the duress he was under to make progress,

Grimmley was certain it felt that way. "Grandmaster, I've never told you how much I admire you."

The Shaman flinched at the sudden change in winds. "I'm not sure what you mean. You've been more than appreciative for what little I've done to help."

"I mean your lifestyle. Living here ... alone ... in this garden you built helping people and animals in need."

"Ahh." The old man's head bobbed. "My life of leisure and contentment, you mean." He chuckled, but his facetiousness was lost on his fledgling apprentice.

"Yes, Grimmley. You never adopted the way of life others expected of you—whether it was from Apothecary guildmasters or the Shaman Dons. You set your own path, lived the life that suited you best."

"And where is this all going?" Grimmley asked.

"I don't think the life of the Dragonbonded is for me, Grimmley—at least not how they lived before. I've been to their fortress, seen how they lived. It's nothing like what I imagined it would be." Conner wagged his head. "That doesn't feel right to me."

"I see. You learned all this in one day, did you? Well, all that is well and good unless the Cosmos has a different plan for you."

In the silence that followed, Grimmley could sense the boy was warming to the notion that the Cosmos had a plan. But whatever Conner was about to say, he never got the opportunity.

Barthox swooped through the window and landed on her perch, then bobbed her head with a few quick hoots.

"What is it?" Conner asked at Grimmley's grave expression.

"Soldiers riding this way, and swiftly." He instinctively gazed out the back window and scanned the trees beyond the lake. "Your dragon?"

"Sleeping among your maples. Skye was too exhausted from the flight here to even tease the mare."

Any words of relief Grimmley favored were cut short by the sound of pounding hooves to the west, so he nodded. "Stay out of sight until I find out what this is about."

Grimmley reached the front door just as three Graystone guardsmen at full gallop pulled up hard at the edge of his porch.

"Grandmaster Rollingsworth," croaked a haggard woman in the lead, hopping from her winded horse. Removing her riding gloves, she dropped to one knee before the Shaman. "I am Hargaile Windstein, first sergeant of the Griffinrock Royal Guard. I apologize sincerely for the interruption and dispatching of any further formalities, but we have sped to you carrying grave and urgent news from Graystone this morn. Late last night, our sovereign Queen Izadora was assassinated. Her body was found moments after the vicious act next to His Royal Majesty and Champion of the Realm, King Jonath Palamuel, who was poisoned while defending his queen. The Royal Physicians have been unsuccessful in reviving His Majesty. Grandmaster, the king sits on the cusp of life and is in dire need of your skills."

*The queen assassinated.* Grimmley pressed his back against a porch beam to steady his legs. "Sergeant, did the Royal Physicians say anything about the type of poison used on the king?"

The sergeant wagged her head, eyes swollen and no longer able to produce tears. "When we rode forth, the king held to life but with shallow breath and pale skin."

Grimmley grunted. "Was the king hot or cold to the touch?"

The sergeant shook her head again, her lips beginning to quiver.

"Was his heart racing or sluggish? Were the blacks of his eyes large or small?"

After several more moments of silence, Grimmley bid her to stand. He would have a long, hard talk with those of the Physicians guild when this was over. They should have sent word the moment they found the king. Now, Jonath's life weighed in the balance of every precious breath. "Very well, First Sergeant Windstein. You and your riders have completed your task with honor. I will take it from here. However, your mounts are nigh to be wind-broke and are in severe need of rest. They are strong in spirit to have traveled so far, and worthy of the king's service. I would attend to your animals, but I fear that I will need my strength for the king." The Shaman gestured curtly around the side of his cottage. "You will find grain and hay in my barn to pack for your return. Gather it quickly and be on your way. However, do not ride them again today."

The sergeant bowed deeply. "We thank you for your generosity, Grandmaster."

Grimmley went inside and began rummaging through the scores of liquids, oils, and herbs stowed in his cabinet of potions. The Physicians had been of no help classifying the poison, and he could not carry every conceivable ingredient necessary to devise a cure. He had to think. "Did you hear?" he asked above the clatter of glass vials.

"Yes," came the lad's solemn reply over his shoulder.

The perpetrator had to have been a highly skilled orderman to so handily and quickly dispose of the king and complete the grisly task before anyone could arrive. That had the vile odor of Assassin all over it. Shallow breath and pale skin further narrowed the possibilities. He would start there. He began placing vials into a large wooden box containing threescore small compartments. "Conner, there is a small green bud growing on a hallerium plant in the garden. Bring that and a few leaves from the haggleweed. Quickly now!"

By the time Conner returned, Grimmley had his box of supplies ready. He placed the leaves and bud on top of the vials and closed the lid. Grimmley turned to Conner and held the young man's wide-eyed gaze over smudged spectacles. "Once the guardsmen have departed, I want you to return to Dragongarde." He raised his hand before Conner could speak. "Conner, truly, I wish we had time to argue, but I must attend to the king. This news could not have come at a worse time. I am sorry, but this changes everything."

For expediency, the Shaman summarized what his young Eastland apprentice was likely not to know. "For the next three days, Griffinrock will be in mourning for the queen. On the fourth morning, there will be a Tournament of the Realm, through which Veressa's lifelong Champion and guardian will be decided. For three days thence, there will be celebration and feasting, ending with Veressa's coronation as the new queen of Griffinrock. Between now and then, the entire realm will be in disarray and confusion ... and likely for some time yet to come. Surely you can see what could happen with the unexpected appearance of someone bonded with a dragon? With the orders actively seeking you out, you're going to have to stay in hiding a pinch longer."

Conner's jaws tightened.

"My boy, nothing would ever get done if we waited until all obstacles were removed from our path. The challenges you are facing are truly formidable. They would be for the most ardent and experienced orderman. But you must have faith that the Cosmos would not have put you here if you did not have what you needed for the task at hand. You must remain stalwart and see this through. You cannot waver. Soon, the realms will need you more than ever."

Unable to think of anything more to add, Grimmley offered the boy a reassuring pat on the shoulder, then walked to the back door. "Barthox, you'd best come with me. Otherwise, I'll come back to find the boy has you making his bed and ironing his socks."

The owl fluttered to Grimmley's shoulder, then swiveled her head to watch Conner with wide, caring eyes. With staff and wooden box of medicines in hand, the Shaman took the walkway that led to the gazebo and his Transit Stone.

In the brilliance of late morning, Conner watched Grimmley disappear in a flash of light, leaving him awestruck by the old Shaman's powers. How could Grimmley so handily wield such elemental forces?

Both Grimmley and Layna believed Conner capable of powers that, according to the old Dragonbonded legends, dwarfed even what he had just observed—forces that would make the greatest ordermen acquiesce to Dragonbonded will. Did he possess such abilities? And if he was able to discover them, how did Grimmley expect him to influence the orders, much less entire realms? For that matter, what could he offer the realms?

He recalled the night shortly before arriving at Grimmley's door, when he had dreamed of the Cravenrock Assassin riding towards him on a black warhorse. In that dream, he had tried to run away, to hide, only to watch the cheers of the crowd below him contort into accusatory jeers and disdain. Even Skye and Caralynn had looked upon him with loathing. And now Conner understood what the dream meant. He could no longer run from his fears, could not run away from whatever future awaited him. What he lacked was a clear picture of what he should be running *toward*.

His gaze shifted to the dark shadow hidden among the maples to the north. He could sense the dragon probing his mind, waiting to see what he would do next. *Yes, Skye. Fear,* Conner thought. *It seems my fate is bound up in that one word.* He recalled what he had said to his bond the day after his dream as he peered out over the Aradorm gorge: *Sometimes, I wish I could be fearless, even for a day.*

Well, Grimmley might not know how to help him access his abilities, but the old Shaman had been right about one thing. With the queen of Griffinrock assassinated, significant changes were coming—and swiftly. Like the pounding of the hooves of his dream-Assassin's warhorse, he sensed the ground rumbling beneath his feet. He had better be prepared for whatever distant specter was coming for him.

He would go back to Dragongarde as Grimmley suggested, but not to run away as he had in his dream. He needed time, time to think, time to discover how to tap into the powers Grimmley and Layna believed him capable of wielding. Dragongarde offered him hope. If anyone was looking for him, it was unlikely they would come to Dragongarde. How many knew where the fortress was, or, for that matter, its entrance? At least the fortress shield would protect him. Grimmley had been right. His chances to find answers lay at Dragongarde.

# A Dark Premonition

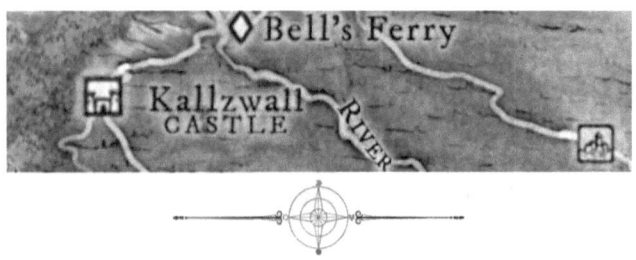

**V**eressa awoke with a sudden jerk and sharp inhale of air, sweeping away all but the faint memory of someone familiar calling her name in a receding dream. She looked about her bed, disoriented, her location discordant with her last conscious thought. Slowly, her reminiscence of blacking out on her balcony brought back the other events of the night—of a huge black beast and its rider. "Oh, Veressa, you are going crazy," she thought as she rubbed at her temple. But the dull throbbing was gone, and the knot had subsided. *How did that happen?* The outlandish ordeals of the past week had left her suspicious as to which memories reflected reality, and which were mere residues of her dreams. But one thing was certain. She could dismiss the dragon and its rider as nothing but manifestations of her sleeping mind.

She recalled an elderly Paladinian nun teacher who had ardently believed such visions were portents. But of what? Veressa struggled to recall how to interpret such apparitions. Finally, she rose and dressed. Antilles remained nearby, his large, caring eyes tracking her every move. Her bond's loud, rhythmic purr helped wash away the worries of her agitated mind. By the time she was dressed, she had concluded that her dream had been an important reminder that she could not hide from her fears and doubts. She needed to face her uncertainties head-on. She would take command of her destiny, tell her parents about what she was going through, and deal with the consequences the best she could. Before going down for breakfast, Veressa packed most of her belongings in preparation for departure later that morning.

She took the long spiral staircase that opened at the west end of the castle's main hall. But something was awry. The bustling vaulted royal halls were oddly vacant of both castle staff and the echoes of their morning chores. Even the kitchen, filled with fragrant aromas of meats and vegetables mixed with scents of Narwalen spices and burning oak, was void of cooks and help. She proceeded cautiously down the corridor, Antilles crouched at her side, and entered the great dining hall. A line of prepared dishes—savory pies, stews, breads, and gravies—adorned the length of the fully set table. But no servants stood at the ready. The only occupants in the muted hall were four forms huddled near the hearth at the far end. The air about them was thick and stale with the anxiety of grief.

Veressa's aunt, the Duchess Mariette, sat with palms pressed to her face, her shoulders hunched and heaving uncontrollably. Duke Regiboldt, always the stalwart soldier, stood at his wife's back with his wax-like face longer even than usual. His large hands lay heavy on her shoulders in an awkward attempt to comfort her. Nearby, Marcantos leaned against the fireplace, his hazel eyes transfixed on the flickering flames, while Friarwood, her protector's ever-present dark shadow, stood idly at his pupil's back with his usual impassive yet observant expression.

"What? What is it? What happened?" Veressa whispered as she crept toward the group.

Mariette blinked up with red, swollen eyes and sniffed. "Come, girl. Sit here next to me," she commanded softly, patting an ornate chair.

Veressa sat slowly, warily.

"This morning, nigh an hour ago, we received the most horrific news from Graystone." Mariette exhaled sharply. "Veressa, the queen has died."

Veressa repeated her aunt's words again and again in her head until she was certain she had heard correctly. An aura of the surreal descended like a fog and settled about her. "How?" she rasped.

"She was assassinated," Duke Regiboldt proclaimed, a slight sneer blemishing his solemn face.

The duchess bowed her head. "Little more is known," she mumbled.

"And father? What of my father?"

Mariette lifted her chin at the girl's query. "Jonath was poisoned. He still clings to life, though it appears only by a thin thread."

Veressa rose in a futile attempt to quell the numbing panic coursing through her. "I must return immediately. I must be with him." She turned to her protector. "Marcantos, prepare our horses. We leave within the hour. I wish to travel fast, so bring as few men as necessary."

Marcantos stared back, unmoved by her demands.

Before the princess could rebuke the man for his sluggish response, the duchess stood and placed her hand on Veressa's shoulder. "What you must do, Veressa, is prepare yourself for the days ahead. There is much to do, some of which will require your immediate and personal attention. You do not have the luxury to go running off to sit beside your father. He will either survive or he won't. Your presence will not alter that outcome."

The duke cleared his throat to dispel the growing tension between the two women. "Veressa, surely you understand that once news gets out, the entire realm will be mourning the loss of the queen. These coming hours are precious, for in them we must determine how best to script the news for your subjects. The words they hear will set the tone for the days to come. There will be time for you to reach Graystone before your mother's memorial and the Tournament of the Realm."

The princess shrugged off her aunt's touch. "What I understand is that neither of you ever cared for my father. I will not linger here while he lies at death's doorway in Graystone!"

"Care for him?" Mariette stifled back her anger, fists of rage at her side. "Jonath is the reason my sister is dead! Protecting the queen was his one duty, and as I predicted, he failed at his task! For years I warned your mother her folly would bring about this ill fortune. I implored her not to get emotionally attached to that … man."

Veressa staggered. "I will not stand by and listen to this. I harbor no doubt he did everything in his power to protect Mother." Her tears flowed freely. "This is not about my mother's injudicious love for her Champion or his supposed inability to protect the queen. This is about the fact my mother fell in love with a peasant serf." She sniffed involuntarily. "I have serf blood coursing through my veins too, Aunt Mariette. Do you detest me as well?"

"Of course not!" Realizing she had said too much, the duchess stepped closer to soothe Veressa, but the princess jerked away again and stood in defiance against them all.

"I am leaving for Graystone, and if anyone tries to stop me, they will regret it for all the years they have remaining on Gaia." With that, she left the hall.

"Highness," Marcantos called to the princess, and caught up with her by the kitchen entrance. "I urge you to consider for a moment your aunt's advice. You are not in an emotional state to—"

Veressa rounded on her protector. "To what, Marcantos? Make sound decisions? Do you think a calmer state of mind would lead me to believe I should not be at my father's side?"

"I was going to say you may not be considering all the risks. We do not yet know the motives of those behind the queen's death. It is possible that you riding out onto the open road with little protection is precisely what they want. At least consider the possibility that your life could be in danger."

"I have thought of that. At least now I know my dream was indeed a premonition."

"What dream?"

Veressa considered not saying anything further, but if her dream was a sign of something personally treacherous, it was best he knew. "Last night, I dreamed I was visited by a Dragonbonded dressed in black and riding a magnificent dragon." The princess bit at her lower lip. "It seems the old fables of such dreams as dark portents were true. If that is the case, you might finally get that opportunity to prove your worth as my protector."

"Given your dream, Highness, it would seem a more prudent course of action is required."

Veressa combed fingers through Antilles's thick ruff. She could feel the urges returning, calling for her to be on the road once more. *Am I being rash? Is this decision driven by wanting again to quench those desires? No*, she concluded. In the past fortnight, she had lost the only two women in her life she looked to for guidance and support—her dear mentor and friend Annabelle and now her mother. Her father was her only anchor to sanity. If she lost him too ...

"Marcantos"—Veressa placed her hands on her hips—"do not waste my time attempting to rein me down a path I do not wish to take. If you plan to stop me, then you'd best get on with it." Veressa waited on the cusp of drawing Air and Earth elementals. She held no hope of successfully defending herself against Marcantos's skills, but she would make sure the battle was not easily won.

They stared at each other for several moments, then the princess gave Marcantos a nod. "Once I charge our horses to be readied, I will finish packing. If you are with me, I suggest you prepare to leave now, or risk having to catch up farther down the road." Veressa felt Marcantos's eyes boring into her back as she headed for the stables.

Lacerus smiled faintly, hidden among the late-morning shadows of the corridor. His subtle suggestions and encouragement were already having the desired effect on the girl. She had great Anarchic potential, which fueled his excitement for the days ahead. In time, as he had done with Marcantos, he would discover what inspired the princess, and then show her how to release her potential.

With his pupil quick on the princess's heels and no time to dally, the Assassin proceeded. "I have come to fetch some supplies from Grandmaster Evinfaire's bedchambers for his journey," he explained to the two guards at the base of the tower's stairs. The guardsmen eyed each other, and with no cause to restrain the protector's preceptor, acquiesced with a shrug.

The Assassin climbed the stairs three at a time to Marcantos's bedchamber landing. A quick glance up and down the stairwell and he was off again, arriving at the summit and Veressa's bedchamber door. There, he entered and crossed the sleeping chamber to the balcony's railing. In moments, he found what he was seeking—deep grooves running the length of several stone balusters, made by claws of something large and very powerful.

Lacerus sighed as he scanned out over the princess's balcony to the western edge of Narwalen Plains. The deep summer greens of Griffinrock's Royal Forest blanketed the rolling hills beyond, the very heart of the Harmonics' soul. First, with the shift of the Cosmic balance, had come Morgas's news of finding dragonfire in the cave where Vault had regrettably made his escape. Then came the sporadic reports from the Anarchic band that a dragon had been spotted along the north central region of the Dragon's Back Mountains. Even together, there was room for uncertainty. But the marks on the stone banister dispelled what little doubt remained.

The marks suggested that the creature was rather small, though when it came to dragons, size could be lethally deceiving. And Veressa's reference to a Dragonbonded? Could this be his errant Vault? There was undeniably something special about the lad. But why would a Dragonbonded visit the princess? And how did the boy even know she was here? Every revelation brought a dozen new questions.

The Kindred could no longer deny that the dragon and its human bond were real. Of course, a problem is only what you perceive it to be, nothing more or less. But with the tasks ahead, the Anarchic band that the Kindred had dispatched would need to ensure that the two did not become meddlesome in the days to come.

Lacerus vacated the room and had begun retracing his steps when he heard steps in the stairwell. *Curse Marcantos and his timing!*

Marcantos pulled up short as the dark form separated from a chair near his bedchamber balcony. Copious, his wretched excuse for a guard, moaned apologetically on his back, but made no motion to remedy his embarrassing pose. The bear gazed up with impish eyes, patiently waiting for a good scratch.

"Blake?" he asked the form. "What are you doing here?"

"Considering this morning's ill news and its ramifications, and as evident in your haste that you are giving the young princess some rein, I thought it best we take a moment to speak privately of the days to come." The student made no attempt to argue, so Friarwood proceeded. "Marcantos, you have advanced considerably under my tutelage, and truly possess all the martial skills necessary to win the upcoming tourney. But more will be tested that day than just your expertise in combat. In the time remaining, you will need to turn your focus inward, to strengthen your fortitude, hone your resolve, and sharpen your wits. You need me with you on that journey, for many snares and pitfalls await."

Marcantos shook his head. "Veressa is no longer princess, Blake, but queen imminent. And I, assigned as her protector, am her Provisional Champion. You know, as do I, the laws under the armistice stipulate—"

"That no more than one from any order may be in company of an imminent monarch—yes, I know. However, that law was intended to protect the orders from undue influence during the pivotal time before coronation. I would hope the queen imminent's safety would supersede such mandates. My skills would be valuable in supplementing yours in her protection." Friarwood moved closer. "You do still want this prize?"

"Of course. I was born to assume the responsibility as Queen Veressa's Champion and would do so willingly. But my foremost duty is to ensure she arrives safely at Graystone."

"That is why you need me—as a constant reminder of the work remaining," Friarwood suggested. "This is your hour, Marcantos. Leave nothing to chance. As Provisional Champion, you could sway the future queen."

Marcantos nodded hesitantly. "I will ask. If she concurs, you should be ready. I fear a moment's delay would bring her wrath down on everyone nearby." The statement had been intended as a warning, so Friarwood's hearty laugh came as a surprise.

# Amid a Nest of Spies

In the two days following his return to Dragongarde, Conner continued exploring the web of fortress chambers and halls, occasionally shadowed by his bond, when the creature was not asleep or hunting. But the forays deep into the fortress yielded only one noteworthy discovery—a fully stocked kitchen directly below the main hall, and adjacent to that chamber, an enormous pantry containing vast quantities of meats, fruits, vegetables, roots, traveling rations, and barrels of ale and water, all in pristine condition. By best accounts, Conner could feast every day for several years on what was there. But by the third morning, when no new treasures had revealed themselves, Conner grew bored and restless. "Let's scout out the valley below. We haven't been down there yet," he suggested loud enough to wake a slumbering dragon—which was precisely what he had in mind.

Skye peered back at him through one glowing eye. Coiled at the mouth of the main hall, he neither spoke nor moved.

Conner persisted. "I've never known a creature to sleep so much. You'd best not be getting lackadaisical on me. I'm wondering if I bonded with a sloth!"

Skye's eye vanished behind the lids again, undeterred by the human's rebuke. "Dragons enjoy naps almost as much as they enjoy eating," he slurred.

"That's only because they don't do anything else," Conner grumbled over the returning sounds of snorts and grunts. Irritated, Conner made his way back to the circular room with the game device, dropped into one of the chairs with a sough, and scanned the hanging murals of young Dragonbonded sitting in thoughtful meditation before the apparatus. What kind of game could hold their interest so? He flicked the golden wheel atop the device. As it spun, a thought came to him.

He leaned closer to study the wheel's bejeweled Cosmic Star design. Each point of the star was inlaid with a different jewel. He called Earth elemental to him, and the wheel began to turn on its own, coming to rest with the emerald-studded star point aimed at him. He released Earth and called Fire. The wheel turned a quarter rotation, stopping with the ruby point in front of Conner. He repeated this for Air and Water elementals, and then Earth again. Each time, the wheel revolved in quarter-turn successions—diamond point, then sapphire, and back to emerald.

What if the device was not part of a game, but a means for Dragonbonded to develop their skills in using elemental forces? And if so, to what end, and how did the device help? With hopes his effort might lead to some new revelation, Conner spent the better part of the afternoon practicing on the wheel. Fire to Air to Water to Earth to Fire—again and again the wheel turned, slowly at first, but faster as his ability to call the elementals improved.

By late afternoon, Conner could no longer deny his complaining stomach. Weariness of eating rations and dried fruit from Grimmley's kitchen gave him the perfect excuse to try out Dragongarde's food supplies and assess the quality of what was in the elementally protected storage. Before long, he returned to the main hall and settled at its opening and the scenic beauty of the Valley of Souls, enjoying his third helping of hot venison stew in an earthenware bowl while awaiting Skye's return from a hunting excursion. He did not have to wait long.

Skye glided through the opening and settled next to him, still wearing the saddle he'd donned that morning. "There are humans climbing the steps to Dragongarde. They will be at the entrance shortly."

"Did they catch sight of you?" Conner asked, scraping the last chucks of stew from his bowl.

"Hemera was at my tail, so I do not think so. They offered no sign of shock or dismay."

Skye's answer did little to allay Conner's concerns. The dragon had not been around enough people to know that stunned paralysis could be a form of surprise. "Thank you, Skye. I'll go see what they're looking for." He hoped at least it was not a *who*. How often did travelers stumble upon the doorsteps of this remote site? How many even knew what the place was? Still, he could not shake Grimmley's notion that people might be looking for him. "Stay here. I'll get rid of them." He slipped clothes over the Dragonbonded armor and proceeded up the long tunnel to the antechamber.

He arrived just as a woman and three men stepped through the entrance. All wore the light, summer pelts common among Alpslanders and sported large swords strapped to their backs.

"Well met, young man," the woman stated pleasantly. "I am Meera Asheborne, and this"—she gestured to the large, muscular man next to her—"is Groegan Briarmede. We have traveled a great distance from the east. I have something for you." The woman removed a small leather sack tied at her waist.

Conner blinked. He did not know offerings to chance strangers were common among these people. "Your present is most gracious, my lady, but I am just traveling through myself. I hope you would not be insulted if I do not accept your gift."

"Ah, but you might find this particular item quite interesting." Smiling kindly, she emptied a half dozen metal bars into her palms, then held them out for Conner to inspect.

Conner leaned forward cautiously in the dim light. The bars were short and slightly curved, and made of dull wrought iron. "They are very nice," he lied, hoping she did not notice or take offense at his disappointment. "What are they for?" he asked politely.

"This," she answered. Calling Fire and Earth, she incanted, *"Hemea ousia synchometallo!"* The metal bars trembled and then shot from her palms, forming into tight, solid bands around Conner's wrists. He jerked away, but he was too slow. He was tossed backward like a doll and slammed into the cavern wall, his arms splayed wide. Fear seized him, and he thrashed, trying to pull his arms free from the manacles now fused to the rock behind him. Memories of the Cravenrock stockade after his beating, his confinement in the Thieves Guild undercity, and being bound by the trackers from Cravenrock all tore at his mind. A steel trap closed about him, and he roared like an animal at the four standing placidly before him.

From down the long hall, as if in response to Conner's growl, came a deep, thunderous reply. Then the floor began to quake like the slow beat of a funeral drum.

"I believe that is your cue," Groegan suggested to Meera, as if meeting an angry beast was her lifelong desire. Neither noticed the two wide-eyed men shuffling slowly toward the chamber exit.

Skye-Anyar-Bello Cloudbender roared his fury at the human blocking his path down the long hall.

"We have detained your bond, noble one," the human stated in Dragon tongue, apathetic to the display of his rage. She bowed low. "An attack on me or any of my comrades will result in his immediate death."

Skye shuddered to a stop. Through the anguish flowing from his bond, he knew she spoke the truth.

Once her statement had had the desired effect, she continued. "My name is Meera-Antala of the family Asheborne, Necromancer of Thanatos. My master, Grandmaster Necromancer Breanen of the family Sagamore, sends her most honorable greetings."

Skye physically shook, fighting back the urge to scorch the pitiful human into ash, for her actions had not been of honor.

As if she understood the dragon's thoughts, she continued. "I humbly regret the subterfuge necessitated to bring about this encounter, but I have need of your full attention, great one." She glanced up. "There are matters of vital importance we must discuss."

Groegan waited for Conner to settle, then motioned to the two behind him. "My comrades and I are of the Barbarians Order. Meera Asheborne, the woman on her way to converse with your bond, is a Necromancer. By your appearance, Eastlander, I assume we can call you ... Vault?"

Conner tensed at the name. It seemed the bad decisions of his past would forever haunt him—now by Anarchist spies from across the Borderlands! "I will not return to Cravenrock," he declared as he tested the shackles with another yank, struggling to gain control of his frenetic thoughts.

The Barbarian smiled at the young man's riposte. "We are well past that stage, Vault, though there is someone you met there who is still keenly interested in you."

"Then what do you want with me?"

"You?" the Anarchist asked. "Do you seriously presume you command the interest of so many Anarchists in the Harmonic lands?"

Conner twitched. "The dragon."

Groegan nodded. "You really have no clue what you have bonded with, do you?"

"Why don't you tell me?"

The Barbarian chuckled at Conner's attempt to redirect the conversation. "And ruin the surprise?" He wagged his head resolutely. "But I can lay a few breadcrumbs along your path toward enlightenment. If you hold any notion of living out your life in the Harmonic Realms, you might find your dragon is of a different mind. Harmonic life is not in a dragon's nature. That is why, during the Great War, the Harmonic Realms struggled for so many years to establish a pact with the Dragonbonded."

"Skye is perfectly fine—"

"What?" Groegan kicked the decayed remains of a chair and it disintegrated into a cloud of powder and dust. "Living like a hermit? If you think that, you really do live in a fantasy."

"They look harmless enough." Gertrum scratched his bristly chin while squinting at the four Alpslanders huddled around the fledgling fire in the distance. Dusk was settling about them and the band was too far to discern any useful features.

Annabelle elbowed the Scouter. "And since when have we known things to be as we see them?" The Ranger had come to like the guildsman's simple but matter-of-fact way of seeing life. "Besides, I find it a bit irregular that they are camped at the foot of Dragongarde. I suggest we err on the side of caution."

Morgas nodded his agreement to Gertrum. "If they are anything but what they seem, I am the most likely to see through their disguises. Assign to me two scouts, and let me go see what they are about." A lone explorer appearing before them in this wilderness would have raised undue suspicion.

Gertrum pinched his lip in annoyance. The strategy would further delay getting to the root of their dragon mystery, but he could find no flaw in their counsel. He motioned to the dozen Scouters eagerly waiting behind. Two came forward. With Morgas leading the way, the three stepped from behind the rock and moved toward the campfire on the knoll.

After several anxious minutes observing what looked to be a congenial exchange, Morgas saluted in Alpslander style and started back.

"So?" Gertrum asked the large Alpslander eagerly.

"You were correct, Ranger Loris, in being cautious. We are going to need a defensive strategy and quickly."

"What? Why?" Gertrum grunted, then peered keenly over the rock. The group had not moved from the fire.

Morgas gazed at the guildmaster with his typical passive expression. "They are Anarchic spies. I recognized one as a Barbarian from the Farlorde camp across the Borderlands north of my village. Further, they would not cross the Borderlands in such a small band nor would the rest of their band have gone far. That means that they are not alone. The rest must be in Dragongarde. Now that we have seen them, they will not take the chance of allowing us to leave this place unmolested. In the next few minutes, we will be under attack."

"Why don't you come back with us across the Borderlands?" Groegan asked Conner as if the idea had just come to him. "It would make all this much easier. Eastlanders are renowned for their honor. Give me your word you won't escape, and we'll leave with the morrow's light. I will show you what Anarchic life is like." The Barbarian stepped forward as if the closer perspective would reveal Conner's deepest secrets. "Eastlander, there is so much you do not yet understand. Nothing is as it appears, and much of what you have been taught is wrong. Come with us, and I promise you will not regret it."

Groegan's warm smile contradicted everything Conner knew of Barbarians, and he shivered. A flash of blue light drew Conner's eyes to the Barbarian's chest, where a gold amulet hung concealed beneath his Alpslander fur jerkin, set with a black stone at its center. "There is nothing I want or need to learn from you. And I will not give up my freedom to live a life of chaos and destruction."

"You Harmonics speak of freedom as if it is a banner to wave at your enemy, to give your efforts just and valorous meaning. You do not know what freedom is," Groegan declared. "Awareness precedes choice, Vault. Those living out their Harmonic lives are unaware that the beliefs they bought on the auction block have been methodically selected and offered by the auctioneer. The illusion of choice is not freedom." He took a deep breath. "Did you know the Eastlands of Griffinrock is only one of a few regions in the Harmonic Realms free from nobility governance?"

Conner shook his head tentatively, unsure where the Barbarian was leading.

"It was explicitly written into the Treaty of Alignment at the end of the Great War that the Eastlands were to remain free from noble rule. And do you know why the Eastlands were so uniquely treated?"

Conner answered with a silent glare.

Groegan resumed his lecture. "Of course not. It is something Harmonics would rather forget. It was a Harmonic concession because the monarchs refused to concede the Griffinrock Eastlands to the Assembly of Anarchists, even though your Eastland ancestors fought alongside the Anarchists against the oppression of Harmonic feudal lords."

"That was six hundred years ago. You cannot possibly know that to be true!" Conner could sense uncertainty and doubt from his bond. What was the Necromancer saying to the dragon? "Skye!" He yelled, jerking hard on the shackles, hoping the pain would keep his bond's feelings from altering his own. "Don't listen to their lies," he whispered.

"It is good that you don't trust me," the Barbarian continued, undisturbed by his captive's gesticulations. "Words can be deceiving. They cloud the mind and veil the eyes and ears from the truth. That is why an Anarchist does not trust anything that cannot be proven through the senses. Vault," Groegan called softly, waiting for Conner to stop fighting and his eyes to settle upon him. "There is so much you need to understand. For the Harmonic orders, power is only a means to an end. If you stay, they will exploit you. You cannot hide here forever, and your desires will not affect the outcome they crave."

"And of course the dark orders would treat me differently." Conner hoped his sarcasm would bolster his doubts, but he felt his resolve slipping—and Skye's. He wanted to refute what the Barbarian said, but he could not, and that made him feel small and stupid. Did he really know so little of the world?

"Yes, Vault, we would. And what you call *dark* is purely a matter of perspective. You would be surprised to find that Anarchic life is not so different from that in the Eastlands. You would be at liberty to choose your own path, free of interference, manipulation, and control by those who fear the powers you will someday possess. That is why you will never reach your full potential in these lands of oppression."

"And if I choose not to go with you, will you release Skye and me?"

Groegan breathed deep again. "If you elect not to go, then we have to consider the possibility that the dragon will fall under the influence of the Harmonic orders."

Conner froze at the veiled threat. "Why should you care?"

"Because soon the Harmonic Realms will declare war on the Anarchic Lands. A dragon's bond under their control, even one not fully realized, could tip the scales in their favor. We cannot allow that." At length, he continued imploringly. "Vault, you should make your decision wisely, so know this. Once the Harmonics declare war—and they will—the long-standing Treaty of Alignment will be nullified. All obligations under that truce will be void, including the mandate that the Eastlands remain free from rule by realm nobility. Your Eastland towns and villages will be parceled off and placed under the thumb of Griffinrock dukes and barons. Then you will see your precious Harmonic Realms for what they truly are."

Another woman in mountain garb, this one young and blond, stepped through the entrance and signaled Groegan urgently.

Conner turned his head away and squeezed his eyes shut. He did not want to listen anymore. Besides, another thought needed his attention. When he looked again, the Barbarian was speaking softly to the woman near the opening.

Shortly, Groegan returned to stand before his captive. "It seems we have run out of time for further debate, Vault. What is your decision?"

"I will not betray my realm," Conner slurred through clenched teeth.

"An unfortunate choice," Groegan sighed. A quick gesture sent the young woman swiftly up the hall toward the Necromancer and the dragon. Groegan spoke to one of the two who had entered the antechamber with him. "Guard the boy. We will make sure our visitors are taken care of." The large Barbarian regarded Conner one last time before vanishing through the entrance with the other guard in tow.

It took some time before Annabelle and Morgas were able to persuade Gertrum that an all-out assault on the Anarchists by the fire was a reckless maneuver and would likely put anyone in the fortress at peril. At last, Morgas was able to convince the determined guildmaster that the Barbarian he recognized could not be the leader, which meant his three comrades were likely Anarchic ordermen as well, sentries for a larger nest of spies. Even with their tactically advantageous location, the element of surprise, and the master Ranger's skills, their guildsman party was ill-matched for what Gertrum fondly called "Anarchist merrymaking." With no time left to nail down details, the three set a desperate plan into motion.

Morgas and the two Scouters proceeded south along a narrow pass while the rest of the party fanned out to take higher ground. At the designated spot, Morgas worked quickly to prepare their decoy camp. Morgas had no more than settled with the first flames licking the evening fire when their camp erupted into chaos.

Annabelle felt the call of Air to the north before the three Anarchists came into sight through the narrow pass. She called on Air and Earth elementals to awaken her thin staff: *"Outher pheto afyravdos."* With her staff morphed into an elemental bow, the Ranger fired half a dozen shafts into the unsuspecting assailants, though only one scored a deadly hit. The Ranger's elemental pull was the signal for the Scouter guildsmen, who felt her call of Earth. The awaiting Scouters drew upon Earth and descended into the fray below.

This was Morgas's cue. Untrained in elemental combat, the large Alpslander would have offered little assistance in this battle. He was to go to Dragongarde to discover what was happening inside. With the Anarchist band distracted, he skirted the mayhem and ran back up the pass. Approaching the base fire, he caught motion to the east, so he huddled with Valmer in the shadows of several rocks and waited as another Barbarian ran past, heading south toward the fight. Morgas and his wolf bond headed upslope, retracing the Barbarian's tracks until they came to a wide set of stairs going farther up. He reached over his shoulder and withdrew his father's sword. Then, testing the leather grip, he eagerly took the steps.

*Vault.* Conner shook his head. Groegan had called him Vault, the name he had adopted when he fell in with the Cravenrock Thieves Guild. What's more, the Barbarian's black onyx amulet with its rippling blue light meant the Barbarian was somehow linked to the Assassin in Cravenrock. But Conner had seen such a gem even before the Assassin, on the ringed forefinger of another man. The specter of this third man needled at Conner. What was that man's connection to these two Anarchists? What good was his accursed memory, if it failed him when he most needed it? He wrenched his wrists against the shackles, once again drawing the guard's stern attention.

Then it came to him—that moment he'd met the third man. Like now, he had been bound, struggling in the thrall of the Cravenrock city guardsmen after his encounter with the Warrior Evinfaire. There was a tall man in black, hidden among the shadows of the entrance to the Keep's ward. But Conner could make no logical sense of such an association. So he began anew, gathering and sorting through all the related facts, weaving and stitching the pieces back together one by one. And when he completed his mental tapestry, he came to a chilling conclusion. He had to escape. And he had to do so immediately, while the Anarchists were preoccupied.

Since the Necromancer had used Fire and Earth to adhere his metal shackles, it seemed logical these same forces would break them apart. He called upon meager amounts of the elementals, then waited. The guard did not stir. His eyes closed in concentration. Slowly, methodically, he probed the metallic bands, his consciousness slipping lightly over the metal bars. Their elemental weave was similar to the shield protecting the fortress, but much simpler. A slight tug on the elemental threads was all he needed to send the shackles tumbling to the dirt.

Astonished by his success, Conner found himself in an unexpected and desperate situation. The metallic clink had drawn the guard from his uneasy stare at the entrance, and the man came at him with lips twisted into a snarl that foretold a terrible reckoning for Conner's defiance.

Conner reached out with Earth, seized the only object his mind could discover—a loose fist-sized rock embedded in the wall—and pulled hard. The projectile struck the guard in the temple with a force that felled him like a tree. Tamping down the sudden urge to flee, Conner took a minute to think through his actions. Somehow, he needed to signal Skye that he no longer was a hostage, but he could sense his bond was under too much stress at the moment to notice. And he did not want to risk encountering the Necromancer in the main hall. He just needed to bide his time long enough for Skye to notice and fly around to get him.

Conner skipped over the prone guard, then bolted through the antechamber entrance. With twilight descending, the light Hemera offered would be fleeting. He sprinted down the weaving path that led to the fortress stairs. But as he bounded around the last boulder, he ran headlong into the Anarchist scout who had left the antechamber with Groegan. Luckily, the man had been preoccupied with whatever was happening on the grassy knoll below. The force of Conner's unexpected impact knocked him to the ground, leaving Conner with enough time to spin and run back the other way before the Anarchist shouted and took up chase. Instead of reentering the antechamber, Conner chose to blaze a trail up the steep eastern slope. But the path soon leveled out and turned north. It was only a few minutes later that he came to an abrupt end at the northern ridge. Conner turned back, only to find the guard coming into view, crouched at the ready. The Anarchist moved toward him with blade drawn, Air and Water elementals swirling about him. There would be no surprises this time.

Any actions Conner might have mused taking vanished when a large Alpslander appeared farther up the trail behind the Anarchist guard. Conner was growing desperate. He needed to buy his bond more time. But before he could act, the big man stepped up behind the guard and plunged his huge sword through the Anarchist's back.

Gertrum hacked wildly at the elemental shield of the Barbarian before him. Like the eight Scouters about him, he searched for any weakness that could be exploited by either his sword or the Ranger's shafts. He bobbed to his right and the Ranger took the opening, firing an arrow that probed deeper into the Barbarian's shield than her previous dozen had. But Gertrum's maneuver had left him exposed, and the Barbarian seized the opportunity. The backswing struck the guildmaster on the shoulder, sending him cartwheeling into the gravel at Annabelle's feet.

The Ranger examined the guildmaster as he rolled to his back with a groan. Her eyes darted north. "We'll need to put these two down and quickly, or it's going to get very ugly very soon."

Gertrum leaped to his feet, hefting his sword once more. "Why is that?" he puffed, shaking numbness from his shoulder.

"A powerful orderman is heading this way, likely the leader of this patrol." Annabelle's arm blurred, and two more arrows took flight. Since her initial surprise volley, none of her arrows had scored a hit, a fact that slowed neither her tempo nor her resolve. She just needed more time.

A nearby Anarchist had reached this same conclusion when one of the Ranger's shafts pierced his elemental shield before glancing away, so he focused his zealous rage on the source of that arrow. Annabelle was so engaged with this fierce attack that she failed to notice Gertrum sprinting up the trail to the north.

Morgas pressed the sole of his boot to the Barbarian's back and kicked out hard, letting the corpse fall away from his sword, its young Anarchic lifeblood flowing out across the rocky terrain. "Vault!" the Alpslander shouted to the thin form silhouetted against the darkening sky.

The boy shuddered, ceasing his backward stride toward the sheer cliffs at his heels.

So, it was him! At last. Morgas slid his bloodied blade into its scabbard and raised his arms wide, fingers spread, hoping the boy understood his gesture for parley. "Come away from the ledge and let us speak. You have nothing to fear from me. I am here with a Ranger and a force of Harmonic Scouters who have been searching for you."

Vault shuffled closer to the edge, peeling off his shirt. "I regret that I have no time to talk. I have a message to deliver. I have to warn the king."

"Warn the king? Warn him of what?"

"That he is amid a nest of spies!" the boy shouted, then leaped backward off the ridge.

Morgas ran to the cliff just as the last glimmer of Hemera's light winked out from beyond the valley. There, before him, a dragon rose, with Vault astride. Tilting to the side, the winged form flew swiftly to the west.

Gertrum sensed the Anarchist long before he came into view, slowing as their eyes met. The Barbarian was large and physically powerful, and held his sword with a skill Gertrum knew he could not match. But it was the pure intensity of the man's stare that truly gave him pause.

Targon growled at his side, the grizzly's muscular shoulder pressed against his side. His bond had accepted whatever fate came as the Barbarian bore swiftly their way. As a young man, Gertrum had committed his life fully to defending the Harmonic way. He had never known retreat. The Scouter would fight this foe with all the will his mind and body could muster. Crouching, he raised his blade before him.

The Barbarian was young and inexperienced, eagerly taking the ruse the Ranger offered. Annabelle ducked the arcing sword that would have taken her head, then with the opening, drove the point of a broken arrow shaft into the man's chest. He staggered back with eyes filled with surprise, and vanished in a sea of Scouters eager to take the last Barbarian down. In moments, the Barbarian succumbed to the will of the Scouters' weapons and ceased his thrashing.

"Where is Gertrum?" Annabelle asked. They would need to work swiftly to regroup and prepare for an attack by the remaining Anarchists.

A young Scouter woman squinted up while attempting to stem blood gushing from a wound in her side. "I saw him running up the trail." She nodded to the north.

The Ranger exhaled hard at the news, sizing up the condition of those still standing. "You!" She stabbed a finger at the eldest. "Attend to her wounds. The rest with me. Let us hope we find that man before he does something foolhardy!"

"You fought well, Harmonic." Groegan smiled down at the master Scouter lying prone at his feet. Carefully, he lifted the point of his sword over the Scouter's chest. "Nothing is grander than to die nobly in a battle lost." The Scouter's eyes glanced to the north, his face suddenly filled with awe and contentment. Groegan followed the man's gaze and caught sight of a dark form winging westerly. A moment later, dragon and rider were gone. So the boy had used the mayhem of battle to make good his escape. Groegan lost his smile.

But the Scouter found it, chuckling and displaying bloody teeth amid his stubby beard. "Excepting maybe to die nobly in a battle won, Anarchist."

Groegan sneered down at the man, lifting his blade higher.

The Scouter's bond roared futilely, trying to rip through the Air shield holding it at bay.

The Scouter lifted his chin, still smiling at the Barbarian. "For Queen and honor, then."

"No," responded Groegan, "for honor without queen," then plunged the sword down toward the man's heart.

Just before the tip of the sword touched the Scouter's chest, an arrow struck his blade, sending the point wide of its mark. His steel found only gravel.

Groegan turned with a jerk to find a master Ranger and four more Scouters crouched near the Scouter's bear. So the master Scouter's purpose had only been to give his troop time. "Well played, my brave adversary. Until we meet again, then." Groegan laughed and tipped them all an Anarchic salute, then vanished into the gloom of night.

"Well, after him! Don't let him get away!" Gertrum bellowed at his flat-footed troop.

Annabelle stepped forward and rounded on those beside her. "Stay your feet! Chasing a powerful dark orderman into the veil of night in unknown territory is a dead man's quest!"

Gertrum sat up with a groan, spitting blood from his lips, then sighed at her counter-order. "Somehow, I had a feeling you'd say that."

# A Journey into the Dark Unknown

Conner's knowledge of the realms this far from home was dismal at best. The only map of Griffinrock that Conner could recall ever seeing hung behind the bar in Estora's Tavern, and that had few details about the territories west of the Narwalen Plains. Eastlanders did not travel far from home, so geography lessons focused on the Eastlands region, and of course, the Borderlands to the east. He had only a general idea which direction to go, so for now, he directed Skye south. Once they were free of the mountains, he would know better how to get to Graystone Castle, or that was what he hoped. At least he no longer cared if anyone saw them. When Skye descended into Graystone's grounds, any remaining wisp of secrecy would be put to a decisive end.

To keep the chill wind off, Conner pressed his chest to the base of Skye's neck and held tight to the saddle. His thoughts wandered through all of the events of that day and all he had heard, and while little could be considered fortuitous, Skye wearing the saddle was something worth appreciation. With the long day, lack of rest, the trauma of their capture and escape, and the boredom of night flight, Conner was soon fighting to keep sleep at bay.

A fitful shudder and tremble nearly sent Conner soaring from the saddle, shaking him from his restless slumber. Even before he was fully awake, Conner knew something was dreadfully wrong. There was another quake, as if Skye had struck something hard. Conner sat up to gaze into the cold night sky and gauge the time. It was nearing midnight.

But there was something more. The stars were spinning. Conner clenched his eyes to fight back his fear of falling, but it did little to ease the sensation. The pit of his stomach pitched with the dragon's next bolt. His bond was in a steep spiral to the rocky mountain ridges below. "Skye, what is it?" Conner shouted, concern lost amidst the rushing wind.

"I need to rest," Skye slurred, then quivered yet again.

Conner watched with wide, timid eyes as the mountains below corkscrewed ever larger and grander. He considered mentioning that maybe Skye should slow his dive, but he did not have enough experience riding dragons to know what a dragon thought to be a safe descent. He would have to trust his bond on this. He bit his numb lip and gripped the saddle tighter.

After several more minutes, the spinning slowed, and Skye tilted his wings to level his flight as they glided toward a ledge near the base of a large mountain. But as they neared, the dragon did not slow. They were coming in too fast and low to make the ridge! Conner's warning was muffled by an awful crunching sound as he was ripped from the bosom of the saddle.

When Conner awoke, he was on his back. He sat up, brushing away freshly fallen snow. He had not been thrown far from the ledge.

"Skye!" Conner stumbled to where the dragon lay motionless, sprawled across the narrow ridge, the end of his tail dangling over the ledge.

Skye let out a soft rumble, but made no attempt to move. Conner could sense that the dragon was in a lot of pain. At a loss, Conner slid down next to his bond and waited.

Nearly an hour passed before the dragon attempted to stand. The wind had picked up, and snow littered most of the mountain surface. But Skye's legs refused to stay under him, and he was forced to use his wings to steady himself.

"And where do you think you are off to? You clearly need to rest." Conner tried to force the dragon back down, but given what he had learned of dragon stubbornness, he would have had better luck keeping a boulder from rolling down a steep hill, or worse, from rolling over him. So instead, he did his best to help his bond walk without getting stepped on in the process.

"I chose this place because there is a cave nearby. Let us rest there." The dragon lurched forward in an awkward motion, teetering between standing and falling forward. Under any other circumstance, Conner would have thought this movement comical, reminiscent of a few people he had seen stumbling out of Estora's Tavern. An hour later, Skye was leaning along the back wall of a cavern not far from the cliff.

With Skye settled, Conner unbuckled the saddle's girth to let Skye breathe easier. As Conner pulled away, he ran his hand over a large scale along the dragon's shoulder and was shocked when a piece of dark blue armor broke away, exposing soft, milky skin beneath. "Skye? What is this?" His voice trembled as he held the chunk of scale. "What is wrong with you?" There was no need to hide the alarm in his voice; his bond would have sensed it anyway.

Skye peeked at Conner through a slit between his eyelids. His head tilted to the side with another low groan. "I am not sure. I have not felt well since we left Dragongarde."

Conner staggered back against the cavern wall, shaking his head, unable to tear his eyes from the gaping wound in Skye's shoulder. Finally, he mumbled, "I did this. This is my fault."

"What do you mean? How are you responsible for this?" Skye asked.

"The Necromancer did something to you! I don't know what she did, but I am sure of it." Conner turned away from the dragon's stare and beat his fist on the rock. "I told them we would not go with them. They warned me they would not allow us to get in their way, Skye. Whatever that ... woman did to you, it is because of my stubbornness and stupidity." Conner coughed back a sob, then stemmed the tide of sorrow threatening to wash over him. "I thought I was doing what was right."

Skye's snort-sniff response turned to a spasm of pain, his leg twitching uncontrollably. At last he settled, and his blue eyes bored into Conner, not as bright as they should have been. "Maybe you should try thinking more about what you are feeling, and feeling more about what you are thinking. Then we would not keep getting into these situations."

Conner nodded. "I cannot change this situation, but I can go get help."

"And what of your message for the king?"

Conner gave the dragon's question no more than a passing thought as he reflected on how best to proceed. "I have to find you help first. I am done running and leaving behind messes others have to clean up. This is my fault, and I'm going to fix it!"

"No, Conner."

Conner rounded on his bond with knuckles pressed on hips. "What do you mean, no?"

"You should not act out of remorse, hysteria, or regret any more than out of anger, fear, or spite. Now, what of your message for the king?"

Conner's hard eyes floated to the cavern ceiling, fighting back frustration with the obstinate beast. At last, he sighed. "From my best guess, we must be near the southern edge of the mountains, which puts us about halfway to Graystone. That's more than a hundred miles of forest between here and there. Even on my best day, I could not make it to Graystone in time to warn the king. He is at the will of the Cosmos now. I cannot help him."

Skye found the energy to give his head a vehement shake. "Somehow, I do not believe you have thought this through. There must be a way to get to the king. You are simply refusing to look for it. This moment is the only one you have to work with, Conner. Live it as you believe you should, no matter how big or small your obstacles may be. To do otherwise is truly a tragedy worse than death."

"I'm done listening to your philosophy." Conner wiped at his eyes. *Do dragons cry?* he wondered. "I have come a long way to reach this place with you. Now you want me to attempt something I know I cannot accomplish, all while I know you lie here poisoned or bewitched, maybe dying? You ask too much of me, dragon!"

Skye lowered his thorny chin to the rocky cavern floor and closed his eyes. Conner heard the dragon's sigh, sensed his bond's resignation. "Maybe you ask too little of yourself. Of course, you must do what you think you must."

Conner was struck with the familiarity of the dragon's words, and was carried back to a time that seemed so long ago, in a cave like this one, when he'd told Skye he wanted to break their bond. He had journeyed far since that day. All his struggles, all the beliefs he had discarded along this path, all the hopes and dreams he had forsaken— surely all his effort was worth something.

He bowed his head and repeated his own words from that day. "I will return as quickly as possible." He picked his way down the closest slope to find a route that would get him off this infernal mountain.

# Tournament of the Realm

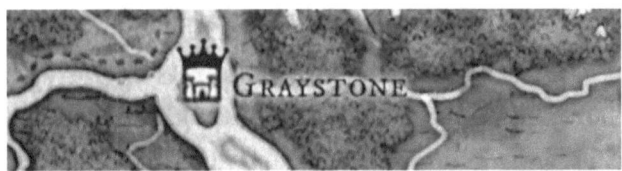

Lacerus stood brooding at the far end of the tourney field, his arms crossed, watching the first rays of Hemera set fire to billowing clouds beyond Graystone's glistening walls. Already, the four other Champion Advocates were finalizing their preparations for the tournament: giving orders to their pages while listening with keen interest to any last-minute instructions their preceptors had to offer. Spectators spilled out onto the field, jostling each other, eager to stake out their claims for the best spots. It was the Harmonic event of a lifetime—the selection of the new queen's Champion.

*Where is that fool Warrior?* Anarchic edginess gnawed at Lacerus. Turning, he moved quickly to Marcantos's tent and ripped back the flaps. "It is time, Marcantos."

Marcantos squinted up from bended knee at Lacerus's dark silhouette. "Do you recall the day we first met? That day you offered your services to guide me in my training?"

Lacerus stiffened, taking note of his student's disheveled appearance, bloodshot eyes that never settled, restless hands fingering the elemental sword he cradled. The Warrior's bed had not been slept in. Lacerus stepped into the tent and yanked the flaps down. He could not afford someone stumbling unannounced upon this discouraging sight. "Of course. You dismissed me with hardly a thought. But why—?"

"I thought I knew everything back then." Marcantos rose slowly before his preceptor. "I believed I had reached the pinnacle of my abilities. I was blinded to what I had become—the product of pampering and grooming by preceptors selected by our order's council, placating me with flowery obsequiousness, anointing me in their fragrant oils of platitude."

Lacerus's mind raced to assess the young Warrior before him, catching only a few words of Marcantos's soliloquy. "You've come a long way since then," he said, though his words lacked conviction. His student's mind had finally snapped.

"I tired of their rancid stench. It's odd, you know. Those lost in the deep desert of false beliefs are the last to thirst for honesty and truth." Marcantos's icy stare fixated on the smoldering embers in his tent's iron burner. "You have to be cognizant enough to see and ask. Most lack such awareness."

"Is this conversation leading somewhere, Marcantos?" Lacerus asked with a sharp edge of displeasure. He needed time to think if he was going to salvage the wreck of a man before him. "You are mere moments from joining in combat with the fiercest ordermen across the three realms."

"Hmm?" Marcantos grunted. "The tournament does not concern me. If the horde of spectators came to watch a long-fought battle, they will be severely disappointed." He twitched a confident smile before gripping Lacerus's shoulders like a vise. "A voice called to me last night, Blake. It said I have much yet to accomplish." Marcantos's eyes misted as if he was suddenly filled with the splendor of a glorious revelation. "I have been so intent on becoming Veressa's Champion that I failed to look beyond this test."

Lacerus shook free and stepped closer. "You heard voices?" He shoved a vial into his student's palm. "Drink this potion," he whispered through gritted teeth.

Marcantos stared at the vial. "What is this? Advocates are not allowed any potions before the tourney. If the council discovers—" But the shrill blast of trumpets in the courtyard cut him short, summoning the Advocates to take the Field of Contest.

"Trust me, Marcantos. This is to help you focus. The Tourney Council will not detect it." Lacerus popped the cork before Marcantos could argue, then guided the vial to the man's lips. "Quickly, so the tonic has time to work."

Marcantos drank the elixir, giving Lacerus a moment longer to reflect on his student's ill state. The Warrior had clearly slipped past the edge of sanity. Trista could not be blamed for this. No, she had done what she could to keep the man's mind intact. Lacerus knew that failing to foresee this ill wind was *his* burden. He had pushed Marcantos too hard, too fast, in preparation for this day. Now Lacerus was paying the price for his own arrogance.

Of course, there was time to save the man, but not here, not now. The potion Marcantos had taken was designed to assist the spirit to reconnect with the Physical body, something Lacerus kept for his personal use to mask the unforgiving effects of Traveling into the lower planes. Of course the triage was a desperate move, but the risk of his pupil taking to the tourney field in his present state was far greater than the risk of getting caught tossing down a mild sedative.

The Assassin worked quickly to gather Marcantos's gear before ushering the young man from his tent. Even then, the other four Advocates waited at the royal dais before King Jonath—brought back to health by the old Shaman—and his daughter, Queen Imminent Veressa. Hundreds of people lined the walls around the castle's grassy inner bailey that had served as Griffinrock's Field of Contest for over five hundred years. Flags representing all of Griffinrock's regions snapped and twisted in the morning breeze.

By the time the Warriors Advocate arrived at the royal dais, Marcantos was once more lucid. And when Marcantos drew lot with the Rangers Advocate and the two ordermen took to the field, even Lacerus was forced to stand in awe at young Marcantos's might. If the Assassin had had any doubts about the Kindred's success, they vanished with the melee's first blow.

# Ripples

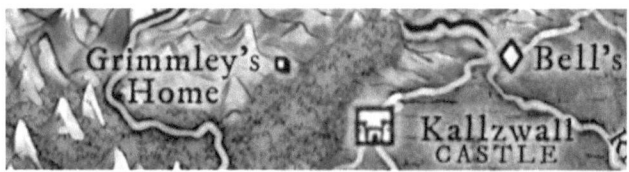

It took several emphatic hoots for Barthox to get the Shaman's attention.

"Hmm?" Grimmley blinked up at his bond. The powerful divination potion he was preparing required a sustained, deep trance, so the interruption was far from appreciated. "Another guest?" He sighed. The previous morning, Layna had arrived with Sara in tow. The Sorcerers Council had selected her to be the order's representative on the Tourney Council, the committee that oversaw all Tournament of the Realm preparations and ruled in cases of grievances or disputes during combat. Her departure for Graystone had offered Grimmley a chance to complete the work at hand. Or so he'd thought.

The Shaman set down his quill. A sharp noise from his garden drew his attention and he turned with a start. "Conner?" He shuffled to the boy filling the doorframe and caught the lad just as his legs gave way. "Why are you here? What happened?"

"Skye," Conner wheezed, unable to find air for more.

The Shaman guided the boy to a chair and thrust a glass of water into Conner's trembling palm. "Drink," he commanded, and took a moment to assess his apprentice's state. Conner was well beyond exhaustion, so given the boy's stamina, he had been running a very long while. He had also been crying. The boy's one word bit at him with angst. "What about Skye, Conner? Where is he?" he asked emphatically.

"In a cave ... the mountains ... north ... poisoned."

"Poisoned?"

Conner yanked weakly on Grimmley's sleeve, tears welling up in pleading eyes. "You have to save him, Grimmley!" he demanded.

"Of course. You know I will do what I can. But I need to know more. How do you know he was poisoned? By whom? What kind of poison?"

"I was on the way to warn the king. But we didn't make it out of the mountains before Skye was struck ill. He found a cave near the southern edge before ..." Conner's eyes went wide with concern, darting about wildly. "I left him there, Grimmley. I had to leave him!"

"Conner, you need to focus. Warn the king? What did you need to warn the king about?"

"The grandmaster Warrior ... Evinfaire ..." Gripping Grimmley's narrow shoulders, he declared, "He's an Anarchic spy!"

Grimmley pulled away instinctively. "That is a very grave accusation you are making, boy. You're going to have to take me through this, and go slow. Tell me everything that happened, and this time, leave nothing out!"

"But Skye! You have to save him!"

"You can't make a statement about Anarchic spies in the very heart of royal affairs without some explanation. Now, out with it!"

Conner choked back a sob and began his tale of how a company of Anarchist ordermen had captured him and Skye, and how the attack by another scouting force had given them the opportunity to escape. After a moment of silence, he continued. "Grimmley, I have to tell you something before I go on, a secret I have been keeping from you. When I was in Cravenrock, before I came to you, I ... I fell in with the city's Thieves Guild. That is, until I discovered the guild's overlord was an Assassin. That is when I fled the city."

Grimmley stiffened and grunted. "The Thieves Guild, you say? An Assassin in Cravenrock? Well, that explains why you were wanted by the city guard, and why you were chased into the mountains before bonding with your dragon."

Conner lowered his eyes under his preceptor's intense scrutiny. "I am sorry, Grimmley, for not telling you this before, but I was afraid of your disapproval. I am not proud of what I did."

"That, boy, is for a later conversation. Go on."

"Though I only saw the Assassin once, and I could not see his face, I noticed he wore a gold ring set with a black stone bathed in blue light. At the time, I knew I had seen the ring before, or one exactly like it, and knew it had to be rare. But I could not recall when or where ... until I met the Barbarian at Dragongarde wearing an amulet with the same kind of stone. Then I remembered the first place I'd seen the ring, and everything fell into place."

The boy gulped down more water with shaking hands. "While I was in Cravenrock, I had an encounter with the Warrior Evinfaire and another Warrior named Friarwood, who I learned later is Evinfaire's preceptor."

"Yes, that is correct."

"It was Friarwood who wore the exact same glowing onyx ring on the same finger as the Assassin. Both ... in Cravenrock ... at the same time. That has to be more than a coincidence. There is only one logical conclusion, Grimmley. Friarwood *is* the Assassin."

With this information, the Shaman let his mind run its course, connecting other recent events. "Of course." He settled timeworn bones in the chair across from his apprentice as the revelation set in. "First, assassinate the queen to bring about the tourney. Evinfaire, the most likely candidate to be Veressa's Champion, would place Friarwood at the very center of the realm. And with an ear, and if necessary, a blade close to a very young and impressionable queen, they could influence, maybe even direct the future of Griffinrock and the Harmonic Realms." And, Grimmley knew, if war was declared against the Anarchists for the queen's assassination, countless Harmonic lives, even the entire war, would be in jeopardy. Sad, old eyes fell on the lad. His heart ached, for what he was about to suggest would wound the boy worse than if he plunged a dagger into his chest.

"It was right that you went to warn the king, Conner. But, today of all days, even with your dragon, you would have had difficulty getting to him in time. And even if you had gained audience, what proof do you possess? No one knows you outside of the crimes you committed in Cravenrock. You would have been branded a criminal and imprisoned for slander against a high-ranking orderman and nobleman. Skye could not have saved you, though he certainly would have raised a lot of eyebrows."

Conner nodded.

"However, it is possible that *I* could get you in to see the king," Grimmley suggested. "I suppose coming to his aid and healing him of the poisoning he received during the queen's assassination is worth something in return."

"Of course. We will go to the castle right after you save Skye. You can substantiate my claim while I tell His Majesty everything I know."

Grimmley shook his head. "No, Conner. We must leave *now* to see the king. We have no time to detour from this path."

Conner stared back in horror at Grimmley's suggestion. "But Skye!"

"Conner, please listen. The tourney is underway as we speak. Even now, we risk failure to block Friarwood and Evinfaire's plans. If we arrive after combat has concluded, and if Evinfaire has been pronounced Champion of the Realm, there will be nothing we can do without hard, physical proof. It will be too late."

His apprentice leaped from his chair and staggered back through the door and into the garden.

Grimmley shadowed Conner to the lakeshore. "You don't understand, do you, boy?"

"Understand what?" Conner asked hotly.

"That this is not about you!"

Conner rounded on his accuser. "You're right! I don't understand!"

The Shaman saw the confusion and distress in the boy's eyes and sighed. He would have to take this slowly. "You keep thinking this is happening to you, as if no one else is involved or affected. But you know that is not true." Grimmley picked up a flat rock and, bending low, tossed it. The stone skidded across the lake's smooth surface only to disappear beneath the water near the far shore. "Conner, there is an aura about you that I have not felt before. You are like that rock skimming over the lake. Each time you make contact with someone, you leave behind a ripple flowing outward across the lands, a wake of change in your passing. And yet you remain like a dry stone." Grimmley gently patted the boy's shoulder. "Someday, my boy, you will have to realize that even the stone succumbs to the will of the water."

Conner's gaze turned north. "All along, you've been telling me about this wonderful Cosmic gift. And now that I am beginning to see it for what it truly is, you ask me to chance losing it. What change could I possibly achieve without Skye? What could a misfit Eastland farm boy touched by the Yearning ever accomplish?"

Grimmley rocked back on his heels with a sudden revelation. He had been pushing the boy too hard, shouldering the responsibility for Conner's actions as well as their consequences. It was time the boy chose his own route. "Yes. I see your point. Both paths are fraught with risks that make divination difficult. This has to be *your* choice."

"I used to believe that I was in command of my own destiny. But since leaving home on my trek, I have learned that I don't really have a say about my future. Everything has been chosen for me. It seems I cannot escape the Cosmos's plan."

Grimmley turned the lad toward him and held the boy's wide eyes before responding. "That is not how the Cosmos works, my boy. No wonder you have been fighting this all along. You *always* have choices, whether you see them or not."

"But—" Conner started.

"Conner, touching that dragon, going on the quest for the silver box, riding Skye, even donning that Dragonbonded armor—these were choices *you* made. The Cosmos is not some powerful force driving us headlong into a preordained destiny. What a pitiful existence that would be! You weren't chosen for this mission because the Cosmos needed some hapless dupe to dump on. Those strong in their convictions often fail to see paths besides the one they stand before, because they never realize something powerful was working inside them to guide them there. If you didn't see any other path besides the one that led you here, to this moment, it is because you would have never taken them anyway."

"And falling into the Cravenrock Thieves Guild? What does that say?"

"As you described it, it says that carrying through on a commitment to another, even one given to the young thief, Bandit, is unbreakable, no matter what personal hardships it may cause. And while I find the news of those days in Cravenrock troublesome, the skills you learned while in the Thieves Guild have proved useful several times since your escape from the city."

Grimmley waited, and when Conner said nothing, he offered one more insight. "Even fighting your bonding with Skye I would say has made you stronger for it. That is what makes the bonding trek so precious. Imagine someone else touching that dragon, someone who was completely convinced they needed to just hop on the dragon's back, fly to Graystone, and proclaimed to a slack-jawed crowd that the Dragonbonded had returned and they're ready to save the realms. Others your age might have done just that. And what would that have served besides stirring up a big mess? I would even go so far to say that your struggle to find how to use your powers has a purpose. Maybe there's a reason you're not ready for them.

"Listen to your inner voice, Conner. Let it guide you now in deciding whether saving Skye or warning the king comes first. I will trust in whatever you decide. I'll go collect what I can to hopefully heal the dragon. When I return, you must have chosen our destination."

The Shaman ambled back into the cottage, leaving Conner to weigh his heavy burden in the quiet morning.

Ripples cascaded across the lake, each wave mixing and mingling with the others, just as Grimmley's words mixed and mingled with Skye's. The stone was gone; even the path that had marked its passing was lost on the once calm, mirrored surface. That no longer mattered. In its wake, the stone had left a stunning display of reflections of Hemera's light.

Conner considers other times he thought he had been compelled—searching for someone to break his bond only to end up being befriended by the best two mentors he could have asked for, and having Grimmley and Layna there to guide him in his search to find his powers.

Grimmley pulled Conner from his solemn reflection. "Where are we heading?"

"To Graystone," Conner conceded. "Though I don't exactly feel dressed for the occasion."

The Shaman pursed his lips while sizing up the bedraggled boy in a black suit, then placed his arm over Conner's shoulder as the two stepped up the path to the gazebo. "There's an old Shaman saying, my boy: 'Once you know who you are, you'll find you no longer worry about how you present yourself.'"

Stopping at Grimmley's Transit Stone, Conner asked, "What is your plan once we get there?"

Grimmley's grunt did little to lighten the mood. "I'm still working out that detail."

# Grimmley's Ruse

"**T**ruly, an amazing feat of skill and elemental prowess!" Jonath declared to Grandmaster Evinfaire, who knelt before him on the royal dais. "The Warriors Order can be rightfully proud of the honor you bestow upon them, this realm, and its people."

Marcantos met the king's gaze with prideful eyes. "I am the one honored, Majesty, for the abilities the Cosmos has graciously bequeathed upon me and for the opportunity to serve this great realm and its citizens. And I humbly accept the responsibility the realm confers upon me."

Jonath lifted the Champion's medallion from his own chest. "Then, let it be struck in the records of Griffinrock's long history that on this day—"

A deep rumble from the far edge of the castle's main keep interrupted Jonath from his prepared speech. The small patch of trees around the Transit Stone shuddered and sparked. Pointing, the king shouted, "Master-at-Arms! Protect the keep from any intruders!"

A grandmaster Sorceress in gleaming blue armor sprang from the dais and sallied across the field, a dozen Queen's Defenders with bows and pikes at her heel. By the time the contingent stood at the ready, the rumbling had ceased. A blinding flash of light heralded a blast of air and dust, buffeting the Defenders and a few spectators who had erred in loitering too close to the Stone.

"Who defies the royal decree by disturbing this tournament?" Jonath shouted into the cloud of dust, squinting as he waited for the two silhouetted figures to emerge from the haze. One was elderly, adorned in Shaman robes, his arms raised high; the other, young and dressed fully in black. A score of paces from the dais, the Shaman stopped and bowed deep to the king. "It is I, Majesty, Grandmaster Shaman Rollingsworth."

"Grimmley?" Jonath blinked and rocked back on his heels. "In the name of the Harmonics, what are you doing?"

"Majesty, I apologize for the disturbance, but I come with an urgent matter that requires your immediate attention. I request but a moment of your time in private to explain."

Friarwood, standing beside Evinfaire, had shifted through a dozen shades of red and purple before he finally erupted. "Majesty! Disturbing the tourney is reprehensible! These trespassers should be detained immediately so that we may proceed unmolested!" Several of the tourney council members nodded in agreement, shouting for the master-at-arms to arrest the intruders.

Jonath stepped from the dais. "Who here has forgotten it was Grandmaster Rollingsworth who brought me back from the brink of death?" His voice rang clear above the others, silencing them all. Turning to the Shaman, he continued. "In respect for your service to crown and realm, I offer you this one liberty, Grimmley. Any matters requiring my private attention will have to wait until our duties here are complete. Otherwise, state your petition quickly and be on your way!"

Grimmley blinked and glanced about. At last, he continued. "As you say, Majesty. I am here to humbly and reverently inform you that tourney challenges have not yet concluded, and therefore, you cannot declare the Warriors Advocate as the new Champion of the Realm."

Jonath waved his arms vigorously for those about him to stop shouting. "What are you talking about? This is complete nonsense, and I have more than half a mind to have you arrested after all."

"Majesty!" Grimmley cried above the growing din of angry voices. Once the crowd quieted, he proceeded. "I would like to present to you Conner Stonefield, Dragonbonded and heir to the once great Order of the Dragonbonded. My King, the Dragonbonded have returned!"

Jonath's gaze turned to the lanky young man in leather armor who had been standing there silently gawking at his daughter. He noted for the first time the blood-red emblem of a dragon on his chest, reminiscent of the uniform once worn by the Dragonbonded. "What nonsense is this?"

The young man in black glared wide-eyed at the Shaman. Amid the stunned silence, the lad barked the word hanging on everyone's tongue. *"What?"*

Some time passed before King Jonath was able to quell the chaos around the Field of Contest enough to assemble the Tourney Council to consider Grimmley's proclamation. While on their way to the royal reception hall, where a special session would be held, Conner was able to process the insanity of this desperate situation.

*Caralynn is Veressa, the queen imminent!* Conner shuddered at the profound revelation. As he recalled his brief encounters with the girl—the night in Pennington Point when he had wrapped his arms around her, the next morning when she tossed him unceremoniously to the ground, the other night on the balcony at Kallzwall Castle—everything made sense. The Master Ranger Annabelle, her protector, had been accompanying the Princess Veressa on her bonding trek. That was why they had been incognito, and why they refused to take their grievance of the attack to the High Chancellor's regional court. Then another thought struck him. *I insinuated that Veressa, the next queen of Griffinrock, was insane and foolish, and then I called her an ungrateful harpy.* He felt his stomach constrict. *How do I get myself in such messes?*

He shook his head hard. He needed to get his mind off the thought and what disaster awaited him down that road, so he turned his focus to a more immediate problem. Besides, Conner needed to have a few sharp words for his mentor. Striding up alongside the Shaman, he whispered, "Grimmley, three days ago, you were telling me to run off and hide so my identity wouldn't be uncovered. And now you go and announce my existence to king and the entire realm? What were you thinking?"

"I had no choice, boy. We had to play the board before us. It was the only move open."

"This is not one of your games of Crowns!" Conner struggled to keep his voice low.

"No, it isn't, though you would be hard pressed to get this illustrious entourage to see it any other way." He gestured to the group walking before them—King Jonath, Queen Imminent Veressa, Layna and the five other members of the Tourney Council, the last remaining combatant, Marcantos Evinfaire, and his preceptor, Blake Friarwood. "But there is one thing you called correctly. Friarwood was livid the moment he laid eyes on you. And he showed no sign of surprise when I announced you as Dragonbonded. He was more ... distraught. He knew—or at least suspected—you were bonded to a dragon, and I believe he is most assuredly in league with those who laid capture to you at Dragongarde."

"So we just have to convince the king of this conspiracy and be on our way to save Skye." Conner could feel his connection with his bond weakening, and he worried it was not only because of distance.

"Unfortunately, I can see but one way to do that now. We will have to play through what I started and see what pieces are left standing when we reach the other side." Grimmley stopped, leaning closer to Conner. "I am sorry, but you're going to have to fight Marcantos Evinfaire."

"What?" Conner gasped, unable to stifle his repeated surprise. "Grimmley, lately you are developing a habit of apologizing to me over this, that, and the other. Frankly, it is becoming irritating. You know I don't possess a lick of combat skill, and yet you want me to stand toe to toe with the man who already bested me once in a heartbeat."

"Yes, my boy, I know. I hold no hope of you winning. But we can hope you get him to show himself as an Anarchist, if that is what he truly is."

"Grimmley, the man won three matches against the best fighting ordermen in the realms. If he was going to show any Anarchic powers, wouldn't he have done so by now?"

"Not necessarily. Anarchic powers can be masked, and he was prepared for those matches. But fighting you ..." Grimmley thought through the coming moves. "You need to get him angry enough that he loses control."

Conner rocked side to side to keep his uncertainties cornered. "Let me make sure I understand. You not only want me to fight the most skilled orderman in Griffinrock, you want me to do it all while he is enraged."

Satisfied with Conner's assessment, Grimmley bobbed his head. "Yes, boy, I'd say that covers it."

"Lords and ladies," Jonath announced once the reception hall doors had been sealed, "Rollingsworth's declaration is spreading through the throng of spectators faster than a fall wildfire on the Narwalen Plains. Rest assured the entire castle and city will be abuzz with the news within the hour. I want to get to the essence of this story quickly, for they will not wait while we sit in deliberation. There will be no more outbursts. Your task is to determine whether this young man, this Conner Stonefield, has the right to be declared an advocate in this tourney." Jonath glared at the Shaman, his irritation palpable. "Grimmley, you had better have an excellent explanation."

Grimmley bowed humbly. "Majesty, let me begin by stating unequivocally that Conner Stonefield is bonded with a dragon. I personally have seen and have even held conversations with the creature."

"So where is this creature?" asked Grandmaster Stiles of the Rangers Order. "If this boy is dragon-bonded as you assert, let him call it forth so that we can see for ourselves that your claim is true."

"Skye is …," Conner started.

Grimmley was quick to finish the boy's sentence. "Currently unavailable."

Marcantos grunted. "How convenient. Dragons haven't been seen in nearly six centuries, so who here could guarantee they would know what a dragon even looked like? Are we to allow the hearsay gossip of a Shaman and his whelp to commandeer the Tournament of the Realm?"

"I believe you meant to say, 'a well-respected and high-ranking Shaman,'" Layna corrected. After a moment, she continued, "Majesty, I also have seen and talked with Conner's dragon." She looked at each astonished face at the table. "And as an authority on the topic, I believe I would know what a dragon looks like."

Grandmaster Reigart, the Warriors council member, rose amid the murmurs, bringing the assembly back to order. "You could marshal an entire company of ordermen before me, all making such declarations, and I would not be convinced dragons still live—if they ever did. I demand physical evidence of this dragon's existence. Let us see this dragon!" Several shouted their agreement.

"Conner, do you have the rock I gave you?" Layna asked.

Conner nodded.

"Place it on the table. Majesty, I believe a demonstration may provide the evidence Grandmaster Reigart seeks, though it will not be a dragon."

Layna drew upon Fire and Water and incanted *"Hetos energi ektrepofanos"* to shutter Hemera's light from the hall. But instead of casting the chamber into complete darkness, the room was bathed in a deep blue pulsating light emanating from the stone on the table. "Majesty, I submit to you: dragonfire. You may recall dragonfire was known to emanate like a blue heartbeat from certain crystals and metals imbued with a dragon's powerful essence. You may also recall that dragonfire fades quickly over time. Therefore, it would be hard to dispute the facts. This stone has been not only in this young man's possession, but very near a dragon, and in the past few days. If any doubt the dragonfire's authenticity, I bid you to examine it with spells to prove it is not a hoax."

Friarwood broke the silence while several inspected the stone more closely. "Proof to being bonded with a dragon does not give this boy the right to claim advocacy for the realm."

"Majesty, if I may continue?" Layna interjected.

Mesmerized by the pulsating rock, Jonath nodded.

"As part of the agreement struck during the Anarchic War with those later to be known as the Dragonbonded, the three monarchs of the Harmonic Realms officially recognized the band of dragon-bonded humans as the Seventh Order. After the war, whether out of reverence for the Dragonbonded's sacrifice or because none in that order remained, the realms never rescinded that agreement. Thus, the Order of the Dragonbonded remains a legitimate Harmonic order. The rules for the Tournament of the Realm, written as part of the Treaty of Alignment at the conclusion of the War of Breaking, simply states, 'Each order is given the right to submit one Champion Advocate for the Tourney.' There just hasn't been a member of the Order of the Dragonbonded here to participate—at least, not for the past five hundred years."

Jonath nodded. "Sound logic, Layna."

Marcantos jumped from his chair and pounded his fists on the table. "You cannot seriously be considering this! I do not recall ever seeing the name Conner Stonefield mentioned for acts of valor, courage, or heroism to crown and realm, which is also required under tourney rules. If so, please correct me." After a moment of silence, he pressed on. "What I do recall, however, is encountering this impudent Eastland farmer when Friarwood and I recently visited Cravenrock. This boy came to my attention while fleeing arrest by the Cravenrock guards for disturbing the peace and other sundry crimes against the city. The last time I saw him, he was being carted away in the arms of the guard to be thrown into the stockade. It later came to my attention that not only did this Eastlander escape, he became a fugitive, an outlaw hunted by the city for crimes of robbery and assault. Truly, he is nothing but a brazen criminal! To allow him to compete in the Tournament of the Realm would bring dishonor and shame to the crown. Never has such a disgraceful offense been suggested in Griffinrock's long and illustrious history. Let us not allow this to happen!"

Grimmley cleared his throat. "Conner, were you ever found guilty of a crime while in Cravenrock?"

"No," Conner replied.

"And were you ever charged with a crime?"

"No."

Grimmley shrugged. "Anyone who has traveled to Cravenrock knows the city guardsmen can be ... fervent ... with their charges." A few murmured their agreement. "The realm is awash with stories of lawful transients swindled at the hands of those sworn to protect them. I also submit, under the realm's due process, that it is unlawful to unduly restrain or prohibit any citizen of the realm from completing their bonding quest. Yet, Conner, as you described to me the events of those days in Cravenrock, you escaped the stockade because you feared being prevented from completing your trek."

"Yes," Conner confirmed.

"Very well," Marcantos shouted with veins thick in his neck. "I will concede the point that there is no proof of this Eastlander's criminal acts. However, absence of unlawfulness offers no credence to bravery or fortitude of character. This boy has no experience in combat, has never held positions of responsibility nor demonstrated bravery in the face of danger. Where are his medals of valor? His badges of courage?

His rank of command? I am afraid the rules of the tourney are quite specific on this matter. He does not meet the criteria set forth."

"I think I can address that, Father," Veressa interjected. "I cannot remain quiet while this man stands in selfless silence before you and those about him defame his very character."

"Veressa?" Jonath asked, surprised at his daughter's interference.

"Father, we have spoken of the recent events that transpired during my time in Pennington Point."

Jonath recalled her account of that night—of nearly being kidnapped and of Annabelle nearly dying at the hands of a gang of thugs. He swallowed hard and nodded.

"What I did not speak of before was that Annabelle and I were not alone that night. It was Conner Stonefield who aided in our escape. It was he who single-handedly thwarted the criminals' plans, protected me from the Sorcerer's spell, and assisted us in our eventual flight from the city without bringing about a royal incident. If he has no badges of honor, it is because he demands no recognition for his deed, though I truly am indebted to him for my very freedom, if not my life."

In the stunned silence, Jonath knew there was more. He wanted to question his daughter further, but faced the young man in black instead. "Is this so?"

Conner nodded.

Jonath took in each contemplative face in the room. He knew news of a human-dragon bond ran rampant in the orders, though none would admit to their secrets here. He had even received a secret message from Ranger Lendfeather of this. But another thought crossed his mind, one so insane he had not imagined it possible even when Lendfeather had given him the news. "Conner, when and where did you bond with your dragon?"

Conner looked up to find all eyes upon him. "Deep in the mountains, Majesty, north of Cravenrock, on Midsummer's Day."

The king inhaled sharply, transfixed with the memory of the Midsummer's Day, when he had been called to the Chamber of the

Oracles to lay witness to that moment of perfect Cosmic balance. What had Oracle Gildamare said? *We believe a significant event is about to happen; one that will, at first blush, be as subtle as a falling leaf, but will most certainly set in motion a cascading series of effects that will ripple through the Harmonic Weave for the next several hundred years, if not longer.* So it had been Conner bonding with his dragon that the Oracles described as the Cosmic singularity. And here the boy stood, creating ripples across the realm. Did the lad even know what he was?

Jonath cleared his throat. "Then I say this deed qualifies as an act of valor that meets the rules of the tourney, for truly I speak from my heart, Conner Stonefield: I am personally indebted to you for what you have done for my daughter and for the realm." Turning his attention to those gathered about the table, he asked. "Does anyone still have issue with declaring Conner Stonefield as member of the Order of the Dragonbonded and that order's Champion Advocate?"

None spoke against the king, though Marcantos shook visibly with rage.

"Highness," Conner bowed awkwardly as the queen imminent approached, then walked beside him back toward the Field of Contest, where a mass of spectators milled about anxiously. "Please forgive me for what I said to you back in Pennington Point. If I had known you were—"

The sound of Veressa's laughter, like the jingling of crystal goblets, interrupted his thoughts. "It is I who should apologize, Conner Stonefield, for now I see you are truly a man who speaks his mind in the face of injustice yet holds his tongue to protect the virtue of another. I can only assume that I also have you to thank for putting me to bed the other night at my aunt's castle." The queen imminent chuckled again when Conner was unable to respond. "Let's keep that as a secret just between us." Then, her face grew serious. "But I do not think you know what you are up against."

Conner glared at the back of the Anarchic spy Evinfaire walking proudly before him onto the field. "I know exactly what I am up against."

Veressa sighed. "I fear my coming to your defense has only served to jeopardize your welfare. Surely you do not think you can win against that man?"

That morning after their departure from Pennington Point, in a fit of anger, Veressa had tossed Conner to the ground like a practice dummy. Of course she would question his sanity fighting someone with even half of Evinfaire's skill. And well she should! He questioned his own foolhardiness for going along with the wily old Shaman. "No," he admitted, then bit his lip, realizing he had said too much.

Veressa stepped in front of him, forcing him to pull up short. "I do not know what you and Grimmley Rollingsworth, and that Sorceress Layna Newstone are about, but I know you well enough to believe that this is not about fame or fortune. I can feel yet again that you come to my rescue, to vanquish some formidable foe lurking in the dark fissures of the alleys ahead—a darkness you refuse to name. Truly, whatever shadow drives you to take such risk frightens me. But"—Veressa's cheeks reddened—"the thought of you getting injured frightens me more."

Conner stood with eyes wide, but he offered nothing further.

Finally, she conceded to his Eastlander stubbornness. "Very well, Dragonbonded. But know this. I cannot explain it, but I believe in you. Succeed or fail in achieving your objective this day, you have won my lifelong trust and friendship. May the Cosmos guide your way to what should be."

And with that, she moved to stand beside her father on the tourney dais.

# Part IV

*It is possible, after many years of practice, and with the right spiritual guide, for a disciple to see beyond the Physical. This is because parts of a Physical Being reside in the other planes. These other parts are, to the Physical self, like echoes to a blind person in a large room. He makes a sound—a clap, a stomp, a sneeze—and if he is aware, knows the room is larger than his Physical body. Enlightenment comes not from hearing the echo, which is always there; it comes from dissolving one's self-image as a creature purely of the Physical. Transcending the ordinary, the normal, the mundane, happens not with knowledge, but with the shedding of the false truths we cling to so dearly. Shed yourself, and then strive to listen.*

*—The Modei Book of Earth (Fourth Book)*

# Conner's Trial

**B**y the time the entourage had returned from their meeting, the spectators had grown to thrice the number as they'd been when the council had adjourned. Conner had not believed it possible so many people could amass in the small area around the field. As he neared the royal dais, a woman pointed and screamed, "Dragonbonded!" In a flash, the placid crowd erupted with ear-piercing shouts and cheers. Those near the wall jumped and craned their necks while men lifted children on shoulders for a chance to gawk at the thin teen in black.

The king and queen imminent took their thrones, and a dozen trumpets roared the crowd to silence so that the master-at-arms could decree the ruling of the council: that the man dressed in black was indeed Dragonbonded. The crowd erupted into an even greater frenzy, and it took several trumpet blasts to quiet them.

While the master-at-arms continued the ruling, Conner fidgeted, scanning the crowd of eager faces staring back at him. That was when his eyes came upon a middle-aged townsman with a large nose and broad-brimmed hat peering over the shoulder of a tall royal guardsman. On his shoulder sat a squirrel.

What first drew Conner's attention was the man's odd smile and sparkling eyes, as if the townsman knew the secret to some joke or riddle. But there was something more that held his attention. Conner had seen him before. He could not recollect when or where, but his features were too distinct to confuse him with anyone else.

The man winked and tipped his hat Conner's way.

"Boy!" Grimmley shouted gruffly.

Conner jumped as he turned to face his mentor.

"You need to focus, Conner. Do you think you can remember everything we discussed?"

Conner shrugged. "There's not a lot to remember. I am to fight a grandmaster Warrior and make him angry enough to show his true form. Oh, and not get killed in the process. That last part I'll try not to forget."

Grimmley was not amused but understood that making light of the situation was the boy's way of dealing with stress.

"Conner Stonefield," the king's voice rose clear over the crowded yard. "You are given rights to carry two weapons onto the Field of Contest." After the king took full stock of the boy's attire, he added, "Of course, if you do not have any on you, you may choose from yonder rack." He gestured to a stand abundant with an assorted array of lethal weapons.

"Majesty"—Layna stepped forward and bowed—"if I may interject, there is no recorded history of Dragonbonded ever using a focal device in combat. As far I know, they also carried no weapons."

Conner moved to ask the Sorceress what she was doing, but she waved him to hold his tongue.

The king appeared almost as confused as Conner, but shrugged his acceptance. "Then advance and prepare to engage in combat."

"Layna, what was that about? Are you trying to get me killed?"

Prodding her frozen student forward, she whispered, "Wielding a weapon you do not know how to use will only prove distracting. Besides, a weaponless opponent is not what Evinfaire expects. Nor do I think he is skilled to handle such a scenario. How better to inflame the man's honor than by forcing him to fight an unarmed boy?"

Conner shuffled forward under the firm guidance of Layna's palm pressed to his back. "I suppose I'd just hack off a toe or slice my hand open with one of those," he said with a nod toward the rack. Still, he longed even for the false security holding a sharp weapon might bring.

When they reached the edge of the Field of Contest, Grimmley gave Conner one of his reassuring pats. "The Cosmos will be with you."

"I don't see how the Cosmos can help me through this situation."

Grimmley peered over the rim of his glasses at his worried student. "It already has, my boy. When there are no truths remaining to rely upon, when all beliefs and opinions have been dispelled, and you are left wondering what is happening and what to do, a little faith can take you a long way."

The loud blast of trumpets cut Conner from his retort. The sooner this was over, the sooner Grimmley could help Skye. So he turned and marched headlong to face the awaiting grandmaster Warrior.

"It seems our first lesson in Cravenrock proved insufficient." Marcantos dropped the point of his sword into the dirt and tilted the grip Conner's way. "Maybe you should take my sword again to better even the odds," he teased, smiling at the opportunity for another lesson.

"That's all right." Conner dismissed the Warrior's offer with a wave. "I think we both know how that would turn out. Perhaps another approach will yield different fruit." He stepped onto the field, hoping his crouching stance did not look as awkward or apprehensive as it felt.

Marcantos lifted his sword into play. Still, Conner saw the man's hesitation, sensed his uncertainty about how to proceed. Maybe Layna had been right. Maybe that was why the Warrior had tossed him his sword during their first encounter. The man had spent his life learning how to fight the most skilled armed combatants across the Harmonic Realms. Maybe the best defense against a man like that was no defense at all.

That line of thinking, as it proved a moment later, had too many maybes.

Before Conner could react, the Warrior closed the two paces of space between them. With a powerful flick of his supple wrist, Marcantos's sword flashed. Conner staggered back long after the attack was complete and felt the sharp prick along his side. His shaky palm came away gleaming a bright red in the late morning light.

"Surely you see that I will not allow anyone to stand in my way of becoming Veressa's Champion. If that means gutting you sternum to hip, then so be it. I offer you just this once—end this charade, yield to me, and leave this place. No one will consider you a coward." Marcantos shrugged his indifference. "Or stand, and risk your very life. It is your choice."

It was the Warrior's cold, unfeeling tone that made Conner shudder. He studied the man before him, standing completely at ease, yet fully prepared to handle any attack Conner might muster. The orderman was in full mastery of his emotions. How could Conner ever hope to complete his mission before being run through?

In this moment of desperation, the memory of that night in the Pennington Point tavern rushed at him—of following Skye's emotional scent. In his mind, Conner stood once more before that emotional conduit—a bright beam of energy streaming from a gaping hole. It was much weaker now. Still, it called to him. He stepped into the stream of energy with his thoughts and felt the same exhilarating rush. His fear passed beyond his mental horizon. His feet walked the grassy field, his eyes studying the grandmaster before him, but his awareness was no longer in his body. He could feel himself rising, floating above the drama playing out below.

Conner could feel Marcantos's unsettled stance and knew something was not right about the Warrior. He rose from his crouch, eyes on the Warrior he was now certain was an Anarchist. "And surely you see that I cannot allow anyone—especially you—to bring harm to Veressa. I know what you are."

Conner could not explain how, but through the shifting pattern around him, he felt the Warrior's pending attack long before the orderman made his move. Conner watched with intense curiosity as his body stepped to the side. Marcantos's sword flowed past. He noted the patterns of light and sound shifting with his movement, new waves flowing out, altering the intricate design around him in subtle ways.

His consciousness rose further as the scene continued below. Still, the beam of energy pulled at him, lifting him to a greater vantage, exposing more of the pattern's weave. He came to a barrier, but his mind did not pause. He pushed through the malleable membrane, and his senses altered, tangling as sight became smells, sounds became tastes.

Conner smelled the Warrior's next assault, heard the shifting patterns, and to these designs he responded. Marcantos's blade drifted past, and Conner leaned back, extending his palm upward. He lightly tapped the underside of the sword as it floated by, altering the arc ever so slightly. Just as on the day under the watchful eye of master Apothecary's Merich Cleaverbrook when Conner created his first a medicinal potion, he watched his catalytic adjustment on the sword play out, cascading through the Warrior's perfectly balanced stroke, doubling and redoubling its effect until ...

Marcantos's body spun wildly out of control. Losing his footing, the Warrior tumbled hard to the ground. His blade torqued from his grip and cartwheeled away, coming to rest near the edge of the field. Onlookers stood in stunned silence. Slowly, the Warrior rose and turned toward his upstart challenger, his face contorted, first with disbelief, then humiliation, and finally with rage. Marcantos drew hot on Air and Water elementals. *"Aetos ousia klisixifos!"* Fury disengaged any limits to self-control. He pressed forward with an infuriated roar, sword flying back across the field and into his extended grasp.

Conner stumbled backward, instinctively calling on Fire, as he had practiced with the bejeweled wheel in Dragongarde. Fire elemental flowed into him, through him, around him, and he staggered under the fierce stroke of the Warrior's elementally endowed steel. But Fire did not stay. And with its passing came Air. His elemental shield shifted form, a new mesh that deflected another powerful stroke before the shield vanished with his next breath.

In a rising crescendo, the Warrior's onslaught came at him. Air elemental whipped at Conner's sides; Water lashed at his legs; steel pummeled him back on his heels. Yet such trivial matters were not Conner's concern. His mind moved with the tempo of the woven patterns shifting under the Warrior's fierce assault. Water came to him, then Earth, then back to Fire once more. In unending succession, Conner met the quickening might of each elemental foray with a new elemental shield. His consciousness ascended to a dizzying height over the weave, and he pushed through a second membrane. Along the pattern's distant fringes, Conner sensed the dynamic motion of dark funnels ripping and tearing at the weave, creating a different pattern in the wake of its destructive force.

Conner flowed through a third membrane and lost all sensation. His senses crumbled and flushed away, and in their wake, a single perception was forged.

The perpetual cycles of elementals came at Conner faster and faster, taking on a life of their own. He fought to control them under the Warrior's relentless assault, to slow their rush. Somehow, he knew his body could not continue absorbing the energy burning through him. But he was lost on a churning sea. Waves swelled and crashed over him, tossing him, driving him under. The bubble between who he was and was not eroded away.

He fought to purge the elemental forces, to channel the energy boiling through him. In desperation, he formed a ball of white light between his palms. Fire sparked and fused with Air, mixing with Water, then churned with Earth. Turning his hot palms out, he sent the light forth.

The ball of light ripped through Marcantos's elemental shield of Air and exploded squarely on the Warrior's chest. A blinding flash sent the orderman reeling backward. Marcantos tried to recover, to reinforce his faltering shield, but Conner struck with a second ball of light. The

Warrior's legs buckled from the impact of the flash. Marcantos shook his head, then with a roar, he staggered forward, sword raised. The third flash sent the orderman to his knees. Before Conner could hurl another blast of light, the Warrior threw his arm up before him, a sign of yielding. "Stop!" he beseeched.

Conner sensed something changing. A new pattern was forming, swirling about him, rising up from the darkness. Confused, Conner hesitated.

It was in this stillness that Marcantos moved. His arm snapped forward like a snake, the venom of his treachery hidden in his palm. There was a flicker of steel in Hemera's late morning gleam.

Conner reacted, but the shifting patterns gave confusing signals. He twisted but not before the short blade drove deep into his shoulder. The morning he received the Calling flashed through his stunned mind—sitting at the Stonefield table, eating the breakfast his mother had made him. He had been so innocent, such a gullible fool. All he had wanted was to find his bond and return home to the Eastlands, to live a simple, quiet life as an Apothecary. Instead, through every step of his journey, he had been directed, controlled, manipulated by everyone he had ever met. He gripped the knife handle and pulled. Pirate, the Assassin, even Bandit had used him for their own personal gain. He groaned as the knife's razored edge slid against his collarbone. "No more," he whispered, and pulled harder, letting the throbbing pain draw him back into his body. He would never be so naïve again.

He thought of Layna, who had promised to help him, but then left him vulnerable to the party of Anarchists. Even Grimmley had manipulated him, telling him he needed to warn the king at the risk of Skye's life, and look where that had led. He had failed himself, failed Skye, failed the Cosmos. How could he ever trust anyone again? "No more," he cried out, and ripped the blade from his shoulder. He let the agony of the wound and the guttural wail escaping his throat cleanse away his errors. Life's energy gushed from the wound. He tried to stem the rush, but hot liquid flowed between his fingers.

The bloody knife slipped from Conner's grasp. "Never again," he exhaled. And, as if succumbing to a long and tiring day of work in the summer fields, he tumbled gently into the grass.

# Awakenings

"**T**ell, look who decided to rejoin the living!" The woman's merry, familiar voice drifted across the edge of Conner's consciousness. "I was beginning to think he wasn't going to wake until he was an old man."

"That's no surprise. You can't give the boy a soft bed in a royal bedchamber and expect to see him up before lunch grows cold," an old man's voice grumbled back.

Conner opened his sluggish eyes and squinted at Grimmley and Layna peering down at him with delight. He tried to rise, but Layna's firm palm held him in place.

"How long ...?"

"Nearly two days." She waited for the news to settle over him before continuing. "Evinfaire's knife severed an artery, and you lost a considerable amount of blood. We would have lost you forever if not for Grimmley's quick actions."

Grimmley hushed the Sorceress with a fluttered wave. "Bah! A lot of people are relieved the tourney is behind them. They'd all be extremely put out if they had to go through it all over again just because the boy up and died."

"Don't listen to him, Conner," Layna said disapprovingly. "He's not left your bedside since the tourney. And you know how he gets when he's tired."

Barthox gave a supportive hoot at Grimmley's back.

Conner turned from their intense scrutiny and banter. "Maybe you should have let me die."

Grimmley and Layna exchanged hard looks of concern.

"I can't feel Skye anymore," Conner said. "There's nothing there. He's gone."

Layna sighed. "I am truly sorry. I searched for the cave you left the dragon in, but found no tracks and had no other means to discover its location." She leaned closer, eyes reflecting more worry than sadness. "How do you feel?"

Conner shook his head, still not ready to meet her gaze. "Normal." But that was what anyone with the Yearning would say if asked. In truth, he could sense a part of his mind had been ripped away, could feel the gaping wound. There was a throbbing silence where he and Skye had once shared emotions. And in that vast silence, he felt alone, an ache he knew would never heal.

Grimmley puffed up his lips and examined him through smudged spectacles. "It is possible you were saved from the Yearning because your bond with the dragon was something special." In the awkward silence, he added, "It seems the Cosmos gave you your wish after all."

In the residual sting of Grimmley's rebuke, remorse took root in Conner's soul. All his struggles to at last accept his bond as the gift it was—all too late. He never had a chance to tell Skye how he felt. Lying there, raw and exposed, shame stripped him of what strength he still possessed. Tears began to flow.

"I know this is of little comfort right now," Layna said, "but you should know you were successful in thwarting Evinfaire. Not only did you defeat him, but during the combat, he showed himself for the Anarchist he is. Alas, in the chaos subsequent to your injury, both he and Friarwood slipped away. The two are outlaws now. They will be executed if ever they show themselves within the Harmonic Realms again."

"Conner, you do understand?" Grimmley prodded. "You defeated Evinfaire. You are Queen Veressa's Champion of the Realm."

As the news took hold, the irony was not lost on Conner's clouded mind. He had sacrificed the bond that had prevented him from pursuing the life he wanted, only to be handed another responsibility as the lifelong protector of the queen of Griffinrock. And it was his bonding with Skye that had made it possible for him to compete against Marcantos in the first place. He would have given everything, present and future, to have Skye back—even with the dragon's stubbornness, incessant questions, and peculiar insights into the human species. He wiped angrily at the tears that would not stop. "Damn dragon," he grumbled.

Grimmley broke the long silence that followed with a chuckle. "I'm not sure I will ever get used to the tranquility at home again. Sara has never been so fit. How will she get her daily exercise?"

Layna joined Grimmley with her own light chortle. "Skye told me bonding with Conner was like having an itch in the middle of his spiny back—constantly nagging and impossible to scratch."

Conner could no longer resist. "Well, you didn't have to listen to his infernal dragonsongs. I swear, for the longest time, I thought the irritable beast was tone deaf."

Once laughter had run its course, Grimmley wiped the moisture from his own cheeks and resettled his spectacles on his button nose. "My first mentor used to tell me, 'The Cosmos enjoys giving us tests, Grimmley. But there's no standard exam. The only tests that count are those that challenge us to grow.'" He tilted his head to study the lad over his spectacles. "Conner, my boy, you should feel blessed you were given a test truly worthy of your abilities."

Conner felt anything but blessed. "And what of my abilities on the road ahead, Grimmley? What am I to make of being an unbonded

Champion of the Realm?" He raised his arms out wide. "And how am I to protect the queen thus?"

Grimmley's face grew grave. Leaning forward, he whispered, "Such inquiries should be neither asked nor answered here, my boy. We will ponder their significance and meaning at a more appropriate time."

Layna thought it fitting to alter the conversation's course. "Veressa's coronation is in two days. And the king still demands evidence of the dragon's existence. If you are able to ride this afternoon, you can take us to the cave where you left Skye."

The thought of seeing Skye's remains chilled Conner to his bones. He swallowed hard. "Of course."

Late the next morning, Conner and Layna, along with King Jonath and an escort of Defenders, arrived at the cave. The king was impatient for answers, so they had ridden hard through most of the night.

"You're sure this is the right cave?" Jonath asked after they had entered the narrow entrance. It was void of anything but a few pebbles.

"Positive, Majesty, though I could have sworn it was larger." Conner pressed his palm against the wall that seemed to have shifted some five paces since his arrival with Skye. "Odd. I don't recall this being here," struggling to make sense of the mystery.

Layna moved to stand next to Conner and lightly traced her fingertips over the surface. Then she began to chuckle. When she was only met with blank stares, she explained. "This is not a wall, Conner. This ..." She gestured at the entire partition. "This is a cocoon camouflaged as a wall, most likely designed for the dragon's protection. Skye wasn't poisoned, nor is he dead, Conner; he's transforming! That is probably why you can't feel him. And given what little I know of dragon metamorphosis, I suspect he will soon emerge a full-fledged dragon!"

# Coronation

**W**hether from shock or exhaustion, Veressa felt completely wrung out from all that had happened over the past week—much more than she'd had time to process. Perhaps that was for the better. From her mother's assassination to the hard ride home to be at her father's bedside during his recovery, to discovering that the man who'd nearly become her lifelong protector was an Anarchist and having one of the famed and long-forgotten Dragonbonded appear out of nowhere to become her Champion—how could she even begin to make sense of it all? And here she stood, high on Graystone's royal platform, mere moments from ascending as matriarch of one of the three great Harmonic realms. If she had been given time to sit and ponder everything that had happened, she was certain her legs would have given out from under her.

Aligned before her, esteemed members of the six order councils waited for the precise moment that Hemera would reach its zenith. As dictated in the Armistice of the Orders, Lord Garrett of the Sorcerers Order, currently the most prominent order in the realm, held the gem-studded tiara of Griffinrock before him in preparation for her coronation.

As rehearsed, the Mystics' oracle Sir Giles gave a quick nod, Veressa's signal that it was time. She tilted forward, but her feet refused to move beneath her. She felt glued to the spot. Obscured by the shadows of the white castle spires towering overhead, panic gripped her, and her mother's voice spoke. *Are you ready to assume this responsibility, Veressa? I will not be there to remind you when you are distracted from your royal duties. I loved you to the very depths of my spirit. But your people need a great queen. That is why I was so hard on you.* What little confidence Veressa had summoned before faltered. Would she ever find a way out from behind the shadow of Queen Izadora's imposing regal prestige?

Lord Garrett's smile wilted in the midday heat, replaced by a look of curiosity.

Veressa needed someone to help sweep away these abrupt doubts. She cast her eyes about, looking for Annabelle's reassurance, until she recalled that the Ranger had not yet returned from her mission in the mountains. She looked to her father standing to her left, his eyes lost in a forlorn, vacant stare, seemingly unaware of her hesitation. Farther on, her aunt Mariette waited stiffly with her husband, Duke Regiboldt. The duchess's eyes had been red and swollen for the past week; Veressa would find no comfort there.

She glanced to her right, and her eyes fell upon her new Champion, the Eastlander Conner Stonefield, looking quite pensive and stiff in his clothes of nobility. He smiled at her, and her heart skipped a beat. His assured gaze filled her with confidence. She took a deep breath. *Yes, mother. I love you too. Thank you for all you have done for me. I will miss you dearly. But I must find my own path. This is my journey.*

Veressa stepped forward, out from the shadows of the towers gleaming overhead and into the brilliant light of Hemera. Accolades from the throngs of people jamming Graystone's streets below filled the castle as she knelt to receive Griffinrock's bejeweled crown.

# Clarity

Conner woke the morning after Veressa's coronation as he had the previous one—with Hemera breaking over the summer carpet of the Royal Forest, proclaiming its arrival through a narrow window in his north-tower bedchamber. But this morning was different.

Conner stumbled out of bed. After a strenuous wrestling match with his new clothes, hopping about the chamber for several minutes with his legs caught in his trousers, he dashed down the winding staircase, crossed the Graystone bailey, and entered a long hall at the base of the southern keep. Even the thick chamber door he came to did not slow his step. Conner applied his slim shoulder to the oak beams and crashed through without even considering a knock.

"What in the name of Ourea?" Grimmley cried at the unexpected intrusion.

"It's Skye!" Conner exclaimed with ragged breath and eyes wide. "I can feel him! He's waking up!"

With the official ceremonies concluded, the Shaman had grown bored and was more than ready to head back to his quiet life in his secluded valley, back to his research and his own cooking. So it did not take near as much time or energy as Conner had expected to convince Grimmley to use the castle's Transit Stone to return to the Shaman's home. Within the hour of informing Queen Veressa of the dragon's awakening, Conner had Sara saddled and was galloping north out of Grimmley's woods.

As Conner neared the cave where he had left his bond, his connection with Skye grew stronger. It was not long after he arrived and built a fire to stave off a late summer chill that Conner heard the hard snaps and cracking of rock emanating from the cave. A moment later, Skye ripped through the remnants of his cocoon wall. Conner stepped toward the cave just as the beast laid waste to the entrance that had become too small for him to pass through.

"Good day to you, Skye-Anyar-Bello of the family Cloudbender. May your days and deeds add honorable verses to your family's dragonsong." Conner bowed low amid the rubble in reverence to the creature that was twice its previous mass. "A lot has happened since you and I entered this cave."

"Like the fact that I am no longer a wyvern?" Skye's head wriggled higher, blue eyes mere slits.

"That I see!" Conner took stock in his remade bond. "Truly, your greatness and stature are more stunning than I could have imagined! Talons of curved steel, scales as black as any night, wings that could shade Grimmley's home," he listed with but a slight expanse of truth. "And *four* powerful legs to boot! You are without doubt a creature to be respected. The females of your kind will surely be unable to resist such a noble physique."

The dragon puffed out his wide chest with pride and snorted. Then his eyes shifted to Sara, tied to a tree near the fire. "And I see you brought me lunch! I do believe you have missed me." He gave his human bond a hungry smack.

"I *have* missed you, Skye," Conner affirmed. He waited for the beast to recover from his rare sincerity before shaking a narrow finger his way. "But don't for a moment think I came bearing gifts to celebrate your joyous return. You'll have to pursue a meal a little farther than my camp if you want to satiate that perpetually empty belly of yours."

Skye chose for once not to argue. He'd be better off conserving his energy to find something to fill his grumbling stomach.

Their days apart had left Conner with his own craving. More than a few questions burned in him, so he squandered no time getting to them. "While you were ... transforming, I was forced to fight a very powerful orderman."

"Forced?" Skye asked with a taste of surprise.

"In a manner of speaking, yes." Conner decided not to speak yet of his new obligation to protect Queen Veressa. That was not the direction he wanted this chat to go. "And I bested him."

Skye sensed Conner did not speak from arrogance. The dragon nodded his approval.

"You once said dragonsongs told of how dragon-bonded humans had to complete some kind of test before they were accepted into the Order of the Dragonbonded."

"And you want to know if this was your test." Skye sighed as he settled his large frame to the rocky terrain. "Is being Dragonbonded all that important to you? Are you any less without such a title?"

Conner jerked at his bond's unexpected questions. Were Skye's references to amphithere and guivre any different? Maybe it was just a name, just a title, but what would be his significance in the realms without such a label? At first, he had thought becoming Dragonbonded was part of accepting Skye as his bond. He understood now that was why he had been so adverse to the idea. He had accepted the Champion's medallion hanging around his neck, and the responsibility that came with it, under the pretense that he was of the Dragonbonded's old order. He had donned their armor, cut his hair, even found himself wanting to be secluded from others, preferring the company of his bond. And he did not argue with those who endowed him with the title of Dragonbonded. It seemed deception was indeed a disease of his species.

"I do not know who or what I am, Skye. But I do know that I faced my fears and somehow I succeeded. Maybe it was because the Warrior was fighting for personal gain, while I fought for Veressa, for her safety. Whatever the reason, I know now that I have the power to choose my own future, one not defined by those who lived in the past. And I am ready to discover what that is. That has to count for something."

Conner was not ready for Skye's response, so he quickly asked a different question. "When we were in Dragongarde, one of our captors told me that Harmonic life was not in a dragon's nature." Conner waited, letting his confusion and doubt flow through their connection, filling in what he feared most to ask.

Skye turned his gaze toward the snowcapped ridges to the north, but Conner felt the dragon's hesitation, sensed his turmoil as he considered how to respond.

The silence grew palpable. Conner pressed on. "The Necromancer—I know she talked to you. I felt it. At least tell me what she said."

The dragon shifted uneasily. Finally, he said, "She asked if I knew where dragons came from. So I told her of our dragonsong that speaks of the four families of dragons being created by the powerful Shaman God Shazarack. She told me that Shazarack was not just a Shaman, but the father of Necromancy."

Conner wanted to scoff at the audacious declaration, to dismiss the notion that people practiced the dark arts of animating the dead as another children's fable. After all, that is how he would have responded a few months back. But memories shuffled stiffly toward him—of undead in the moon-shaped cavern gripping at him, clinging to him, pushing him off the ledge of what he knew to be real. He shuddered. "And you believe her?" As soon as he had asked the question, he wished he hadn't. Lies were second nature to humans, not dragons. Truth or not, the dragon believed her.

Conner felt this new possibility settle around them like thick morning fog. An ethereal dampness clung to his skin, dulling his mood. He wanted to refute the Necromancer's claims, but he was afraid to delve into his doubts about everything he had been taught about Harmonic and Anarchic life. There was one person who could enlighten him—the Necromancer Meera Asheborne. He had heard rumors the Necromancer had been captured was being brought to Graystone, to be held prisoner at the Shamans temple. He would need to find a way to speak to her.

Conner stepped close to his bond, noting the dragon's wider forehead and thicker black scales glistening an iridescent blue in Hemera's light. Sharp bone spikes the size of Conner's thumb grew from Skye's crown. "You were right, Skye. You are the only one I can truly trust."

"And what of your great Shaman tutor?"

Conner shook his head slowly. "I will continue my studies as before. But I no longer hold any illusion that Grimmley can help us. Nor can the Sorceress Layna."

"So we are on our own once more," Skye surmised what Conner had already concluded.

Conner reached up and patted the dragon's hot muzzle. "So it seems, my dear friend. So it does seem."

# Imprisoned

"**A**nnabelle!" Veressa leaped from her throne and ran to the Ranger.

Before Annabelle could react, the queen engulfed her ex-preceptor in a tight embrace just as the hall's doors clanked shut. Alone, Veressa found no need to conceal her delight. "It is good to see you again. I have missed you so," her voice muffled by the Ranger's green cloak. The odor of dirt, smoke, and horse assaulted her, but Veressa found the smells comforting.

It was several minutes before Annabelle could peel Veressa away. Cocking an eyebrow, the Ranger held the young queen at arm's length. "So your longing for company is the reason I received an urgent summons to the queen's reception hall, even to appear before you as I am?" The Ranger's hands flowed downward before her, exhibiting her bedraggled appearance. "Majesty, it has been eight days since I left Dragongarde with our captured Anarchist in tow, and many more days since I departed Dreadcreek. Surely my queen could have delayed her request until I had a chance to bathe?"

Veressa laughed as joy bubbled up from within. "And what an adventure it must have been." She took a regal pose, her jaw tilted upward, and commanded, "I will want a full and detailed verbal report of every moment of your quest." Failing to hide the smile painting her entire face, she added, "After you have had an opportunity to rest, of course."

"It is nice to know my queen cares for my well-being."

"And what of your Anarchist prisoner? This grandmaster Necromancer?" Veressa shivered at the sudden thought of having to courier a powerful prisoner back to Graystone.

"Meera Asheborne. We captured her at the foot of Dragongarde itself. With her Barbarian friends either dead or scattered, and with no cadavers about to call to her defense, she surrendered without so much as a ruckus. After dropping out of the mountain pass north of Kallzwall, we met up with a team of Shamans dispatched to assist with the prisoner. She is being held at Graystone's Shamans temple until she can be relocated to a more secure location."

Suddenly, Veressa reached out and gripped Annabelle's arms tight. Her smile faded. "Annabelle, I have asked you here for a very specific reason," she whispered. "One of utmost secrecy, for I cannot share what I must say with any other."

"Of course, Majesty," Annabelle responded with a hint of concern. "I am always at your service. You know that. But I am obligated to first mention that my status within my order is far from exemplary. Even being here, visiting you alone at night, you risk being accused of nepotism."

"Yes, about your status." Veressa sighed, deciding it best to get that business out of the way first. "You should know that I submitted a royal request to the Rangers Council to reinstate your position and status in the order. And, as queen, I informed your order's council that I would also be conferring upon you a medal of valor for helping my new Champion of the Realm escape the Anarchists. It was only by the efforts of your band of Scouters that he was able to return here and expose the Anarchic conspiracy for what it was."

Annabelle's expression grew dark. "Veressa—Majesty—why do you not listen to me? With the growing talk of declaring war on the Anarchists, you cannot afford to have the orders distracted by displays of favoritism. This one act, no matter how unpretentious as it may seem, could drive a wedge between the order councils when you need to find ways to bring them together."

"You do realize that your own argument works against you?" Veressa stood defiantly before the Ranger. "You have always been more concerned for the welfare of others, always striving to see the greater picture, even at extreme personal cost. Which is why I need you here with me, especially now." Unable to wait longer, Veressa called Air to her. With a slight hand gesture, she incanted, *"Aetha energi kalyptholos."* The air about them shimmered for a moment. Noting Annabelle's wide-eyed stare, the queen smiled. "Do not be concerned. I warned the guards outside not to be alarmed if they sensed any spells."

"Your ability to control elementals is improving swiftly, I see. But it frightens me that you have something to say that requires a dome of silence?"

Taking Annabelle's hand, Veressa returned to her throne and waited for Annabelle to take the oak chair at her side. With a deep breath, she began to tell Annabelle about her journey from Cravenrock back to Graystone. She was not sure where to begin or what to tell, but once she started, the words were tripping over themselves to get out. Too much had been pent up inside, worries and fears about what she had felt and what it might mean. In the end, she left nothing out.

Annabelle listened intently, encouraging Veressa to continue with occasional nods of the head as Veressa spoke of her first nighttime excursion into the wilderness, and then her second. Veressa described her angst over these growing urges to connect with the natural world, and how Friarwood—or whatever his true name was—had come to her offering his support, detailing what he had suggested, and what she had tried on the excursions that followed.

"I am worried that I have done something ... depraved," Veressa concluded. "Was he trying to turn me into an Anarchist?"

Annabelle, who had been looking troubled through Veressa's tale, finally spoke. "I see now why you felt a need to have me near, Majesty.

First, do not be imprisoned by your suspicions. You should not worry yourself. It is likely this spy's intent was merely to soften you to be more receptive to his suggestions. I can see nothing sinister in what he suggested, nor in what you did.

"He was right on several points," Annabelle continued. "First, you have indeed bonded with a powerful animal, one that has and will continue to influence your emotional state. But we knew that on the day in Cravenrock when you told me of your dream vision. More importantly, these urges you have been feeling are certainly related to this unique bonding. I have no doubt that your bond is feeding these desires to be out in the wilderness. But Antilles was a gift from one of the great Djinn to help guide you on your path. You were accessing your elemental abilities while tapping into your connection with your bond. I see no harm in acting on these urges, though I agree that some supervision would be prudent."

Annabelle shook her head slowly. "I heard nothing in what you said that demands any urgent action, my queen. But I will need rest before I can fully process all you have said." Annabelle stood slowly and stretched away a stiffness that would only abate with a good night's sleep. "We will endeavor to get to the source of this, Majesty. I will check in tomorrow afternoon to discuss our way forward." Bowing, Annabelle left Veressa to consider her words of confidence.

Annabelle moved down the long hall with a weariness she had never known. Her heart was heavy from her queen's distressing tale. She had fought hard to keep her alarm hidden. Like her father, the girl had always been observant.

Annabelle's knees went weak and she buttressed herself against the wall, her head hung low. Tears welled in her eyes. Her father used to say that change was like water filling a pail from a leaky roof: it never happened all at once. She sensed Veressa was unsettled, but that could be for many reasons. She also had to consider that what Friarwood had been attempting with Veressa was no different from how Marcantos had come to use Anarchic Sight.

Annabelle pushed away from the wall and stumbled on, replaying Veressa's words, letting questions bubble to the surface. Why would Friarwood risk exposing himself just to assist Veressa? Was he seeking information that he could exploit with a young, impressionable queen? What information had he gleaned about Veressa on the long road to Graystone? How had a Warrior been able to sense her Ranger potential? Could Veressa have slipped up during their encounters and made mention of her dream vision? And lastly, with Friarwood still free, who might he have already told the queen's secrets to?

The Ranger stepped into her bedchamber, Peron taking a perch near the window. Pressing her back against the thick door, she slid the bolt into place. She would sleep on all these thoughts and hope her subconscious had something to offer up with Hemera's first light.

# A New Promise Made

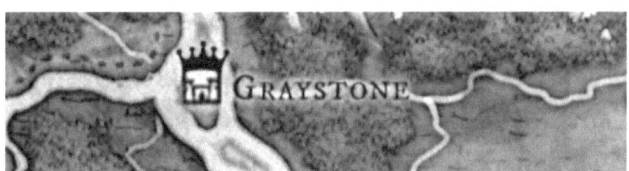

**C**onner crept down the musky stairs, his pulse heavy in his ears. Darkness and the reek of death called up unwelcome memories of his days in the underbelly of Cravenrock. He could conceive of no sound reason he would be summoned to such a gloomy place, so his only thought was to be done and leave as quickly as possible. With a steadying breath, he proceeded through the dank hall, a moth drawn to the meager light ahead. After several twists and turns, the narrow path flushed him out into a large chamber. He made neither sound nor motion until his eyes adjusted to the stream of timid light offered through a large stained-glass window along the far wall. Tightly spaced about the circular room was an array of stone coffins. Upon each was the exquisitely chiseled stone figure of a woman, lying as if captured in immortal sleep. He had reached Griffinrock's Tomb of Queens.

The movement of a dark form hunched near one of the coffins drew Conner's attention. "Majesty," he exhaled, unsure whether he should disturb the king. "Are you alone?"

"Ahh, Conner," the form's raspy voice echoed. Still, the form did not move. "Yes, of course, why?"

"I thought I heard you talking to someone. My ... my apologies, Majesty."

Behind each coffin hung a large, brightly painted tapestry depicting a woman in queenly garb and tiara placing the Champion's medallion around the neck of a kneeling form, some men, others women. Conner moved to get a closer view of the tapestry hanging near the king, Queen Izadora holding the bejeweled medallion—the same one that now hung around his own neck—before the image of a young King Jonath upon bended knee. But it was the look of love and admiration in young Jonath's eyes that drew his attention.

Following Conner's gaze, the king nodded. "She was a beautiful woman. Even then, I could not hide my feelings for Veressa's mother." He turned his intense stare back on Conner. "It is the same look I saw in your eyes when Veressa placed the medallion around your neck."

"Majesty, I ... I ..." Conner fumbled for something to say that would not lock him into a lie but would ease the growing discomfort of being discovered—for in truth, he was developing deep affection for the queen. He could only hope the light was too weak to show his crimson cheeks.

"I made a most grievous and perilous mistake," the king interrupted, seemingly uninterested in any explanation Conner might muster. He nodded at the tapestry. "I was inexperienced, rash, and deep in the self-adulation of a fertile love. I was filled with the false belief that I could be both protector and lover to the queen. I needed to be the first so that I could become the second."

Conner opened his mouth several times, but no sounds emerged. He did not know why His Majesty, the king of Griffinrock, would share such private matters with him.

"Unprecedented change is coming, Conner. Your very existence is assurance enough for me. And you, young man"—he shook a knowing finger at Conner—"you will be in the middle of it, maybe even its very instigator." He held his hand up to stay Conner from responding. "I would never presume to be able to rule over another man's heart. By the Cosmos, I was not even able to rule over mine. I know the futility of such commands. But I do worry what this could mean for my daughter's

... for your queen's safety. Surely you see that the closer you are to Veressa, the more you will draw her into the dangers swirling around you. If you care for her as I suspect you do, you will not want that."

"Of course not, Majesty."

The king nodded, but waited as if expecting more.

Conner thought it strange that he had not mentioned his betrothal to Pattria. It offered the best defense to the king's charges, but he knew the king's accusations were true. The memory of the words he'd said to the Warrior Evinfaire on the Field of Contest came to him, one of the last things he remembered of that day. "And surely you see that I cannot allow anyone—especially you—to bring harm to Veressa." *Yes, anyone. Including myself,* he thought. He held the Champion's amulet in his palm before the king and decreed, "As Veressa's Champion, and in honoring my lifelong commitment to her health and welfare as queen of Griffinrock, I solemnly swear that all my words, manners, and deeds will be for the queen's protection, including divulging any feelings of affection I have for her."

Conner saw Jonath relax in the waning light. And, even if only for a moment, the king's lines of worry softened.

# An Old Promise Fulfilled

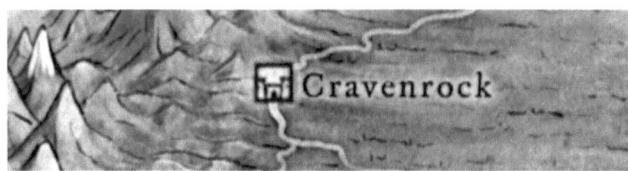

**C**onner huddled tight against the saddle to combat the damp night gale assaulting him. The Narwalen grasslands just a few paces below the dragon's wings rushed by in a blur. They had departed Graystone shortly after dusk with Erebus but a waning gibbous on the eastern horizon. Now the Orb of Chaos was high overhead, and still Skye showed no signs of fatigue. His bond's newfound strength was truly astounding.

Skye had sensed his bond's eagerness for the outing, but despite the dragon's torrent of questions, Conner had declined to say anything more than that he needed to fulfill an overdue promise. Conner smiled at his own cunning. Nothing held a dragon's attention longer than an unsolved mystery, and Skye was not going to get an answer until they reached their destination. So on the dragon sped.

The wind rustling over Skye's wings slowed. Conner hazarded a peek across the moonlit horizon ahead. Cravenrock was coming into view. Signals from his heels and hands sent his bond into a lazy spiral around the dark walls of the massive city, then he gestured for Skye to take the large landing just inside the southern gates.

Those loitering late in the courtyard vanished into the shadows at the sight of the great beast in corkscrewed flight—all except for one guardsman bent on tormenting a transient woman whose crime had been venturing too near the gates for the guard's liking. The woman stumbled away under his heavy boot, her eyes wide in fear. The guard laughed with self-importance. But a strong blast of dust and grit against his back and a quick glance over his shoulder was all he needed to dispel the boredom of the evening and draw him from his habitual horseplay. He tried to run. Unfortunately, his legs tangled with his leather scabbard and he tumbled to the dirt.

"You there! Guard! Stop where you are!" Conner commanded before the guard could rise to take another step. Conner slid from the saddle, using Skye's shoulder and front leg to step down into the shadow of the gate's lights. He recognized the guardsman immediately as the pompous sergeant who had taken a keen interest in Conner at the marketplace the day he'd arrived in Cravenrock. The same guard who had orchestrated Conner's chase through the city streets, directed his capture, exacted his frustrations on his ribs with his steel boot, and stolen all his coins. "Do you know who I am?"

"I do be knowin' ye, sire," came the guard's muddled reply. "Word of the new Champion of the Realm arrived days ago, a dragonrider of the great order. Ye be the queen's own Champion."

"No." Conner stepped into the light. "I mean do you know *who* I am?"

Bent low, trembling, the guard squinted up.

Words were not necessary, nor could they express Conner's feelings in that moment of priceless silence, as the guard's confusion turn to recognition, then slowly to understanding. Conner nodded with thinned lips, then with a taste of vindication said, "You owe me money. Thirty coppers to be exact."

"Thirty, sire?" The guard whimpered, quickly fumbled through his pockets, certain his very life hung in the balance of fulfilling this debt. "I have but twenty-two, mi'lord." Beleaguered, he held his offering out with shaky hands.

Conner snatched the coins away. "Then it seems you are still indebted to me." He scanned the area about them. A few inquisitive souls were venturing back into the courtyard; soon there would be many more as word of his arrival spread through the streets. "My dragon and I have flown all the way from Graystone this night. He is tired and hungry, and becomes short-tempered in such an ill state. You are to stand guard over him while I am away on an errand and ensure no one ventures too close to either head or tail. If he eats anyone, I will hold you personally responsible. Is that clear?"

Skye followed enough of the exchange to offer a timely smack of his lips at the man quaking before him.

"How ... how can I be stoppin' him from eatin' someone, mi'lord?" Sizing the dragon's teeth, the guard nearly wailed while gesticulating, indecisive whether groveling on knees or full prostration was needed to alleviate this cruel situation.

"Are you not a guard of the city and realm? So, guard him!" Suddenly embarrassed by his own behavior, Conner patted his bond's neck. Leaning close, he whispered, "Don't be too hard on him, Skye. I will return shortly."

The Champion of the Realm moved quickly north, the crowd of onlookers silently parting like a herd of sheep before a working dog. As he passed, they muttered questions to one another, whispering their uncertainties, but none spoke to him. He recalled their looks of indignation during his first visit to the city—how they had measured him, judged him, reaching radically different conclusions than they did now. Was he not the same person he had been then? Were new clothes and a jeweled amulet all that were required to change how he was treated? He moved north to be free from their repugnant stares. Some tried to follow, but he knew the night city, the alleys, and their shadows better than most residents. Soon, their muffled voices and gasps of wonder were lost behind.

Conner stood in silent reflection for a moment above a hole in the floor of an abandoned building, then smiled. The last time he stood here, he was being escorted to the northern section of the city by Bandit. That was the last time he had seen the lad. Not that long ago, Conner had made a promise to not leave the boy behind. It was time to fulfill that promise. Certain he was alone, he descended the stairs and began backtracking through the labyrinth of corridors beneath the city. He hoped the added weight of a certain small thief would not be an inconvenience for his bond. He needed to be back in Graystone before Hemera's crimson gaze tolled on the morrow's horizon. It was time to test the limits of his bond's new wings.

## Two May Be Company, But Three's a Pack

"**C**hampion of the Realm!" Pauli declared with a shake of his head. He gave his crudely fashioned willow fishing rod an expert snap and sent the cork bobber and hook in a lazy arc back into the eddy near the river's bank. Satisfied with his third catch of the morning, he proceeded with the litany of titles he had heard bestowed upon his fishing mate since arriving in Graystone two days before. "Member of the legendary Dragonbonded! Orderman of the Dragon! Dragonrider! The greatest fighter in all of Griffinrock! Guardian and Defender of the Harmonic Way! Herald of the Omen, whatever that means, and the bravest hero ever, who single-handedly uncovered and defeated a dozen evil Anarchic spies and traitors infiltrating the very heart of Griffinrock!" He leaned forward with a wink and whispered, "I overheard that last one just this morning by a fine lass." He settled back once more against the massive willow trunk. "And here I sit on the banks of shining Graystone Castle, chatting him up like he was my best friend." Pauli jerked upright as if pinched. "Oh wait! He is my best friend!"

After a short chuckle and no retort from his best mate, Pauli plowed on. "You know, it's hard to believe I spent my entire life besting you in every form of combat I ever devised. Do you suppose if I wrestled you here and now until you screamed 'Give!' they'd confer upon me that fine bejeweled necklace and let me flounce about behind the queen?"

"I don't think that's how it works," Conner said. He glared at his own bobber, which had not moved since he had tossed it in an hour ago. Maybe there was an elemental spell he could use to get fish to bite. He filed that thought away for his next lesson with Grimmley. "And I definitely don't flounce about behind the queen," he added with false annoyance.

"That's okay," Pauli replied with a toothy smile as he wiggled his large frame into his usual fishing pose next to Conner. His fingers clasped behind his thick neck, Pauli's eyes were lost in the willow above. "I don't think I could ever get used to all that gaudy getup. Besides, it's more fun watching you flounce about."

Conner joined his friend in a hearty chuckle that kept his anxieties at bay. "I think you're going to discover very soon just how many forms of combat even you, with your astounding prowess, could not devise."

"Yeah!" Pauli bolted upright again. "How about that? Me, a member of the Warriors Order!" He paused, then added with a touch of impatience, "Once I bond, of course." His eyes sparkled when they fell upon the large gem hanging from Conner's neck, then took on a far-off gaze. His voice became curiously distant. "From what I've heard about the city, it won't be spring before we'll be in all-out war, you know. No one knows exactly what that means, and that makes them all as skittish as crows in a windstorm. They need someone they can look to, a true hero and leader. You breathe hope where it's sorely needed. There's inspiration in what an Eastland farmer can accomplish. We can't all be heroes, you know, but we can each do our share. I was born for this, and I'm ready to pay the price for freedom if I must."

Conner squinted up at the willow branches shading the brilliant blue sky beyond. Pauli's loyalty and the full weight of the Champion's medallion choked him. Hero? Defender? Leader? He doubted he was any of these. And he loathed pretending to be something he was not.

He remembered almost nothing of his challenge with Evinfaire past stepping onto the Field of Contest, and he continued to fail at summoning whatever forces he had apparently used to defeat the traitor, even with Grimmley and Layna's concerted efforts. Conner believed Grimmley when he said that both queen and realm would be in grave peril if that truth was ever exposed. He was learning the Harmonic games of intrigue and politics all too quickly. So he turned this newfound skill to good use.

The noblemen and ordermen at royal court, constantly vying for the new queen's notice, were masters at this game. Every decision, word, and action were honed with meticulous precision to maximize their positions of power and influence. Conner knew there was something more than just Pauli's abilities that had placed him in the Warriors Order sights, but he was at a loss for how to warn his always exuberant but gullible friend. "It seems to me if you have to pay, then it's not *free*dom."

Pauli pruned up his face and stared back. "What's happened to you lately, Conner? You become the great Champion of the Realm and suddenly you get all philosophical? I think you're spending too much time with that crazy old Shaman."

Before Conner could defend his preceptor, a shadow eclipsed Hemera's piercing rays.

Pauli was first to welcome the new arrival. "Well! There's our little thief!"

Kriston Heldcrest dropped to the grass and gave Pauli an offended expression, but it quickly morphed into a smile. With a sudden flick of his thin wrist, a large knife with a bone handle appeared in his hand. He began whittling on remnants of Pauli's fishing pole.

Pauli's eyes bulged. "Hey! That's my knife!" he exclaimed, and snatched the blade away. "Now I know why you have him looking after your dragon, Conner. It's the only creature in Graystone that doesn't have a pocket to pick."

"That's not why I chose Kriston as my page, Pauli. Besides, he's given up his pilfering ways." Conner offered Kriston's bony shoulder a reassuring pat, though the twelve-year-old boy was already proving himself worthy to take on Pauli toe to toe. In truth, Conner had owed the boy a big debt. Kriston had helped him escape Cravenrock and the Assassin. "It seems our young friend has a real knack for languages. And if that wasn't enough, Skye's developing a real fondness for him."

Pauli pointed at the ex-thief's ribcage with the tip of his recovered blade. "You sure the beast isn't just waiting for him to plump up before he eats him for a snack?"

"Stop it, Pauli. You know dragons don't eat people," Conner snapped.

Pauli huffed. "That's not what I heard. *Sane* dragons don't eat people. If your dragon ate Kriston, then you'd discover I was right all along: that beast is more than a bit off."

Kriston cleared his throat, eyes narrowing. He was quickly tiring of the Eastlanders referring to him in the third person. "You do be needin' to have ..." He took a breath, then started again, slower. "You really need to have another talk with that dragon."

Conner sighed. He had felt Skye's melancholy mood all morning but chosen to ignore it in hopes it would resolve itself without another intervention. Not long after Conner had returned to Graystone with Skye, he had realized trouble was looming. Everyone from queen to city serf wanted to gawk at the dragon, and this, quite literally, made for a flammable situation. The twitch of the jumpy dragon's tail, not to mention an awkward cough, would put everyone in his vicinity at risk. So Layna had suggested that the dungeons beneath the castle, those that had served the Dragonbonded during the Anarchic War, might offer Skye some privacy. It was the perfect ruse to keep the dragon in hiding until Conner could rediscover how to control elementals. Unfortunately, the dungeons had been sealed for security reasons shortly after the war. After five hundred years, excavating them had proven more challenging than expected. This had left Conner busy for days soothing and consoling his impatient bond. "I thought he was happy with the arrangements for his new home. The queen went out of her way to have those tunnels cleared quickly. What's troubling him now?"

"From what I can tell, he's fed up with being around our kind and keeps going on about wanting to return home for a stretch."

Pauli snickered. "I bet when the dragon says, 'our kind,' he means you, Conner. There was many a time I thought the same thing after a few days staying over at your farm." He turned to Kriston. "You really understand what that beast is saying?" Pauli asked.

Conner's mind began to wander as the other two continued their banter. Since emerging from his cavern cocoon, Skye had become insufferable. Conner could not fault the dragon for wanting to return home; he too felt homesick. But at least he had friends to alleviate his pangs, and his parents and Pattria were expected to arrive in Graystone in a few days. Still, the dragon's timing could not have been worse. Though one Anarchist plot had been thwarted, the queen's life could still be in peril. He needed Skye, if for nothing more than the queen's security, and that was grist for the dragon's irritation.

The queen. As if there weren't enough to consume his every conscious thought, he had to contend with his growing attraction for Veressa. Conner could not explain how he had known she was high in Kallzwall Castle that night of the queen's death, but he had felt Veressa's anxiety and turmoil as if they were his own. He knew she felt the ties as well, though they had never discussed it. And their physical closeness only heightened the sensations. Even now, he could feel her eyes upon him. He turned and glanced up at the gleaming white castle tower behind him.

But the king's advice had been as clear as Conner's promise was indelible. His feelings were a distraction to the path before him. Failure meant disaster for everyone, so he would double his efforts to keep them at bay.

# Tangled Knots

Veressa took a stuttered step away from the tower window. Conner had stared straight up at her, as if he could sense her watching him, as if he had read her very thoughts! Was clairvoyance another of her young Champion's powers? Trembling fingers tugged at the creases of Royal Chamberlain Nantree's latest version of a dress. *If silk dresses are so great, why don't men wear them?* she wondered with a bite of frustration. But the fidgeting did nothing to unknot the tension, so she lowered her head and sighed.

Antilles appeared at her side, pacing in figure eights, rubbing his shoulders against her leg, purring to soothe her.

Forgotten in the far corner of the queen's study, the green-cloaked Ranger cleared her throat.

The queen tensed and spun, painted smile once more returning. "I'm sorry, Annabelle. What were you saying?" she asked with a thin voice.

Annabelle sniffed. "I think that cord of thought can wait just a few minutes. Right now, I am concerned with this infatuation you are developing."

Veressa gave the Ranger her best regal look. "Infatuation? Whatever are you talking about?"

"You can drop the veil, Veressa. It won't work on me. It is impossible for one woman to hide feelings from another when it comes to love. I see how you look at your young Champion, and how you act whenever he is around. If it's not infatuation, then what is it?"

Veressa bit her lip. Her mentor's arrows always sailed true. The allure that shadowed Conner's physical presence was disconcerting. But what could she share and not be thought crazy? "Am I the only one in the castle amazed that not only a long-forgotten Dragonbonded has returned, but is here, with a dragon, right beneath our very feet? Or that this young, untrained Eastlander handily bested one of the greatest ordermen in several centuries, and acts like it was nothing special? He is truly an enigma, Annabelle. That is all." She waved her hand and waited as the Ranger weighed her every word, measuring them against the woman before her with the precision of Nantree's eye for measuring lengths.

Finally, Annabelle nodded. "My mother used to say, 'Today's remedies are tomorrow's ailments.' It seems we have traded Marcantos Evinfaire's treacheries for a new set of mysteries. Not that we are worse off, mind you. But it seems only time will reveal if we are better."

Her heart sank as she said Marcantos's name. Traitor, spy, and outcast wanted by High Law—labels a fortnight ago she would have never imagined possible for the man. She knew he had changed, had sensed his mental agitation the day they had met in Cravenrock. But a highly decorated Warrior an Anarchist? She shivered at how that might have happened, and how her own feelings had blinded her from discerning the truth.

"That is why you must stay, Annabelle. There is so much I will need your help with," Veressa beseeched.

"We've covered that ground already, my queen. I am grateful that you helped reinstate my position within my order—"

"If you hadn't helped Conner escape, Marcantos's deceit would not have been discovered, and he would be serving as my Champion, with that horrible Friarwood at his heels," Veressa interjected. "How could I stand by and not do something?"

Annabelle smiled kindly. "At least now you appreciate what you set in motion by conferring upon me this medal. The Rangers Council could no longer deny me the right to advance to the next level."

Veressa's cheeks crimsoned, but she accepted the Ranger's truth with a nod. "*Grandmaster* Annabelle Loris does have a nice tone. And it is a title you well earned."

The Ranger ran fingers lightly over the thin staff balanced across her lap. "I haven't earned it yet. There are Modeic runes to engrave, spells to learn, powers to acquire. But do not fret. You and I have time remaining before I am called away for my studies. We will continue with your lessons on how to control these urges you are having." She hesitated, deciding it best to leave out helping Veressa unravel whatever residual knots the Anarchist spy Friarwood might have left within the new queen. That would require more time. Instead, she gestured to the large cat still pacing about its bond. "And how to adapt to your powerful link with Antilles." She leaned forward, adding, "Which is why you need to attend to my advice about your father."

Having recaptured Veressa's attention, Annabelle continued. "I worry King Jonath slips deeper into remorse and guilt over your mother's death. He has spent much of his time since the coronation in the royal tomb with her remains. He eats and sleeps little. Thrice he has called upon the Shaman Dons to commune with her reclaimed spirit. And thrice they have refused, fearing he will not move past the loss, worsening his ill state of mind. If this continues, he will not be able to guide and support you in his duties as king." While Annabelle talked, she watched the young queen's hands fidget with the creases of her dress. Veressa was so much like her mother.

Antilles sensed his bond's distress and began his usual pacing across the chamber.

"The fortnight of lament has passed, Veressa. The kings of the other two Harmonic Realms grow impatient waiting in the royal reception hall. They both grieve for your mother and seek retribution for her murder. As with the councils of all six orders and your subjects, they have made the necessary overtures; they will back you in what is to come. Never has there been such an outpouring of support. But only you, the rightful successor to the crown, have the right for a Proclamation of War."

Veressa did not move.

"You cannot wait on this, my queen. Hesitation shows weakness. And there is much that needs your attention before the proclamation is signed—the establishment of new agreements with the six orders and their guilds to begin constructing arms and weaponry, the strengthening of our network of spies to discover how the queen's assassination went undetected, and the conscription and training of Harmonic forces, just to name a few."

"But we still do not know what the Anarchists' motives were."

"And we may never know," the Ranger conceded.

"My people, the kings of the other two realms, the orders—everyone is so quick to seek reprisal. They wrap it in a nice package and call it justice so they can sleep at night."

"Do you truly believe that knowing why the Anarchists sent an Assassin to kill your mother will change anything? Or do you seek another solution because the one you and I know you must take is too hard to accept?"

"I ..." Veressa choked back a sob, eyes scanning the room as if she had lost something valuable and desperately needed it back. "I don't want to be the first queen in six hundred years to lead her people into war."

"It is not fair such a responsibility is thrust upon anyone's shoulders, especially a sixteen-year-old having just bonded and lost her mother." The Ranger saw the torment and loss in the queen's eyes and recalled what Veressa had said in Cravenrock when she'd told

Annabelle of the dream vision. But something else nagged at the Ranger. Was Friarwood's meddling with the queen the reason she was resistant to declaring war on the Anarchists? Annabelle came to Veressa, and for the first time, was moved to hug her.

After a few minutes, Veressa stiffened and pulled away. She wiped away the sadness staining her cheeks. "Please fetch Gareth Nantree, Annabelle. I may need the Chamberlain's assistance choosing a dress appropriate for this occasion. And then inform the kings of Elvenstein and Grenetia that I will attend to them shortly. We have much to do."

Annabelle bowed and departed in heavy silence.

# In the Light of a New Day

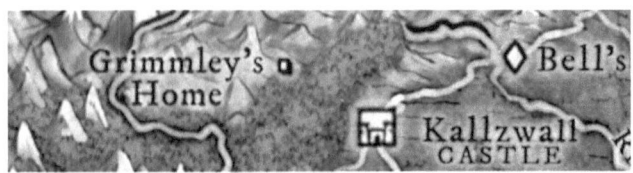

In the late morning light, Layna took note of Grimmley's tightly furrowed eyebrows as the Shaman puffed on his pipe. The dullness in his gaunt, hollow eyes betrayed the anxious, weary mind lurking behind. He was troubled, but not by her move an hour before that had decisively turned the tide of the game of Crowns in the Sorceress's favor. Finally, she broke the silence. "Are you planning to just stare at the board till dinner?" But the worry evident in her tone blunted her attempt to shake him free of his apprehensions.

Grimmley looked up. "Hmm? Oh, yes. Yes, I should make a move." A wrinkled hand appeared from his loose, bright-blue robes and hovered over the board, touching several pieces but moving none.

Layna sighed at being forced to take the direct approach. "Grimmley, you are not alone. It has been five days since the coronation. Maybe the time is ripe for us to share our thoughts and concerns." In truth, the Sorceress was bursting at frail seams to share hers.

"Yes, yes, I suppose we should." The Shaman pressed his back to the chair and closed his eyes. *"Hemea ousia fragidomatio."* The cottage was sealed from eyes and ears.

With a settling breath, Grimmley began. "I know you, Layna, and know you have thoughts you wish to share, but before we delve into our situation, I first must tell you a story, a mystery that continues to confuse and confound me, an anomaly that most certainly will rear its ugly face when we least desire."

"This must have to do with the silver box," she probed.

"How did you know?"

Layna waved at the cottage's organized mess. "Because it is missing."

Grimmley nodded. "I returned it to its rightful owners. After you and Conner rode off for Dragongarde, I went to the Paladin's Stronghold of Aldemeer, and held audience with the order's Grand Clergy." After a draw from his pipe stem, he added, "And to see what more I could learn about the enigmatic box. As it turns out, I learned more than I'd expected to.

"The Clergy had known immediately what I had in my possession, or they would not have agreed to meet me in such short order." An impish smile formed on the Shaman's face. "At least, they thought they knew what I had."

Layna smiled back. "So they were quite upset the box was empty."

"Oh, you could say that. All eleven had disappointment tattooed on their faces as clear as the Cosmic Stars tattooed on the crowns of their heads! They did not need their detailed records to know what the box was or what it had once contained. But that was just the first discovery."

The Sorceress could feel the Shaman's exuberance grow as he proceeded with the tale.

"You see, there was not just one silver box, but at least *two*. I am now certain the box I returned was the one Shazarack had taken ... or stolen. You'll recall that we were under the impression that the last ten stones had mysteriously vanished. Yet the Clergy thought I was returning a different box, one containing nine stones given by the Clergy a very long time ago to a Shaman named Alicia Farclave."

"And have you ever heard of this Shaman?"

Grimmley's eyebrows furrowed. "No. But I did not let on that I had not. As you know, under the Canon of the Orders, all exchanges of goods and services between members of different orders are recorded, mostly to ensure balance in trade. If a Shaman had received such a magnificent gift, there should be a record in my order's archives at Manor Caltarus. So I traveled there, and I can state unequivocally that no such record exists. Paladins hold the prizes from Shan-Grail to be priceless. That left me with a perplexing question. How could a lone Shaman convince the Grand Clergy to willingly part with nine of their greatest treasures? And more importantly, what did she do with them?"

"But this doesn't explain how you know there are two boxes. This Shaman could have given the box to Shazarack."

"Yes. I thought that at first, too, so I looked up the records of this Alicia Farclave. She lived over two hundred years after Shazarack supposedly died. I found nothing particularly special about her. She reached the rank of grandmaster early, but no further details exist. She did not take any apprentices, nor did she teach. There was not even a record of her reclamation. She simply vanished."

After several moments, Layna broke the silence with growing impatience. "I'm at a loss to see how this mysterious tale ties into our situation."

"Yes. I suppose now I should stitch these pieces together." Still, he forced Layna to wait while he lit new tobac in his pipe. "After Conner escaped the Anarchists on the night before the tourney, the lad filled in a lot of details that had previously been missing. At the tourney, you heard about our industrious young pupil's illicit behavior in Cravenrock." Grimmley raised an eyebrow. "The link Conner drew between the Assassin he'd met there and Friarwood involved a certain gold ring he wore, which bore an onyx gemstone with flowing bands of blue light. Conner made this connection after observing that the leader of the Barbarians who detained him at Dragongarde had an amulet with the same kind of gem."

"Fettering Stones," Layna filled in.

"Anarchic ordermen in possession of curious, rare, and likely very powerful stones," Grimmley sighed. "Something sinister is going on, Layna, and that is very worrisome. I sense the Fettering Stones this Shaman Farclave was given are related. If I could get my hands on just one of those stones, I might be able to understand what powers they possess, and possibly discern what is happening."

"Well, until that happens, it seems you've pushed that rock as far uphill as it will go." Layna had her own itches that needed scratching, so she redirected the conversation. "Grimmley, it was a perilous move divulging Conner's existence at this stage, not to mention pitting the boy against Marcantos Evinfaire. Not only is the human-dragon bond common knowledge now, but so is the boy's ability to use four elementals. Don't misunderstand. I don't argue with the ends, only the means you used to achieve them. The lad could easily become a lightning rod for what lies ahead. It seems we have stepped into a quagmire deeper than we would have had if we'd exposed Marcantos after he had been named Champion of the Realm."

Grimmley's head bobbed as Layna spoke, for he found no fault in her logic. "I can see why you are concerned, but consider this. We know Marcantos's near ascension to Veressa's Champion and the simultaneous arrival of an Anarchic force at Dragongarde to waylay Conner and his dragon involved individuals with the same rare Modeic stones. These two acts required more than just coordination and timing; they needed a significant amount of information. How did an Assassin infiltrate and rise so easily within the Warriors order? How did the Anarchists discover the existence of Conner and Skye? And how were they able to reach Dragongarde before the Harmonic scouting force carried out the same objective?"

Grimmley sighed as he considered where this was leading. "Layna, all this has the makings of an intricately devised plot, one likely spawned years if not decades ago. And we don't know how deep this goes. We have to consider the possibility that there are more spies embedded deep within the Harmonic orders."

A numbing chill settled over Layna. She did not know how to respond.

Grimmley relit his tobac and continued. "Exposing Marcantos after he'd been named Champion would have required that I divulge the story of the stones, driving any other spies further underground and making it nearly impossible to root them out. Until we learn more about this conspiracy, we cannot trust anyone nor let on to what we know."

"Well, Grimmley"—Layna gave a faint chuckle—"if we must be involved in a conspiracy against the realms, at least we can say we picked a good one."

The Shaman grunted, failing to see the humor. "I assume you also refer to Conner's struggle to use elementals."

"On our trip to Dragongarde," Layna said, "Conner asked me about the Omen of the Dragonbonded. I told him the Mystic Oracles were not always right." She frowned gloomily at her bewildered friend peering back over the board. "I am not proud of lying," she continued, "but I worry Conner's inability to remember his fight with Marcantos stems from a mental block over this foretelling, that he denies his destiny because of what it divines. It has been my experience that one needs a sense of hope to navigate through epiphanic transformations such as this. We can offer the lad support, but only he can find his way to a vision for his future." Her frown turned to a grimace. "And we don't have long. Of that, I am certain."

"Well, no one wants the boy and that infernal dragon out of this valley more than I. At this rate, there won't be enough maples left to make syrup for my hotcakes this winter," the old Shaman lamented in a futile attempt to mask his true affections. "But there are several factors working in our favor. These subversive specters have suffered a serious setback thanks to the lad's actions. They will need time to lick their wounds. But, more importantly, a great many tourney spectators saw Conner handily best one of the most powerful ordermen of our time. Such a feat should give anyone pause in planning injury to the queen. With all this in our favor, I still believe there was a reason the

Cosmos dropped this lad in our laps, Layna. Do not lose faith. The Cosmos will continue to guide us."

The Sorceress leaned close and tapped pipe ash into the bowl on the table. "These are perilous waters, my old friend. If Conner's inability to repeat what he did on the tourney's field is ever exposed, it would put him, the new queen, and us both into great peril. Yet not seeking assistance could lead to the same outcome. It is quite a conundrum."

"That is why I don't see that we have a choice but to continue with this ruse."

Layna knew their thoughts ran in tandem. It did not take a Mystic Oracle to ordain that the skies could soon be filled with dragons and their bonded humans. They would need a leader and preceptor, someone strong of heart and character, one who understood the ways of the Dragonbonded, grounded in the old, yet carved in the new. Conner had that potential. But with a clandestine conspiracy and a war brewing, who could predict what would happen?

Other questions bubbled up into the Sorceress's thoughts. How could Conner wield such powerful spells with neither incantation nor focal item? And why had she never found any historical records or notes about the original Dragonbonded being able to manipulate all four elementals? It would have been apparent to any observant orderman of the time. But most of all, she pondered the notion that dragons might have been created by the Necromancer, Shazarack. If that were true, he must have been incredibly powerful. She had a few new theories regarding why so little was known about the eclectic order, but she would need time to reflect before sharing anything further with Grimmley. He had enough to consider. For now, she would keep them focused on the most immediate need.

"Grimmley, I believe we must bolster our efforts to help Conner build a bridge across the void between what he has been and what he needs to become. And may the Cosmos help us deal with whatever materializes in its wake."

# Epilogue—Homecoming

**"T**he Dragonbonded?" asked Sovereign Prince Galan, head of the Necromancers order. Annoyed, he studied the long faces of the other members of the council, then turned to his wife. "You said you could keep this young man out of the way, Breanen. Now he is the queen of Griffinrock's Champion?"

Lady Breanen shrugged, unconcerned by Galan's volatile temper. "You worry too much, my husband. The Cosmos shifts in our favor." But her recondite response did nothing to quell his storm. So she took a more direct approach. "Plans do not always go as expected. Even in the capable hands of someone like Meera, there will be setbacks."

Galan had considered sending a member of the council on the expedition to deal with the young Dragonbonded, but they were all needed in Thanatos at this critical juncture. It was Breanen who had pushed him to send the less experienced Meera Asheborne. "You should have foreseen this!" Galan had known Breanen from the time they were both fledgling apprentices at the Necromancer academy a half century before. Even then, her powers of divination and innate skills of necromancy were incredible. She had even predicted Galan's rise to Sovereign Prince of the order. But she was not infallible. He shook his head at the unfathomable thought. "A Dragonbonded changes everything."

"The Dragonbonded changes nothing!" Breanen rose to her feet, her hand gripping the amulet hidden beneath her flowing gray hair. "Since the Great War, the Harmonics have refused to abide by the armistice, flagrantly building holds in the Borderlands and sending militia into our territories. Now, war boils in their hearts. The other orders still need our necro-army before spring is full if we are to successfully defend the Anarchic Lands. We cannot disrupt that process."

"And what of Meera Asheborne? She is more than just a loss to our order; as you well know, she holds many secrets. If she is forced to talk, the damage could be immeasurable."

"Wheels are already in motion to take care of that problem," Breanen stated flatly.

Before Galan could ask for her to elaborate, a hesitant rap at the council chamber door drew their attention. A young adept appeared and bowed low. "Sovereign Prince, Lady Breanen, apologies for bothering you at this hour, but you should come straightaway to the gates. There is a ... situation that demands your attention."

"Where is your master?" Galan demanded of the mob of undead clustered inside the fortress gates. Most were rotted beyond utility, with body parts and bits of armor dangling and swinging to and fro as they milled about aimlessly. The stench of dirt and decay was thick around them. He scanned but found no necromancer directing them.

One of the creatures near the ancient bronze likeness of their Supreme Lord Shazarack turned to inspect Galan with a lidless stare, half its face atrophied into a perpetual grin. Thin white hair hung in wisps over moldy, gray robes long since rotten. "You have rebuilt the fortress just as it once stood, and added to it as well!" The undead gave the Prince a nod of satisfaction.

"Spirit, I asked where your master is!"

"Master?" The gray-hooded undead seemed shocked by the question. "I serve no master," it gasped.

"What kind of trickery is this? All undead serve a master. Who was your summoner?"

The undead shuffled closer. A gurgling sound escaped its dangling jaw, but it fell silent when it looked upon Breanen. Turning, it pitched toward her, raising a bony hand.

"What *are* you doing?" Breanen asked.

The undead drew on Earth and Fire elementals and rasped, *"Ourera ousia anypkosmima."* Breanen's amulet floated up from beneath her flowing gray hair.

Breanen inhaled and staggered back, but several undead lurched forward and gripped her fast in their sinewy arms. "Stop!" she screamed, her face contorting in uncontrolled terror as the undead caressed the amulet's thick gold chain. Her thin body jerked and twisted as she fought to break free from the vise-like grips.

Galan quickly cast a spell of protection: *"Ourera psychi prostatepsychi!"* Several others shouted and quickly began casting spells of command and protection against the undead intruders, but the creatures were immune to their efforts. Ignoring the mayhem and Lady Breanen's screams, the gray-robed undead lifted the amulet from about her neck. The onyx stone flashed a brilliant blue, and the old woman's violent convulsions stopped.

The undead studied the sparking blue flames in the onyx stone. With a flick of its hand, its undead companions released Lady Breanen. Her body tumbled to the dirt.

Prince Galan ran to her, cradling his love's still form. Turning his gaze upward, he whispered, "Who are you?"

Exalted, the undead held its bony arms wide to the sky in mimicry of the statue behind it. "I am Nartesis Shazarack, Supreme Lord of the Necromancers!" it declared in a hollow voice. "I have finally been awakened from my deep slumber in my mountain cave. At last, I am home!"

*– THE END –*

# CHRONICLES OF NARTESIS SHAZARACK

After a thousand years, Nartesis Shazarack has returned home to Thanatos, the City of the Undead. This man may be long remembered as New Cronoa's heinous Father of Necromancy and the one person powerful enough to defy death itself. But very few are aware that, without his vision as a young man, both villainous and heroic, the valiant Dragonbonded would never have existed.

Before you read about his attempt to restore his place as the Supreme Lord of the Necromancers in book 3, "Army of the Dragonbonded," you should know his past and how he fundamentally directed the course of New Cronoa's history.

Be sure to pick up a copy of "Chronicles of Nartesis Shazarack" by JD Hart, available Summer 2018, before the release of the next book in this incredible series.

# BOOK 3: ARMY OF THE DRAGONBONDED

Conner's secret is out: he is the first human to bond with a dragon in over five hundred years. And with the proclamation that the Dragonbonded have returned, the Harmonic Realms are poised to declare an all-out war on the Anarchic Lands. In the wake of a stunning new revelation, Conner volunteers to go on a dangerous quest, one that holds opportunities to get answers to troubling questions.

Veressa is adapting to her growing ability to use elemental powers. But as a queen preparing to declare war with the Anarchists, she can't help being distracted by political wrangling and order rivalries. As the meaning of her dream vision becomes clear, she chooses a path that will forever alter the Harmonic way of life.

Both Conner and Veressa struggle to keep their mutual affections in check while they work to build their own futures. Both will soon learn that even when life seems bleak, things can always get darker.

Be sure to visit the Dragonbonded website to find out more about upcoming books or to sign up for the monthly newsletter:
**http://www.thedragonbonded.com**

# ABOUT THE AUTHOR

JD (Jim) Hart's own fantasy adventure began when, during college, *The Hobbit* was literally dropped in his lap. With the turn of that book's first page, he was forever bound to worlds of magic, dragons, and epic adventures. After many years working as a software manager, engineer, and organizational change consultant, he has decided to leave the fast-paced, high-tech world behind. His new adventure is writing imaginary tales that explore humanity's immense diversity in philosophy, and our connections to each other and to the natural world. Jim lives in North Carolina.

His debut series, **The Dragonbonded Return**, introduces readers to the distant lands of the Harmonics and the Anarchists, home to Shamans and Necromancers, Rangers and Assassins, Warriors and Barbarians, Sorcerers and Warlocks—and, of course, those who bond with dragons.